2⁰⁰

THE GUNROOM

This commentary on the hardships of life in the pre–World War I Royal Navy, published in Great Britain in 1919, is a story so unsettling it was suppressed by the British Admiralty and is only now being published for the first time in America.

Praise for Charles Morgan and his novels

THE FOUNTAIN

"A superlative novel."

The New York Times

THE VOYAGE

"Mr. Morgan writes with assurance in the grand tradition."

The Daily News of London

THE JUDGE'S STORY

"A wise and profoundly moving book."

Saturday Review

THE RIVER LINE

"Attempt[s] . . . to investigate the forces influencing existence."

The Christian Science Monitor

Also by Charles Morgan:

MY NAME IS LEGION
PORTRAIT IN A MIRROR
THE FOUNTAIN*
EPITAPH ON GEORGE MOORE
SPARKENBROKE
THE VOYAGE*
THE EMPTY ROOM
ODE TO FRANCE
THE HOUSE OF MACMILLIAN
REFLECTIONS IN A MIRROR (first series)
REFLECTIONS IN A MIRROR (second series)
THE JUDGE'S STORY*
THE RIVER LINE
A BREEZE OF MORNING
LIBERTIES OF THE MIND
CHALLENGE TO VENUS

Published by Ballantine Books

THE GUNROOM

Charles Morgan

BALLANTINE BOOKS • NEW YORK

ISBN 0-345-34581-9

Manufactured in the United States of America

First Ballantine Books Edition: July 1988

Preface

Nearly half-a-century has passed since this first novel by Charles Morgan was published. It now makes its first reappearance; all the more a period piece because the conditions described in the Royal Navy were those of c.1911. The date is emphasised by the novel's original jacket which depicts a Naval officer and a lady wearing an Edwardian hat, seen against the bows of a warship in dry dock.

The reviews at the time of publication (1919) were encouraging, although one weekly newspaper *(The Nation)* surprisingly listed it among "Christmas Gift Books for Boys," together with *The Harley First XI* and *The Boys of Fellingham School.* But most reviewers took it seriously. Edgar Wallace, for *The Sunday Chronicle,* headed his notice THE MIDSHIPMAN'S HELL: Amazing Charges in a Remarkable New Naval Novel. "From time to time," he wrote, "we get a book with a purpose . . . designed to show up some social or national abuse." After mentioning Dickens and Alec Waugh he continued, "We now have a novel written by Mr. Charles Langbridge Morgan who shows the method of training the young midshipmen in a manner which both surprises and alarms."

Among the book's most interested readers were the senior and junior Naval officers of the day, and Service opinions varied not over the accuracy of what was told, but rather whether it should have been told at all. During his lifetime the writer never allowed *The Gunroom* to be reprinted. "Not because it was anything else but deadly true about the Navy as I knew it," he wrote thirty years later, "but because I think the love story was weak and therefore the novel is not very good as a novel."

The process of humanising gunrooms, according to one

naval authority, began soon after the First World War, and it is very possible that this first book from the pen of the young, indignant Charles Morgan helped to bring about a change of climate which makes some of the incidents here related as remote from the modern Navy as are stories of the press-gang in Nelson's day.

Of Morgan's pride in his first profession there can be no question. Not for nothing had he been made Chief Cadet Captain at both Osborne and Dartmouth. Having resigned from the Navy in 1913, it was for Naval Service that he volunteered in the first days of August, 1914. Again, with the outbreak of the Second War, he hastened to offer himself to the Admiralty.

The Gunroom was written during the First War when its author was an interned prisoner in Holland, one of the Naval Brigade which took part in the attempted relief of Antwerp. Some 500 men, cut off from retreat to the coast, were forced to cross into Dutch territory. Charles Morgan spent his twenty-first birthday in a moated fort not far from Leyden. After an abortive attempt at escape, prisoners were placed on parole, and Morgan shared a cottage with other naval officers at Rosendaal near Arnhem, on the estate of Baron van Pallandt. The background is accurately described in *The Fountain* (published in 1932). "The fates had suddenly given me Time Out," he wrote afterwards of those years, and he used it to set down this story of his life as a midshipman.

Charles Morgan had entered the Royal Navy in 1907 at the age of thirteen. Of his time at sea the only surviving letters are from his Cadet ship in the Mediterranean. They were written to his father, a civil engineer, and are the letters of an eager boy, keen and anxious to succeed in his chosen career. Of his two next ships the only record lies between the covers of this book. They were the *Good Hope* (here called *King Arthur*) in the Atlantic Fleet, and the *Monmouth* (here called *Pathshire*) on the China Station. The Senior Sub-Lieutenant of the *Monmouth* was Christopher Arnold-Forster (later Commander), under whose beneficent rule all barbarous customs, such as were practised in the gunroom of the *Good Hope*, were firmly suppressed. His portrait appears in this story as Sub-Lieutenant Hartington. The encounter between him and Midshipman Morgan was a turning-point in the life of one, and the beginning of a life-long friendship for them both.

Over twenty years later *Sparkenbroke* was dedicated

To Christopher Arnold-Forster
Who lent me courage to seek my trade

The trade, of course, was writing, and the theme of *The Gunroom* is equally divided between the "Evolutions" practised on junior midshipmen, and the genesis of a writer. Chapter VI describes the conflict in the mind of the chief character, John Lynwood, who resolves to "banish poetry from him as men banish a drug."

> Keats should go; and Blake, and Milton's prose, and Burke's speeches. . . . . . From his sea-chest he disinterred battered notebooks on Machanics and Heat and Steam . . . . . This was to be a grand burning of the boats. But the boats would not burn; the memory of the abandoned country would not perish.

By 1913 decision had been reached. Charles Morgan's father informed the Secretary of the Admiralty that his son wished to resign from the Service. "It appears he is happy in his present work, and all his surroundings. The reason he gives for desiring to retire from the Service is that he wishes to follow a literary career." Home from China, the young man set about taking his examinations for Oxford; the doors were opening, to close again with the outbreak of war. By October of that year he was a prisoner in Holland.

"The Gunroom," wrote Morgan long afterwards, "is, I think, a good book in so far as it gives an account of the lives of midshipmen in the Royal Navy. These parts were written in blood and reflect my own experience." Recollection of these trials was fortified by the company of the two naval officers sharing his internment, since in the gunrooms of their separate ships both had undergone similar experiences.

A documentary rather than a novel perhaps describes the book in its first form, and it was this version which went down irretrievably in the North Sea when the ship in which Morgan returned on parole to England in 1917 was torpedoed and sunk within seven minutes. Picked up by a British destroyer, he landed in England, a sick man, to lead the shadowy life of a prisoner on parole for one more year of war. He re-wrote his book; he even re-wrote it twice in order to introduce a love story. This was "foolishly added," he told a French critic many years later, "and is extremely bad."

What novel, one wonders, could stand such treatment? Yet its reappearance is justified by reason of its passionately held beliefs, and the occasional beauty of the writing.

I have called it a period piece; it is also a fragment of social history. Much of it portrays our world before 1914, yet it was written at the same time and often in the same mood as the poetry of the First War. There are passages which recall the last poems of Wilfred Owen, born a year earlier and also a lover of French thought and language.

Charles Morgan, in the forced seclusion of his internment, was deprived of both the agonies and the fulfillment of the poets of the trenches. His muse had not been fertilized by the suffering and comradeship of that long and terrible ordeal; he was not, in Edmund Blunden's words on Owen, "plunged into the abysses of the breaking of nations. But he has seen the grim beginning, and apprehended its shocks and amazements." After three years' absence he found much in the England of 1917 that was hateful.

"What *are* we fighting for? Not for freedom, surely, not for peace. All that has been forgotten long ago." Morgan wrote that in a letter to a Quaker. In another letter to this same Pacifist friend, written on the day after the Armistice, he says, "My sense of the moment tells me you were wrong— and even now I think I should volunteer again; but my sense of Eternity tells me that you were right."

In this frame of mind *The Gunroom* was written. It is a young, angry book and a revolutionary one, looking forward to a new world which will abide by the Sermon on the Mount. "It can't go on like this," cries the girl in the story. "We must substitute the motive of Sharing for the motive of Gain. It's the only way out. It's the only way to stop the cruelty everywhere."

She continues, "I suppose it does mean a revolution for Christ." In later years Charles Morgan might have added, "and for the great spiritual teachers of mankind."

Perhaps such a book as this may be understood better today than it was in 1919. It is an uneven work, but alive with a "sense of worlds outside our own and of time beyond our time."

EILUNED LEWIS

Contents

Chapter I
The Shore Recedes

I

Late on an afternoon in September a boy, wearing a naval mackintosh and a felt hat, came out of Torquay railway-station and hailed a cab. His figure, his voice, and his manner, which was nervous and a little self-conscious, suggested that his age was about eighteen. He took a handful of change out of his pocket, and, when he had selected from it, with momentary hesitation, a sixpence to give the porter who had brought his luggage, he cast over the few bystanders a look almost of resentment, as if he thought they had been watching and criticizing him. If an older man had intercepted this glance its character might have puzzled him. He would have asked himself how, in eighteen years, a boy, who had obviously known nothing of the poverty and hard usage that age the street urchin, could have made the discoveries about life which were reflected in the face he saw. Not that a man's experience lay in this boy's features; rather did he seem to have lost too early the swifter wisdom of a child. He had developed a faculty of suspicion before the years had taught him what he should suspect. He had faced sorrow before he had learned to distinguish clearly between sorrow and bitterness. A child's pride and the humility that springs from discipline; a love of freedom and an acquaintance with restriction; a hatred of cruelty and a knowledge of its refinements—all these had been mingled in him to the destruction of simplicity. He stood there, on the outskirts of the strange naval world into which this cab was to bear him, a boy whose premature manhood might have caused a perceptive woman to fear for him. She would have seen that he was not physically delicate, and have been glad that his body, at any rate,

1

had power to endure; but she would have noticed, too, and trembled for her discovery, that the boy's lips and eyes suggested an imagination which could throw ugliness as well as beauty into relief.

The cabman, his face screwed up and his cheeks blown out as a protest against the driving rain, looked queerly at the luggage he was hoisting on to his roof. It consisted of a green canvas trunk, bound with wooden splines and leather, and an oblong tin case. Their pattern, which the cabman recognized as uniform, betrayed at once their owner's calling, for they differed in nothing but the name they bore from the boxes that were invariably brought with them by midshipmen joining their ships. On them was printed in white letters:

JOHN LYNWOOD, R.N.

"You'll be goin' to the 'otel, sir, same as the others, I expec'?"

"Yes; you recognize the luggage?" Lynwood answered.

"Ay, sir. It ain't often the young officers joins their ships 'ere in Torquay, but I knows that tin box an' the green one, sir, as if they was my own. There's no mistakin' 'em."

"No, I suppose not."

"I'd just done with three other young gentlemen," the cabman when on, "when I came back to the stand to catch more of 'em off this train."

"Well, you've caught one," Lynwood said, with a smile at the phrase.

"The mare, she's bin servin' 'is Majesty to-day, she 'as. Old army pensioner, she is." He shook a stream of water from his oilskin cape and ran his hand over his dripping beard. "Old sailor meself, sir," he remarked, as he picked up the reins.

Lynwood settled himself among the thin cushions as the cab's loose wheels rattled into the street. This, in his childhood's dreams, was to have been the beginning of adventure—this "going to sea." It was not thus he had imagined it. The books he had read had conjured up pictures of bright sunshine and blue water, of admirals who welcomed the new-comer in a fatherly manner, of petty officers whose ambition it was to teach him knots, splices, and cutlass drill. All this was to have been but a prelude to a life among friends, who would share with him glories, perils, and promotion, and whose kindliness would make all things pleasant for him in strange and gaily coloured lands. And now, looking forward, he saw none of these delights. His experience at Osborne and Dartmouth and, above all, in the training cruiser had taught him what he might reasonably expect. He had done well as a cadet. He had taken firsts in his passing-out examinations, and—for what it was worth—had been a Cadet Captain in both colleges. There was no reason why his promotion should not be as rapid as that of any of his contemporaries. But the element of romance had to be excluded—unless there were a war. Those who had lived through it had given him to understand, with a clearness that could permit of no further disillusionment, that the naval officer's life was as mechanical and monotonous as that of a book-keeping clerk. There were drills and watches, tactical exercises and coaling. There was a discipline of iron, and a requirement, equally inelastic, of absolute efficiency. Faults were not pardoned nor weaknesses forgotten. Motive was a matter of small account, for only success and failure appeared on the final balance-sheet.

This, Lynwood had come to recognize, was inevitable in a service conducted with one object alone, the object of victory in battle. Never, even in the bitterest of criticisms, had he heard one word against the Navy's efficiency. It was a perfect machine, as inhuman as a machine, as pitiless as perfection. The object of its training was the production of a war personnel, and this implied the production of human beings who possessed certain definite qualities and in whom certain qualities were not found. If a required quality were lacking it had to be instilled; if a surplus quality were present it had to be removed. The process was often painful. Not infrequently men were broken by it, and went; or rebelled against it in their hearts, and went likewise. Many, though broken, were forced by circumstances to remain.

Lynwood remembered having asked the officer who had given him this summary of the naval system how it was, then, that so many of the officers he had met at the colleges had been visibly happy, and, within certain limits, contented. "To start with," his informant had replied, "the officers who are appointed to Osborne and Dartmouth are picked men—men who, because they were born with most of the required qualities, haven't had their natures badly damaged. The colleges are star billets. You don't meet there—or, for that matter, in the society from which most civilians draw their conclusions—the two and a half stripe salt-horses who will never become commanders or the engineers who have sweated their souls out for the sake of a family which attains the ultimate glory of a Portsmouth suburb—in short, the underworld of H.M.S. And you don't meet the drunks. But there's another reason. The Service does its training young, on the principle of flog a dog while it's a puppy. And if you get through that stage—well, you're probably shaped to the mould like the Chinese women's feet, and you forget, and it doesn't do you any fresh hurt. But if you break while the pressure is being applied, you break—that's all. A good thing you broke so soon. If you can't afford to leave it, the Service has your measure. It knows you broke, and your promotion is not rapid. . . . Of course," he added, "there are a few who are neither broken nor shaped. They go on in the Navy, successful up to a point, dabbling in something else they might have been masters of. Or else they go—often too late."

And now Lynwood looked forward to the inevitable pressure of the mould. It was applied, he knew, to junior officers for the Service's and their own good. The customary phrase was: "Junior snotties must be shaken." The system was unofficial; indeed, its more obvious extremes had been expressly forbidden; but it was a recognized system, of whose existence the whole Navy was aware. No protest against it—and this had been particularly impressed on cadets—would gain any sympathy from any rank. So the Navy had been created, and so it must continue. Conditions, said the senior officers, were much better than in Nelson's time—much better, indeed, than in their own days as midshipmen. Comparatively, modern midshipmen were wrapped up in cotton-wool. The senior officers, in their Wardroom armchairs, didn't know what the Service was coming to!

Some captains, it was rumoured, made a stand against the system in their own ships, on the ground that it was not, in fact, essential to the efficiency of the Service. Some sublieutenants, too—and they had more control in this matter than any captain—stood out against the system in their own Mess, simply because cruelty disgusted them. But these well-intentioned people dared not proselytize. They resisted the system quietly within their own domain, and, lest they should be considered old women, said as little as possible about their resistance. Their number was said to be increasing. Whether a junior midshipman did or did not experience the extremes of the system depended nowadays on the ship to which he was appointed and the sub-lieutenant who ruled his Gunroom. The system, to the accompaniment of the shaking of many conservative heads, was said to be dying.

But it was by no means dead. Lynwood had decided that, if he was subjected to it, the system should not break him. After all, its greatest violence was unlikely to last more than a year. In his second year he would be partly exempt from it; in his third, he would be in a position to enforce it, if he wished, upon others.

The cab drew up at the hotel door. As he stood on the pavement fumbling for money he looked out across the harbour. The railings were jewelled with raindrops. Beyond them a sea of dull green tossed itself into livid foam and spray. Further from shore all colour was lost. No horizon was distinguishable from the opaque sky. Once he thought there became visible the ghostly form of a warship, infinitely lonely and apart, but a moment later he could see nothing.

"Good luck t'ee, sir," said the old sailor, and, as the boy turned towards the hotel, he added under his breath: "And Gawd 'elp 'ee."

Lynwood heard, and looked over his shoulder. Then he pulled himself together, gave his instructions to the hallporter and walked quickly into a ground-floor sitting-room, to the door of which was attached a temporary notice written in blue chalk:

REEVE & CO.

Mr. Reeve, though he had never held a commission, was one of the great personalities of the Navy. He described himself as a tailor and outfitter, but he was more than that. He had taken charge of Lynwood—as of almost all cadets—from the beginning of his career. From Mr. Reeve's descriptive pamphlet Lynwood and his father had drawn their first ideas of life at Osborne, at Dartmouth, and at sea. A telegram signed Reeve had told of success in the entrance examination long before any official intimation had been received. Reeve had advised as to equipment, and had provided it. Reeve had been on the Portsmouth jetty to explain the intricacies of a strange uniform on that great day when seventy new cadets were inspected by an admiral before they crossed the Solent to Osborne and their destiny. Nothing seemed outside Mr.

Reeve's scope. He had made himself responsible for the
transport of the great sea-chests from Osborne to Dartmouth,
and from Dartmouth to the training cruiser. He had laboured
exceedingly in things large and small, and had prospered
exceedingly. And now, here was his representative, again in
charge of the sea-chests and the luggage, prepared to aid his
charges as they entered upon the next great stage of their
careers. A room had been taken and a placard attached to the
door. Within was Mr. Binney, "Reeve's man," helping the
midshipmen to change the plain clothes in which they had
travelled for the Number One uniform, with dirks, in which
they were to join their ship. Mr. Binney unpacked and re-
packed their bags for them. He undertook the sending of
telegrams for things forgotten. He answered innumerable questions, and, with an odd sympathy which showed he knew
they had cares enough, promised to have their luggage taken
to the landing stage at which the *King Arthur*'s boat would
call. Certainly, sir, the luggage would be there in plenty of
time. Where were the sea-chests? Already, as if by a miracle,
they were at the head of the steps. In the rain? Yes, but they
would come to no harm. Had all the young gentlemen got the
keys of their sea-chests? It would be awkward to arrive on
board and not be able to open them. In case any young
gentlemen had forgotten or should lose his key, he had a
skeleton which would open any chest. Perhaps they would not
mind sharing it? . . . Yes, he had heard that the *King Arthur*'s
captain was a very good captain; and the rear-admiral—of
course, everyone knew that he was one of the coming men:
not that the captain or the admiral would make much difference to them. . . . Before long they would have to coal
ship. . . .

Mr. Binney had remarkable information. Moreover, he
talked and made discreet jokes to such effect that silences, in
which there might have been time to think, were pleasantly
avoided. . . . Was it true that Mr. Reeve had a son who was
going to enter the Service? Ah! that he didn't know. Was the
sub of the *King Arthur* a good fellow? That he couldn't say.
Mr. Binney knew exactly what things he ought to know and
say. Personalities—save in a complimentary context—were to
him an abomination.

Lynwood found that he was absurdly sorry for Mr.
Binney—so eager, so capable, so warm-hearted a man and
yet a tailor's assistant! What, in the terms of this world, was

his reward for all these excellencies? Lynwood pictured the little man's family, the boy for whose education he had saved, the girl for whose happy marriage he was already laying plans. What were Mr. Binney's castles in the air? He was too good a man to have none. . . . Then Lynwood's thoughts shifted abruptly. He became envious of Mr. Binney, who would not have to go into that bleak ship, who would return comfortably to London—though it were in a third-class compartment—who would dine that evening among friends, who would sleep that night, not in a strange hammock, but in a familiar bed. Mr. Binney's future was at least certain. Lynwood glanced at his kindly eyes. He saw the beads of perspiration which much stooping had produced upon his red forehead. Mr. Binney was tired, very tired.

Three other midshipmen—Sentley, Cunwell, and Fane-Herbert—were in the room when Lynwood arrived. He knew them all intimately, for they had served their training as cadets in his term. Sentley was small, dark, and a little pompous in manner. An unimaginative conscientiousness was written plainly on his face. Cunwell was of a heavier type, square headed, square bodied, and coarse skinned. He had loose lips that were usually wet, and self-assurance that was aggressive. He possessed, however, a certain force, not of intellect—for his flat, almost concave, forehead proclaimed his stupidity—but of personality, a personality impervious to satire. It was not his habit to think more deeply than mere physical action demanded. He was neither an observer of himself nor an analyst of others. To him nothing was a symbol, everything a fact. He treated the mind with suspicious hostility, as if it derived its strength from witchcraft and the evil powers. Mental capacity seemed to him no more than an unfair advantage over himself exercised by others in examination-rooms, and he did not allow himself to be troubled by his own deficiency in this respect. He brushed it aside characteristically. "You brainy fellows will soon learn that exams don't count for much."

In Fane-Herbert the effect of good breeding was conspicuous. When he smiled, his small white teeth and dancing eyes could not fail to cast a spell. In anger he became cold and aloof, refusing the easy relief of passion. He faced injustice and humiliation with an air of scornful pride which served him ill by irritating his oppressors. Intellectually he was unremarkable; but he was expert in all physical exercises that required quickness of eye and subtlety of wrist rather than force and speed. His whole manner was slow, almost languid. His reserve was not easily pierced, and only to his most intimate friends would he speak of himself. Upon the rest of the world he looked calmly, seeming scarcely to expect that others would be interested in him. Lynwood knew him well, liked him well, admired him for a dozen qualities; but he felt that in Fane-Herbert there was an element, not deliberately concealed, which was, however, never fully in the light of day, and therefore not entirely comprehensible.

"How did you get here?" Sentley asked. "You weren't in our train, Lynwood?"

"No, I came across country—not from London."

"Did any of the others come with you—Driss, or Dyce, or any of the senior snotties?"

"No, I came alone."

"They'll come by a later train," Cunwell declared. "They can go off by the seven o'clock officers' boat. You bet the senior snotties anyhow won't go on board before they must. I shouldn't have come so early myself, but——"

"Aren't the senior snotties on board already?" Fane-Herbert asked.

"No, of course not," explained Cunwell, who knew everything. "The five senior snotties are also joining the *King Arthur* to-day. Didn't you know? They've been doing their destroyer time, and things like that. Now they are coming back to a big ship for a year before their lieutenant's exams. But I believe there are four intermediate snotties there already— second year people, one year senior to us."

"I expect they won't be too pleased with the seniors' coming," Sentley remarked.

"Oh, they'll take it out on us," Fane-Herbert said.

Lynwood was talking to Mr. Binney, and beginning to undress preparatory to getting into uniform. His round-jacket was lying on the table. Cunwell picked it up, and ostentatiously examined its sleeves.

"I say, Lynwood," he said, "I can see the marks where your Cadet Captain's stripe has been."

"Can you? I can't help it."

"Well, I shouldn't let the senior snotties see it, if I were you. My brother told me that when he went to sea for the first time, one of the snotties who were with him had the marks of his stripes showing, and he got a dozen cuts once a week till they disappeared—just to teach him that Cadet Captains at Dartmouth have got to learn their place when they go to sea."

Lynwood, who was well aware that Cunwell had been bitterly disappointed because he had never been made a Cadet Captain himself, knew what triumph lay beneath the friendly appearance of his warning. Cunwell delighted to impress upon him the indisputable fact that he had fallen from relatively high estate.

"Well, I expect you are glad now, Cunwell," he said, "that you were never made a Cadet Captain? You won't get beaten once a week—not for that reason, at any rate."

"All right," Cunwell exclaimed angrily, "you needn't be sarcastic about nothing. I thought you would like to know; and then you lose your temper because I warn you. You are an extraordinary fellow! My brother——"

"Oh!" Fane-Herbert interrupted. "For four years and a half we've heard about your brother. You told me all about him the first night we were at Osborne."

"You're another of the Cadet Captains. Are the marks of your stripes showing? . . . At any rate, my brother is one of the best officers in the Service. The men love him."

"I dare say."

Sentley, as did all save Cunwell, resented this wrangling. To him it was as if prisoners insulted one another on their way to the scaffold. Moreover, youthfully conscious of his dignity as a naval officer, he felt that such disputes were not for the ears of Mr. Binney.

"It doesn't really matter now," he said mildly. And then, determined to be cheerful at all costs, he added: "Do you think we shall get leave at Christmas?" and Fane-Herbert echoed him: "It doesn't really matter now."

But the question set Lynwood looking across the months. "It's a long way off," he said.

"Not longer than a Dartmouth term."

"No."

"But you won't get four weeks' leave, as you did at Dartmouth," Cunwell said. "Of course, snotties sometimes get both watches of leave, but I shouldn't count on it."

"Don't you want leave?" Lynwood asked.

"Of course I do; but I'm not so damned homesick already as you are."

There seemed to be no reply to this, so silence fell for a moment. Mr. Binney interposed quickly:

"The *King Arthur*'s pretty good about leave, I think."

"Is she?" Cunwell turned on the others. "One might think you fellows weren't keen on the Service. Don't you want to go to sea?"

"Why not wait till you get there?" Fane-Herbert said coldly.

"Yes, you just wait!" Cunwell warned them. "I can tell you, Fane-Herbert, your smiles and your cricket won't help you there; nor your English and *x*-chasing, Lynwood. That isn't the kind of thing Commanders look for."

Even Cunwell's voice became less strident when at last they had left Mr. Binney with their luggage, and, under his directions, had gone into the street. Their best uniform, in which they were bound to report themselves on board, added to the discomfort caused by wind and rain. Soon their trousers were wet to the knee.

"I say," said the careful Sentley, "do you think the Commander will mind our trousers being like this?"

"I can't help the Commander's troubles," Fane-Herbert answered. "What makes me swear is that our cap badges will get spoilt."

"What do our cap badges matter? You should see my brother's cap, and he says——" Derisive applause checked him.

"Do you hear the water from the gutter roaring below that grating?" Lynwood said. "Those must be the steps. Yes, I can see our chests standing there."

Sentley stopped suddenly outside a chemist's shop. "I say, hold on a minute. I want some shaving soap."

They turned to look at him. "Oh, Sentley, do *you* have to shave now?" and they laughed good-humouredly till the colour rose to his cheeks.

"I shall have to very soon—at any rate, for Sunday Divisions. Will you wait for me while I get it, Lynwood?"

"Don't stand about in this deluge," Cunwell put in. "The messman will keep shaving soap. Most messmen do. You can get it in the ship if you want it."

They left the chemist unvisited, and pressed on to the head of the landing-steps. Here they wrapped their mackintoshes round them and sat down on the wet lids of their chests. Someone began to drum his heels against the painted wood.

"If you kick off all the paint," said Cunwell promptly, "you'll be in the soup at Captain's inspection."

The heels stopped, and silence fell. Presently their luggage was brought on a barrow chartered by Mr. Binney. The sea was splashing and hissing on the stone steps. In a little time, out of the mist of rain, the bows and funnel of a picket-boat became visible.

"That's our boat," said Cunwell at once. "She has a sailing pinnace in tow—that's for our chests."

A bell rang clearly four times; the engines slowed. It rang once, and the throb of machinery ceased; the tow-rope slackened.

"Cast off the pinnace! Take the pinnace inside, coxswain. I'll come outside you."

"Aye, aye, sir! . . . Get them fenders out, Micky."

The picket-boat's engines roared astern as the midshipman brought her bows round in readiness to come alongside the pinnace. In a couple of minutes both boats were in position.

"Are you the snotties for the *King Arthur?*"

"Go on, Sentley, you are senior—you answer."

"Yes," shouted Sentley.

"Down into the boat, then . . . No, not in the pinnace. Get into the picket-boat's cabin."

They clambered across as they were bid.

"This must be one of the intermediate snotties," Lynwood said to Fane-Herbert.

"Yes. Don't you remember him at Dartmouth? Ollenor?"

"Ollenor, is it? I haven't seen his face yet under his sou'wester."

The picket-boat's cabin was divided into two parts—an outer section, comfortable, light, and clean, which in fair weather was adorned no doubt with white-covered cushions with blue crests; and an inner section, dark and ill-ventilated, wherein were kept signal lamps and all manner of spare fittings. They seated themselves in the outer section because they came to it first.

"Do you think we ought to sit here? Suppose some officers come down?" Sentley suggested. In the training cruiser it had been the custom for cadets to sit on the cabin's roof.

"Well, so long as there is room for them it's all right,"

Fane-Herbert said; "and if there isn't room, then we can go into that inner cabin. I'm not going out on to the roof in this weather and these clothes."

"Yes. . . . I know that sounds reasonable enough, but don't you think that, as we are junior snotties just joining the ship, it would be better to move off into the inner cabin *anyhow* if any officers come—whether there is room for them or not. You see, there isn't much space where we are, and it might get us a bad name to start off with, and——"

"And you are the senior of us," Lynwood laughed. "Poor Sentley! The sins of us all will be visited on you as well as on ourselves. . . . Let's move in if any officers come. It's as well to be on the safe side."

While they spoke the boat's crew were getting their sea-chests down into the sailing pinnace.

"Any more to come?" Ollenor shouted.

"All on board, sir."

"The luggage too?"

"All on board, sir."

"All right. Jump in. . . . Pinnace, get your painter aft, and shove your bows out."

At this moment a thin, pale man, wearing a bowler hat, appeared at the top of the steps and began to descend them with what speed their slipperiness would permit.

"Hold on," said Ollenor.

The man came across the pinnace and jumped into the picket-boat's cabin. Sentley glanced at him, hesitated a moment, and then retired into the inner cabin, whither the others followed him.

"Who do you think that is?"

"An engineer, probably."

"But does even an engineer officer go ashore in a bowler hat?"

"I don't know."

"I don't believe it's an officer at all."

"It must be. He's wearing plain clothes."

"At any rate, we are on the safe side—coming in here," said Sentley.

The atmosphere was vile. The little fixed windows were flush with the upper deck. Through them could be seen, now the grey sky, now the brown, hardened feet of one of the crew. Ollenor's voice repeated his former orders; the bell rang, and the engines turned slowly. Then the tow-rope grew taut, the pinnace swung out abruptly, and both boats circled towards the open sea. Land and the old life receded. Through the narrow stern door of the inner cabin, beyond the pale face and the bowler hat and the tiller vibrating above the propellor, beyond the tow-rope and the sailing pinnace, which came sometimes into sight as the helm swung over, Lynwood could see the hazy outlines of the roofs of Torquay. Soon a change of course banished even these from view. Lynwood found himself longing for respite, for a break in this dream that brought them nearer and nearer to the ship. He wanted the tow-rope to part! His eyes travelled to it as if there were a chance of its doing so. But no god intervened. . . . No word was spoken. They sat still, avoiding each other's eyes. Soon Ollenor's voice was heard once more shouting instructions to the sailing pinnace. The engine-room bell rang, and rang again. The propellor cast up new foam, and the picket-boat quivered as they went astern. And now they rocked at the foot of the *King Arthur*'s port after gangway.

The pale man stood aside that they might be the first to leave the boat, but they had no eyes for that. As they reached the quarter-deck they saluted as they had been taught, and looked round for the officer of the watch to whom they should report themselves. His childish pictures of a shining sunlit quarter-deck flashed irresistibly across Lynwood's mind. Here the planks were stained to dark patches by the rain. The turret, with its unbroken surface of flat grey, wore a hard blank expression, which was somehow similar to that of an intolerant and dull-minded human being. Ropes, cheesed down into neat spirals on the deck, were black and sodden with wet. Over all, casting its shadowy gloom on brass and steel, lay the sloped awning, from whose edges the rain dripped and splashed with miserable monotony. The quarter-deck was like a vast gymnasium, bare, and cold, and sombre.

Ollenor had followed them up the gangway, and stood now in conversation with the midshipman of the watch.

"Can the picket-boat make fast and go to tea?"

"Yes; you have nothing, so far as I know, till the seven o'clock trip."

"Come on, you fellows," said Ollenor; "you'd better come and report yourselves to the Commander. Then come along to the Mess. . . . There's the Commander's cabin."

Sentley knocked.

"Yes?"

Sentley took off his cap, drew back the curtain, and went in. The others were following him when the Commander broke out: "Who are you?"

"We've come on board to join, sir."

"Speak for yourself. . . . And you in the rear there, stand at attention! What do you mean by lolling about in my cabin?" No answer was expected or given. "Who told you to come into my cabin? Get out of it. When I say 'Come in,' come in—not before."

They withdrew, and Sentley knocked again.

"Come in. . . . Well? Don't stand there like a dumb thing? What do you want, boy?"

"We've come on board to join, sir."

"Will you speak for yourself? Now, report yourselves properly, one by one. What's your name?"

"Sentley, sir."

"Are you the senior?"

"Yes, sir."

"Are these all the junior midshipmen? I thought we were to have six of you."

"Two haven't come off yet, sir."

"Send them to me when they do. And see they know how to behave themselves before they come into my cabin. Understand?" The others then gave their names in turn. "Very well," the Commander went on, "clear out now. I dare say I shall learn your names as soon as you care for. Go on—out of it!"

The last command was shouted at them. It rang in their ears as they walked toward the Gunroom.

"I wonder if he's always like that?"

"Lots of Commanders are half mad with overwork," Cunwell said. "They chase everyone—lower deck, snotties, Wardroom—everyone."

"But have you ever heard anything so absolutely without cause?" asked Lynwood; "a screaming rage all about nothing."

"It's part of the system, I suppose," said Fane-Herbert, "and all for the good of the Service. It's no good to take it too seriously."

II

When the midshipmen had left his cabin the Commander picked up his pen and stooped once more over the letter he was writing to his wife.

". . . Means more drive," he wrote. "All one's life is an amazing drive. The R.A. never tires. He must be made of iron. It is his affectation—" The Commander crossed out the sentence and wrote: "He considers it necessary to be entirely unsparing of himself and others. It's like running a mile race at a hundred yards' pace. He acts as if there were going to be a war to-morrow. Of course, we all act similarly—and that means a smart ship. But if you knew how I should like to relax the pressure on the men—even for one day! But what the R.A. does we must all do. I have that promotion to think of that you and I are waiting for.

"When you met the R.A. you thought him charming, didn't you? And so he was. You should see him in the ship. And I hope you think me even more charming than the R.A.? You should see me in the ship. I wonder if the men think I am always like this. I'm sure the snotties do. I've just cursed some new ones till they fled, and I suppose they think—and I don't wonder—that I'm an inhuman beast. What's more, I'm afraid they won't ever have much cause to think otherwise. I shall curse them and drive them whenever I see them—just as the Admiral, a bit more politely, drives me. (It doesn't hurt me, because I can see *through* it all.) It must be done. It really is necessary. Probably the R.A. excuses himself to *his* wife on the grounds that the Vice-Admiral drives him, and so on up to My Lords Commissioners at Whitehall, who would put the responsibility on the Germans, and they return it. It is a circle!

"I'm sorry. I oughtn't to fill all my letter to you with grousing. The Service is a fine service, and Peter shall go into it if you'll trust him to Commanders even fiercer than myself. But we shall have to talk it over about Peter. I'm not quite sure that the Navy is the best place. Your father was an artist, and if any of that has come through to Peter—well, we eat artists. I know you want it—but then you know the Navy ashore, and you have a husband who is going to be an admiral, haven't you? Do you know anything of the Jesuits of old time and their methods? I feel rather like them sometimes. But then, of course, the Service is a really fine 'end'—that makes all the difference.

"When I come home . . ."

The midshipman of the watch tapped at the door. "Eight bells, sir."

"Sound off!"

The bugle sounded. The pen worked quicker now. The last four words were crossed out.

". . . I'll write again. I want to get this letter ashore. I'm sending in an extra boat after Quarters. Quarters is sounding off now. I must go."

He thrust on his cap and walked out on to the quarter-deck. Here the Marines and the Quarter-deck Division were falling in.

"Where's the midshipman of the Quarter-deck Division? . . . Mr. Ollenor, in future you will come up from the Gunroom in time to see that your Division falls in smartly to the bugle. Look at them! They're a damned disgrace!—all talking when I came. . . . Don't answer me. Go to them."

The Commander was shouting. He swung round on his heel to cover a queer smile. The sergeant-major, who missed nothing, wondered what joke there was; but he knew nothing of the Commander's letter.

At that moment the Rear-Admiral emerged from his quarters. With his hands clasped behind him he walked to the after-rails and looked over the stern.

"Commander!"

"Sir!"

The Rear-Admiral pointed upwards to where the white ensign had become entangled with its staff. "Your ensign's foul. It looks bad for the rest of the squadron." Then he strolled away.

The Commander's lips tightened. "Midshipman of the Watch!"

"Sir!" The midshipman came running, stopped and saluted.

"Look at that ensign—disgusting! The Admiral noticed it. Why can't you keep your eyes open instead of standing about doing nothing? What do you think you are here for?"

"It was cleared a little time ago, sir. The wind——"

"Damn it! Don't argue. It's your job to see that it's always clear. Don't let me find it like that again, or your leave will suffer."

He dashed for'ard, swinging a telescope. The midshipman knew his cue.

"Sideboy!" And the sideboy, a wizened little creature as yet too young to be an ordinary seaman, came running in his turn. "Look at that ensign! The Commander noticed it."

The sideboy looked; and gulped while he summoned his excuse. "I cleared it just afore quarters, sir," he said. "The rain an' the wind——"

"It's your job to see that it's always clear. Understand?"

"Yessir."

"And put your cap on straight."

"Yessir."

"Now go and clear the ensign. Get a move on!"

The midshipman tucked his telescope under his arm and watched for the Commander's return.

Chapter II
Seen Through Steel

Before they reached the Gunroom after their interview with the Commander, Lynwood and his companions met a tall midshipman, whom they immediately recognized.

"Hullo, are you the new snotties?" he asked. "I'm Reedham, three terms senior to you—probably you remember me at Dartmouth? You are Lynwood, aren't you? Weren't you the fellow that was made a Cadet Captain first shot?"

"Yes," said Lynwood, and added quickly: "We've just come from the Commander."

"Oh have you? Did he bite your heads off?"

"We seemed to do something wrong."

"You always will seem to do something wrong whenever the Bloke's about. . . . But where are you going now?"

"The Gunroom. Ollenor told us to go there when we had reported ourselves."

"Well, I shouldn't, if I were you. Quarters will be sounding off in a minute or two. You had better come up for them. Ten to one, if you don't, the Bloke will jump on you for shirking. He's bound to be on the look out. Really you ought to have twenty-four hours to sling your 'ammicks in—standing off all duties; but that theory is a back number with our people. . . . Are your chests on board yet?"

"No; they have only just come off in the sailing pinnace."

"Then you'll have to go to Quarters in the rig you have on. You ought really to change into monkey-jackets, of course. Anyway, I should unship those dirks. Chuck them down behind somebody's chest for the time being—out of sight, though."

When they had followed his advice they trailed behind Reedham on to the upper deck.

"Of course, you haven't been told off for Divisions yet," he said. "It won't matter where you go this afternoon so long as the Bloke sees you somewhere. You come to the Foretopmen with me, Lynwood, and the remainder had better take a Division each."

Under this friendly guidance they went through Quarters without mishap, and, immediately afterwards, went below with Reedham. On their way to the Gunroom they passed through the Chest Flat, an ill-lighted section of the main deck, flanked on the port side by cabins and on the starboard side by the Gunroom and the Gunroom pantry. The whole of the centre of the flat was occupied by the Engine-room casing, on either side of which passages led, for'ard to the men's quarters, and aft to the half-deck. Through a door in the starboard passage they entered their new home.

The Gunroom was a long, very narrow room, about seven feet high, built almost entirely of steel. Its outboard wall was the curving side of the ship, and was pierced at intervals by scuttles, which visitors referred to as windows. Its inboard wall, which it had in common with the Chest Flat, contained the doors. The after-bulkhead was unbroken, and for'ard were the pantry hatch and the serving slab. The furniture, though not elaborate, occupied most of the floor space. A long, narrow, leather-cushioned seat, always called the settee, was attached to the ship's side. Parallel to this a table was screwed to the deck. Between the doors stood a sideboard, covered with innumerable weekly and daily papers; and overhead, screwed to the walls, was a series of small wooden lockers, between which and the beams above were kept such sextants as were not for the moment in pawn. A stove, a few chairs, and a piano completed the Gunroom's regular equipment.

The place had an air of hard usage, and bore witness in a thousand ways to the manner of its occupants' lives. The only decorations were a few cheap prints, some of Transatlantic and some, perhaps, of German inspiration, representing ladies who were not merely insufficiently clothed, but who seemed, oddly enough, to have definitely completed their toilette when they had donned a pair of silk stockings or a diminutive undergarment. In their eyes invitation was conveyed by means of a formula, having no connection with art or life, which seldom fails to produce commercial profit. They hung there, eternally grinning, eternally brandishing their insistent legs, the remarkable substitute for womanhood which our generation has learned to recognize and accept. Near them, as if to throw them into overpowering contrast with reality, oilskins, which smelt strongly, hung with dirks and belts from pegs on the wall. The deck, the stove, and the settee were littered with papers, books, pipes, tobacco-tins and cigarette-ash. At the end of the table, on which cards, a dice-thrower, and a couple of empty glasses were grouped incongruously with teacups, the Sub was sitting.

"Hullo, Reedham," he exclaimed, "who are your young friends?" Then he pointed a finger at Sentley. "You with the innocent face, are you the new warts?"

Not yet accustomed to this usual description of very junior midshipmen, Sentley hesitated before he answered: "Yes, sir!"

"Lord Almighty!" the Sub cried, smiling despite himself, "don't call me 'sir.' Who the deuce taught you to call subs 'sir'?"

"No one."

"I should hope not. . . . Well, don't do it again."

"No; I'm sorry."

"And don't be so bloody polite. This isn't a dame's school. . . . Had some tea?"

The Sub pressed a bell that swung from a cord above his head. The pantry-hatch opened with a click, and a pale face appeared—the face of the man in the bowler hat to whom they had yielded place in the picket-boat.

"Tea for these officers, messman," said the Sub.

Lynwood and Fane-Herbert exchanged glances, but they were careful to say nothing. They knew that they would be wise to keep the knowledge of their mistake locked away in their own hearts. But Cunwell perceived that he might score a point.

"I told you so, Lynwood," he said, so that all might hear.

"What did you tell him?" the Sub asked, wondering if they had been betting against the Sub's offering them tea.

"When we were coming off the picket-boat," Cunwell began, "the messman came down at the last moment, and" —Sentley kicked him vigorously, but he continued, nevertheless—"and Sentley and Lynwood and Fane-Herbert thought he was a Wardroom officer, and cleared out for him."

Ollenor, Reedham, and Norgate, the midshipman who had kept the afternoon watch, roared with laughter at this.

"That's good!" the Sub exclaimed. "The Wardroom would

rejoice to know that Wickham was mistaken for one of themselves. And you—what's your name?''

"Cunwell.''

"And you, Cunwell, what did you do?''

"Oh, I went with the rest of them; but, of course, I knew——''

"Of course you did. I see we have a smart young officer here, Ollenor, competing for a medal.''

The dog-watches passed without event. The Sub having gone to his cabin and the others on to the upper deck, Lynwood was left in the Gunroom with Reedham and Fane-Herbert. They fell at once to a discussion of personalities and prospects, and Reedham, wearing the quiet smile that was habitual to him, answered questions, volunteered information, and gasped at examples of ingenuousness. The Sub, it appeared, was named Winton-Black. Reedham described him as a good enough fellow if ever he did anything—which happened infrequently. He was to leave the ship in a few months' time, and was careless of what happened in the interval. Almost all his spare time was spent in his cabin, so that he seldom appeared in the Gunroom except for meals.

"Then we ought to be all right," said Fane-Herbert.

"Oh, don't you believe it. You would be much better off, I assure you, if Winton-Black *did* put in an appearance. He's an easygoing old thing, as lazy as they are made, and it would be too much effort for him to chase you much. But his being away leaves the senior snotties' hands free, and the five seniors we are going to have include some pretty tough customers. I believe Krame, the senior of the lot, who will arrange all our duties and dispose our lives, is—well, Ollenor knows more of him than I do, and *he* says he's as bad as we could hope for. Howdray has a name through the fleet—Bull Howdray. He's usually tight, and pretty violent. Tintern is musical—a bit of an artist, but untrained, of course—quite a decent sort in a mild way; but he sozzles to console himself for the might-have-beens. The other two, Elstone and Banford-Smith, I don't know much about.''

"But how will you intermediate fellows come off, Reedham?''

"We?—oh, we shall be all right, I dare say. We've had our share of the worst of it. You see, there are four of us: Ollenor and Norgate you've met, and then there's Tommy Hambling, who is keeping the first dog-watch at the moment. If we went quietly we shouldn't come to much harm, but

Norgate and Hambling are always making asses of themselves. They came off to the ship absolutely blind to the
world the other night. We thought we had got them down
safely, but the silly fools showed the effects next morning.
Hambling went bright green in the middle of School, and had
to retreat and be sick, which angered the priest; and Norgate—
much about the same colour—went off to sleep in the middle
of Baring's Seamanship Lecture. The whole story came out,
of course. It seems that Baring saw they were tight the
evening before, but didn't know how bad it was. At any rate,
he decided to say nothing about it if they were fit for duty the
next morning; but then, when they collapsed during his own
lecture there was hell to pay. He told Winton-Black to give
them a dozen cuts each, and has stopped all their leave, wine
bills and extra bills till further orders. Now they talk about
breaking out of the ship when they get to Portland. Norgate
says he has an amateur there, though Heaven knows where he
finds her. And so it goes on. . . . Of course, that gets everybody's back up against us four, and will give Krame an
excellent opportunity to make himself objectionable if he is so
minded.''

"But who is the officer in charge of midshipmen?'' Lynwood asked.

"The Snotty Walloper? Baring.''

"Won't he see that Krame and the others don't go too
far?''

Reedham grinned at them while he lighted his pipe.

"You people *are* fresh from Dartmouth, you know! A
Snotty Walloper doesn't look after snotties as a Term Lieutenant at the colleges looks after cadets. Baring's job is to
see we keep our watches, run our boats, work out our yearly
sights, and do our instruction. He signs the Leave Book, and
occasionally he invites one of us to dine with him in the
Wardroom. That's all. You don't go to him with your troubles. When you come to sea you have to look out for yourself
and square your own yard-arm. No one interferes except in
matters affecting discipline. Your private life is your own so
long as you don't make a public exhibition of yourself when
you go ashore. . . . Oh no, don't imagine that Baring would
trouble his head about what Krame does to you. It's none of
his business. And what's more, nobody wants the Wardroom
to interfere in what the Gunroom does. You don't want it
yourself. Etiquette about that sort of thing is very strong.''

For some time the conversation drifted away to Dartmouth days, but Lynwood's thoughts ran on. The prospect of independence, of complete emancipation from leading-strings, attracted him. He compared his life with that of boys of his own age at public schools, and found, almost to his surprise, that he would be unwilling to accept their comfort and security in exchange for the privileges of responsibility. All midshipmen regard schoolboys with a certain contempt. They are launched into the world while their brothers are but preparing for it. They command, not a football fifteen, but a boat's crew. They have experience of men and women whose very existence is not yet, and perhaps never will be a reality to the shore-going folk of their own class. And daily, in the ordinary course of routine, they carry—though it does not strike them in this way—their own lives and the lives of others in their hands. All this begets a rare pride, the pride of one who for the first time signs his own cheque and rejoices silently in the possession of his own banking account.

Lynwood awoke from a day-dream to find himself staring at one of the pictures above Reedham's head.

"Those pictures," he said suddenly, "aren't they appalling?"

"They are pretty vile," Reedham agreed. "But they are a Gunroom custom. I don't see what other pictures you could have. Really good ones would look horribly out of place. Besides, the kind we have is what most people like."

"Well, if ever I'm Sub of a Gunroom," said Lynwood, "I'll have good pictures or none at all."

"Probably you will think differently then," Reedham answered, with a smile of experience. "One's ideas change at sea. One gets accustomed, you know."

Later in the evening the five senior midshipmen arrived and burst into the Gunroom, followed by the two remaining juniors, Driss and Dyce. The place was soon full of the noise of greetings, the ringing of bells, and the ordering of drinks. When dinner was over, Krame made out a preliminary list of the duties of each midshipman, in which it was laid down who were to run the boats, who were to keep watch together, and to what station each was to go for the ship's evolutions. Then began a series of questions. Krame, a dark, large-eyed youth, whose good looks dissipation had been powerless to destroy, seated himself on the table.

"Now then, Warts, how many of you are teetotallers? Prove!"

They proved by bending their arms at the elbow and holding out their hands in drill-book fashion. Krame counted.

"One, two, three, four. . . . Driss, aren't you a T.T.?"

"No."

"Why not?"

"Because I don't want to be."

"I'm not going to ask you to sign the pledge, you know. You can drink yourselves dead when you go ashore for all I care. All I want to know is, how many of you are not going to use your wine bills on board. Then we can use them—see? What about you, Cunwell? Aren't you T.T.?"

"I don't want to sell my whole wine bill," said Cunwell. "I may have to stand a boat's crew a drink or something."

"Thoughtful and righteous youth!" laughed Howdray.

It was decided that the ten shillings' worth of drink, which each junior midshipman was allowed to consume in a month, was to be transferred, in four cases out of six, to the seniors. Driss was allowed to keep his because he insisted upon doing so with an Irish vigour that amused them, and Cunwell surrendered only two-thirds of his share.

This preliminary having been settled to Krame's satisfaction, many drinks were called for with which to celebrate it. The musical Tintern was urged to the piano, and an impromptu sing-song, which was one vast chorus, was begun. It started in decorous fashion with the original version of *Riding down from Bangor*, followed with much greater enthusiasm by its parody. The standard then fell, and the enthusiasm rose until, when the time came to close the Gunroom, a dozen and more young gentlemen were gathered round Tintern, shouting, between pulls at drinks and puffs at pipes, songs that their sisters—but their sisters have nothing to do with the Gunroom. And Tintern, with a glass at his right hand from which he complained he had not time to drink, played and smiled and sozzled, as Reedham had remarked, to console himself for the might-have-beens.

Chapter III
A Chapter Without Name

I

On the morning of his first full day in the *King Arthur* John Lynwood enjoyed the luxury of a lie-in until a quarter-past seven. In the course of ordinary routine, he and all midshipmen not engaged in other duties would by this time have done half an hour's physical drill on the quarterdeck; but Krame, trusting that the Snotty Walloper would be unobservant on this occasion, had sent a messenger for'ard the previous evening to tell the Physical Training Instructor that the midshipmen would not require him in the morning. Therefore, when he turned out of his hammock, John went immediately to his chest, took off his pyjamas, wrapped a towel round his middle, and pattered barefoot down to the bathroom.

Here the senior midshipmen, who had already secured the shallow hip-baths, were sliding them over the tiled floor towards the cold water tap, disputing with vigour as to whose servants had brought the cans of hot water, shouting for soap, and calling down curses upon the heads of those who had presumably stolen their sponges.

"Damn that marine," Ollenor's lazy voice was saying, "he has taken my soap again. I hid it in the corner of this locker yesterday. . . . Shouldn't mind so much if he ever looked as if he used it."

John waited his turn, bathed, dressed, and went into the Gunroom for breakfast. The senior midshipmen seemed to be in good humour, the sun was shining, the coffee was hot, and John, in obedience to one of those moods of his of which it was always difficult to discover the cause, was a thousand times more cheerful than he had been on the previous night. When Prayers and Divisions were over, the Chaplain, who

25

was also a naval instructor, came into the Gunroom to conduct School. John learned much of him before his arrival. He had hoped that the Chaplain would be a scholar, a little precious, it might be, but possessed of an uninformed mind, more pliant than routine, simpler than discipline. He had met one Chaplain of such a kind, and had been grateful for the relief that his contrast afforded. But this man, it seemed, was above all a Wardroom officer. Ollenor summed him up: "He is always trying to bowl you out," he said. Only Reedham, who had a good word to say for everybody, spoke in his defence. "I dare say he means well. We don't give him much chance. We're not exactly Padre's blue-eyed boys, are we?"

John saw at once that the Padre, when he entered, looked around him in expectation of hostility.

"There you are," said Hambling, in an aside that was intentionally audible, "he hasn't even the decency to knock."

"Will you young gentlemen please keep silence when School has begun?" said the Padre. He looked round him. "No duster, no chalk; blackboard not in position. Who is the Senior Midshipman?"

"I am, sir," said Krame.

"Then you will in future see that the Gunroom is properly rigged for school *before* I come in."

"That will be your job, Cunwell," said Krame abruptly.

The Padre continued in his even tone. "And you will give your instructions at a proper time, please, and not interrupt me when I am speaking."

By this time the Gunroom, which, in the manner of Gunrooms, resented nothing so much as cold superiority, was determinedly hostile. If the Padre had ever hoped to win the midshipmen he had set about his task wrongly, and had definitely failed. Of all soil the Gunroom is to a chaplain the most stubborn. Few attempt to cultivate it; fewer succeed in such an attempt.

The navigation lecture became a mere occupation of time, the teacher being as mechanical as the pupils. When he talked, they let him talk, asking no questions. When he drew on the board, they watched him, for he had a habit of turning quickly to discover the direction of their eyes. For this amount of attention, because it was a part of discipline, he made a rigid demand, but so long as their answers to his questions were not flagrantly irrelevant, he seemed to care not at all for the direction of their minds. His manner was a strange contrast to that of the masters at Dartmouth. And here—from the pupils' point of view—there were no marks to be won, there was no competition, no incentive but the fear of the examinations for the rank of lieutenant, which were yet comfortably far off.

When the lecture was over, the Padre interrupted the thud of books thrown ostentatiously aside to say he wished every new midshipman to come in turn to his cabin. He would see the most junior first. "And I hope," he added, "that the Gunroom will learn to behave itself at an early date. If ordinary persuasions, which ought to be sufficient, fail, there is always the Leave Book. You understand me, Krame?"

"Quite, sir."

In his own cabin the Padre was more tolerant. John found him sitting at his desk with a heap of papers before him.

"With regard to Voluntary Subjects for your lieutenant's exams, Lynwood—what are your tastes? You can choose three or less of the following: Higher Mathematics, Naval History, Mechanics, German, French, and Electricity." John examined the paper that was handed to him, while the Padre went on: "Most midshipmen, when they come to sea, regard it as an opportunity to abandon all their study. I admit that the ordinary circumstances of their lives—boat running, watch-keeping, crowded quarters, and—er—so on—do not make book work easy. Commonly, the work that should have engaged them for three years is left to the last three months. That is not necessary. It is merely a question of character and concentration. I want you junior midshipmen to choose your Voluntary Subjects at once, and to work at them and at the compulsory subjects consistently from the beginning."

In this speech is was easy to recognize the intonation of a formula. The man spoke without enthusiasm, apparently without the least hope that his advice would be followed. He was doing his duty, that was all. John chose as his three subjects, Higher Mathematics, French, and Naval History; the first because it was necessary in Gunnery, and the last because it was a subject after his own heart. The examination consisted in the writing of an essay with the aid of books. There were three years in which to write it. He intended, as he said ambitiously in a letter home, to "write a big essay in chapters, and if possible to publish it later as a book." When he suggested this to the Padre, the Padre smiled.

"I am afraid you have literary tendencies," he said.

"I like books," John answered.

The Padre looked away from him and talked into the open scuttle. "It would be better from the Service point of view if you liked mechanics. They promise very rapid promotion to those who specialize in Engineering."

"I don't think I should do well as an engineer, sir."

"Perhaps not. Make your own choice. . . . Do you care for poetry?"

"Yes, sir."

The Padre looked at him sharply, an odd expression in his eyes, as if memories were pressing on him.

"I have a few books there," he said, pointing to his cabin shelves. "Borrow them if you like, but don't leave them sculling about the Gunroom—they wouldn't like volumes of verse. And don't give too much thought to them, old man. They won't make you happier here."

"Why not, sir," asked John, "if I like them?"

"Because—oh, never mind why not. . . . Think over the question of Voluntary Subjects, Lynwood, and send in the next midshipman, will you please?"

II

The next two days were spent in sailing to Portland and in coaling ship. On their first evening in Portland the junior midshipmen had their earliest experience of Gunroom Evolutions. In this instance the Evolutions were comparatively mild, being in a manner introductory to the more serious business which was begun when the *King Arthur* put to sea. But these preludes, which began on a Thursday and were repeated on the following Saturday and Monday, were enough to provide for the junior midshipmen an engrossing subject of conversation whenever they were beyond the hearing of their seniors. John and Fane-Herbert landed together on Tuesday afternoon.

"Thank God," said Fane-Herbert, "we are out of that for a few hours."

"Do you think it will happen again this evening?"

"I don't know. It can't happen every evening. . . . I shouldn't mind so much if it were a punishment of some kind—if they even pretended that we had done something wrong. As it is, they chase us for an hour, and then offer us drinks, and then chase us again."

"I think I would rather that," John answered, "than that they should be avowed enemies. One feels, at any rate, that they are not doing it out of any personal spite against us. They seem to do it largely because they feel they must."

"But why must they?"

"It's the tradition, I suppose."

Fane-Herbert, who had uttered no word of protest while the Evolutions were going on, and who, when they were over, had quietly washed the dust and blood from him and had turned in, broke out now. He was talking to his friend. He could afford to let the mask drop.

"I'm keen on the Service," he said, "keener than most people, I think. I don't expect a soft life. I don't care how much I am chased on duty by commanders and officers of the watch. Probably that makes you do your job better—at any rate, it's all in the day's work. Every junior is chased by his seniors in one way or another. . . . But I swear one has a right to a certain part of one's life. The Gunroom is our Mess. It is the only place we can go to, or write or read in, or do any of the things we want to do when we are off duty; and it isn't as if the day was slack. Heaven knows, what with School, and watches, and boats, and signals, and divisional work, and sketches, we have enough ordinary work to do. But then at the end of the day our own Mess is made hell for us."

"I know. It's no good thinking about it."

"I suppose when you and I are Subs there won't be any of it in our Gunrooms."

"No."

"And what about the other fellows—Dyce, Cunwell, Driss—do you think they will carry it on?"

"Probably. Possibly we shall when the time comes. It's the Service custom. It has come down through generations. It's the devil of a job for any Sub to stand out against it. It might mean his quarrelling with all his senior snotties, and probably the Wardroom would be up against him. Every time a junior snotty did something wrong the Sub would be blamed because the Warts weren't properly shaken in the Gunroom."

Fane-Herbert reverted to the personal consideration. "Reedham told me we haven't had a proper dose of it yet. He said we had better stand by for the first night at sea. Krame is planning great things."

John thrust the thought from him. "Don't let's talk about it," he said. "We shall have to go back to the ship presently.

We shall have enough of it then. . . . What are you going to do when we get leave? Didn't you say your people were leaving England?''

"It's rather in the air at present," Fane-Herbert answered, "but there's some talk of my father's going to Japan to represent his armament firm out there. My mother may go too, and take Margaret with her. . . . Do you remember Margaret, when my people came down to Osborne years ago? She must have been about fourteen then.''

"Of course I remember her. She stood on the canteen steps with a huge basket of strawberries over her arm. And as everyone passed she looked at them and, if she liked them, she said: 'Are you in Fane-Herbert's term, please?' and if the astonished cadet said he was, she went on: 'then will you take some strawberries, please?' ''

Fane-Herbert laughed. "I never knew about that. It was a good idea of hers only to be generous to our term. She's a wonderful person.''

"Yes; I remember coming out to lunch with you and going to Carisbrooke for tea. She talked to me the whole time. It was a windy day. Her hair was blowing about.''

"She has good hair," said her brother shortly. "She has put it up now. . . . When we get leave you must come home and see my people. I think you would find it interesting. My mother was a Stardyke before she married, so we have dozens of political and literary people about the place. That is in your line, isn't it?''

John said it was; but he was chiefly interested in Margaret, whose hair had made so strong an impression on his boy's mind. He loved hair—the colour, the line, the scent, the touch of it. He saw the wind blowing through Margaret's, though he had forgotten her features. And, from searching in the past, his mind went out suddenly towards the future. His sense of beauty, so acute, so creative, must not be allowed to develop. It had power to arrest and overwhelm him, to transform some swift manifestation of loveliness into an essential of tremendous importance, capable of dwarfing all the other realities of the world. And then, when the world insistently broke in upon him, he would be haunted by that flash of appreciation as by the ghost of one beloved. A moment would light the years, laying them bare, exposing aspects of existence that he had been happier not to recognize. The movement of a beautiful hand, for instance, once seen and realized by him, would become a light in which to consider the movements of all hands. A phrase of poetry that had once captured his mind would dwell in it and gather significance from his experience. Margaret's hair—though he had forgotten Margaret—had become for him a symbol; and yet, not her hair as a whole, but her hair as he had seen it at a certain instant. In his memory the association of colour and light and movement never varied. He had no recollection of the appearance of her hair at any time but at this moment which his imagination had endowed with permanency. . . . John realized that it was necessary for him to blunt this sense, which was for ever creating within his imagination a background to the immediate circumstance. He put it to himself in this way:

"Seeing that I am to be a naval officer, the sooner I shape myself to Service conditions the better." Then he added aloud: "It's better not to think too much about those other things."

Fane-Herbert looked up in surprise. "What other things?"

"The things outside your job that you can't ever reach. If I were to have a painter's training and could ever paint that hair, or a writer's and could ever describe it, then——"

"Are you still thinking about Margaret?"

This renewed associating of personality with his symbol startled John. "No," he said, "I wasn't thinking about your sister. It might have been anyone's hair for that matter."

As they turned into a shop to have tea, John said suddenly: "You remember that I told you how the Padre offered to lend me poetry and then said I should be happier if I didn't read it? . . . I've just understood what he was driving at."

III

If the conditions of John's life are to be understood, Gunroom Evolutions must be once described. The detail of this part of his and his companions' training need not be referred to a second time.

The Evolution evening of which an account is to be given was not an isolated or exceptional incident in the junior midshipmen's lives. It was part of a persistent treatment to which they were subjected, with fluctuating vigour, so long as they remained in the *King Arthur*. It was not applied every night. Sometimes there was an interval of over a week between two successive applications, and, indeed, towards the end of their service in the *King Arthur* there were intervals even greater than this. The lengh of the intervals depended upon the leisure and the inclination of the senior midshipmen. But the treatment, though not regular, was never definitely suspended. It was seldom possible to say with certainty on any afternoon, "There will be no Evolutions to-night." They were always likely to occur, and when they did there was no way of escape. The junior midshipmen grew to expect them, to remember suddenly in the happiest moment of an afternoon leave what the evening might have in store. The dread of these Evolutions permeated their waking life, entering their minds when on or off duty, interrupting their work in School, colouring their speech, inspiring their manner with furtiveness and bitterness, with resentment and fear. Only from the letters they wrote home were the Evolutions excluded, for they did their utmost to make their people believe that they were happy.

The *King Arthur* sailed for Gibraltar early in October. During the day the midshipmen carried out sea routine, keeping their watches on deck or in the Engine-room. Krame made his arrangements for the evening with so much success that, as a result of careful interchange, the midshipmen who, from eight to midnight, kept the first watch below and on the bridge were three of intermediate seniority, Norgate, Hambling, and Ollenor. Reedham, the only one remaining of the intermediate group, left the Gunroom after dinner at the same time as Winton-Black, and purposely did not return. So it happened that, when mess was over, and when the midshipmen of the Last Dog had finished their later watch-dinner, the five senior and the six junior midshipmen were left in the Gunroom together.

"Warts, fall in! Howdray, you are the mate of the ship's biscuits. Elstone, you might look out for the water."

"Water? What the hell do you want water for?"

Krame pointed to where the junior midshipmen stood in single rank. "These six young gentlemen," he said "have not yet been christened. They are—what's the word?—unregenerate. As I, being Senior Midshipman in this 'ere Gunroom, am responsible for the young gentlemen's spiritual, bodily, and moral welfare, I propose to christen them. Therefore water, Elstone."

"I knew all about that," said Elstone, "but what I mean is, why not christen them in crême de menthe? It's stickier."

Howdray's great voice shouted in protest. "And whose wine bill is to go down the young gentlemen's necks?"

"Besides," said Tintern solemnly, "it would ruin their shirts, you know."

"Damn their shirts!" Krame answered. "They can buy new ones, can't they? They ought to be rich enough. They don't spend their money on anything, so far as I can see—no women, no card bill, no extra extras, no wine bill to speak of. . . . But I'm with you, Howdray. We won't waste crême de menthe on them."

"It might go down to themselves," Banford-Smith kindly suggested.

"Lot of good that would be," Howdray grumbled, "seeing that we have their wine bills."

"Water be it," said Krame. "The jug's on the slab, Elstone. Howdray, the biscuits are in my locker, just above your head."

From his place in the line John watched Howdray climb on to the settee and fetch the material for the christening. Krame and Elstone sat at the end of the table, Elstone next the pantry hatch and Krame nearer the ship's side. On Krame's left was Howdray, now sliding back into his place and arranging the huge ship's biscuits on the table in front of him. Further for'ard, sprawling on the settee, and engaged in a competition of blowing smoke-rings at their liqueur glasses, were Tintern and Banford-Smith, who seemed less interested than the others in the business of the evening. Elstone regarded it, perhaps thoughtlessly, as a tremendous joke; Howdray was frankly a bully of the old fashion, great in bulk but not in strength, good-humoured on occasions, happy-go-lucky, for ever at war with authority, a creature of vast appetites and weak control. Only Krame seemed to derive genuine pleasure from the proceedings. He possessed a quick, almost brilliant mind. He was handsome, popular in polite shore-going circles, an efficient officer, admired, on account of his easy manner and soft, smiling lips, by women and by men whose acquaintance with him was but superficial. He enjoyed Gunroom Evolutions. He used to tell his dance partners about them. It pleased him to play the autocrat in Oriental style, to see human beings—no matter at what cost in pain to themselves—subjected to his will. Even as John watched him, he called the junior midshipmen to attention and stood them at ease again half a dozen times in quick succession, not because by doing so he served any purpose, but because he liked to hear his own voice giving orders. He smiled complacently to see them spring to attention at his behest. He pretended that they had not moved smartly enough, and turned down the corners of his mouth in an absurd grimace of disapproval.

Over the table the electric lights beneath their yellow shades swung with the slow motion of the ship. The air was swirling and blue with tobacco smoke that clung in long wreaths to the nap of the red and black tablecloth. The temperature was high, and the atmosphere foul with the odour of food, for a threatening sea had caused the scuttles to be shut, and no one had troubled to open them again.

Krame left his place and seated himself regally on a chair between the table and the door. On his right stood Elstone with a jug of water, on his left Howdray, clutching an armful of ship's biscuits.

"Now, first Wart forward. At the run!"

Sentley, who was on the right of the line, hurried from his place and stood at attention before Krame.

"On the knee! . . . 'Shun! . . . On the knee!" The spectators roared to see Sentley clambering from one position to the other. Howdray picked up a thick cane from the sideboard and hit Sentley as he knelt.

"Come on," he said, "get a move on. 'Shun! Now, at the order 'Kneeling position—place,' you'll drop on your knees—understand?—drop, not let yourself down like an old woman. . . . Kneeling position—place!"

Sentley went down. His knees brought up hard against the deck. He kept his body and head erect, his hands to his sides. Banford-Smith and Tintern climbed out of their places on the settee; one perched himself on the edge of the table behind Howdray, the other found a convenient seat by the piano.

"The child," said Krame, after the manner of a gunnery instructor, "will incline the 'ead forward in a reverent attitood and assoom a mournful aspect. 'E will now repeat the Warts' Creed."

Sentley repeated that parody of the Apostles' Creed which had been given to each junior midshipman earlier in the day. "I believe in the Sub Almighty, master of every Wart, and in

Peter Krame, 'is noble 'elp, our Lord . . .'' and so on to the end. No senior midshipman protested against this Creed, no junior midshipman refused to repeat it.

When he was silent, a ship's biscuit, thick and tough, was beaten and beaten on Sentley's head until the biscuit broke. Howdray was about to pour water from the jug when Banford-Smith restrained him. ''Cut out the water,'' he said, ''it will make such a damned mess on the deck.''

Each junior midshipman came forward in turn, dropped on his knees, was struck with Howdray's stick if he dropped not fast enough, bowed his head, repeated the Creed, and had a biscuit broken upon him. John, because he stood on the left of the line, came last. When the ceremony was over, Krame glanced behind him.

''Now let's have a hymn,'' he said to Tintern.

''What hymn?''

''Any old hymn—something to celebrate the young gentlemen's regeneration. Lynwood will lead the singing. All Warts will support him.''

Tintern emptied a glass of port, squared himself to the piano, and beat out the first chords of No. 165. Not only the Warts sang it; the senior midshipmen, tired of the many repetitions of the christening ceremony, were glad of a chance to make a noise.

''*O Gawd, our 'elp in ages pa-ha-hast.*'' This prolongation was in response to Tintern's improvised chords and runs. ''*Our 'ope for years to come.*'' The voices swelled to a roar, and paused for breath. In the momentary silence the ship rolled deeply; the sea came surging over a scuttle and receded, leaving wisps of luminous foam. ''*Our shelter from the stormy bla-ha-hast, And our eternal——*''

Tintern was beating the keyboard with his doubled fists as a kind of desperate finale. The wild discords screamed under the steel bars overhead. A locker flew open, and by a lurch of the ship all it contained was shot across the Gunroom. A Manual of Seamanship, a ''Child's Guide,'' a writing-case, a Gunnery Drill-Book, and a box of instruments, lay scattered on the table amid a pile of crumpled letters. An Oxford Bible was open and face downwards on the deck. Near it a bottle of ink, streaming its contents, rolled to and fro. Finally, there fell from the locker a photograph of Driss's mother. He started forward to gather up his possessions.

"Fall in, damn you!" Krame shouted. "Who told you to fall out?"

Driss went on.

Krame stood up. "Come here, Driss. Did you hear me tell you to fall in?"

"Yes."

"Well?"

"I am going to pick up my things before they are spoilt."

"Why don't you keep your locker properly shut? Look at the ink on the deck. I've a damned good mind—by God, you shall lick it up!"

Driss's face was pale, his Irish eyes dangerous. Tintern leaned sideways in his seat and took Krame by the arm.

"Dry up, you fool!" he said in an undertone, and turned back to the piano. He had tact, moreover.

"O Gawd, our 'elp in ages pa-ha-hast . . ." Before the chorus was ended Driss had secured his locker and quietly fallen in again.

The next Evolution was known alternatively by two names—one, "The Angostura Hunt"; the other, which was sometimes attached in other Gunrooms to an Evolution slightly different, "Creeping for Jesus." John was the first taken. Thrust on his knees near the serving slab, he was blindfolded with two handkerchiefs. He could hear the senior midshipmen's voices. "Lay it here. . . . No, not under the table. We can't get at him under the table. . . . There, that will do. Replace the bitters, Elstone."

"Can you see?" asked Krame.

"No."

"Can you smell?"

"Yes."

"Can you feel?"

"Yes."

"Well, that's what is wanted—a good scent, and probably a bit of feeling before you're through with it." He cleared his throat. "Now, Lynwood, somewhere in the Gunroom is a piece of bread on the deck. Between you and the bread is a trail of Angostura bitters—pungent, so as to make it easy. You've got to find the bread by scent and pick it up with your mouth. No feeling with your hands, mind you. Put his nose on the trail, someone."

Hands seized John's head and thrust it downwards. "Got it? Smell it?"

"Not yet."

"Give him a sniff at the bottle. . . . Got it now?"

"Yes."

"Right. Wait for the order to commence. . . . Stand by. Go!"

John began to crawl along the floor. They were shouting at him to go faster. "Get a move on. Good dog. Good dog.———! the beggar isn't trying. Let him have it, Howdray."

A cane sang through the air and fell upon John's legs, sang and fell again. The blood ran to his head. The smell of corticine and dust sickened him. The blows were falling rapidly now. Someone other than Howdray seized a stick and sent the pain shooting through John's body. He saw now the reason for this creeping position—the excellence of the target it provided. If he could but regain the scent and get to the end of it! But the scent was gone, and he could not steady himself. The weight of his body on his hands was making his wrists ache. The noise was deafening. On his palms the dust seemed inches thick. When he tried to rise, they thrust him down again. . . .

Behind the bandage on his eyes was scarlet blindness, and he was visited by a sense of the desperate impotence of the blind. The words of those shouting above him conveyed no clear meaning to him now. They were giving him guidance, he thought. There was a medley of cries: "Port! Starboard! . . . He doesn't know his port from his starboard hand." A stick fell again.

"Give him a chance, Howdray. Still a moment; I'll put him on the trail." This was Tintern's voice.

But help was unavailing. Perhaps some foot had extinguished the trail; at any rate, even with Tintern's guidance, John could not detect the scent. He groped forward to no purpose. Banford-Smith, sliding from the table, stood unintentionally on his fingers, causing him so much pain that, though he was now too bitter to cry out, he reeled from his track. A moment letter his hand touched something wet—perhaps the blood from beneath his crushed finger-nail, perhaps no more than Driss's ink. He neither knew nor cared. In his head, which he dared not raise from the ground, it seemed that fire was burning. His temples and his eyes were throbbing as if they would burst. He paused bewildered, and instantly sticks fell on him again. . . . It would never, never end. Perhaps he was going to faint. He wished he might. That might end it for the evening at least. That might end it all.

Shouts, forcing themselves upon his consciousness, suggested that he was near the bread he was seeking. He groped in the dust with his teeth and tongue, hoping he might end his quest. The grit was about his lips and in his nostrils.

Then the bandage shifted, and he saw the bread. He did not dare to seize it immediately lest they should guess that he could see, but he worked slowly towards it and picked it up between his teeth. A great burst of cheering followed, vague cheering, such as he remembered having heard when, down and out in a boxing competition, he had been dragged by his seconds to his corner. Presently he found himself leaning against the table, the bandage having been pulled away. The sweat was dripping from his forehead and stinging in his eyes. His whole body ached. He stooped, brushed the dust mechanically from the knees of his trousers, and tried to smile to show that he was "taking it well." And there was Fane-Herbert's face, indistinct as though seen through a heat wave, wearing that proud, resentful, unforgiving look.

"Have a drink," said Howdray, his stick still in his hand. "Dry work on the deck, eh?" He rang the bell. "You did it in pretty good time, too."

"Pretty—good—time?" said John slowly, as if he did not understand. "Pretty good time? I thought it was ages."

Soon he was taking a glass off the tray that the steward held out to him.

"Cheer-oh!" said Howdray.

"Cheer-oh!" John answered, and drank thirstily. He sat on the extreme edge of the table, watching, with set eyes, how the others repeated his performance. The shouts and the crashes of the canes came up to him as from a dream. Soon Cunwell was beside him, drinking too. Fane-Herbert refused to drink. Sentley came last of all.

"Fall in again," Krame was saying. "Fall in!"

They stood in line, awaiting the resumption. It seemed as though more would be unendurable; but John's glance at the clock, combined with his knowledge that the Evolutions would continue until the Mess was compulsorily closed, showed him that as yet they had but begun. Hitherto they had been called upon only to act singly, and the Gunroom's limited space had added nothing to their troubles, but now an obstacle race was being planned. Of this John had had previous experience. He knew that it meant fighting with his own friends in an attempt not to be last.

The course, as designed by Krame, was long and difficult. They were to go out of the Gunroom, aft through the Chest Flat, through a watertight door on the bulkhead, on to the half-deck, into the Smoking Casemate, round the pedestal of the gun, out of the Casemate, for'ard through the Chest Flat and into the Gunroom again by the after door. Arrived there, they were to pass between the stove and the wall, over the table from port to starboard, between the settee and the table's edge, under the table from starboard to port, along the deck to the Gunroom's after end, under the table from aft for'ard, over it from for'ard aft, and out of the Gunroom once more. They had then to go by way of the Chest Flat ladder on to the upper deck and to the after twelve-pounder gun in the port battery. Here they would find a signal pad, from which each was to detach a sheet. With this prize they were to run to the Gunroom, and, as Krame remarked, the Lord help the hindmost. . . .

The six of them started together. They fought at the narrow door of the Gunroom. They sped through the dim light of the Chest Flat, doubled up and with knees bent that they might pass below the hammocks slung there by the marines. In the Casemate it was impossible for more than one at a time to pass between the pedestal and the armour beneath the gunport. Elstone stood above them as they wriggled through the narrow space, thrusting each other aside, tearing their clothes, hitting their heads and knees and elbows against the projections of brass and steel. They reeled out of the Casemate, not now packed close, but divided by the intervals that the delay at the gun-pedestal had created. John was the second to reach the Gunroom. When, having passed behind the stove, he was about to go over the table, he heard them shouting at Fane-Herbert, who had entered last. But none dared pause. Over the table they went, and headforemost on to the deck beneath it; under and aft, under the table again, canes urging on those in rear, and falling haphazard across knuckles and arms. Already John was spent; all were spent. Their legs trembled beneath them. They coughed amid the dust. Under a hail of blows they battled at the Gunroom door, swept beyond it through the Chest Flat for the third time, and rattled up the ladder into the cool, sweet air of the upper deck. At the battery gun, during the few moments he had to wait before he could tear his sheet from the signal pad, John caught sight of the great phosphorescence of the sea. Above him the masts tapered to a dark, clear sky. Smoke drove ghost-like from the funnels. For'ard the lamps were gleaming in the charthouse windows, and near at hand, in the uncertain light of the battery, seamen stood smoking around their spitkids, gazing with an expression of amusement and contempt at their officers being licked into shape.

As John raced away with his sheet of paper he heard Fane-Herbert muttering to himself: "Oh be damned to them! I'm last, anyway. I'm not going to hurry any more."

They burst into the Gunroom, thrust their sheets of paper into Krame's hands, and stood there trembling with exhaustion and pain. Dyce seemed to be on the verge of losing control. His face was working. They had fear that his nerves would yield, that he would break, as can even the strongest men, into ungovernable tears. The atmosphere was charged with a strange emotion—the emotion that, as it were a sudden fever, sometimes grips a mob, cutting it free from the restraints men impose upon themselves, casting it back into the primitive conditions of self-defence and self-assertion. If Dyce had given way, his collapse might well have been a signal for forgetfulness of the difference between senior and junior midshipmen, for a complete abandonment of control. Near him John could hear Driss—of all of them the youngest in appearance, the most clearly a simple-minded, high-spirited boy—saying over and over again to himself: "My God, I want to kill! I want to kill!" His fingers were twined among the tablecloth, as if thereby he held them in check. Now he was making odd, inarticulate sounds in his throat. John saw his face, and turned quickly from the flaming bitterness he read there. There were passions streaming through Driss, passions utterly foreign to his apparent nature, fierce desires, called up from God knew what animal depths, upon which it was not good to look.

Last by thirty seconds, Fane-Herbert entered without signs of haste. And they put him over the table, and pulled out his shirt, and tried to flog the pride out of him. He did not move through it all, and when it was over, with his fine mouth set, he turned away from the faces grinning above the canes.

"Fall in again!" Krame said. "Fall in, I say!"

Evolution followed Evolution: the obstacle race in reverse order; an affair called Torpedoes, that consisted essentially in hurling the junior midshipmen's bodies along the table against the for'ard bulkhead; and half a dozen others, the product of Krame's ingenuity. Even the flame in Driss died down. There comes a time when resistance, even mental resistance, disappears. The limbs move as they are told.

At ten o'clock a ship's corporal tapped at the door and announced that it was time to close the Gunroom.

"Last drinks," said Krame, and rang the bell. "Warts fall out!"

Somehow they opened their sea-chests, got out of their clothes, scrambled aft, and swung themselves into their hammocks. Once in his, John lay as he was, not caring even to creep between the blankets. He lay staring at the white-painted T-bar within a few inches of his face, listening to the rifles, which were stored near by, clicking to and fro in their racks with each roll of the ship. The half-deck sentry passed him now and then. Somewhere a pump groaned continually. From the open door of the Wardroom came the sound of voices and laughter and snatches of song.

John did not sleep. He lay inert, capable of no consecutive thought. He went on repeating catch-words to himself, counting the groans of the pump, counting the sentry's footsteps, sucking his damaged finger, running his hand over the rough surface of the canvas hammock. Despite his efforts to banish so tormenting a vision, again and again he saw himself crouched in the window-seat of a sun-strewn library, now looking out to the hills, now turning the pages of a book. He saw the excellence of open print; almost he heard a clock ticking. . . . In less than two hours, Ollenor, who had been keeping the first watch, shook his hammock.

"Lynwood!"

"Yes, I'm awake."

"About ten minutes to eight bells. Your middle watch."

"All right; thanks."

He swung out on to the deck, went to his chest, and put on watch-keeping clothes.

On the bridge Ollenor turned over to him such information as he would need for his watch. When Ollenor had gone, John glanced at the dim figure of the officer of the watch on the upper bridge. Then, passing the Quartermaster at the wheel, he stood by the semaphore and looked aft, beyond the funnels and the boat deck, at the lights of the next astern. Presently he turned his face for'ard and took off his cap, and let the wind blow among his hair. Soon he must take a sextant on to the upper bridge and help the officer of the watch keep station; but now he stood inactive, one hand on the cool steel of a searchlight. The incomparable peace of the wide sky; the throb of the main engines; the rising and dipping lights of the fleet—there was sweet, timeless monotony in these things. Far below him the cut foam was hissing against the bows. Behind him the pipe of the boatswain's mate was shrilling and shrilling again.

And Krame was asleep, and the hand of God over the sea.

Chapter IV
War, Carpets, and Candles

I

The fleet put in to Arosa Bay, and, in less than twelve hours, sailed thence without regret. On the day following their departure an event occurred which, for the time being, changed the lives of every member of the *King Arthur*'s company. Late in the forenoon watch a wireless signal was received and immediately submitted to the Rear-Admiral. This much of its contents became public: that the Admiralty had ordered the Cruiser Squadron, which at the time was making common speed with the battleships, to proceed independently to Gibraltar at sixteen knots. This speed, unusual and uneconomical enough to suggest that there was serious reason for it, combined with the tension already created in men's minds by the happenings at Agadir, gave wonderful import to the news, which spread with almost magical rapidity from the bridge to the officers' messes, from the fo'c's'le to the boiler-room depths. Speculation as to the meaning of the order was anxious and eager. Rumours of war had in times past been so frequent as to colour all prophecies with scepticism, but hope remained—hope that now at length the consummation was at hand. The Rear-Admiral unbent so far as to jest with the officer of the watch. The Yeoman of Signals overheard him, and repeated his words on the lower bridge. The lower bridge handed on the tale to the boatswain's mate, who, having embellished it, shared its marvel with the lower deck. In a quarter of an hour the Rear-Admiral's good-humour had permeated the ship. A Pay-master celebrated it in the Wardroom Casemate by paying for a round of drinks. The Senior Engineer put on clean overalls and went smiling below. The stokers grumbled no more, but fired their boilers and slammed

their furnace-doors with vigorous enthusiasm. They were not
going to Gibraltar now to carry out gun-practice in Catalan
Bay, gun-practice in Tetuan, gun-practice in Catalan again.
"Sixteen knots!" remarked a Chief Stoker, with emphasis
that made explanation unnecessary. "Sixteen knots!" said
one of the carpenter's crew. "Looks as if we shan't need
them targets wi' the little red sails."

Even in the Gunroom, comradeship displaced boredom.
The Chaplain relaxed discipline during School. Baring came
in to drink a glass of sherry and to share Wardroom opinion
with Winton-Black. Midshipmen, senior, intermediate, and
junior, looked towards the future from a common standpoint.
The Clerk saw his ledger shrouded in the mists of the past.
His action-station, he said a dozen times, was with the
Dumaresq. "You won't see much of the show from the
Dumaresq," said Banford-Smith, and the Clerk replied hum-
bly, but with complete happiness: "No, but it's better than
the Ship's Office."

There was, too, a wonderful moment in which Krame
seemed to forget that John was a Wart whose duty it was to
tidy up the Gunroom, to polish the stove-pipes, and to do
scuttle-drill when the sea ran high and ventilation became
necessary.

"Come on deck, Lynwood," he said. "We had better have
a glance round our guns for minor defects."

They strolled on deck together and visited every casemate
in their group. In that time they were friends, officers charged
with a common responsibility. The great game was about to
begin, the game for which the whole Service had been training for many weary years. All routine, all hardness, all
drudgery had become suddenly worth while. Spirit had entered into the flesh.

At no time while he served in the *King Arthur* was John
happier. He and Fane-Herbert, knowing nothing of war, con-
gratulated themselves upon the fact that it had come to them
so early in their careers. "And isn't it amazing what a
difference it makes?" said Fane-Herbert. "The Gunroom is
changed. All the senior snotties act as though we were their
friends."

"I expect they would be better in the ordinary course,"
John answered, "if they got more leave clear away from the
ship, and weren't so infernally bored by unbroken routine."

But the excitement and its excellent effect endured not

long. When they arrived at Gibraltar nothing happened. The next day, while they coaled ship, hope waned. "Come on, lads," cried a petty officer to encourage the grimy workers, "that's about where Agadir lies." He pointed a finger towards Africa. But they laughed at him and glanced at the coaling flags that told them how their work progressed. "Six 'undred more to come," they said; "six 'undred more ton. . . ."

And when they sailed from Gibraltar, their destination was Catalan Bay, their prospect gun-practice. The ship's company added another memory to their list of war scares, and suffered from the inevitable reaction.

II

The essential element in gun-practice and range keeping exercises is waiting with nothing to do—waiting till the target is ready, waiting till the ship's turn comes, waiting while a passing merchant ship fouls the range, waiting while the important people in the controls make abstruse calculations with which the men at the guns have no concern. The monotony is varied by gun-drill, but even gun-drill palls. The hours pass slowly. The eyes stare at the expressionless breech of the gun until, tiring of that, they stare at the red wheel above the ammunition hoist. Often they stare at the bugler as he passes the open door of the casemate, and prayers go up that ultimately he may sound the "Secure." The captain of the gun, sick of the limited topics which can be discussed within the hearing of the officer whose head is in the sighting-hood, produces rags and a tin, and proceeds to polish bright work already immaculate. Then he puts away his rags and tin, and watches the bugler again.

Coming into Gibraltar for a week-end, John played in a cricket match, in which, for lack of training, the batting was poor and the bowling without sting. Gunroom Evolutions had long begun again. Krame had forgotten the incident of the "minor defects," and the junior midshipmen were Warts without cease. In Tetuan Bay the natives ashore appeared, to those who watched them through telescopes, to be carrying on warfare. There were rifle flashes and smoke, and bodies of men moving hastily hither and thither. No one cared very much. To the midshipmen it meant something to record in the personal logbooks they submitted each Sunday morning to the Captain. . . .

It was in Tetuan Bay, too, perhaps during the warfare, perhaps during some other similar week after peace had been declared, that the ship's company bathed—the officers from the starboard after gangway, the men for'ard from the port lower boom. John, as midshipman of the watch, was on the quarter-deck, watching the clock for the time at which he should recall the men from the water by ordering the bugler to sound the "Retire." Suddenly, on the port quarter, he caught sight of the unmistakable fin. Sharks were not then to be expected in that part of the world. He looked again, this time through a telescope. "Quartermaster, what do you make of that?"

The Quartermaster borrowed the telescope. "Yessir. Shark, sir."

John wheeled round. "Bugler! Sound the 'Retire' and sound the 'Double.' Go on sounding it until you are sure that all men in the water have heard. Sound it first to the officers on the starboard side. . . . Boatswain's-mate! Go and pipe by the lower boom: 'Shark on the port quarter. All hands return to the ship.' Warn the boat."

John called for a megaphone and summoned courage to address the Commander, who, in the water, was very much like the rest of mankind. It was bad enough to have sounded the "Retire" at him.

"Commander, sir!"

The Commander, much to John's surprise, held up his hand to show he had heard, just as John himself, had he been away in a boat, would have held up his hand to indicate attention to the Commander's orders.

"Shark on the port quarter, sir!"

The Commander raised himself an instant from the water and made a funnel of his hands. "Get the men out," he shouted, and swam towards the ship. The other officers followed him. He met John on the top of the gangway.

"Like shouting at the Commander?" he demanded.

John had not liked it. He had thought twice about doing it, but it had seemed inevitable. Apparently he had done wrong. "I thought, sir——" he began.

The Commander grinned and shook the drops from him. "Go on, boy. I'm not an ogre. You did quite right. Very smartly, too."

III

Early in November, when the day of joining the *King Arthur* seemed to be separated from the present lifetime, instead of by little more than a month, of experience, and when the prospect of Christmas leave, not infinitely remote, coloured even the present with hope, John had an adventure in night boat work. For him the day had been more than usually strenuous. The *King Arthur* had been at sea for Commander-in-Chief's firing. From half-past eight in the morning until half-past seven at night, John had been almost continuously on duty. It had happened, as sometimes it must happen, that when he was not on watch he was required in a duty boat, and when neither in a boat nor on the bridge, he had had to go to his gun. At dinner he thought his day was over, and, Krame having chosen a sing-song that night in preference to Gunroom Evolutions, he settled down to read as best he could among the choruses. But soon after nine a cutter was called away again. Banford-Smith, whose duty it should have been, had advanced too far into a cheerful evening to venture out into the night. Some midshipman must run the boat, and the choice fell upon John.

Fortunately the evening was fine, for the trip seemed likely to be long. It appeared that the *Vera* was bringing or had brought into harbour a target of which the *King Arthur* stood in need. This target required repairs and a new sail. "And first of all," added the officer of the watch, "you've got to find the thing."

"Where is the *Vera* lying, sir?" John asked.

"The Lord knows! The bridge seems to have lost her. She hasn't come to her buoy yet. But go to the dockyard wall first. The target is probably there already. If it isn't, you'll have to look round till you find the *Vera*, and make enquiries."

John ran down the gangway into his cutter, seated himself on the "dicky," and gave orders to shove off. The oars dropped into the water and the boat drew away from the ship. On one hand, the many lights of the Fleet winked at their reflections in the smooth water; on the other, the great rock, magnified by the night, and speckled with the illumination of innumerable windows, rose, dark and gigantic, against the sky. When the wall was reached they searched in vain for the target, and turned to cruise the harbour in quest of the *Vera*.

Although he was tired and needed sleep before the morrow's coaling, he was glad that he had come. The click of the oars' looms and the hiss of their blades, the spring at the beginning and the slackening at the end of each stroke, the ripple and suck about the stern, the regular breathing of the crew and the synchronous creaking of their stretchers, bespoke a romance that was not the romance of steel ships. The cox-swain sat motionless, his hand on the tiller, as rugged as a statue rough-hewn in wood. Clustered in the stern sheets, with their bags of glistening tools, the carpenter's party lent emphasis to man's silence by their occasional whispering. John's gaze strayed for'ard; the white gleaming of the crew's faces and of their hands curved over the oars grew more and more indistinct towards the bows, and the line of gunwale shrank to a delicate thread.

Swing, catch, and an easy stroke; the gleam, the dip, and the swirl of blades; the hidden faces and the arms outstretched, the arms drawn in and the faces raised. And he, above them, commanding them, passed among the shadows of great ships into the darkness. On either hand the little bow-wave ran out lapping, and flattened itself wide of the stern.

"Don't see no *Vera*, sir," said the coxswain.

"Not yet."

" 'Adn't we better arst, sir?"

"Ask? Where?"

"Report at the ship for orders, sir."

"The orders were to find the *Vera*." John had no intention of returning to the *King Arthur* and confessing himself defeated.

"Don't think we'll find 'er, pullin' round the 'arbour, sir—not to-night, anyway."

John had made up his mind. He would seek information elsewhere. The helm was put over a little. At no great distance from him, lay the *London*. At first he thought of going alongside her and asking her officer of the watch for the position of the *Vera*, but he dismissed this idea when he realized that this was no polite hour for midshipmen to pay calls. Moreover, a story of his being lost might easily become a jest in the Wardrooms of the Fleet.

"Goin' alongside the *London*, sir?"

"No. When she hails, answer 'passing.' I'm going to stop under her bridge."

Came the hail: "Boat ahoy!"

"Passing!"

Judging the amount of way necessary to carry his boat to the forebridge, John very quietly gave the order: "Oars!" The rowing ceased, and the water licked at the sides. Presently the cutter was still.

"Hail the bridge," John said, "and ask the signalman of the watch for the *Vera*. Hail quietly, so that they can't hear you aft."

The coxswain stood up. "*London*"—a thick sound, for it is no easy thing to hail quietly. Then a little louder, in a tone almost melodramatic: "*London . . . London . . . London—*bridge!"

The bowman could not resist it. "Change at the Elephant an' Castle!"

The crew heard. The crew choked down a laugh hurtful to the coxswain's dignity. He turned on them.

"Knock orf chawin' yer fat there," he said angrily, and silence fell. Someone peered over the bridge rails.

"D'you know where the *Vera* 'angs out?" the coxswain asked quickly, before the other had time to hail him.

"Lyin' outside at anchor. Comin' to 'er buoy to-morrer."

"Outside the ruddy 'arbour?"

"Yes."

"Gawd!" The coxswain sat down disconsolately. "We shall 'ave a night of it," he observed.

The music of the oars began again. They pulled slowly between the ships, beyond the ships, out of the harbour. Soon the *Vera*, an outpost of twinkling lights, beyond which lay the open sea, was hailing them. Much to his surprise, John was welcomed by the officer of the watch.

"That infernal target?" he said. "It *is* alongside the wall—right at the far end. What an hour to send you out after it! I'm afraid you have a long job of repairs; it was knocked about a bit. Come down into the Wardroom before you start."

John went below and accepted whisky and soda, an illegal proceeding, for by regulation he was too young to drink spirits. They offered cigarettes, and when he refused to smoke one because his crew was waiting, they gave him a handful to take away with him.

"You'll have time to smoke them all before you get home to-night," said the Gunnery Lieutenant. "Well, so long. You will have luck if you are turned in before the end of the middle watch. Sorry you have had so far to come."

A long pull shoreward brought the cutter at last to the

target. John turned out the carpenter's party and all the boat's crew save one, whom he kept with him as a boat-keeper. John soon found that in the man he had retained he was to have a remarkable companion. He came aft, seated himself in the stern sheets, and looked up expectantly.

" 'Ave a smoke, sir?"

"Yes; carry on smoking."

" 'Ave a cigar, sir?"

John hesitated. He would have felt safer with one of the *Vera*'s cigarettes. He was not inured to cigars, but for company's sake he took one and lighted it.

"Funny thing, sir," the man said, "these night trips always make me feel mysterious-like. You feel more powerful some'ow in the dark. Do it take you that way, sir?"

"Powerful?" John asked, wondering how much this had in common with his own sensation.

"Same as you feel, sir, when you're alone, an' there ain't no one to see 'ow small you are. I always thinks then o' the things I might do if I liked—but it don't seem a fair advantage to take o' folk what aren't made the same way."

"What do you mean?"

"It's this way, sir. You see, I can make people do things— anything. I don't rightly know what the name of it is— 'ypnotism, or mesmerism, or the like. It don't make much odds what they call it. But I can make people do things all right, I can, an' 'ere they are makin' me do things all day. I'm a proper bad 'at, I am—always on the carpet. I get to feel angry like, knowin' the power I 'ave. I did a turn at a ship's concert once—afore you young gen'lemen joined—an' the Commander, 'e won't 'ave doin' it no more."

"Could you make me do things now?"

The man held up a finger. "I could make you 'op into the water, sir." John looked over the side, and the voice went on. "An' if I went up close to 'em, I could make the ruddy carpenter's party stand on their ruddy 'eads an' stop there. An' if I stepped out in front of 'em, an' the ship's police kep' their 'ands off, I could make the Captain an' the Commander to a cake-walk at Sunday Divisions, I could."

"Why on earth don't you?" said John.

"Oh, it wouldn't never do, sir. That ain't Service, sir— —the orficers cake-walkin'. I should be doin' detention for the rest 'o me mortal. . . . Besides, that ain't what I likes doin'—sing-song turns, an' funny stunts, an' the like." He looked away, and his words drifted into vagueness, being no longer addressed to an audience. "I likes talkin' to a crowd an' seein' 'em all comin' round, comin' round gradual-like, not knowin' 'ow or why, all of 'em comin' round to my way o' thinkin'. They don't agree to start off, but soon I sees 'em noddin' their 'eads, an' smilin' an' smilin', an' sayin' 'Aye, aye,' an' ' 'Ere, 'ere.' An' their faces looks strange some'ow till they douse the glim." He paused, shot out both hands in an expansive gesture, and let them fall again to his sides. " 'Ere I be, Able Seaman, 'undredth class for conduck, 'undredth class for leaf, an', Gawd Almighty! I might 'a bin Prime Minister of All England, wi' the Albert 'All risin' up to me, jus' as if I 'ad 'em on strings. . . ."

Together they sat there, dreaming vast dreams. Above them the carpenter's party was driving in nails. John held his cigar close to the water, and watched the diffused red of its reflection. When he dropped it, as if by accident, it fizzled sharply.

"Dropped yer cigar, sir?"

"Yes."

" 'Ave another, sir?"

"No, thanks."

Silence again. . . . The work on the target was at last completed. Tired men climbed back into the boat. Oars were got out lazily. It was five in the morning when they reached the *King Arthur*. A bugle was calling the hands to coal ship.

IV

The year dragged towards its end. The novelty of night firing wore off. John was soon to cease watchkeeping on the upper deck and to join the engineering staff for a period of training. He wrote to his mother, asking her to send him a pipe, for among the boilers even midshipmen under eighteen can console themselves with tobacco. Once, with Gunroom Evolutions in his mind, he wrote: "I think we may have had the worst of our time in this ship. For a whole week now we have been left pretty well alone." But the next evening his hopes were shattered, and the old business began again. The need of leave, of an interval, however brief, in which there would be no Krame and no Commander, became imperative. When they went ashore the junior midshipmen found a place of refuge in the Garrison Library. There, having paid a small monthly subscription, they could read the newspapers without fear that Krame would enter suddenly, and, because one of them was reading *The Times*, exclaim: "Who has *The Times*? I want *The Times*." There they could sit in comfortable chairs, and enjoy teas marvellously inexpensive, certain—quite certain— that, until the clock told them they must go, their time was their own. No one would shout at them to pick up paper. Howdray would not make them put away their letters and write out his Division List for him. Elstone would not tell them that he wanted a sketch for his log-book done immediately. In the Garrison Library there was peace. They could talk without continually glancing over their shoulders lest someone should enter by the Gunroom door.

They did talk to their great relief. It was good to plan rebellion, though they knew nothing could ever spring from their plans. It was satisfactory to hear, from midshipmen of other ships, that these things went on not in the *King Arthur* alone. It was amusing to compare method and detail, and to congratulate themselves because certain Evolutions usual in H.M.S.——and H.M.S.——had not been devised by Krame's inventive mind.

One afternoon someone brought in news that what was happening in a Home Fleet ship had leaked out. A complaint had been made to the Admiralty. A Court of Enquiry had been ordered. Great things were expected to result from this—perhaps a general reformation.

"No," said Fane-Herbert. "Probably they will keep it out of the papers. And anyhow, people will say: 'Oh, it's all an exceptional case. How terrible! but it's just an exceptional case.' There may be a court-martial. The Sub or someone may get dipped. And then it will blow over and be forgotten. It won't make any difference to us."

The great day came at last. "This time to-morrow we shall be on our way home."

"They will give us hell going across the Bay. It's always worse at sea. No one is away on late leave."

"Oh, what does it matter now? Next week we shall be out of it. Think, sleeping in a bed, and people who don't shout, and no tidying up the Gunroom, and no Krame for days on end!"

"And London. . . ."

"And pictures, and carpets, and flowers. . . ."

"And think of meeting a lady again!" said Fane-Herbert.

They laughed at him for that. "Aren't there ladies at
Gib.?"

"Yes; but they know the difference between a Lieutenant
and a Wart. I mean a—a *civilian* lady. . . . By the way,
Lynwood, you must come round and see my mother and
sister. Why not stay with us in Town the first night of leave,
and go down to your own home the next day?"

John nodded. "Thanks, I should like to. . . . Think of a
day with no routine!"

And they laughed again.

V

On that first night of leave for which they had been laying
innumerable and contradictory plans, Fane-Herbert came into
John's room while he was dressing. He sat down on the bed.

"Do you know we are to have a great man to dinner
to-night?"

"I thought you insisted that there should be no dinner-party?"

"So I did. This isn't a party. He's the only guest. My
mother knows him very well, and, strangely enough, he
appears to be an old friend of your mother's. He heard you
were going to be here to-night, and invited himself."

"Who is he?"

"A novelist, a poet, a writer of biography; a very important person indeed. Can you guess? He has the Order of
Merit, the only literary one except Thomas Hardy's."

"Wingfield Alter, of course. That's rather terrifying. What
is he like?"

"I haven't met him for a long time. He used to give me
shillings when I was a small boy, and tell me stories. But that
was ten years ago; he may have changed since then. Margaret
likes him, though, so I expect he is all right." Fane-Herbert
went to the door. "Shall I tell him you write poetry?" he
asked laughingly as he went out.

"No; for the Lord's sake don't be a fool!"

On his way downstairs John met Margaret.

"Have you heard of our guest?" she asked.

"Alter? Yes. Is it an ordeal?"

"Oh no. He is really a delightful person—tremendously
interested in everything. The only people he can't endure are
old ladies with salons who pat the lion. Mr. Alter won't be
patted."

"Of course he is pleasant to you," said John. "But, if he knows anything of the Navy, he won't have much use for junior midshipmen."

"Why not?"

John did not wish to explain. "Oh," he said vaguely, "junior midshipmen are rather looked down on in the Service."

"Only by senior midshipmen or their equivalent," she answered. "You will find that Mr. Alter doesn't take much notice of rank—rank of any kind, I mean, except that of ability."

At the foot of the stairs John's attention was arrested by a portrait in oils that hung there.

"Who is that?" he asked.

"My great-grandmother—on my mother's side."

"She is extraordinarily like you. Is there a portrait of her when she was your age?"

"No, I'm afraid not. That was done some time after her marriage. She was about twenty-six, I believe."

The subject of the portrait looked younger. She had Margaret's wide-set grey eyes, her dark hair, her clear skin, to which colour flowed richly only in emotion. And the resemblance went further than the physical, for John saw above him that expression, so remarkable for its vitality and yet so comforting in its repose, with which, when he turned his head, he found Margaret regarding him. In her eyes, though, was the brightness of laughter, and her great-grandmother had been a grave sitter.

"Is it so astonishing?"

"It is a wonderful portrait. You are sound evidence for the artist."

"I had her hung there," Margaret said, the light of laughter flickering out—"I had her hung there, at the foot of the stairs, so that I might see her whenever I came down to a dance or a dinner, and each morning before the day began. She looks so extraordinarily alive—so interested in all the world. And now—well, now, so far as the world is concerned, she's a picture on the wall and a name in a genealogical table."

"And so you use her as a text?"

"Not that. I don't attempt to weave philosophies around her. I suppose it's an odd form of superstition—at any rate, you can call it that, if you like. She seems to keep a certain balance—— " Margaret paused suddenly.

"Isn't that morbid?" Not till the question was out did he realize that he had spoken to test her.

"Morbid?" she repeated. "That's an easy word with which to dismiss the things you are afraid of. I'm not the least afraid of great-grandmother. . . . Besides, I don't think of her as dead. She is the best of great-grandmothers—extremely practical. She makes compliments transparent—on her stairs, at any rate." Margaret laid her hand on the panels. "And she makes me glad I can *feel* the grain in this oak." She turned away and walked to the bottom of the flight. Then she glanced up at John with a quick smile. "And sometimes, when I have been lazy, she sends me to my room again to change my dress."

She took him to admire a lacquer cabinet that stood in the hall.

"I expect you like looking at and touching these things? I know I should, if I had been long in a warship."

John rejoiced in her understanding. "Carpets," he said, "are the unceasing wonders; and the sound of dresses, and candles!"

"Candles? Do you remember that phrase in a poem of yours—'the spear-head flames'?"

"Yes. How did you see it?"

"Hugh sent home the copy you gave him. And—do you mind?—I showed it and other poems of yours, without your name, of course, to a friend of ours, a man whose judgment people believe in."

"I'm very glad. What did he say?"

"Good things. I'll tell you when there is more time."

"Who was he?"

"I'll get you to meet him some day—if you are not for ever out of England. . . . Why didn't you ask me what I thought of the poems myself?"

"I thought you would tell me."

"I'm scarcely a year older than you."

"Does that matter? It depends on what you were born and what you have read."

"I have read——" She broke off suddenly. "But no; I am sure poetry depends very much on what you have been through."

There was a pause.

"Mr. Alter, if he heard us, would say we were very young," John said.

Margaret looked back over their conversation and laughed.

"Have we been taking ourselves so seriously? Look at my great-grandmother. She is telling us to get along with us into the drawing-room."

There they found Wingfield Alter and Mrs. Fane-Herbert. Hugh came in a moment later. Alter had his back to the door as they entered, a square, broad back, full of determination. When he turned his head there were legible in the deeply lined face, with its high forehead and proudly carried chin, a self-confidence and directness of purpose which made it almost unnoticeable that Alter was a short, ungainly man. He wore a spare moustache and a pointed beard which began so far down his chin that his lips were unobscured by it. He waited for no introduction, but took John's hands at once, welcoming him as his mother's son, and looking at him closely.

Even at dinner John felt those deep-set eyes turned continually upon him, searching, he supposed, for points of resemblance to his mother. Mrs. Fane-Herbert, tall and slim at the end of the table, was a clever woman and Alter an eager listener. She turned the conversation to the Navy, and for long he was a willing and appreciative pupil. Hugh instructed him with great zest.

"How long is it, sir, since you were in a warship?"

"It must be four or five years. I have been in Russia since, and have lost touch. I see I must renew my acquaintance. I want to see what I can of the officers produced by the New Scheme—all my friends were *Britannia* cadets. Your education has been broader, less rigidly specialized than theirs. What is the effect on efficiency?"

"There must be a danger," said Mrs. Fane-Herbert, "of encouraging ideas and tastes, good in themselves, but ill-suited to the naval officer as such."

"I often wonder about that," Alter answered. "The Service is very exacting, very highly specialized, narrow in a sense. And boys enter it very early, knowing nothing of what they are or what they will become. They enter it in much the same spirit as that in which they choose the career of an engine-driver. Tendencies undreamed of then are bound to develop later—diverse tendencies, probably opposed in a thousand ways to Service requirements. Am I right?"

"Every word," said John, leaning forward a little.

"For example," Alter continued, "what on earth would have become of that young man whose work you showed me,

Margaret, if he had committed himself to the Navy at the age of thirteen? Of course, any critic would say those poems were immature. So they were; the technique of the sonnet was awry; the scansion was often loose; here and there they were too sonorous, too strained for the sake of effect. But so many of the essentials of poetry were there—real feeling, real imagination, and observation of the kind that's worth having. Never an adjective that he had not thought out with his eyes tight shut or wide open. If he can write like that before he is twenty—why, given a chance to develop, he might do anything. But if he were shut up in the Navy, burdened with the sameness of routine, brought into contact only with men whose minds are highly specialized for one purpose, war——" He interrupted himself with a gesture. "And there must be people of that kind in the Fleet—not poets necessarily, but men who, for one reason or another, need—need desperately—intellectual space. Most of us need it, unless our minds are very limited—that's the worst of the tragedy, *most* of us need it. And in the Navy, so far as I can judge, it must be almost impossible to obtain—at any rate, it is probably to be purchased only at the price of resignation or professional failure."

John did not hear the conversation that followed. His thoughts were proceeding by strange paths, now of pride and gladness, now so steep and dark that he could neither see nor imagine any end to them. Later in the evening Alter spoke to him alone.

"I'm unspeakably sorry," he said. "It was stupid of me not to have guessed; but Margaret ought to have warned me—she, with her mysterious poet whose name she would conceal in order to tantalize me. It's of no use to ask you not to let my words unsettle you; they are said, and I meant them, and there's an end of it. But I shall feel responsible now. Will you let me help you, if I can? I don't mean with master-keys to editors' rooms—you must win them for yourself. But I can give advice and criticism for what they are worth. I should want to help in any case now, but the more because you are my old friend's son. Will you remember?"

John thanked him as well as he could. When Alter had gone Margaret came to him.

"I never guessed that he might talk of it to-night," she said. "But you have heard his opinion yourself, and I am glad of that. Was the rest of what he said true?"

"Yes—in a way. I never thought of it in those terms before."

"And now you will go on thinking of it. You mustn't, you mustn't—but I know you will. And if it hurts, I am the cause of every hurt. I made you see clearly." She looked straight into his eyes, her own eyes glistening. "Whatever comes of it all, will you try to forgive me?"

"Perhaps I shall thank you some day," he answered. "After all, it is better to see clearly, isn't it?"

"Great-grandmother would say so. But it's the bravest thing of all."

She gave him her hand and said good-night. Presently he was sitting in the smoking-room with Hugh, still conscious of her touch and hearing her voice, still seeing her dress flicker between the banisters as she went upstairs.

The next morning he went into the country to his own home. He told his mother that he had met Wingfield Alter.

"He is a very dear friend of mine," she said. "I knew him before I met your father. He was married then, and poor, with no literary reputation. I saw him last soon after your father's death."

"But you never mentioned him?"

"London is so far away."

With a little sigh, she returned to her embroidery.

Chapter V
Two Worlds

A few days after John had rejoined his ship at Portsmouth, Mr. Baring, who was keeping the first dog watch, turned his telescope on to a shore-boat of shabby appearance which seemed to be approaching the *King Arthur*. Reedham, who was midshipman of the watch, likewise inspected the craft, which seemed to have the impudent intention of boarding the ship, not by the port gangway, which was, as it were, a back-door for the use of all and sundry, but by the starboard gangway, which, with its elaborate handrail of mahogany and brass, was the front-door of the exalted.

Though an officer less reserved might have said, "Who the devil is this?" Mr. Baring contented himself with looking from Reedham to the shore-boat and from the shore-boat to Reedham, for all the world as if Reedham were responsible for the incursion and for the unseamanlike appearance of the boat itself. And Reedham looked at the Quartermaster as if to say, "Well, what are *you* going to do about it?" And the Quartermaster did nothing but finger his boatswain's pipe.

There was, in truth, nothing to be done. It is possible to shout at a Service boat that is committing a breach of etiquette, but a shore-boat, though it lack varnish and leave lanyards and fenders hanging over the stern, cannot be so readily reproved. If it is known to contain a tradesman or some other dependent of the ship, then the megaphone may be called into use, but where a double exists caution is advisable. Who knows that it is not an admiral's guest who approaches? Admirals have queer guests.

This boat, as it drew near, was seen to contain, in addition to the oarsman, a small person wearing a bowler hat and a grey overcoat. There was no attempt at smartness. The hat was old and the coat older, though both were neat and respectable—so neat and so respectable, in fact, that Mr. Baring dismissed the idea that this might be an eccentric, and yet worthy, visitor.

"You had better lie off for the time being," said the small person to his boatman, when the craft had reached the gangway, and he, with a small bag in his hand, had disembarked. "I may need you to take me back. More probably I shall return in a ship's boat. If so, I will call you alongside and pay you."

"Return in a ship's boat, will he?" thought Mr. Baring. "We'll see about that. . . . Some commercial, I suppose."

The small person climbed the ladder slowly. As he stepped on to the quarter-deck he raised his hat in obedience to a Service custom well known to him. Mr. Baring, incredulous of such knowledge in a "commercial," accepted the salute as if it had been addressed to himself.

"Well," he said, "what can we do for you?"

"My name is Alter," said the small person, "and——"

"Indeed!" Mr. Baring interrupted, determined to enliven an uneventful watch at the expense of this innocent. "And what is your line?"

A few moments passed before Mr. Alter understood this question. Then, as he realized that he was a "commercial," his eyes twinkled.

"Books," he replied.

"Oh, what kind?"

"Various kinds—novels, biography, poetry."

"I'm afraid there won't be much sale for them on the Lower Deck. Have you a card?"

"Yes. . . . But it wasn't the Lower Deck that I was seeking."

"The Wardroom? The Gunroom?"

"The Gunroom, as a matter of fact. I wanted to see——"

"But the Gunroom officers, as well as the Lower Deck, use the Ship's Library. We *have* a Ship's Library, you know."

"Yes, I know. I'm very glad of it."

Mr. Baring extended his telescope in the direction of Mr. Alter's bag. "Where is your stock? Not in that little bag?"

"No; as a matter of fact some of my stock is already in the Ship's Library."

"Come, come," Mr. Baring exclaimed, "that won't do;

that won't wash at all. The Ship's Library isn't bought from casual booksellers, you know; it is a Service issue.''

"Dear me," answered Mr. Alter, putting down his bag on the deck, and selecting a visiting-card from his case, "but I don't think I have made a mistake."

"Then I must have made a mistake," Mr. Baring remarked with sarcasm. This was a persistent little fellow, he thought.

"Well," said Mr. Alter, "perhaps we have both made mistakes. I should have told you my full name and my business at once—in truth, I intended to do so, but you didn't give me much chance. I haven't come to sell. I should like to pay a call, if you will allow me. There are friends of mine in the Gunroom—Fane-Herbert and Lynwood. I am Wingfield Alter. I write books, you know. That's the card you asked for.''

It was as if some visitor, unknown by the name of Bennett, had added, "Arnold Bennett; I write books you know." Mr. Baring knew now only too well. So this odd creature, with a bowler hat and a hand-bag and a pointed beard, was Wingfield Alter, the friend of many admirals, an honoured guest in times past at combined manœuvres. Mr. Baring had an unpleasant vision of great men telling this tale to one another in the corridors at Whitehall. "And Baring took him for a commercial traveller. Baring must be an ass!"

"I am very sorry, Mr. Alter," he said quickly, still feeling that it was Mr. Alter's fault—as perhaps it was. "It was your little bag that deceived me. However, it will make a good tale for you to tell.''

"But I never tell tales against myself," Mr. Alter answered.

At this moment, Reedham, who had disappeared quickly and discreetly when Mr. Alter handed his card to the officer of the watch, and who had been engaged meanwhile in awakening a somnolent Gunroom, and urging its occupants to "clear up some of the mess and stow away the *Winning Post*" before the arrival of a literary Order of Merit—Reedham returned panting to the quarter-deck, and gazed over the side while he attempted to regain his breath and to look as if he had never been absent. His face was still pink as a result of his exertion when he was ordered, as he had known he would be, to escort Mr. Alter to the Gunroom.

But they had not gone far together when Mr. Baring called him back.

"Reedham! . . . One moment. Excuse me, Mr. Alter. . . .

Look here Reedham," Mr. Baring continued, while Mr. Alter waited out of earshot in the starboard tunnel, "have you warned the snotties down below?"

"Yes, sir."

"Gunroom tidy? Look decent?"

"Pretty tidy, sir. Hadn't much time, sir."

"That's all right. The best way with the British Public is to let them see what's good for them, you know. . . . And, Reedham, just drop a hint to some of the snotties to—er— moderate their language a bit, and not to offer him too many drinks. It might create a bad impression. You can never tell with these writing chaps—even the most respectable of them."

"I imagine," said Mr. Alter slowly, as he and Reedham went down into the Chest Flat, "that the officer of the watch is also the officer in charge of midshipmen?"

"Yes," Reedham answered, "he is. But what made you think so?"

The Gunroom had been transformed to greet the Almighty Pen and the gold-laced visitors who might be expected to accompany it. No one was asleep. There were no glasses on the table. Howdray was reading, in the second volume of a Manual of Seamanship, the eighty-seventh page—the page at which he had happened to open it. Elstone was working industriously, with a pen which he dipped from time to time into an empty Indian ink bottle, at a log-sketch which Dyce had completed for him a week ago.

The seemliness of the place was the seemliness of a school-boy, who, being dressed for a midnight escapade, jumps into bed boots and all as he hears the master's step near the dormitory door. The newspapers and magazines were thrust together into a pile, from which, as specimens of the whole, the title-pieces of *Punch* and the *Morning Post* had been made to protrude. The *Winning Post*, which was not hidden even for the Captain's Sunday inspections, and *La Vie Parisienne* and *Le Rire*, which were decently covered on such occasions, were now not to be seen—unless the inquisitive eye perceived one of them poking out its thumbed edges from beneath the leather cushions of the settee. And on the pile's summit, chosen to occupy so conspicuous a position by Krame's quick spirit, lay the *Hibbert Journal* that Elstone had long ago received from a kinswoman who "thought, my dear, you might care to pass your long watches with some magazines," and a copy of the *Daily Chronicle*, which he had hastily borrowed from Wickham, the messman, in case, as Krame remarked, old Alter had Radical tendencies.

"This is Mr. Wingfield Alter," said Reedham. "He has come to see Lynwood and Fane-Herbert."

"How d'you do?" said the senior midshipman. "My name is Krame. This is Elstone—Howdray—Driss. I'm afraid Fane-Herbert is ashore on leave, and won't be back till dinner. Lynwood is in the Dockyard with the Engineer Commander. They were expected back before Quarters. They may be here at any moment now. . . . Will you sit down and wait?"

"Thanks. . . . There's one thing, though." He turned to Reedham. "Perhaps you would manage it for me? Would you ask the officer of the watch if I may go ashore in the officers' boat, and if he says I may, will you pay off my boatman with this?"

Reedham took the money. After a moment's hesitation, seeing no opportunity to convey Mr. Baring's warning, and, indeed, feeling no inclination to do so, he went out of the Gunroom, not a little envious of those who might remain. It is exciting to see the Name that for years has stared at you from advertisements, and has twinkled at you from the gilt-lettered backs of books, come suddenly to life, take off its hat, put down its bag, and seat itself in your chair. The Name, by coming to life, assumes responsibility for many illusions.

But Mr. Alter, seated in the chair Krame had offered him, and explaining that he had had tea and would not have a whisky-and-soda just at present, was not conscious of being an idol, good or bad, or of being responsible, however indirectly, for another's self-respect. He wondered, with a puckering of his eyes, whether he were wiser to apologize for having disturbed his hosts, or to pretend that, within his experience at any rate, midshipmen had always sat, during the dog watches, in Gunrooms tidy almost to primness, reading Manuals of Seamanship. It would be pleasant if they would all go to sleep again and not worry about him. He was an old man, he thought, forgetting to count his three-and-fifty years, an old man and a restraining presence. He had broken in upon an hour peculiarly their own. He felt a nuisance, in fact, as age so often feels in the presence of youth, and did not realize that youth, in this instance, was tremendously interested in him. And so, while he hesitated, and while their tongues were momentarily paralyzed by the thought of his

great works and of the thousands of words they contained—
all wiser, no doubt, than any they could speak—a little wall
of silence grew up, over which, so soon as he perceived it,
Mr. Alter leaped at a venture.

"Wondering about that bag of mine?" he demanded. "Others have wondered. Feel its weight—books and papers. I
brought them here for Lynwood, who is a friend of mine, and
they shall revert to the Gunroom when he has done with
them. Do you read much?"

"Nothing very solid, I'm afraid," said Krame.

"But these aren't solid—at least, I hope not. Some of them
are my own. Now, I wonder if you could find time to read
one or two of them—the naval ones, for instance?"

"I think we have all read those time and again," said
Krame.

Mr. Alter smiled—pleased as he could never now be pleased
by a column in a newspaper. "I'd dearly love to have your
criticism, if ever you care to go over any of them again. My
publisher's address will always find me. Look, here's *The
Lower Deck*. That was an early effort."

Howdray turned it over.

"Are you going to write another book about the Service,
sir—the Service as it is now?"

"I don't know. It attracts me as the impossible always
attracts. I shall never get the essence of it though. Of course,
it is not necessary as a general rule to live a life in order to
describe it. But still . . ."

"The Service doesn't like being described," said Krame.

"The Service is like no community on earth. Its members
have two distinct natures, one when they are inside the naval
boundary, the other when they are outside it; one when they
are in contact with Service people, the other when they are in
contact with Non-Service people. Very, very seldom, for all
my watchfulness, have I gained any real insight into the
essentials of the Navy from words addressed to me by any
officer ashore or afloat."

"But," Krame remarked, with a smile that confirmed Mr.
Alter's declaration, "you have lived in ships?"

"As a visitor."

"Even as a visitor you must be able to see—well, how we
live, what work we do, and things of that kind."

"But not how you think, and not how you would act if
there were no spectators from the world outside. That's what

any writer has to discover about the persons of his drama—not what they do before the footlights, but what they were thinking before the curtain went up. Otherwise he can't make them live.''

All the world loves to hear itself discussed as a mystery, and Mr. Alter's mysteriousness produced at least a part of the result for which he had hoped. Howdray and Elstone were awake now; Krame was delighted to find a whetstone on which to sharpen his wits; and Driss—Mr. Alter felt the glow of his personality for the first time, saw him lean forward and listen intently, though, in the presence of his seniors, he hesitated to speak. Mr. Alter wanted him to speak, wanted them all to come out of their shells; but he saw that as yet they were not ready. He, by talking himself, must give them material they might afterwards care to pull to pieces.

''Have you ever noticed,'' he said, ''how Portsmouth and other naval ports differ from the rest of the world?''

''Lord Almighty! have we not!'' Howdray exclaimed in his great voice. ''Pompey, Queensferry, Gib., Sheerness—they are all the same, curse them.''

''And even Arosa Bay and Vigo?''

''Just the same.''

''Although they are south of the Bay and Pompey north of it? Doesn't that strike you as strange?''

''I believe,'' said Driss, ''that if you could drop the Fleet into the middle of County Carlow it would bring its own atmosphere with it.''

''That's what I mean,'' Mr. Alter exclaimed, pulling out a pipe. ''Its own atmosphere—it has a definite atmosphere of its own, enveloping it, hiding it from outsiders. And the atmosphere they breathe changes naval officers only so long as they breathe it. Once outside it—once in the train from Portsmouth to London, for instance—they are so much like the ordinary civilian that he fails to recognize them as visitors from another world. He notices something a little strange about them—something he can't define, something that, in nine cases out of ten, he dismisses with the catchword 'breezy.' ''

''Breezy!'' groaned Elstone. ''Don't we look breezy?''

''No, you don't—not here and now, because you are within the atmosphere, though my presence disturbs it somewhat, I dare say. But if you went ashore to-night, outside Portsmouth, away from naval people—what then?''

"Ask Krame. He is the poodle-faker."

"Poodle-faker?"

"A payer of polite calls," Howdray explained. "A balancer of teacups. An opener of doors. An eater of small morsels. A maker of small talk—in short, a specialist in drawing-room duties."

"But poodle-faking is quite different," said Krame.

"That's the whole point," cried Mr. Alter, encouraged by this admission. "A man who works in an office all the morning and goes into polite society in the afternoon preserves the same nature throughout the day. He may alter his manners a bit, just as he puts on a clean shirt, but he doesn't change essentially. You people do. And why? Isn't it because in the Service circle, within the Service atmosphere, you have standards of life that are unrecognized elsewhere?"

Krame smiled. "I suppose we do see things differently from other people. But doesn't that apply to almost any profession?"

"No; take the Bar—as distinctive and self-contained as any civilian profession, surely. You hear men talk of the Legal Mind as if it were a thing apart. What does it mean, after all? A little added precision of thought, a yearning after precedent, a reluctance to change—certainly nothing necessarily foreign to unlegal minds. But the naval officer's attitude towards the essentials of life—so long as he remains within the atmosphere—is altogether different from the attitude of other human beings. Isn't that so? In a ship and in a naval port, don't you think of women, for instance, in one way, and when you are at home, don't you think of them in a way quite different?"

"Oh, I don't know," said Krame. "Of course, one meets here a different kind of woman. One treats her differently. She doesn't fill the same part of the horizon as the women one meets at home."

"You are side-tracking," Mr. Alter objected. He let the pages of a book run through his fingers. "I am not comparing your treatment of harlots with your treatment of women who are not harlots. That contrast is obvious among men in every path of life. Put it this way: A naval officer in London; his mother, his sisters, all his womenfolk in Scotland—out of the way; he spends an evening with an old and intimate friend—a Cambridge man, let us say. Then—for the contrast—the same naval officer spends an evening in London with a naval friend. He goes to the same places, let's imagine, sees the same people, speaks to the same women as when with his Cambridge friend. Now, isn't it true that, though the outside circumstances are the same in each case, the naval officer's outlook upon them changes completely? In one instance, his companion is another naval officer, and the Service atmosphere is undisturbed; in the other, he is with a civilian, and the atmosphere is entirely altered. Not only his action or his speech concerning women, but his inmost thought of them, his whole attitude towards them, undergoes a change. And it's the same with Religion, with Charity, with Ambition—with all the constituent parts of life itself.''

"I suppose that's true," Krame answered. "We go out of one world into another."

"And all the rules and customs of citizenship change."

"Yes. You see, in ships we are in a strange position—monks with no vows."

"The rigours of a severe Order and none of its spiritual support?"

Krame thought over this in silence. Then, from behind him, Driss broke in suddenly: "Isn't that rather like prison? Don't men deteriorate in prison?"

Mr. Alter brushed aside a suggestion so dangerous, though it revealed to him much that had hitherto been obscure. "At any rate," he said, "it is not a natural condition, and is bound to produce phenomena of which we outside have no knowledge, no understanding. Men speak of the Silent Service because they cannot understand the language it speaks. . . . And there's one fact more amazing than any other in this connection—that men who are living the Service life, who ought to be able to tell the truth of it, when they sit down to write, write—not the truth as it appears to their naval minds—but the truth as it appears to their minds adapted to civilian conditions. They feel they are talking to civilians. The atmosphere is disturbed. They write what the civilians expect to hear—'breezy' stories. Their sailors are, figuratively speaking, for ever hitching up their trousers by the back, in accordance with the civilian music-hall tradition. Have you ever seen a sailor hitch up his trousers by the back? Usually what they do with regard to these particular garments is to curse them because they are so tight and uncomfortable. Why don't the naval writers say so?"

"Well," said Howdray, "I was shipmates with one of the fellows that write these magazine yarns, and he said——"

"Yes? What *did* he say?"

"I remember he had just finished one of them, and chucked it across the table for me to read. When I had read it, I said, 'Yes, I think that ought to go down well. But why are all your Lieuts. R.N. of the kind that sings at breakfast and plays the banjo in its bath? And why, when your snotties have their leave stopped, are they such infernally cheery devils that they regard it as a joke? In fact,' I said, 'why do you lay on the pretty colours so blazing thick?' 'My dear old thing,' he answered, 'the people who read me like the banjo-playing. You have just said yourself that the tale ought to go down well. That's the main point, seeing it is going to pay my mess-bill this month. Besides, the public has been taught to picture indomitably cheery "middies" with blue eyes and pink cheeks. It's no good to tell them about bleary eyes and safety-razors. It doesn't pay to foist one thing on to them when they are expecting another.' "

"But why shouldn't the public be asked to admire what is really admirable in the Service? Heaven knows, there's enough of it," Mr. Alter said. "Your friend's attitude, if I may say so, was the attitude of the young journalist who despises art, and he is a man even more intolerable than the young artist who despises journalism. Moreover, being confessedly a journalist, he appears to have despised the public—which is absurd. I'm afraid I shouldn't like your friend. . . . There's fineness in the Service that would amaze the world if it were known. Englishmen are eager about the Service, it's a part of their national life, it's their proudest tradition—incidentally, they pay for it. They are entitled to know about it. But they will never discover the real good in it so long as you people blind them with the magazine tradition. You must destroy that first. You must stop putting sugar into the wine if you want the vintage to be appreciated."

"You mustn't blame us, sir," said Krame, laughing at Mr. Alter's vehemence. "We don't write stories; that's your job."

"Yes; but I live outside the atmosphere. I am no good. But, to be sure, as you say, you don't write stories, and here am I attacking my hosts. It reminds me of how——"

And the conversation drifted into stories of East and West, of land and sea, Mr. Alter being carefully silent when any midshipman showed a disposition to talk. Darkness fell, lights were switched on, and near the time of gin and bitters and the departure of the officers' boat, John returned. He explained that the Engineer Commander had kept him in the Dockyard.

"So I shan't have a chance to talk to you," said Mr. Alter. "I must go to London to-night. I have been staying with some Hampshire friends, and thought I would look you up on my way home."

They went out on to the after shelter-deck.

"What do you think of the Gunroom, sir?" John asked; "and of the people you met there?"

"As for the Gunroom," Mr. Alter replied, "I have lived in worse quarters—but of my own free will, which makes a difference. The *Hibbert* lends it dignity and repose. . . . And I liked Krame and the rest."

"I knew you would."

"Because I'm a civilian?"

"For a variety of reasons. I like them myself, oddly enough. . . . How are Hugh's people?"

"They are going East. I believe that's fixed."

"And is——"

Mr. Alter took no notice of the interruption. "Margaret is going with her mother," he said.

"Oh—I see. . . . There's your boat called away. You will have to be going soon. Thanks for coming, and thanks for the books. I wanted them—very badly."

Chapter VI
Strain and Relief

In a ship there is neither bud nor fallen leaf. There is no ploughing of furrows, no scattering of seed. The winds are never sweet with the fragrance of broken earth. Fingers of sunshine touch no grass to vivid green when a shower is over and the clouds have blown away. Rain does not whisper among trees or press the dust of long, white roads into little pits of darkness; it lashes at grey steel, hangs in beads on the metal rims of scuttles, envelops topmasts in an unsteady mist. The seasons are marked by the Navigator's instruments and by variation in the colour of the waves. On a fixed date white cap-covers are taken out, on a fixed date they are put away again; and thus does summer begin and end. When snow falls the Watch for Exercise banishes it with squeegees. Christmas Day comes when the December wine bills are nearly exhausted. Nothing flowers and goes to rest; nothing is ever born again.

Spring, when the calendar bids her come, comes obediently, but to ships of war she brings few gifts. Even that essence of her which makes men ashore lift their heads and say that spring is in the air, reaches ships changed by the tang of salt, or often, in port, corrupted by the smell of harbour scum. By no visible or tangible promise of her future glory does she give to seamen credit with which they may tide over the lean, harsh months of the early year.

Through January and part of February John struggled hard and honestly to settle down, to convert the inevitable into the desired. Long years ago he himself had chosen to enter the Navy, and now, though he wondered at the decision, he knew he must abide by it. His mother's means, he felt sure, were too small to re-educate him as he would need to be re-educated if he left the Service. He must put away from him the thought of change. He must make the best of things as he found them. He must work, work and forget, work at naval subjects, and awaken somehow new ambitions, new enthusiasms, new desires, which should stand between him and the old. He would put no pen to paper save the pen of a naval officer. He would banish poetry from him as men banished a drug. Rosebery's *Pitt,* Morley's *Gladstone* and *Walpole,* Lecky's *Democracy and Liberty,* all should go back to the Chaplain's cabin; for were not the lives and dreams of statesmen a part of that old world which was to be left behind? Keats, too, should go; and Blake, and Milton's prose, and Burke's speeches. One afternoon of resolution he piled them together and carried them off. Still Mr. Alter's books remained, and these he lent, urging the borrowers to keep them as long as they wished. From his sea-chest he disinterred battered notebooks on Mechanics and Heat and Steam. From the Gunroom shelf he dragged down Sennett and Oram's standard work on the Marine Steam Engine. This was, indeed, to be a grand burning of boats.

But the boats would not burn; the memory of the abandoned country would not perish; the new enthusiasms, like a constitution hastily formulated, never broke the bonds that their own artificiality imposed upon them. The strength of materials and their curves of elasticity; the names and properties of lubricants; the hundred and one "little dodges" by which the Engineer Commander hoped to save a few pounds of coat—none of these things interested John. He did his utmost to interest himself in them. He even reached a point at which he could say that he liked engineering and believe that this was true. Nor was it altogether untrue. Engine-room watches were less troublous than those on deck. The Commander was out of the way. But these advantages were powerless to awaken in him the saving enthusiasm he desired. The engineer officers for the most part treated New Scheme midshipmen with good-humoured tolerance, convinced that, as they had not received the old-fashioned training, they could not be made into efficient engineers. "I don't know what the hell's the good of those Upper Deck snotties wasting their time down here," they would say. "As soon as they're beginning to learn something they are whisked away to their seamanship again." No one except the Engineer Commander himself—and he was too busy to see much of them—took any interest in the engineering midshipmen, and their work resolved itself, partly through their own fault, into a wearisome keeping of watches, a writing-up of notebooks, an uninspired observance of rules. Sennett and Oram returned whence they came.

Then John made a second attempt to sever himself from the past and to engross himself in a naval future; but this, partly because it was a compromise and partly for other reasons, failed as the first had done. He turned to Voluntary Subjects, to French and Naval History. He tried to persuade himself that he was carrying out his original intention to devote himself to Service subjects. If French and Naval History were subjects for a Service examination, surely they were within the limits he had prescribed? That they were also, by reason of the literary aspect they presented, without those limits, John would not allow himself to recognize. He shirked that issue. He quieted his conscience by telling himself that French and Naval History appeared in the official syllabus. He would not admit, what was indeed the truth, that he read Balzac, not because the reading would help him to pass the examinations for the rank of lieutenant, but because Balzac was an artist. He concealed from himself the fact that his love of Naval History centred in the noun rather than in the adjective, and he refused to acknowledge, even to himself, that he cared more for the prose than for the substance of his essay on the Dutch Wars, more for the writing of it than for the examination marks which were to be his ostensible reward.

The result of this, as of all self-deception and confusion of motives, was disaster. As it were a stimulant, it strengthened John for a time, but left him weaker than it had found him. Balzac, Corbett, and Mahan temporarily filled the gap which, by denying himself all but Service books, he had created. Then the Home Fleet came south to carry out combined manœuvres. The *King Arthur* was much at sea. The pressure of Engine-room watches became so great that French and Naval History had to be abandoned. The drug was taken away. The whole deception was suddenly exposed. During the long hours in the Engine-room John stared at the pounding piston-rods, or at the greasy steel floor on which he was standing, or at the iron bars of the gratings that lay tier upon tier above his head. He listened to the talk of stokers, and to the unending tales of drink and harlots with which the artificer-engineers tried to lessen the tedium of the watch. He liked the stokers; he liked the artificer-engineers who were, he knew, doing their utmost to be pleasant and entertaining. But he grew very tired of steel and oil, and drink and harlots. He revolted against them, not in anger or contempt, or anything like a spirit of righteousness, but because they were unavoidable, because they were ever at hand, because those sights and that conversation were *all* that, for hours at a time, life had to offer him. And in the intervals there were Gunroom Evolutions and Krame.

Of all the junior midshipmen Sentley alone had settled down. He was not happy, but he looked forward to the satisfaction promotion would bring him. He lived by rules, and was tempted neither by strong emotions nor by a strong imagination to break them. They were too well suited to his placid, dogged temperament. He would never be a great naval officer, but he had no desire to be great. If very reasonable expectations were fulfilled by his becoming a captain he would not be disappointed by failure to fly his admiral's flag. He was by nature contented, hard-working, moderate in his somewhat formal religion, moderate in his vanity, moderate in all things. His life in the Gunroom was unpleasant; but when he was flogged, it was the pain that troubled him—not the humiliation, and his resentment vanished with the pain. In speaking, even in thinking of his superiors in rank, he never used the expression "ought not." He seldom used it at all except in a formally religious sense, and then his condemnation ended when his conscience had been stilled by a mild utterance of protest. It was not in keeping with his policy, nor was it within his power, to stand out in opposition to anything. He drifted easily with the tide.

Driss was very calm. It was impossible to pierce his reserve or to tell what course his mind had taken. Dyce was frittering away his soul, now resisting, now yielding, now seeking the easy consolations, now dragging himself away from them, knowing that very soon he must return. He laid no plans, and deliberately avoided looking into the future. His duties were performed perfunctorily, and to no one's satisfaction, least of all to his own. Sometimes a chance remark, a flash of wit in his conversation, would display the true worth of a mind that was fast becoming dulled. He was a generous friend, a bitter but ineffectual enemy, and an amusing companion. If he had had money, and leisure, and independence he would have ended his days at the head of a country-house dinner-table, passing port to numerous and frequent guests.

The senior midshipmen had absorbed Cunwell. He did his best to please them. On Sunday mornings he produced a polishing pad, which he had bought ashore for this very purpose, and offered to give Krame's boots "just a rub over before Divisions, as I am doing my own, you know." Then, when he had finished rubbing and breathing from a broad mouth, he would look round apprehensively to see what the junior midshipmen had been thinking of him. As a reward for these attentions Krame spared him a little and patronized him much. Sometimes he would say at dinner, "My old friend Cunwell will have a glass of port with me?" and Cunwell, glowing in the joys of privileged familiarity, would shout back, "Thanks, old Krame, don't mind if I do." Krame would keep his lip from curling, but his eyes flickered his laughing contempt.

Cunwell did not like Krame, who, he said, sneered because he thought himself clever. As a model he chose Howdray, whose doings were chronicled and laughed over throughout the Fleet. But the imitation was not successful. It was as a ragtime played laboriously, for Howdray imparted to his vice a certain glitter that Cunwell could not reproduce. Cunwell, when he drank, became immediately dull and sick. He had no pleasure in risk, no spirit of adventure. His dealings with women were usually ridiculous, so that the women themselves sniggered at him behind his back. Soiled collars and a dimness of eye were the outward signs of the change in him.

Manœuvres, contact with the Home Fleet, and a rumour that the *King Arthur* might not return to England to refit, depressed the spirits of the whole ship's company. The Commander was impossible to please. The defaulters were numerous. The relations between Wardroom and Gunroom, never cordial, became more than usually strained. The Chaplain preached a bitter sermon on the virtue of contentment. The Captain, who was a kindly man, regretfully sent more prisoners to cells in a fortnight than he had condemned to that punishment in the previous two months. Gunroom Evolutions and floggings became more frequent and severe. When the men went to physical drill after Divisions, and were commanded, in accordance with custom, to double round the batteries and quarter-deck, they ran, not eagerly and good-humouredly as when paying-off time is near, but at a Service double such as discipline demanded. And the speed and spirit of this morning procession is generally a good indication of the temper of a ship's company. The Commander wrote to his wife that the commission was stale. The men needed general leave, he said. And Tintern paused suddenly one night in his playing of the Alphabet—

*"With a Glory Allelujah in the morning,
In the morning by the gaslight,
See——"*

"I'm not going to play any more," he wailed, in imitation of a spoilt child.

"Oh, come on, Tintern; there's no one else to play but you. You'll stop the whole sing-song. Why won't you play?"

"Why? Because the poor old Konk"—he was referring to the monarch after whom the ship was named—"because the poor old Konk is bloody-minded, and so am I."

It was when affairs had reached this stage that, to the junior midshipmen, relief came, sudden and unexpected.

II

One forenoon the Captain's messenger came to the Gunroom to say that the Captain wished to see Mr. Sentley. After an absence of ten minutes, Sentley returned. They read in his face that he had good news. In his hand he carried a sheet from a signal pad.

"We are all to return to England immediately," he said. "We shall have about a fortnight or three weeks of leave. Then we are to join the *Colonsay* for passage to Colombo, where we are to recommission the *Pathshire*, China Station."

"All of us?" said Howdray. "What do you mean?"

"We junior snotties."

"Not the others?"

"No."

"Oh, damn! You lucky, lucky little devils!"

That night the Mess dined the junior midshipmen. As the Gunroom had been drawn together once before by the hope of battle, so was it now united by the prospect of parting. Wrongs were forgiven, enmities forgotten. Soon they would be saying of one another: "I was shipmates with him *once*." If an association is to end, let it end sweetly.

Speeches were made. Titern said, "I've always thought it odd that the Service should have a special name for a ship that isn't mouldy and at cross-purposes. It sounds as if such ships were rare. And so they are nowadays, west of Suez. But the China Birds say that there are still Happy Ships on the China Station. A Happy Ship is a ship in which all the Messes get on with one another—a ship in which, among other things, there isn't bad blood between Wardroom and Gunroom. And I hope the young gentlemen will get one. I ask you to drink to the health of the *Pathshire*, and may she be a Happy Ship!"

When the toast had been honoured and the wine passed once more, the Mess shouted at Krame for a speech. He rose slowly, and looked round him.

"As Tintern has been talking about a Happy Ship in the future," he said, "I suppose the young gentlemen think it's up to me to say something about their somewhat lurid past. There's not much to be said—no excuses, or apologies, or that kind of thing. But there is this: a Happy Ship is a happy ship right through, and contrariwise. Nothing that has happened here has happened because of personal ill-will. It has happened because—because—Lynwood, what was that line I picked out of some stuff you were reading? I remember now. It has happened because we are 'in the fell clutch of circumstance.' I hope that in the better land to which they are going the young gentlemen will have more leave—not a few hours at a time, pub-loafing at Pompey or Gib., but real leave, clear away from the ship, and long enough to give them a chance not to be bloody-minded. Long leave is what the Service wants, gentlemen, says I, beatin' the tub! Long leave is what we wishes the young gen'lemen, says us, liftin' our glasses."

Krame sits down amid a roar of applause. Presently Tintern goes to the piano and plays all the familiar songs. To-morrow this sing-song party will break up, never to reassemble again. Every tune is made richer by wine and sentiment—the *Alphabet*, *Napoleon*, *Farewell and Adieu*, *Screw-Guns*.

"If a man doesn't work, why, we drills 'im and teaches 'im
    'ow to behave;
  If a beggar can't march, why, we kills 'im an' rattle 'im
      into 'is grave.
  You've got to stand up to our business an' spring without
      snatchin' or fuss.

D'you say that you sweat with the field-guns? By God,
you must lather with us. 'Tis! 'Tss!
For you all love the screw-guns. . . ."

Thus Mr. Kipling to the tune of the *Eton Boating Song*. And now a round of drinks, and song again—a song whose immortal words are unpublished, whose tunes are various, whose name is the *Barrack-Gate*.

". . . Then the wily Gym. Instructor . . .
Just outside the Barrack-Gate."

There follows a swift catalogue of the merits of a certain Princess whose home is in a few manuscripts of an Opera, rhymed wonderfully by the hand of a master, and sung to music by Sullivan. From this obscurity a swift return is made to the simplicity of *The Wives*, in which it is told how the Parson's wife, strangely clad, decorated her hat with the midshipmen's astronomical observations—

"And in one corner of her hat
She carried the Yearly Sights.
She carried the Yearly Sights, my boys,
And every one was there;
And in the other corner
Was the Book of Common Prayer."

The evening wears on. *Mandalay* is sung as a tribute to the East. The room is heavy with smoke. The yellow lampshades that swung to and fro on those nights of Evolution seem to be swinging now, though the ship does not roll. The ship seems to roll though the sea is calm. The past is receding. Voices are loud. The rosy flush of wine takes all the sadness from farewell. . . .

The Gunroom is being closed. The group that was leaning over Tintern's shoulder has scattered. In the Chest Flat Ollenor's voice is heard repeating the last chorus, and at the piano Tintern, almost alone now, is singing to himself a song that is not a Gunroom song:

"Home is the sailor, home from sea,
And the hunter home from the hill."

Chapter VII
Margaret

I

During their passage to England, John and Hugh heard many golden legends of the East, but, apart from these, they had a reason of their own for looking eagerly towards the future. Mr. Alter had said that Mrs. Fane-Herbert and Margaret were going to China. This news, which, while he himself expected to remain west of the Straits, had promised Hugh nothing but that he would spend in strangers' houses what little leave he might obtain, now made his good fortune seem more fortunate. It meant that his own people would be often accessible to him. And into John's imaginings of the East Margaret persistently entered. Though his acquaintance with her was so short, he never thought of her as of a stranger. The very brevity of their contact made vivid his memory of her. Her personality appeared to him as a thing apart, strangely complete, and significant on account of its completeness and its independence of the rest of his life. The impression she had made upon him was an impression of contrast. His own existence was set about with a wall of steel. A door had opened for a moment, and he had seen her. When the door was closed, still he saw her, an occupant of another world, the citizenship of which was denied him. For all the interdicts he had laid upon himself in his attempt to settle down where Fate had cast him, he made from time to time dream-sorties into that other world, and on these occasions of secret adventure it was Margaret whom he encountered. But the country in which he found her was strange to him. He was conscious always of having overstepped his boundaries. To stray, even in dreams, beyond his steel wall was to expose himself to forces outside his experience, and now life seemed indefinably dangerous as it had never seemed before.

It is this sense of danger, experienced by all natures neither utterly animal nor merely trivial, that gives to love both its dignity and its finest colour. It is never more acute than in minds that have been isolated or confined, for to these the new world is new indeed. John was so much a stranger to the perilous country that as yet he did not call it by any name. In childhood his shy reserve had withheld him from close friendship. His mother had been an invalid—"too frail to be hugged" —and it was not until circumstances had placed her beyond his reach that her strength had in some measure returned to her. His nurse, unusually free from a mistress's supervision, had been too occupied with her own affairs to accept the devotion which John would have given so eagerly. He had no sister upon whom to expend his affection. For lack of outlet, emotion had accumulated within him until its force could no longer be resisted.

Margaret had seem so inaccessible, by reason of her own position and of the distances which must always divide him from her, that John had never regarded her as a prize he might hope to win. The thought of her was as a clear bugle awakening the finest legions of his mind—thoughts which had slept long, and, being aroused, were masters of the evil in him, masters of sorrow and loneliness and pain, as faith is master of us all while faith endures.

And now, though the difficulty of her position remained, the miles between them were to be swept away. For on the China Station ships remained long in one port, and leave was more generously given than elsewhere. John listened gladly to the tales that were told of Yokohama and Tokio, of Hong Kong and Shanghai, but repeated to himself, happy in the possession of his secret, "She will be there, and there will be no London to absorb her." It was almost incredible that the news which, when it was given, had seemed disastrous should have become the substance of his happiness.

Then doubt arose. The first letters Margaret wrote to Hugh on the subject had confirmed Mr. Alter's tale; both her father and mother had been in favour of her going. Then her tone had become less assured.

"I don't know whether I shall go to China after all," she wrote. *"Father is discovering difficulties—or, rather, Mr. Ordith, who has been to China, is discovering them for him;*

and now he talks of taking mother with him, and leaving me in the charge of some aunt—I don't know which aunt."

And in a later letter:

"Father seems to have decided now that I am to stay in England. I am horribly disappointed. It may be the only chance I shall ever have of seeing the East—and the East is changing so fast. Mother is still on my side, I think, though she doesn't like to say very much. It is so difficult for her and for me to argue, because neither of us knows anything about China, and Mr. Ordith, who has been staying with us again, is full of facts and figures. I wonder why he is so much against my going. He is always pointing out difficulties. He has a mind like a blue-book, all tabulated and accurate. You can almost hear him saying, 'Section Two, Sub-section Four— so-and-so; Sub-section Five—so-and-so.' What can an ordinary human being do in face of that? Of course, father is tremendously impressed. He says it is so refreshing to meet a young man with an orderly mind. There's no doubt that Mr. Ordith is clever, and very attractive—in a way. I dare say he is right about the Chinese horrors, but, even if he is, there's no need to tell the truth so often. But I still have hopes. Nothing is definite yet. Perhaps if I light enough of father's cigarettes and warm his Times for him every morning, he may relent. Or perhaps all the aunts will refuse to have me, if I get my word in first."

When these letters arrived Hugh paid little attention to them. He had made up his mind that his family was leaving England, and he refused to be deluded by false hopes. But now, when his attitude towards the matter had been changed, he read over with real anxiety such of Margaret's letters as he had not destroyed.

"This fellow Ordith," he said to John, when the extracts had been read aloud, "seems likely to be an infernal nuisance. He is a Gunnery Lieut. R.N.—a star-turn at Whaley, an inventor and that kind of thing. My father's firm, Ibble and Company, has a lot of Admiralty contracts. I suppose that's how they met."

"What has your sister said about it since?"

"I tore up the letters before we left the *King Arthur*. I kept these only by chance—mixed up with some books. But, so far as I can remember, she hasn't said anything—certainly nothing definite. And she hasn't mentioned Ordith, I'm sure. It's odd, isn't it?"

"I don't know."

"Do you think she has had a row with him?"

"No; but—— Anyway, we shan't know anything until we get home to England."

Hugh laughed. "I believe you are just as keen as I am that my—that my people should go to China."

John answered quickly: "You see, I am counting on your invitations to give me an excuse for leave."

II

After spending nearly a week at home, John came up to London on the first Friday of his leave. He was to stay with the Fane-Herberts, who were giving a dance on the following day, and before he returned to the country he and Hugh were to go together to Mr. Reeve's London branch and order the clothes they would need in China.

"I am afraid it is no good," Hugh told him. "It seems to be definitely fixed that Margaret is to remain in England."

But at dinner that night they were thrown once more into perplexity. Mr. Fane-Herbert was away in the North, and was not expected home until Saturday afternoon, when he would bring Mr. Ordith with him.

"I believe Mr. Ordith is a wonderful dancer," Mrs. Fane-Herbert said.

"From all accounts," Hugh replied, "he must be wonderful at everything."

"My dear Hugh, you speak as if you disliked him already, without ever having seen him."

"I don't dislike him, but I can't see what he has to do with our affairs."

"Our affairs?"

"Margaret's going to China. It was all fixed up before Ordith came on the scene."

Mrs. Fane-Herbert smiled. This was a chance better than she had hoped for. "Now," she said, "shall I show you how wrong you are? I had a letter from father this afternoon, and, so far as I can judge, for he is not at all definite, he has been thinking it all over, and has come to the conclusion——"

"That I am to go after all, mother?" Margaret interrupted. "Do say I am to go!"

"Well, dear, I don't want you to be disappointed again, but I must say that father seems to incline more towards

taking you. . . . So you see, Hugh, how little Mr. Ordith
had to do with the matter. It is very foolish to make rash
judgments.''

"But why has father changed his mind?"

"It doesn't matter why," said Margaret. "The point is that
he has changed it."

Hugh shrugged his shoulders. "It beats me, I confess."

His mother allowed Hugh's suspicion to fade into silence.
To have attempted to remove it would have been to empha-
size it, and this she wished to avoid. Her husband's letter had
given her two pieces of information, the last of which explained the first. *"I think,"* he had written, *"that, after all,
Margaret had better come with us when we leave England.
Edith might not to be burdened with her. I know you
would like to have her with you, and that she herself is
anxious to come. There are many obstacles, but, if you have
really set your heart on taking her, none that I am not
prepared to overcome if I can. We will talk it over when I
reach home."* Mrs. Fane-Herbert, when she read this, was as
astonished as Hugh had been when he heard of it; but at the
end of the letter, separated from her husband's decision by
more pages than he usually troubled to write to her, was a
brief announcement which made it all clear: *"Ordith has been
appointed to the* Pathshire *as an additional Gunnery Lieutenant. Isn't it a strange coincidence in connection with Hugh?"*
To Mrs. Fane-Herbert it was an illumination uncomfortably
brilliant.

She established at once the connection between her husband's change of mind and Mr. Ordith's change of plan. But
would Margaret establish it? If possible, that must be prevented. Mrs. Fane-Herbert was tempted to say nothing of the
contents of her letter, to leave her husband to make the best
of it on his return. But his best, in this instance, would, she
knew, be bad indeed. He thought of Margaret as a child
without perception. He would not trouble to deceive her.

Mrs. Fane-Herbert realized that she herself must give these
two pieces of information to Margaret in such a manner as
might prevent their being connected with each other. The
responsibility and the chance of failure made her nervous and
troubled. Dinner was to be an ordeal. She wished that her
husband was not so successful a man—at any rate, that
success had not blinded him to so many things she would
have liked him to see and value. She wished that Mr. Ordith

had not so much ability and charm; that she could bring herself to dislike him frankly, and so to form a clear policy with regard to him. He might make an admirable husband. She did not think so. But what was there against him? Nothing but her instinct and Mr. Alter's saying that the young man had a systematized soul. Her husband wanted him in Ibble and Company. She had seen, scribbled on a blotting-pad in the writing that, years ago, had filled her love-letters, the words "Ibble and Ordith—Ordith and Ibble," as if the amalgamation was already accomplished and a dispute about the nomenclature had begun. Mr. Ordith would leave the Service and succeed his father, Sir George Ordith, as head of Ordith and Co. The plan was cut and dried, as were all Mr. Fane-Herbert's plans. But she hated the whole project. Even if the result were excellent, she hated this involving of Margaret in the affairs of Ibble and Co., for Ibble and Co. had already robbed her husband of the qualities she had loved best in him. She disliked it the more because her husband had never dared speak openly of it, and because *she* had never dared mention it to him. She knew how he would answer. Was he trying to force the girl? Absurd! He was trying to give a fair chance to a young man whom he liked—surely a reasonable and proper course? Oh, yes, reasonable and proper! Mrs. Fane-Herbert thought helplessly. But wrong, she felt—wrong in motive and bad in effect. If it were not wrong, why did it already compel her to fence with her own children?

Hugh had helped her at the beginning of dinner. The first piece of information had been naturally given, she thought. Now for the second, which was the test. She led the conversation into new channels, and talked much and well—just as Mr. Fane-Herbert had written those intermediate pages in his letter. But too long a delay would draw attention to itself. Margaret would wonder why she had put off speaking of Mr. Ordith. When should she speak?

She waited until dinner was ended. Then she paused in the open doorway.

"Oh, and Hugh, father said in his letter something of Mr. Ordith's being appointed as additional Gunnery Lieutenant to the *Pathshire*. Isn't that an odd chance?"

"Ordith, *too,* going to China?"

"I suppose so."

Mrs. Fane-Herbert made her way towards the drawing-room. She knew Margaret was watching her. Why, oh why, had Hugh said, "Ordith *too?*" Or was it her imagination and not his voice that had so laid the emphasis? She did not look round to search Margaret's face, though her desire to do so was almost too strong for her. In a moment Margaret would speak, and her tone, even more clearly than her words, would indicate how much she had guessed.

But as they entered the drawing-room Margaret said: "If I am to go East, mother, I shall want dozens of new frocks, shan't I?"

And Mrs. Fane-Herbert was left without enlightenment.

III

Mr. George Ordith, later a baronet, and head of the great armament firm honoured by the serious jealousy of Ibble and Co., had trained his son Nicholas with extraordinary care and consistency. He had been terrified lest Nick, who was to inherit all that a life's toil had accumulated, should value it little and dissipate it rashly. Therefore, almost as soon as Nick's fingers were able to close about the coin, a penny had been thrust into his palm, and, when he had held it a little while, been taken from him and dropped loudly into a money-box bearing his name. Nick enjoyed the tinkle, and crowed in accompaniment. The process was repeated every Saturday morning, until at last, because he was never allowed to play with them, Nick came to have a respect for pence. The money-box was cleared annually, its contents supplemented by a sovereign, which was George Ordith's Christmas gift to his baby (for it was left to womenfolk to present what were described as "baubles and gewgaws"), and the whole was added to Nick's deposit in the Post Office Savings Bank. By the time he was out of dresses he was a capitalist. Only Mrs. Ordith's earnest entreaties saved her son from being taught to read from the financial columns of the newspapers. At school, Stocks and Shares were to Nick an exciting reality, and, at the age of fifteen, he withdrew from the Post Office all his money except half a crown, gave it to his father in return for a cheque drawn in favour of the parental broker, and instructed this gentleman to purchase on his behalf certain Meat Shares in the Argentine.

From this it must not be deduced either that George Ordith was a miser or that he wished his son to become one. He said a thousand times that money was not everything; that it could not purchase happiness; that, though it was a blessing to wise men, it was a curse to fools. And Nick said, "Yes, father," and asked, as other children might ask for a coveted toy, when he might have some of those coupons that were cut off with scissors. George Ordith had acted upon a theory that the sons of hard-working, careful men are often wasters. He had wished to nip in the bud any natural tendency in Nick to become a waster. And he erred in this, that Nick had been so made that waste would in any case have been repugnant to him. If George had not provided a money-box, Nick would have been impelled by instinct to manufacture one out of the first empty tobacco-tin whose lid he could pierce. If George had not built up the firm of Ordith, Nick would probably have established it.

Thus had nature and training, instead of counteracting each other's effects, as Sir George Ordith had intended, been allies in the production of the young Gunnery Lieutenant in whom Mr. Fane-Herbert found so much to admire. He had taken firsts in every examination in which it had been possible for him to take firsts; he had created a reputation for himself at Whale Island; he had played cricket and Rugby football for the Navy; he had smiled and danced himself into the favour of innumerable hostesses; he had a nice taste in wines, a beautiful touch in billiards, a safe seat on any horse, and an inexhaustible supply of words, which flowed like oil from his lips. He was tall, dark, and technically handsome. Moreover, he had a level head—a head so level that business men, while they admired him, looked back sometimes to the days of their own youth, and reflected that, after all, young Ordith must be missing a great deal. They would have liked an opportunity to raise their eyebrows now and then, and to say, "Ah well, boys will be boys!"

But Nick never gave them a chance. He condescended so far as to appear gallant and rash in the presence of women who he thought would like that kind of thing; but in the presence of men from whom something might be expected he gave no judgment which was not a considered judgment, offered no opinion without quoting his authority for the facts upon which it was based, relapsed into thoughtful silence when he had no opinion to offer, and added little by little to his reputation for soundness.

In a book to which he made frequent reference he wrote down such details concerning his friends' habits and tastes as might aid him in his dealings with them. A glance into this volume reveals much of the writer.

"FANE-HERBERT, WALTER.—*Proud of cellar. Always offers to pay for things—don't let him. Likes to be taken aside from large company as if conversation private and important. Sharp business man—try no tricks. Wants me in Ibble's—obviously with view to amalgamation. Be dense about this. Probably fond of daughter when it comes to the pinch. Personalty (authority, K.S.K.), over 700 thou. One son in addition to daughter. Pleased with his feet—ask size of boots occasionally. Eton best school in the world. Expectancy of life, 15 yrs.*

"FANE-HERBERT, MRS.—*Avoid cynicism. Ask her advice often. Points for flattery: upbringing of children; fineness of bed and table linen; acquaintance with Parnell—touch this carefully; Irish descent, rather remote. Keep off subject of husband's success. Keep business in the background. Money not mentioned—except in connection charitable purposes. Acute woman. Guesses about Ibble and Ordith, and about daughter. Private income probably small. Ought to die well first.*

"FANE-HERBERT, MARGARET.—*Exceptional, requiring exceptional treatment. Flattery must be restrained and veiled. Probable points for flattery: shape of fingers; piano; knowledge of books; power to see through pretences. Certain points for flattery: imperviousness to it—and ability to keep secret. Necessary to cultivate literary conversation. (Literature Primers, Edited by J. H. Green, and English Lit. by Stopford Brooke, Macmillan and Co.; for contemporary lit. try Bookman—? something more advanced.) Be careful not to split infinitives; also use singular after none—e.g., 'none of them is. . . .' Introduce ideals into all talk of the future. Might talk of improving the conditions of Ordith's workpeople, and thus establish* secret *between her and me—but make quite sure bunkum of that kind doesn't spread and make things awkward at Ordith's. Probably make good hostess. Not extravagant, but might develop philanthropic tendencies. To me very attractive: keep this clear in mind, as it may be dangerous. Don't touch* her *too much; guard eyes. Go slow. Impulsiveness would probably be effective, but I am not good at this, so better act judiciously.*"

Nick Ordith clearly perceived his own weakness. He wished that Margaret, the girl, were less important to him, and that he could regard her as no more than a link with Ibble's and a beneficiary under her father's will. This amalgamation was to be a big affair, and he would have preferred to approach it with a cool head—with a head, that is, not inflamed by any passion that disputed his customarily perfect control. But, though you bind the Devil hand and foot, he will lash you with his tail. All Nick's care to restrict every tendency in him that might interfere with his material success could not prevent him from losing command a little in Margaret's presence, and he knew that some day, at a moment when he least expected it, that command might break down altogether. He thrilled at her touch; he thought of her at night when he ought to have been thinking of fire-control instruments. And he knew he stood in danger of revealing all this. Women, a few women, had so twisted him before. He had no confidence in his ability to handle Margaret as if she were built of the cool ivory of a chess-piece. She was young—ten years his junior, and she was unspoiled. Youth and the unspoiled had for him an attraction more powerful than his will. There might come a time when he would lose the game as a result of his reluctance to sacrifice his Queen. Certainly she would exercise an undue influence upon his strategy.

He determined to dance with her that Saturday night as often as he dared neglect more urgent business, and at dinner primed himself for brilliance. Mr. Hartfeld of the Foreign Office and Mr. Street of the Admiralty were present, and treated him with more deference than the ordinary naval officer has a right to expect from Government Departments. Mr. Fane-Herbert established himself with his back to the smoking-room fire when dinner was over, smiling at Street, Hartfeld, and Ordith, and glaring at Hugh until he suggested that he and John should go and play billiards. At last the four great men were left alone to discuss the prospects of the Empire overseas.

The detail of their conversation is not for the ears of the less fortunate who hold no stock in armament firms, but the spirit of it may be revealed in its conclusion.

"Of course," said Mr. Fane-Herbert, "it is understood that we shall act with the greatest reserve. Ordith's presence out there will appear accidental—or at any rate, whatever they may think, no one will dare to say that it is otherwise. He will be my friend and personal adviser—in no way personally interested."

"The Foreign Office has nothing to do with it," said Hartfeld.

"Nor the Admiralty," Street echoed.

Street flicked the ash from his cigarette. "It is of the utmost importance that we should be committed to nothing."

"But we can rely upon your support?"

Hartfeld nodded. "Speaking for myself alone; I can't answer for others."

"Isn't that a little nebulous?" Ordith asked.

"We can do no more than promise to do our utmost," said Street, in the pained voice of one whose offer of his life's blood has been scorned.

"We shall be grateful," said Ordith.

"Most grateful," Mr. Fane-Herbert added solemnly. He knew how foolish it was to ruffle officials. "Another brandy, Street? A cigar?"

"But, apart from the question of gratitude and the gentlemanly preamble," Ordith continued, "let's see exactly how we stand. As I see it——"

"My dear fellow," Hartfeld exclaimed, flourishing a delicate hand, "why this passion for black and white? Everything depends upon the fluctuations of circumstance——"

"Lord help us! why not say of 'Change'?"

Mr. Fane-Herbert gave him a glance which advised that, since these were not business men, they should not be treated as such. They must be allowed to talk if they wanted to. "You were saying, Hartfeld—the fluctuations of circumstance?"

"Upon the fluctuations of circumstance and the—er—signs of the times. Definite commitments in affairs of this kind are always dangerous, and are only to be obtained at the price of elasticity."

"In other words," said Street, "we want to give you the freest possible hand."

Three of them nodded wisely. Ordith's fingers moved lightly on the arms of his chair. He had not wanted these people brought into it. "They can't help," he had said. But Mr. Fane-Herbert had taken him by the shoulder; "No, they can't help—granted. But they can hinder. Look on their talk as the price you pay for a retainer, see?"

"Then what it comes to," Ordith said, "is that you are concerned in these contracts that we hope to obtain simply from the point of view of the national interest, eh?" So far as he knew the question was meaningless, but he felt that it would please them.

"Exactly," they answered together.

"And you afford facilities?—a diplomatic phrase, surely?"

"Every facility."

Mr. Fane-Herbert's approving eye was upon him. "Then success ought to be assured so long as there are no competitors." That was the point.

"Competitors?" said Hartfeld. "We can't answer for foreign competition."

"No; I was thinking of competition from home. Ibble's is not the only firm in the British Isles."

"By no means," said Street gracefully.

"Oh, I can answer for Ordith's; we have arranged that. There are others."

"I'm afraid we couldn't possibly interfere with legitimate commercial competition."

"No one would ask it of you. But your attitude towards us will be at least benevolent?" Ordith said.

"Certainly," Hartfeld answered.

"Good."

"It will be a brilliant success!" Street exclaimed.

"Success," said Ordith, "depends less upon genius than upon an adequate appreciation of the platitudes."

This faith, so authoritatively expressed by a successful young man, was put to the test soon after the dance had begun. He saw Margaret dancing with John—her eyes shining with happiness in a manner that might have caused another lover a little uneasiness. But Ordith did not for a moment feel insecure. He could see that John had gained ground, that the first ramparts of reserve had been overpassed; but he had no fear. "Unlike poles attract," he repeated, choosing his platitude, and confident of his power to carry attack upon that line to a successful issue. So, before seeking out the important lady he had seen among the crowd and had chosen for his immediate favour, he stood gazing at Margaret's neck and shoulders and admiring her movement with the eye of an anatomist.

He did not know that John had advanced farther than the first ramparts. In the morning, when he and Hugh had gone together to buy their China equipment, Margaret had come to offer feminine advice on materials. She had watched them turning over shirts, and hesitating, and retracting decisions in the manner of men at the counter. Women and their shopping? Oh, but men were infinitely worse! They had so small a field of choice, and yet they got lost in it. She laughed at this and a thousand trifles, and laughter is the truest ranging-arrow in love's quiver. London, too, with its bright sun and sky, and the cool wind that stirred up the sweet scent of her furs, had conspired to bring them together. Hugh joined the conspiracy by accepting an invitation to lunch with an old friend whom he met in Mr. Reeve's shop. John and Margaret came home by way of Marble Arch and a diagonal cut through the Park. The dying winter was old and weak—so weak that he could not gather up and hide away in his dark box the coins of gold scattered beneath the trees by the sunshine or the strands woven among the grasses. And, as they went, they talked of all the things on earth they held most dear—their nurseries and old toys, terra-cotta flower-pots, the summer sound of lawns being mown, firelight in mirrors, books, the silky touch of dogs' ears—each as the centre of some tale which seemed peculiar to their own autobiographies, though, at that moment, it was being remembered afresh, in one form or another, by every young creature—and every old one, too, who wasn't too stupid to value such things—from Kensington Palace to the western pavement of Park Lane.

John and Margaret, like all the other young creatures, had no idea of this. They felt as if they were telling each other secrets—which is the best known of love's tricks. In truth, they were but beginning to discover the secrets of themselves, and had not yet had time to become so confused as the rest of us in life's attempt to draw a boundary between the soul and the body. Dust to dust, ashes to ashes! There was no dust, there were no ashes, their hearts argued; therefore all—her lips and the colour the wind had whipped into her cheeks, his frank eyes, and brown, fine-cut hands—all must have something of the soul in them. What reason had they to doubt? They were not afraid, and fear goes hand in hand with the Devil. Their happiness was of the clean kind they would have liked to sing about to all the world.

So it happened that they danced together that evening with all the memories of daylight and keen air to lend magic to the flowers and the sparkling lamps and the murmur of stringed instruments.

"I love the little pointed shadows under everybody's feet," she said, "and the vague pools of light in the polished floor. It's better than fairies on the village green."

"That's not an absolute opinion," he answered, laughing.

"Shouldn't we be on the side of the fairies if we were dancing on green grass now?"

To him it mattered only that they were dancing together, and her silence acquiesced in his mood.

"There's any number of people," he exclaimed, "who are wishing the music would stop. It's strange to think of other people being tired and bored."

"Perhaps this isn't the music they care for."

"The old people?"

"Yes; probably they remember other tunes. Shall I ask the orchestra to play something that was heard all over London thirty—forty—fifty years ago? Shall I?"

They are for ever asking each other questions.

"Do you think anyone would dance to it?"

"I don't know. Would we dance to *this*—fifty years on?"

He brushed aside the unimaginable future. At this moment she was his, her voice speaking close to him, the curve of her cheek and forehead clear beneath his eyes. He imagined suddenly that he would remember this instant, that his future would be full of it; and it took to itself already some of the glamour of history.

"Oh," said she, "there's Mr. Ordith watching us!"

The charm was lifted. He could not endure that another should peer over his shoulder into the history-book of fancy, or that a stranger's eye should witness the building of this magic temple in which the moment was to be preserved against the assaults of all time. Soon the music faded into silence. A few feet slid on, and then stopped. The room filled with human voices.

"That's the end," she said softly, and he did not find the remark unnecessary. They sat down somewhere and talked little, each aware of anticlimax. John was almost glad when Ordith, graceful and self-confident, came up and took her away.

Perhaps her own emotion was communicated to Ordith; perhaps he, perceiving it in her, realizing—as she did not— from what source it flowed, and trying to take advantage of it, was himself entrapped. He pursued a policy of what he described to himself as "talking big"; he played upon an imagination already excited.

"I can't bear to leave London," he said. "And you are actually eager to go! Life centres here. The people in this room have their fingers on the pulse of the world."

"The politicians?"

He smiled over her shoulder. "Yes. I know it is a middle-class fashion to despise them. I can't despise men with power and knowledge. And not the politicians only. Everybody is here—the artists who matter, the thinkers who are in touch. And at this moment, a crisis in the history of the world, I am to go away."

He made it sound a tragedy.

He knew that to Twenty Years the present is always the opportunity of mankind—and an unpromising Twenty Years it would be if it thought otherwise. He knew, too—for his shrewdness went deeper than the surface—that Twenty Years has an understanding of many truths that Disappointment, not Philosophy, describes subsequently as illusions. But, so far as his immediate purpose was concerned, it mattered nothing whether the ideas that dominated Margaret were illusory or not. Only the fact of their domination was of importance to him, for they were to be a means to his own dominion. He spun a web of dreams that he might entangle her in it. His voice, which he could tune to the very ring of sincerity, told her how the future was to be glorious. There was to be battle against all the powers of evil—a new political outlook, new relations between state and state, and between governors and governed. That was the mission of their generation.

"We must grip the essentials," he said. "We must permit no compromise. And, above all, we mustn't lose ourselves in mere talk—we must act temperately, and according to a clearly-conceived plan. . . . And women!" he exclaimed. "What a tremendous chance! Your influence is growing every day; soon it will be direct as well as indirect. And then the best of you will not be content to manipulate the party strings at dinner-tables. You will be cutting them where they are obstructive. You will come with free hands—no stale tradition—no fear of precedent—no corruption of ideals."

He felt proud when he had delivered himself of this. It would win him laurels, he thought, among the forward young men, with their pamphlets and loose collars, their carpet-slippers and their political ikons. And Margaret was in a mood to question little. Cynicism and doubt had small influence over her that night. Was not Mr. Ordith her father's friend?—and, Heaven knew! he was no vague idealist. And had not Mr. Ordith a reputation for soundness and level-headedness where such a reputation was most difficult to

win? She paused neither to doubt nor to believe. It was
enough that his enthusiasm awakened in her a sensation of
warmth and brilliance, of assurance and power. And, though
she danced with him a second and a third time, and though
intervals elapsed between the dances, the sensation endured,
and grew in intensity, grew until—so inflammatory are wine,
ideals, and the contact of dancing—Ordith, too, became aware
of its heat, and flamed amazingly, so that he was cool-headed
no more. The conflagration, he found, gave him greater
power over her—though power of a new kind. He was too
wise to speak personal endearments to her, even the lightest,
but his voice assumed a lower, more intimate tone, and
vibrated now with a passion that was not artificial. He spoke
of the foolishness and selfishness of other women, their blindness to ideals—how he loved that word!—their fear of sacrifice, their failure to understand the *real needs* of the world. It
was implied that she was wonderfully different from them all.
How many and far-reaching were the victories within the
scope of a mind inspired by her motives! Somehow he was to
be her ally in these victories. "We," he said, and "I," but
never "You," thereby binding her to him without emphasiz-
ing her submission to the bond. The reality of triumph is in an
opponent's ignorance of his own defeat.

But control was slipping from Ordith. After a brief struggle
he let it go, and rejoiced in his freedom. His eyes, looking
down on her, lost their breadth of vision, and saw none of her
surroundings. Her proximity obscured all else; his touch on
her overwhelmed every other sensation. His muscles tightened his grip, but it seemed to him only that her body was
laying a heavier and heavier weight upon his arm. He danced
faster, but was aware only of greater rapidity of movement
and breathing close to his heart.

Slowly this extraordinary concentration of his mind produced its effect upon her. First she became conscious of
having, in his view, lost individuality, of having been rele-
gated somehow to the position of an instrument. Her will was
to revolt against that, but revolt was contrary to her inclination. She found a certain pleasure in the strength of the
current that was bearing her away, even while she feared it.
She said something; he did not answer. She repeated it; and
from his silence understood that his mind would not receive
her words. It was as if a wave, sweeping over her head and
robbing her voice of its effect, had roused her to resistance.

His arm had grown firmer about her. Her feet were scarce touching the ground. She wanted breath and foothold. She became frightened, active, determined to break free.

"Why are you dancing so fast?" was all she contrived to say.

But he heard, and looked down to drink in her powerlessness, to exult in his own power, to strengthen his grip again. He could not talk. His imagination was running on and on, dragging him with it. His thoughts, which had no traceable sequence, were presenting to him pictures of such vividness that he screwed up his eyes as if he might physically see them.

"I am tired," Margaret said, shrinking into the conventional. "Shall we stop?" Then, a moment later, with a flash of determination that compelled his attention: "I want to stop."

He let her go suddenly—too suddenly. Her eyes were raised questioningly for an instant, and, as he met them, were abruptly turned away. He took her out of the crowd. He wanted to get beyond the range of the many eyes that he imagined were turned upon him. She sat down where he told her to sit.

"Listen," he said. "I told you just now that I was sorry to leave England. I want to tell you why. There's so much to do here—so much danger to be warded off. And this going away is"— he paused feelingly—"is somehow shirking the fight. My father and I don't agree on all points. I should like to see Ordith's run differently—the position of our labour improved. I am on their side. . . . They know it. . . . Further, the whole attitude of armament firms must be changed. As matters stand their ambitions are warlike; their influence on political action is—well, you can understand that. And my chance to change all this is unique. No other young man has my opportunities. But I stand alone, absolutely alone. I——"

"But why are you telling this to me?"

"Because—oh, don't you feel as I do? Don't you——"

"But why are you telling it to me now?"

He was seized by an impulse to put away even this rattling imitation of reason, to make his spring now. All the world was moving so swiftly about him that he felt only force and sensation could keep pace with it. It pleased him to see that her eyes were frightened, and that, though she wanted to go away, she could not move. This was power; but he would not use it yet; he must not use it for months to come. Now he would go on saying something while he watched her.

"Can't you understand why I am telling it to you?"

"You talk so fast," she said, her hand travelling to her forehead.

"Then I'll talk slower."

"No," she said, under her breath; but he paid no attention. His voice continued—to her ears as inexplicit as music.

"Between us we will lay great plans," she heard him say presently, and her protest against being thus included was never uttered. "Out in the East—the home of all philosophy— we shall have time to think. Margaret, you will help me to get all this clear in my mind?"

All what? He didn't know or care. It sufficed that he had bound her to him by some tie, the more difficult to break because it was so vague. Moreover, his use of her name had been resisted only by a quick intaking of breath.

"You will help me?" he repeated. "You must—you must." Then, too confident, he stooped over her and reached with his hands for hers. By his lightest touch the spell he had laid upon her was broken. She started up, the blood tingling in her. She knew that she had acquiesced in something she had not considered, as if she had spoken in her sleep. His ascendancy was revealed as menacing—a cloud that overshadowed her, and, while it held her attention, warned her to take shelter.

"I can hear the music again."

"But the next dance is ours."

"No."

"You promised. Look—your name." He offered his programme, sure that she would not examine it or remember the number of the dance.

And she said without looking, "I can't dance now."

He answered as if he were stroking her. "Ah, you are trembling. What is the matter? Have I frightened you?"

"Frightened?" The sound of her own laugh restored her calmness. "What is there to be frightened of? But see," she went on, holding out her programme, "I am sure you have made a mistake. This dance is Mr. Lynwood's."

John was coming up the stairs towards them. "Then I will find you again a little later," said Ordith, and disappeared.

"What has happened?" John asked, looking into her face, which had now grown pale.

"Happened? Nothing—oh, nothing. I was a little tired, that's all."

And, in truth, Margaret knew of no cause for an effect so overwhelming. Looking back, she wondered how so strong an emotion had taken hold of her. Why had she been afraid? and why now was she conscious of having escaped, of having awakened—of having lost something, too?

"Let's go and dance," she said.

"No, not now," John answered, "not if you are tired." He led her away, and stopped opposite two chairs. "There," he said, "sit there for a little while where it is cool. Don't talk or worry."

When she was seated he moved away a few yards, wishing to give her the time she needed. Gradually she realized that the cloud charged with so much power over her was indeed gone. The atmosphere seemed less stifling. Freedom of thought and action was returning. Presently she remembered John and was grateful because he had taken her away from the place where she had been with Ordith; and grateful, with warmth of gratitude, because he had known how to be silent. Her look summoned him.

"You don't know how good you have been," she said.

"I hated to see you hurt to-night of all nights."

"To-night?"

"Because everything seemed so good. I was looking forward to China and seeing you there. To-night seemed a kind of celebration of the future."

"But that remains," she said, as if the recollection of the fact surprised her. She could not forget Ordith's power, or, for the time, think of any part of her existence as being altogether free from his influence. Where was he now? Was he near her? Involuntarily her hand went out to John's sleeve.

She tried to thank him for what he had done. Her sense of relief, of safety after danger, made his chance intervention seem the result of his kindness of heart; and every word she spoke, hesitating and tremulous, between tears and laughter, was marvellous to him.

"Tell me," he said, "what can I do? You haven't told me the facts. Do you trust me a little?"

"There are no facts."

"But he——"

"Oh, leave him!" she exclaimed. "Let's go down to where all the people are. What time is it?" she added suddenly, as if awaking from a wild dream to the surer business of the day.

He told her, but was certain she did not hear, her thoughts having fled great distances by then. As he followed her, he realized dimly with how great a force he had to contend, but he did not understand how indirectly this force could act. He felt sure that Ordith must have been in some manner definitely violent—have tried to kiss her, he angrily imagined. Then her "Oh, leave him!" echoed in his ears.

"Margaret," he said, "I haven't been trying—to find things out. I wanted to help if I could."

She turned to him with a little movement of confidence which was a full reward. "I know. Don't think I am ungrateful. I shan't ever forget. Your coming made everything different—and secure again. I would tell you about it if I could—if there was anything to tell; I think telling would help. But there's nothing—nothing tangible, at least." She shivered, as if something cold and flat had touched her. "Only a feeling of having been caught and of having broken free again."

Together they went into the ball-room, where faces, still smiling their response to some jest spoken a moment earlier, seemed out of touch with reality. This colour, this light on chin and throat, this flash of jewels and gleaming of shirt-fronts, was as a picture in oils that had hung unnoticed while life pursued its course swiftly, and to which, now there was breathing space, attention had reluctantly returned.

Chapter VIII
The Net

On Sunday, John and Ordith were much with Margaret, and even when she contrived to be alone she found she could not exclude them from her mind. To think of either was disquieting, and she needed peace. She felt that John was watching her. He knew how she needed help and was eager to render it would she but indicate a means. Her failure to indicate it was being interpreted by him as a lack of trust for which he blamed himself. He could not understand, his eyes said continually, what he had done or left undone that repelled her confidence. And that he should attribute her silence to a fault in himself added to her uneasiness. She could not speak her mind to him; she could not ask him to help her with a problem the terms of which were not yet clear to herself. She felt that he was waiting for her to speak, and reproaching himself with some dullness or hardness that, as he imagined, was sealing her lips. Several times she tried to speak—if only to tell him that she was aware of his sympathy; but words would not come.

Moreover—and this itself was an element in her difficulty—was not John weak with her own weakness? Together they were set about by forces stronger, infinitely stronger, than themselves. There was comradeship in that, but not help. It was as if they were two children side by side in a darkness that contained a menace, of which both were in different measures conscious, but which neither was able to grapple or even to define.

For a time, while she was in church, her trouble had been less. The air of security, of permanence, of prosperity about the place, and the absence of any kind of tumult within it had lulled and comforted. "The peace of God which passeth all understanding. . . ." She had bowed her head with the rest, mistaking the decorous silence for peace indeed. But, as she rose from her knees, her eyes encountered Ordith's which seemed half-laughingly to search and accuse her; and, as if following a suggestion of his, she began to think that the support she had received from the service had been based, not upon faith, but upon the extraordinary beauty of its prose. The hymns, with their redundancies and bad rhymes, had meant nothing to her, despite their devotion, and to the modern prayers on contemporary subjects she had given no heed. The balance and completeness of the Litany, the Lessons' direct beauty, the Collects' vigorous restraint—upon these her attention had been concentrated. Though the matter of the Benediction had remained unchanged, it would have brought no comfort to her if it had been expressed differently—by the Archbishops, for example.

"Hadn't old man Cranmer a wonderful ear for words?" Ordith said lightly, cutting Margaret to the quick. She felt that he read her thoughts, or—and this with a pang of fear that was reflected in the eyes she suddenly raised—that he had imposed his thoughts upon her.

"You don't like my saying that?" he asked, looking into her face. And even as she moved her lips to reply, to express somehow the resentment that was burning in her, his power asserted itself and drove her back to say, scarcely of her own will:

"Yes; it's quite true."

Like a pleasing, habitual vice, Ordith frightened and controlled her. Her father had chosen him as her husband, and her mother seemed to acquiesce in the choice. She pictured herself saying "No" to Ordith, and "No" to her father and mother. She would be very calm, very determined, and then all would be over, the battle fought and won. Surely it would be easy to say "No." One word to be spoken, one definite resolve to be kept—that was all. Nowadays coercion was impossible; the time of starvation, and imprisonment, and whips was long past. What she had to do was to look Ordith in the face, say "No," and stand by her decision. It sounded easy.

And, on the other side, was the tradition of obedience to her father, hard to break she knew, for she had failed often to break it, but not unbreakable; and there was one thing more.

Of this she thought, as men think of all things that are too vast for their imagination's canvas, in a concrete, limited manner: so are we compelled to picture God in the form of man. She thought of it as Ibble's works and yards as she had seen them when she had gone with her mother to the launching of ships—bare tracts of granite setts, buildings in common stock brick that had the motley appearance of disease, sheds of corrugated iron, cranes that groped above her head, railway-lines that tripped her feet, cables coiled up like gigantic snakes, flames from darkness, the mutter of machinery and the creaking of belts, the glass roofs through which the light came blurred and thin. The foundries, where the molten metal grumbled and spat and threw up scum on the runner-cups, had been her childhood's conception of hell. The whole place filled her with terror. She had seen the workmen, with their sullen, yellow faces streaked with machine-oil, and eyes dulled by labour into which imagination had never entered. Her life had been overshadowed by Ibble's, and not her life only, but her father's and mother's lives. Her parents had been omnipotent in her nursery. What power was this, then, that stood behind *them* and dominated *them?* She learned to think of Ibble's as a tyrant inexorable because unapproachable; an immovable background against which alone the movements of life were visible, and in contrast to whose darkness life's colours shone out. As she grew older she discovered that Ibble's did not stand alone, but was a unit in a complex system, a string in a universal net. The nature and extent of the net itself were not clear. These facts stood out: that nearly all the world was in its meshes; that somehow inclusion in it was profitable; that those who thought to break it were fools and dreamers; that at any rate, though it was delicate and fragile so that the winds of fate blew it hither and thither, it was impossible to break. That was the first article in a traditional faith—impossible to break. Margaret had seen her own mother fight to get out of it, and seen her fail. This acquiescence in the matter of Ordith was the seal upon her failure.

This intangible, this invincible force, that swayed all she knew, swayed Margaret also. Though she denied it to herself, saying that she was young and her life her own, she believed it in her heart. All her experience contributed to this belief— the house with the wonderful attics and passages which she and her mother had wanted to buy, but which her father had rejected because its reception-rooms were not magnificent enough to receive the guests of Ibble and Co.; the sending of Hugh into the Navy because, since his intellect seemed unlikely to qualify him for inclusion in the firm, it would be as well to have a representative among the customers of Ibble and Co. Ibble's was their God. Even her father, who was said to have the controlling interest, was himself controlled, working in sickness and health, growing tired and hollow-eyed and nervous, all for the sake of Ibble and Co. Once he had been seriously ill.

"I wish you would retire, Walter," her mother had said. "Surely we have money enough? Haven't we every material thing we want? Couldn't you come out of it now? Couldn't we go back to the old days before Ibble's——"

"Come out of it!" her father had answered. "My dear, I can't give in yet. Besides, I have my duty to do by Ibble and Co."

They had thought Margaret too young to understand, but she had understood something of the tragedy, for already Ibble's foundries were her Hell; and now she remembered it. And she was to play it out with Nick Ordith. Some day he would be, not Ordith the individual, but Ordith's, the firm and the tradition. Ibble and Ordith, Ordith and Ibble. . . . She had read in her mother's mind concerning the amalgamation, and knew what was planned but not spoken of. Her marriage likewise was planned but not spoken of.

After all, she asked herself, making a little kick within the mesh, what had her marriage to do with Ibble's? But what, too, had the attics and passages in which she would have liked to play had to do with Ibble's? She had but to say "No" to Ordith, she repeated—one word, one resolve. Often, when her thoughts returned to this point, she would laugh at herself as we laugh when we know we have uttered an empty boast; and sometimes while she laughed there were tears in her eyes.

Chapter IX
Quartered on the Kingdom

I

After leave which extended longer than any of them had hoped, the junior midshipmen, who had parted at the *King Arthur*'s gangway, joined the *Colonsay*. In the sense that in their new ship there was none senior to them they were junior midshipmen no longer. The Gunroom would still have to be tidied by them, but, instead of Clearing-up Stations at Krame's command, there would be organization based upon common consent. When the atmosphere became foul at sea, they would have to open and shut the scuttles if they wanted fresh air, but this would not be Scuttle Drill. Between them and an emancipation essential to what happiness they might find in the *Colonsay* and *Pathshire* there stood only one doubt. Of the Sub-Lieutenant they knew nothing but that his name was Hartington. He was not on board when they joined, and all the questions concerning him that they put to one another remained unanswered.

"Anyhow," said Cunwell, "if he kicks up a dust it will be easy enough for us—there are six of us—to keep him steady."

It sounded easy; but the Service tradition was against it.

"That's bluff," John answered. "We might be able to stave off obstacle races and Angostura hunts if we were prepared to make a Gunroom Revolution of it, but, as a matter of fact, we shouldn't try. You know we shouldn't when it came to the point. If Hartington wants to make it Hell for us, he can, though he is alone. But if he wants to live in love and charity with his neighbours, we ought to have the best time of any snotties in the Service."

Hartington came on board late that evening, and, after an appearance in the Gunroom too brief to give any indication of

102

his character, disappeared into his cabin. On his way thither he had passed John and Hugh in the Chest Flat.

"I wonder if he realizes what an immense difference he can make to us all," John said. "Think, a two years' commission in China, with no one in the Gunroom but ourselves and a Sub we get on with! I don't believe he could spoil it all, if he knew."

"I dare say we shall shake along, anyway," Hugh answered. "But it would be good—even if he were just neutral and didn't go out of his way to worry us."

The anxiety was universal. All the midshipmen were discussing him in whose hands their future lay. Then came Driss.

"I think Hartington's going to be all right," he said. "You know that, for some reason, they have put my chest down outside his cabin—it will have to be moved in the morning. Well, Sentley was standing by my chest while I was looking to see if I had some pyjamas there—I came later than the rest of you, so my trunk and tin case are still on deck. I left them there, thinking I had in my hand-bag all I should want for to-night. And, while I was cursing because I couldn't find my pyjamas, Hartington put his head out of his cabin. I had clean forgotten he was inside, and I thought he was going to let me have it for making a noise. But he just asked what was the matter—quite civilly, you know."

Driss paused to allow the others to be sufficiently impressed by the fact that the Sub in such circumstances had been quite civil.

"So I told him I should have to go up on deck and get my trunk down. 'What do you want?' he said. 'Pyjamas? Come in here and choose a pair of mine. Blue silk or white silk? They are rather attractive, don't you think?' "

"He lent you some?"

"So might dozens of Subs!" Cunwell exclaimed scornfully.

"Yes," said Driss eagerly, "so they might; but not in that way. I swear he treated me as—as, an ordinary human being in a country house might treat another ordinary human being who was short a pair of pyjamas. None of the being-generous-to-junior-snotties touch. You wouldn't have thought there was such a thing as seniority. I believe he must come from the South of Ireland—though I've never heard the name there," he added solemnly.

"That sounds promising," Hugh said. "I wonder. . . .

Oh, wouldn't it be great, Driss, if Hartington were like that all through!''

"I believe he will be," Driss answered. "I'm almost sure he will be. He didn't even give me the pyjamas and have done with it. We talked for quite a long time—about where we should put his photographs, and pictures, and writing-desk—he has an old writing-desk that he's very keen on, and an odd taste in pictures. And we talked about other things as well, all off the ordinary track, just as if there wasn't any Service at all.''

But even then they could not believe that nothing aggressive lay beneath this apparently pleasing exterior. Driss, who had seen and heard, found it impossible to carry conviction in face of the others' deep-rooted scepticism. The next day routine was irregular. Hartington went ashore soon after breakfast and did not return until the dog watches, when he took over the duties of the officer who had been keeping the Day On with John as his midshipman.

"Have you been keeping watch all day?" Hartington asked.

"Yes, sir, on and off. I've been below a good deal when there was nothing doing on deck.''

"Tired?''

"No, not very; I'd much rather keep Days On than the regular four-hour watches.''

"Is anyone coming up to take over from you?''

"I don't think so.''

"Well, you may as well go below. I'll look out up here. I'll send down a side-boy if I want you.''

In the Gunroom John found everyone busy appropriating lockers and bringing in their books and papers from their chests.

"There's enough room for two lockers each, and three for Hartington," Dyce said. "Those are your two, Lyynwood, in the corner—the worst billet of the lot. . . . No, we didn't just push you into them because you were away. We cut round— someone cut for you—and you were lurked.''

"I don't mind," John said. "Two lockers anywhere are luxury. I'll get my books in. By the way, Driss, I think you were right about Hartington. He took over the watch just now; asked if I was tired, and sent me down.''

"Of course I was right," Driss answered, smiling. "Did you happen to discover where he lives?''

"No; we aren't on a personal footing yet. I called him 'sir,' being on watch."

They unpacked slowly, pausing often to sit on the table and discuss the most suitable stowage places for sextants and Inman's Tables and Seamanship Manuals. They had a feeling of spaciousness and independence that was altogether delightful—so glorious did it seem to dispose their own dwelling-place in their own way, instead of availing themselves of whatever odd corners were left over by Krame and Howdray. On the table was a pile of John's possessions—books, instruments, and innumerable manuscripts which, though he had no hope of being able to shake them into publishable form, he had not the heart to destroy. There was a foolscap book with marble covers into which he had copied such poems as he had completed; there were penny exercise-books in which novels had been sketched and begun; there were bundles of papers tied together with tape; and sheets of all colours and sizes, some of them but half covered with writing, upon which he had set down pieces of description, scraps of narrative and dialogue, and sentences from imaginary political speeches—fragmentary records of fiery and ambitious dreams. How little his best friends in that Gunroom knew of the things that were written there! How they would laugh if they read them, for many were evidence of absurd imaginings! John turned them over. Here was the peroration by which the *King Arthur*'s able seaman, " 'undredth class for conduck, 'undredth class for leave," was to bring the Albert Hall to its feet—"jes' as if I 'ad 'em on strings." And here was John's own speech to the House of Commons on Home Rule; here his reply to the Foreign Secretary's pronouncement on the imminence of war with Germany—and in the corner of the manuscript he had written the great sentence from John Bright's speech on the Crimean War. On the back of an old Torpedo Sketchbook he found his notes on Lawrence's *Principles of International Law*—part of the equipment of a Foreign Secretary's critic, he remembered with a smile, and among the notes was a passionately eulogistic review of Mrs. Lynn Lynton's *True History of Joshua Davidson*. Some of his essays had progressed no further than their motto—perhaps the fire within him had dried up his pen, perhaps a boat had been called away. . . .

"Midshipman o' the Watch 'ere, sir?" said the voice of an invisible side-boy.

"Yes."

"Orficer o' the Watch wants you on deck, sir."

"All right."

"I'm going down to have a cigarette," Hartington said when John reached him. "Let me know if there's a panic."

For an uneventful hour John walked up and down at the top of the gangway. A hand touched his arm, and he turned to find Hugh beside him.

"John, what do you think has happened?"

"What? Something to do with Hartington?"

"Hartington has been reading some of your stuff."

"Lord Almighty! How did he get hold of it?"

"Found it on the deck in the Gunroom. He picked it up to see what it was. Then he asked if it was private. Cunwell said No, you often let people read it."

"Some of it," said John, "and some people."

"I know. But we couldn't do anything. Hartington smiled, and said that, seeing it wasn't letters and was sculling about the deck of his Gunroom, he thought he had a right. We couldn't do anything," Hugh repeated. "But I thought I'd better come and tell you."

John thought for a moment.

"What was he reading?" he asked.

"I don't know—verse, I think."

"In a marble-covered book?"

"Yes, he had that. He said it looked more like a formal volume for the public service than the odd bits of paper."

"Well, I'd rather he read the volume than the odd bits. . . . But isn't it perfectly damnable—the Sub's getting hold of that right at the beginning! What comments?—the usual remarks about long hair?"

"He hasn't spoken a word."

"Oh well," John said, "it can't be helped now. It was my own fault—leaving it on the table. I suppose I shall hear about it from Hartington for ever and ever, Amen. I wonder why it is regarded as an almost criminal offence to try to write verse?"

Left alone, John tried to think out smooth answers to the remarks the Sub would make when he came on deck. So far as the Sub himself was concerned, the damage was done, but it might still be possible to prevent him from sharing his intelligence with the Wardroom. Of course, the news was certain to spread sooner or later. If Hartington had not made his discovery now, he would have made it in a week's time, and if the fact of there being a poet in the ship were not laughed over in the Wardroom to-day it would be laughed over to-morrow. But John knew it was important to gain time. If the *Colonsay*'s officers learned first to think of him as an ordinary midshipman who discharged his duties with reasonable efficiency, they would tolerate his writing of poetry as a superficial eccentricity. If, on the other hand, he was made known to them primarily as a poet, it would be extraordinarily difficult to rid himself of the stigma and to win back his good name.

When at last Hartington reappeared he spoke only of Service matters. John wondered what was coming. Perhaps he had not realized that his midshipman of the watch was the author of the verse he had been reading. Perhaps he thought the whole affair so unimportant that he would not trouble to refer to it. John clung to this last possibility as long as he could, but from time to time he noticed that Hartington regarded him curiously, with eyes that seemed to laugh at his apprehension and discomfiture.

"Lynwood," he said suddenly, "I shouldn't leave my manuscript sculling about the deck, if I were you."

"It was all on the table," John answered quickly. "I hadn't time to put it away when you sent for me. I'm sorry it made a litter. If I may go down for a moment, I'll get Fane-Herbert to put it into my locker for me—I should be back almost at once. Then everything will be tidy——" He stopped helplessly.

"I wasn't objecting to the untidiness," Hartington said.

The silence seemed unending. John had never felt so uncomfortable, so utterly at a loss. He knew the contemptuous thoughts that must be passing through Hartington's mind. He tried haltingly to minimize his error.

"I do it only—only in my spare time," he said, "just as other people do—do other things." He wanted to explain that he meant no harm by his poetry, but he could find no words. The poetry itself was the harm, he knew. There was no explaining it away. "Do you mind very much?" he asked nervously.

Hartington smiled. "Mind?" he said. And then he added, "Why should I mind? Is it contrary to the King's Regulations and Admiralty Instructions to write verse?"

"No, but——"

"The point is, that most Subs would have made you read it to the Mess after dinner, and very probably beaten you at the end of it—if not on that pretext, then on some other. So it wasn't very discreet of you to leave it about, do you think?"

"No."

"And there must be a penalty," said Hartington, taking John by the arm. "I suppose I must be a very bad Sub in some respects—at any rate, not in accordance with pattern: you'll find that out, I expect. But there must be a penalty. So after dinner, when we have turned over to the Officer of the Night, you will report yourself in my cabin with the manuscript you are going to read to me, and two whiskies-and-sodas. . . . Do you mind reading to me?"

"Of course not," said John, amazed. "I should like to."

"And I want to hear more of it. So that's settled."

II

That evening John went to Hartington's cabin for the first of many times; but the first, because it was so unexpected and so full of promise for the future, was perhaps the most marvellous evening of all. It did not end until long after the Gunroom had been closed and the other midshipmen were turned in. By then the ship had become very silent and peaceful. As he climbed into his hammock, after a glance at the curtain behind which Hartington's cabin-light was still shining, John's thoughts returned to the *King Arthur*, and to the nights when he had turned in bruised, bleeding, and covered with the filth of the Gunroom deck. He remembered the hopelessness of his outlook then, the sense he had had of confinement worse than physical confinement, of being surrounded and shut in by a wall which he could never, never break. And now—he thrust his face deep into his pillow—now he had found at last one living soul in and of the profession to which he was bound, in whose eyes the things he cared for were not all dust and ashes.

Upon youth the mass of men's opinion lies heavily. He who stands alone in faith doubts at last; but two in faith are a sufficient army. And John had begun to doubt. His central beliefs were these: firstly, he believed that Art was a fine thing, a major force in life, not merely a slave to fan merchants or naval officers when they came, hot and tired, from their business in the City or on the bridge; secondly, he believed—to use a term as unrestrictive as his own opinion upon this matter—in political unselfishness. He had found the phrase once when driven into a corner during a trivial Gunroom argument about a newspaper article. Do you believe this? do you believe that? they had shouted at him; and he, because he could not accept all the implications of unqualified assent, and because he knew they would not listen to qualifications, had answered "No" and "No" and "No" again. Are you a Unionist? Are you a Liberal? No. Are you a *Socialist?* How could he tell them when he had never read Marx or opened one book written by a Russian. They hurled all the old arguments at him. If they sent ashore a naval landing-party, that would soon settle the strikers. Surely a man like the Duke of Westminster, with a real *stake in the country*, was entitled to more votes than his butler, who had no stake at all? If women were given votes, soon they would sit in Parliament, soon they would be running battleships. Once give way and you always gave way. What was wanted was a firm hand.

"I don't believe it," John said.

"Then what on earth do you believe in?"

The question was more searching than they knew—extraordinarily difficult to answer. Yet it had to be answered. Then John had struck upon his phrase. "I believe," he had said, "in a certain political unselfishness at home and abroad. At least, that's the spirit of the thing. I can't explain it any better. It's of no use to ask me what I should do if I were Prime Minister. I haven't his experience. I don't know how he is placed. But I don't believe in your firm hand and land-parties. All the blind destroyers have worshipped them. . . . I can't go any further than that now—just political unselfishness."

"That's all very well as talk, but what would you *do?*" asked Cunwell, the man of action.

"I don't know. I admit I don't know. When I've had a chance—if ever—to read History and Economics, and—oh a dozen things I never shall read, then perhaps I shall have a more definite creed."

And as to the other part of his belief: they didn't laugh at Shakespeare—he had been a school subject, and was a tradition. They didn't laugh at him any more than at the crests on their family note-paper. But, they asked, where would Shakespeare have been without Drake and Howard of Effingham? It was a question of values. To them, Art was the camp-follower of Action; to John it was Action's equal and honour-able ally. They thought of books as ministers to the tired warrior in his leisure hours, worthy only if they soothed him. And they liked poetry whose rhythm they could mark with their feet.

The effect of unanimous opposition had been to make John doubt himself. People so far divided by circumstance and experience as Cunwell and Mr. Fane-Herbert agreed on these points at least—that political unselfishness was the talk of ignorant agitators, and that Art was a handmaiden. Were they right after all? They said: "Wherever you look in the world to-day Physical Force rules us. Can you reject universal Evidence? Isn't it just stubborn and foolish to refuse to do homage to a Force which, if you don't bow your head, will cut it off? Isn't it wiser to support the side that has already won?" John had begun to think that this victory must indeed be final. All his friends acclaimed it; scarcely a book he had read, except the New Testament, seemed to challenge it. Many of the poets sang it: not Blake—but Blake was ac-counted mad.

And now, though they had spent the evening in all the happiness of vigorous disagreement, John had found in Hartington one who denied the finality of this victory. He had been introduced, moreover, to authors who denied it uncom-promisingly. Hitherto, such authors had been, within his experience, few, and these few had failed and were dead. They had seemed to have no heirs. That night he discovered that their flame was still guarded and honoured and fed. He had turned over pages, written by living men, that were lit with it. In France, in England, in Germany there were eyes that saw by it. In Russia the sky was red—perhaps with its light.

So, after all, the whole world did not believe that an Army of Occupation must be quartered for ever on the Kingdom of God.

Chapter X
Eastern Seas

It was not long after they sailed from England that the mid-shipmen decided that many of their dreams were coming true. The *Colonsay*, though she was a poor ship to look at, passed the great lowering battleships of the Home Fleet proudly, almost with a little toss of her head. They might frown contemptuously at her, but soon they would be buried in the Northern mists, ploughing up and down eternally, keeping station on the Flag, the bondservants of the wireless at Whitehall; and she would be away for a holiday. True, the wireless could reach her too, but it would not take the trouble. To Colombo and back she would be her own mistress, bound to drop a curtsey only now and then to other people's admirals whom she might meet at ports of call.

And those who sailed in her might look further than Colombo. There they would take over the *Pathshire* from her homeward bound crew, and depart towards the freedom of the East. A small ship with its implied intimacy and informality; long cruises independent of even the ladylike China Squadron flagship; few fleet exercises; coaling with shore-labour; new countries, new faces, new interests—this was their prospect. It changed them all, and put new life and hope into them. For two years they were to be outside the vice whose jaws were Gibraltar Straits and the Shetland Isles. It was the release of their lives, a visit of slum children to the open fields. From the Home Fleet they came, and to the Home Fleet they would return, and they were all determined to make the best of the time that was to intervene.

"It's extraordinary," John wrote to his mother, "the contrast between this ship and the *King Arthur*. Ordith is odd to

111

me—but nothing on earth to complain of; and the other two-stripers treat the Gunroom almost as equals off duty. Even on duty they are always polite, except when they let fly in moments of justifiable excitement, and that does no harm. And often they yield points of strict etiquette in a way that makes four hours on the bridge pass like two. I don't know how long all this will last. I dare say that as the end of good things draws near, the good things themselves will deteriorate. But now everyone is so pleased with life that all goes well. Hartington, the Sub, I like immensely. You don't know how much happier I am. There's always something to which to look forward. I think the absence of that was the trouble of the *King Arthur*, and the trouble of all the unfortunates in home waters.''

The *Colonsay* put in to Arosa Bay to drop ratings who were taking passage to other ships, and of these the ship's company took farewell with the air of schoolboys who, going out into the playing-fields, leave comrades to do impositions in class-rooms. At Gibraltar they did not tarry long. Soon after the Rock had gone down over the western horizon they were overtaken by a storm, which continued with extraordinary violence until they were within a few hours of Valetta. To reach the bridge was a formidable task. In the batteries, where the fo'c'sle gave shelter against the head wind, progress was comparatively easy, but, once over the break of the fo'c'sle, the trouble began. There was a space of several yards between the head of the battery ladder and the foot of the ladder that led to the bridge. Across this space had been stretched a rope, by clinging to which it was possible to avoid being whisked off the deck and blown, but for the friendly intervention of a davit or a sighting-hood, into the mountainous sea. John, heavy with sea-boots, and with skirts of oil-skins clinging to his legs, held this rope and tried to advance, but the combined strength of legs and arms could not move him. While the boatswain's-mate, secure under the lee of the bridge ladder, smiled at his attempts, John pulled and pulled but went forward not an inch. Then, suddenly realizing how ridiculous he must look, he burst out laughing, and swiftly choked because he had opened his mouth to the gale. And it was not until the boatswain's-mate—himself securely lashed to a stanchion—came to his assistance, that John could move at all.

"Is this an official hurricane?" he said to Dyce, whom he was relieving.

"No, not yet. We are logging the wind as eleven. A hurricane is twelve." He turned over the details of his watch. "Which battery did you come up?"

"Port."

"Is that the driest to go down?"

John laughed. "There's devilish little to choose. I think the port's the better."

Dyce ran his fingers over his face. "I'm sticky all over with it," he said. "I feel as if I should crack if I grinned. It stings after a time. All the same, it's exciting on watch. You never know when the foretopmast will go over the side. . . . Well, d'you know everything you want to know? Will you take over now? I'm going to the Gunroom to fug."

"We've just had a green sea in there," said John, "so the fug is considerable."

The *Colonsay* entered Valetta white with salt. Ashore there, after coaling, John met Reedham and Ollenor, whose joy in having got so far East was overshadowed by the thought that, when their old shipmates had sailed for Port Said, they themselves would go westward again. "I'd give a year's seniority to be coming out with you," said Reedham. "Come and have a drink."

An ankle twisted while playing grommet hockey on the quarter-deck prevented John from going ashore at Port Said, Suez, or Aden, and his knowledge of these places extended no further than the tales told by other midshipmen of the marvellous things they saw there. Already they had entered the atmosphere of the East. Colours had grown brighter, near outlines more distinct. In the Canal they went into half-whites, and as they entered the Red Sea blue monkey-jackets were discarded altogether, and for the first time they wore white tunics as well as white trousers and boots. The heat made the outboard wall of the Gunroom too hot to lean against. The midshipmen who were working in the Engine-room came up from the watches, not red with heat, but white and trembling with exhaustion.

"This ship," said Hugh, "may have a thousand advantages, but its engines are not among them. The Tiffeys say they are the hottest they have ever served with—and the Lord defend them from hotter!"

"What watches do you have to keep?" John asked.

"Now only one four-hour watch each day. It doesn't sound much. You try it. The indicator diagrams are the worst business—one set to be taken every watch. I suppose I'm slow, but I can't take a set—allowing for mishaps—in much less than half an hour; and the temperature up there, on the top of the cylinders, is anything from 135° to 160°. It's a real relief to get away into the boiler-rooms for a spell. And the more warm and sooty lime-juice you drink the faster you sweat, so that's no good. But, barring odd jobs, we have to ourselves twenty hours out of the twenty-four, which is a recompense for most evils."

There were tales, too, of the stokers on duty on the evaporators, of how they worked in a temperature of 126°, and how they had fainted at their posts within three-quarters of an hour.

From Aden across the Indian Ocean the way was calm and blue. The sea was an enormous, flat, highly-polished sapphire, and its surface was so still by day and so luminous by night that it seemed hard like a jewel. Astern, the wake was thin and regular, and visible almost to the horizon. The ship, and all life in the ship, seemed to John somehow theatrical. The brillance of colour, the flash of white uniforms in the sun, the absence of most of those Service activities that ordinarily distinguish a warship from a yacht, contributed to this effect. Superficially this life corresponded closely to that led by puppet naval officers on the civilian stage. Here were sea and blue sky, white ducks still new, the gleam of sun on gold-laced shoulder-straps and gilded buttons. It was all pleasant and unreal.

"This," said Hartington, "is very like a poster advertising for naval recruits. It catches the eye but doesn't convince the mind."

"It gives one the idea of the stage, or of toys," John answered. "The ship goes through the water like a toy boat that you pull by a string across a bath—nothing to interrupt quite regular bow-waves that go oiling on and on to the very edge."

Hartington leaned across his bunk towards his cabin scuttle. "Listen, now," he said. "Down there—by the water-line—not a muffled swish of waves, but, clear and distinct, the touch of particles of water on steel. Almost you can hear each bubble split and scatter. . . . You seem, as you go East, to be able to look at everything very close, every detail like a minutely accurate miniature—or, as you said, a toy that you can pick up and hold under your eye. I remember, when I was a small boy, I loved to pick up a toy horse and cart, or an engine or a house—just for the fun of feeling like a god. I was Destiny brooding over the nursery! I could throw a divine boot at my sister's dolls' tea-party—but I didn't, because of the crockery. But often, when one of her dolls was ill, and the doctor had failed, and the bottles were empty of physic, I used to remove the roof of the house—my dramatic mode of entry—and take the patient from her bed, and cure her, and put her out in the garden. Nine times out of ten my sister approved the miracle; but now and then, when she had had ideas of her own about that cure—probably a journey round the world from the night-nursery to the schoolroom—she used to weep because I had spoilt everything. I remember her nurse asked me what I meant by interfering, and I said solemnly that I had meant well—which was quite true—but that I had been 'playing at God.' I shall never forget the effect of that remark.''

"And here and now,'' John said, ''one has a feeling of being in the doll's house one's self.''

"And a horrible idea that someone is 'playing at God' not very far off—Someone whose Hand might come suddenly out of nothing and pick the painted ship up out of the painted ocean and—and drop it into the nursery fire. I used to send tin soldiers to Hell that way.''

John smiled. ''Is that the 'fatalism of the East?' ''

"No: it's a Cockney picking up an idea of Time and Space and the other capital letters. *'O Time and Change they range and range From sunshine round to thunder.'* . . . Have you written more verse?''

"No.''

"What have you written?

"Nothing. It's too hot.''

They sipped Irish whisky and lemon beneath the electric fan whizzing and vibrating in its cage.

Chapter XI
Away From the Ship

At Colombo the exchange of crews between *Pathshire* and *Colonsay* was effected as an evolution. With the exception of a few hands left behind for indispensable duties, both ships were simultaneously emptied into their boats. As they met and passed the men tried to cheer, but silence was immediately restored. There would be time for cheering, perhaps, when, with her new freight, the *Colonsay* left for home.

To John, who was too junior to have seen anything of the traditional "spit and polish" in the old Channel Fleet, the *Pathshire* was a revelation. In China, where time was less precious than in the North Sea, and where the menace of Wilhelmshaven was more remote, Gunnery, Torpedo Practice, and Fleet Exercises had not made good their claim to undivided attention. The *Pathshire* was full of bright work, which in home waters would have been obscured by Service grey. Her paint and enamel glistened in the sunlight so that her after-turret was a mirror; her stanchions were burnished like a knight's armour; her dull metal was overlaid with silver gilt; everywhere were decorative turk's-heads and whitened lanyards; her upper deck was spotless as a yacht's.

"Think of Cleaning Stations in this packet!" said Sentley. "It must have cost her Commander and Number One about a third of their pay to provide all the paint and enamel in excess of the Service allowance."

The Gunroom, they discovered, was but half a Gunroom, their quarters having been cut into two parts by a temporary bulkhead. One part was given over to the Warrant Officers, but, in compensation for this, Hartington obtained permission from the Commander to use as a smoking-room the after

116

main-deck casemate on the starboard side. There had been no midshipmen in the previous commission, so that all furniture other than the scanty Service fittings had to be bought with the Mess Fund. A few wicker armchairs, a couple of cheap card-tables, and several ash-trays—these things being regarded as essentials—were obtained at Colombo, and all else was left, at Hartington's suggestion, until they should reach the wider market of Hong Kong.

Nearly a week was to pass before they sailed again, and the midshipmen were given leave. John and Hugh went together to Kandi. They avoided the obvious hotel which other officers were likely to visit, and chose a place that consisted of three small bungalows, almost hidden among the trees that covered the hill on the less popular side of the lake. Here came men whose experience of the "best hotels" in the East did not tempt them to strain their finances—quiet folk, who were chiefly remarkable, in John's eyes, for the matter-of-fact way in which they regarded what to him was novel and amazing. And the hotel itself, save when a breath of wind stirred the branches that overhung it or the sound of gong or bell came up from the lake below, was deeply silent.

After dinner on the evening of their arrival, sitting together in the verandah that ran the whole length of the three bunga-lows, and watching their cigarette smoke twist and disappear against a sky of so heavy a purple that the stars seemed to be embedded in it, they discussed their plans for the morrow—discussed them happily and at leisure, knowing that their time was their own, and that any decision made to-night might be freely reversed in the morning. As they were on the point of leaving the *Pathshire* an English mail—the first to reach them since they left home—had been distributed, and each had brought his share to Kandi unread. "Let's keep them," John had suggested, "until after dinner to-night, when we shall be alone and quiet, and clear away from the ship." And now they brought out their letters from their pockets and began the reading they had so long postponed. Soon there was little sound but that of pages being turned. From far down the verandah came the murmur of indistinguishable voices, and from time to time the hiss of a match or the sharp tinkle of a liqueur glass.

Among John's letters was one from Margaret, which he did not open until all the others had been returned to their envelopes. Then he read it slowly. When he began he was content with the moment. This evening's beauty and quietness, so wonderful a contrast to the nights he had spent in the *King Arthur*, seemed a satisfaction of all his desires. For two days he was independent of routine—free to control his own movements, to read, to sleep, to go in and out according to his will. He and Hugh were filled with the spirit of content that visits all men at the beginning of their holiday. There had seemed no need to look further, to question motives or consequences. The night was pleasant; this letter of Margaret's would add pleasure to the night.

But, as he read, he began to remember many things which the freedom of his new life from persecution had caused him to forget. She spoke of London, of political plots and rumours, of the strength or weakness of new movements, of the expansion of new ideas. New books, new expressions of opinion; the words of men who had been her father's guests; fears of a strike at Ibble's—her letter was extraordinarily suggestive of keenness and activity. Much had happened, more was about to happen—and this in a London many weeks away. What, Margaret asked, had he been doing? What had he written? He looked back over weeks of inactivity. He had done nothing but talk to Hartington. Days had slipped by—precious days. Since he left England he had read little, had created nothing, had not tried to create. The storm of the *King Arthur* being over he had relapsed into lazy content. Time had sped.

To youth, consciousness of the passage of time comes seldom, but coming, it brings with it pain by which age is not affected—pain unsoftened by any acceptance of the inevitable. Still the chance; still the opportunity to make good; still the feverish casting about for means! And middle-age growing nearer—a vision of the insignificant man going to and fro between his home and office, of the two-and-a-half stripe lieutenant many, many times passed over! John saw that he had been wasting his life.

Then he saw, in a flash that left him blind, that, unless its whole course were changed, he would continue to waste his life. Waste—and at the end old age, looking back upon years empty of achievement. "If only I had my time again! If I were but eighteen once more!" It was as if this foreseen wish had been uttered and fulfilled. He was eighteen now. The future was still his.

The letter fell with his hand on to his knees.

"Finished?" Hugh asked. John looked up to encounter his

laughing eyes. "I have been watching your face," he went on. "It seems to have been a disturbing letter."

"It was," John answered. "It reminds me how far we are out of the world and how infernally slack I have been."

He held out the envelope that the writing might be seen.

"Margaret!" Hugh exclaimed. "What has she been saying?"

"She has made me think, thrown me back on things I had forgotten. It was so good to be free of the *King Arthur* that, during the whole passage out, the world has seemed the best of all possible worlds. It isn't—or it won't be long. Oh, Hugh, it's all very well—a happy ship, a good Wardroom, a good Sub, and no Gunroom persecution; but what does it all lead to? I want to do other things—things I shall never be able to do—and to meet other people."

Hugh, believing that John was thinking particularly of Margaret, said: "At any rate, some of the 'other people' will be out East before long."

"You dear old fool!" John exclaimed. "That isn't what I meant. . . . No; it's just restlessness, I suppose. I feel that all the work we do is so like a housemaid's—to-day's routine the same as to-morrow's. We never build or make anything. For all our work we leave nothing behind."

"I don't see your trouble," Hugh said. "So long as life is pleasant I don't want to leave anything behind."

"We are missing so much. We get out of touch. In whatever progress there is we have no part."

"I know we are missing a great deal. Every letter I get from outside makes me jealous of the people at home. They can go about and see things, and we are shut up day in and day out."

"How they would shout if they heard you say that!" John broke in. "Mostly they imagine that it is they who are shut in and we who go about—as they say—seeing the world. It's all wrong. The world doesn't consist in places but in people. And the only boundaries are boundaries of thought. Think of the people your sister listens to, the books she reads, the opinions that count—coming to her first hand. Men and women from abroad—Germans, French, Americans—she is beginning to be in touch with them all. But the Service boundaries are desperately close-drawn."

Hugh leaned back in his chair and yawned. "I suppose we are all much the same,'" he said. "We all feel shut in—or shut out, rather—though perhaps for reasons different from yours. Sentley wants plants and birds—being a naturalist; and there's not a plant or a bird in H.M.'s ships. Driss wants Ireland; Driss is almost sick for Ireland sometimes and he can't go there. And do you remember Tintern?—he was starved for music. He said to me once—dead serious—that if he could get music he would never get drunk. He used to dream about going to Germany and being educated—'start life all over again with the five-finger exercise,' he used to say. . . . And the strange thing is that officers of the Old Navy didn't feel like that. I suppose they were made of harder stuff. Last leave I asked an old retired Admiral about his snotty days, and he said, 'No, we didn't hanker after shore life as you young fellows do. Of course, we were keen enough to get ashore when we could—better food and beds—but I think we were all of us glad in a way to get back to the ship.' "

"But the Navy was smaller then, and more independent of the outside world," John said. "I dare say your old Admiral felt an almost personal affection for it. But you can't have affection for a vast machine that is itself only a unit in a greater system of machinery; you can feel loyalty, perhaps, but not affection. It's like trying to fall in love with a Board of Directors. The Service is too big and impersonal to love. Moreover, it isn't a free agent. You know as well as anyone what lies behind it."

"Ibble's?"

"And more."

"And Ordith's?"

"More than Ibble and Ordith's, more even than the whole armament ring. Behind the armament firms are the mines, behind the mines is shipping, behind shipping—oh, it goes on for ever expanding and expanding. It goes out in every direction, and drags in every individual in the world—shareholders, banks, the financial houses at home, international finance—there it is, fully expanded again. Your sister, viewing it from her own angle, sums it up as a Net. We are all shut up inside it, and everyone who thinks is swimming round and round trying to find a way out. Discontented devils—so we are! Every novel that says anything is full of protest, and every speech—public or private. The papers call it Industrial Unrest, the Foreign correspondents European Unrest. The whole world's affected as it was not in your Admiral's time. . . . And in the Service we are shut up in a corner pocket of the Net; we haven't the chance even to swim round and round.''

"Margaret will never accept anything," Hugh commented. "Father is always telling her that if only she would watch the world as it is instead of thinking of the world as it might be she would get on much better."

"You wouldn't care much for a sister who sat down placidly to watch the world as it is," John observed.

"No—it wouldn't be attractive. I don't mind so long as she doesn't go to hopeless extremes," added her cautious brother. "But she won't do any good. The net is there, and the net will remain."

"Until it breaks," John said.

Two men and a woman with a shrivelled face passed along the verandah into the hotel. One of the men was chinking the coins in his pocket. A dog rose sleepily from under the table by which they had been sitting, stretched himself, sniffed the warm air, and pattered after his master.

Chapter XII
The Captain in Confidence

I

On the afternoon of the first Sunday after the *Pathshire* sailed from Colombo for Singapore, Hartington was sitting alone in his cabin when a double knock sounded at the door and the curtains were drawn aside. A pale face, with thin lips, watery, protuberant eyes, and a pitted forehead fringed with straight, clipped hair, was thrust into the cabin.

"Hullo, Aggett! Come in."

Aggett smiled, exposing the gaps in his teeth, and entered awkwardly. He was an Engineer-Lieutenant of the older, rougher school. Round his neck, instead of a collar, he wore a white scarf that was not clean. The creases in his fingers and the thick cuticles which grew high on his nails were stained with oil and dirt. But that scarred forehead and those strange eyes which had the extraordinary opaque appearance of great age—almost as if they had done service once before to some other being now dead—proclaimed their owner's intelligence. A flabby vicious little man, but no fool, this Aggett appeared. And, to one who cared to seek further, to contrast the darting movements of his hands with the cumbrousness of his feet, or to remark how strong and decided a voice proceeded from that poor body, Aggett seemed more than intelligent. He possessed force and wariness, a rare power to stake all at need, combined with a distrust of his fellows, which was valuable because it was discriminating. He was a man whom it was impossible to imagine as a child. No lasting affection of wife or mother could be easily thought of as connected with him. He could have no home, no ties. He passed, surely, from ship to hotel, from hotel to ship, making hundreds of acquaintances but not a friend, despising and

122

using all he met, never introspective or lonely, sufficient unto himself.

He threw over the cabin a quick glance of disapproval. It irritated him that anyone should take trouble to decorate his habitation; and he was the more irritated in this instance because Hartington's taste, unlike that of many officers who tried to make their cabins "tiddley," could not be easily scorned as effeminate. The few photographs, in the simplest of wooden or silver frames; the books, with their appearance of dignity and quietness; the pictures—here a Medici reproduction of a Dürer drawing, there a water-colour landscape of the hills about Fiesole—were such as no woman was likely to have chosen. Aggett wanted to say what he said usually to officers whose walls were not so bare as his own, "This place is like a whore's boudoir;" but his sense of the appropriate overcame him, and he said:

"Well, Hartington-me-lad, sittin' in your country residence, eh? Let's ring for the family butler."

"Which means you want a cocktail? Put your head out and ask one of the snotties in the casemate to send for Ah Foo."

Aggett did as he was bid, sat down on the edge of a chair, and took a cigarette from a paper packet concealed in his breast-pocket.

"Ordith wants you to come in to supper to-night in the Wardroom. Can do?"

"Yes. I shall have to leave you early, though. I've got the Middle. I shall want some sleep first."

"Right. . . . Ordith asked me to come with the invite. He's workin'—always workin'."

"Gunnery?"

"Yes. Fellows in the Wardroom don't know how much work he puts in. I know him better than most. I *do* know. They think he's slack 'cause he only takes a watch now and then. But I give you my word"—he leaned forward and smacked Hartington's knee—"I give you my word there's not a man in this ship or any other damned ship who does more work than Ordith."

"I believe it. And he has brains."

"Brains!" Aggett exclaimed. "I should jus' say he has. One o' the smartest men alive. And no slop or sentiment. On and on like a well-lubricated engine. And an eye to the main chance—why, I'll tell you." He hitched up his chair closer to Hartington's, and continued with slow emphasis: "Ordith's a man worth watchin'. Head an' shoulders above the Service truck. All the powers have an eye on him. Ordith and Co.? Why, you mark my words, Ordith's goin' to control more 'n that some day. . . . Good fellow, too. Think so?''

"I like him," Hartington answered, "though I don't know him well. None of us knows him well, so far as I can see. He keeps to himself.''

"He keeps to himself where the blamed fools are concerned. An' he looks round slow, an' takes his pick o' the best.''

Hartington laughed. "So it's a particular compliment to be asked to supper?''

"Well," said Aggett slowly, "I wasn't thinkin' o' that. But I dare say you're right. He's not a friend to be sniffed at.''

Ah Foo, light-footed and blue-clad, came in with cocktails.

"Rum crowd of snotties in your Gunroom," Aggett said, when he had sipped his drink and thrown a slice of lemon-peel into the wastepaper basket. "They want shakin', I think.''

"Why? What have they done wrong?''

"Oh, nothing in particular; but they seem to take life too easy to my way of thinkin'. Got a nice, thick stick? A taste o' that would do 'em good.''

"Well, you look after them in the Engine-room," Hartington said, "and I'll see about the Gunroom; then we shan't quarrel.''

Aggett emptied his glass and rose. "Don't think I'm tryin' to poke my finger into your pie. You can mollycoddle the young gents to your heart's content, for all I care. But you'll find it doesn't pay in the long run. You mark my words.''

And he went out of the cabin, leaving Hartington to wonder what lay behind this visit and this invitation. He had noticed that Aggett was much in Ordith's company, and had marvelled that one so uncouth should be so well received in that quarter. What was now afoot? What reason had Ordith to cultivate the acquaintance of the Sub of the Gunroom? And why had Aggett been sent—for it was plain that he had been sent—to sing Ordith's abilities and importance.

When he left Hartington, Aggett went immediately to Ordith's cabin. He found Nick in white trousers and a singlet, mopping his forehead so that sweat should not run down on to the drawings over which he was bending. At Aggett's entry Nick looked up, a pair of dividers held between his fingers.

"Well?" he said.

"O.K. He'll come."

"Get a drink?"

"One cocktail."

"Seem well disposed?"

"Fair to moderate. Likes you; doesn't like me. Thinks I'm a coarse brute."

Nick smiled. "Well, you're not a fairy, Aggett. He's a delicately nurtured young man, you must remember. Old county family, and God knows what!"

"I know about that," Aggett answered. "I don't go much by the fruit that grows on the family tree."

"That's where you are at fault."

"Fault be damned. Then is that what you are at—makin' the most of the Hartington family connection?"

Nick laid down his dividers and turned to face Aggett. "No," he said. "That particular connection doesn't happen to be of any use to me."

"Well, what is it then? Look here, Ordith, I'm in with you in all your pretty little schemes—or am I wrong? No? Very good, then. I give you expert engineering advice—and you won't find a better combination of theory and practice than there is in me. I help you all I can. Probably I get nothing out of it. I'm prepared to risk that. I'll chance your caring to remember me when you are Ordith and Co. But I want to know right now what you are up to. Why are you bringing in this Sub? What the hell use is he to be? Tell me straight."

"I will tell you straight, although, so far as you are concerned, it's a side issue. Haven't you observed that Hartington's popular with the snotties? Haven't you seen young Lynwood go into Hartington's cabin evening after evening?"

"I dare say. Well?"

"Lynwood's friend is Fane-Herbert. I foresee that when old Fane-Herbert and his wife and daughter come out East we shall see much of Lynwood, Hartington, and, of course, the son himself. Now Hartington may not appeal too strongly to old Fane-Herbert, but unless I'm much mistaken the women will take to him. He talks well. He may be persuasive and have influence. And I'd rather have him a friend than—the other thing. That's the long and short of it."

Aggett shot out a glance of suspicion; then covered it with a smile. He felt that even the cautious Ordith was looking uncommonly far ahead. Hartington to Fane-Herbert the snotty; the snotty to the women; the women to Fane-Herbert the father—it was a circuitous approach. He did not know that Ordith was now thinking, not of contracts but of personalities, not of the father but of the daughter. Aggett knew nothing of Margaret. His partnership with Ordith was a business partnership—loose and informal at that.

"I suppose you're right," he said. "Anyhow, I leave it to you."

Nick turned to his drawings when Aggett had gone, but did not immediately begin to work. Aggett—what a dirty little man he was! But full of knowledge and energy which was useful now, which might be even more useful some day. It went against the grain that he should be even remotely connected with Margaret. He didn't know; he should never know. And yet—those searching eyes would see, that alert brain form its conclusions. Probably Aggett would come and make his oily jokes about love and women and masculine weakness. They would be hard to endure. Nick thought for a moment that he would banish Aggett from his confidence, do without him. He was a mean creature; why not break with him? Then Aggett's virtues rose up in his defence. He was a wonderful fellow to pick holes in an idea, to expose the impracticable in a theory—a destructive critic of great ability. And Nick knew how much he stood in need of informed destructive criticism. At night he would discover some improvement in breech mechanism, or a perfected driving-band or a brilliant new system of fire-control. When he rose in the morning he would be blind with enthusiasm, aware only of the excellence of his own idea. But the thing would need to be threshed out. Talk was the only method, so poor a critic was he of himself. And Aggett could talk admirably. He could put his finger instantly on a weak spot. . . . Yes, Aggett was indispensable. Sly jokes and indecencies, those unpleasant teeth, that grating laugh—they must be borne. Margaret or no Margaret, Aggett was necessary.

"Don't be a fool," Nick said aloud. "Don't give way to your prejudices."

He dipped his head into cold water and dried himself vigorously with a rough towel. Then he picked up his dividers, and, commanding concentration as others switch on an electric light, began to work quickly.

II

After supper, in a corner of the Wardroom Casemate, Nick and Hartington sat drinking whisky-and-soda. In front of them was a vacant chair, from which Aggett, ten minutes earlier, had been summoned to the Engineer's Office. Now he returned.

"Just had a star-turn in Number Four stokehold," he remarked. "Stoker off his chump."

"Mad?" Nick said.

"Fightin' mad. Up with his shovel and started layin' about him. But they brought him down all right—no damage, except to him. He's unconscious. They've got him in the Sick Bay, but they can't bring him round. All over with him, I'm told. Only a question of hours now."

"That means a funeral," said Nick gloomily. "Burials at sea are depressing affairs."

"Don't wonder he went mad. The heat's fierce, an' four hours in every twelve isn't a kid's job. Hope it don't take the others the same way. We're short enough o' stokers as it is, without 'em dyin' off."

"You can hardly blame them for dying, Aggett," the Commander put in from his distant seat.

"You stand rebuked," Nick said.

Aggett drained his glass. "The commander hasn't got to run the boiler-rooms," he observed. "It would be different, wouldn't it, sir, if the Chief Boatswain's-mate kicked the bucket?"

"Nothing to jest about."

"No, indeed."

"No, indeed," the Commander repeated, and, picking up an illustrated paper, rattled his shirtcuffs as he turned its pages angrily.

A man appeared at the Casemate door.

"Mr. Hartington 'ere, sir?"

"Yes."

"Captain wishes to speak to you, sir, in the after-cabin."

Hartington rose. "Sorry, Ordith."

"All right, my dear fellow."

The Commander threw aside his paper. "Hold on a minute Hartington. . . . You say this stoker is going to die, Aggett?"

"Probable."

"What's his name?"

"Hammond, Zachariah Peter, Stoker First Class."

"Right. I'll just go in and tell the Captain, Hartington, before you begin your pow-wow. I shan't be a second. Come along with me."

They went aft together, and, while Hartington waited, the Commander passed into the Captain's quarters, and presently reappeared.

"All right, Hartington. He's waiting for you."

Hartington entered. The Captain, a tall, grave man, who, but for his beard and moustache, might well have been taken for a judge, was leaning back in an armchair, his feet thrown up on to the fender that surrounded the empty fireplace.

"Ah, come in, Hartington, and sit down. You will find cigarettes on the small table."

Hartington offered him the silver box.

"Will you have one, sir?"

"Thanks, no; I never smoke. You light up, though. I want a few words with you."

An uncomfortable silence followed while Hartington lighted his cigarette, took an ashtray from the mantelpiece, and sat down.

"Now," the Captain said, "I want to talk to you about the Gunroom. I don't know what your own views may be upon the treatment of midshipmen. I hope you have views. I hope you have thought the matter out. The Sub of a Gunroom, you know, holds a position of responsibility."

"Yes, sir."

"Well, what is your policy?"

"Put shortly, sir, my idea is to make the Gunroom tolerable."

"You think it likely to be intolerable?"

Hartington paused before he answered. He had no knowledge of the Captain's own views on this matter. Was he of opinion that midshipmen should be shaken? Was this interview to be an intimation that the *Pathshire*'s midshipmen were not being shaken enough? It would be dangerous to cross him. The Old School was strong, wonderfully tenacious, intolerant of heresy. It would be easy not to commit himself until the Captain's attitude was made plain.

Then he saw the Captain's eyes watching him, but their expression conveyed nothing save enquiry and interest. He decided to take the risk. Many and many a time he had wanted to test his views by laying them before a man with long experience of the Service. He said:

"A Gunroom can easily be an intolerable place, sir."

"Still? I suppose the Service doesn't change very fast."

"There was a case before a Count of Enquiry only a few months ago, sir. I have heard that was pretty bad. The junior snotties in that ship were in the same Term as ours, so I have heard a good deal of it indirectly."

"But perhaps that was an isolated case."

"I don't think so, sir. The Home and Atlantic Fleets——"

"Stop a minute." The Captain took his feet from the fender, and raised himself in his chair. "That's what I want to get at. I want to be quite frank, and I expect frankness from you. I know—of course I know—that this chasing of midshipmen goes on. But it is very difficult for one in my position—a Captain of a ship is more isolated than, perhaps, many of you imagine—it's difficult to find out the exact extent of the evil. How much of it is genuine? How much exaggeration? And, more difficult still, what is the cause of it? Young officers nowadays are different from the old—differently educated. Osborne and Dartmouth aren't the mill that the old *Britannia* was. They come to sea less prepared for—for whatever harsh treatment they may receive. You mentioned the Home and Atlantic Fleets. I'm afraid I interrupted you, but I think you were going to limit the system—to a certain extent, at least—to those fleets. Isn't that so? Well—now, what's the cause of it all? What is there behind it? Is it the drive at home, or is it something—something more fundamental, something in the very veins and arteries of the Service."

"You are better able to judge of that than I am, sir."

The Captain leaned back. "I want your opinion."

"I think it goes on for three reasons, sir. First, it's the Service tradition. There are hundreds of officers who believe—honestly believe—that it is necessary to chase snotties in order to bring them to a right frame of mind, in order to produce efficiency. Second—the reason you suggested, sir—the pressure of work, the feeling one has of living from day to day until—until something happens to break the tension—that makes us not quite ourselves. We never trouble about the effect on the snotty. A long view is impossible—there isn't time. And so we do without thinking what we should never do if we thought."

"And the third cause?"

"It's rather complicated, sir."

"Never mind."

"And I'm afraid you may think it fantastic—not quite a practical view to take."

"Let me have it, all the same. You seem to have thought out this matter, Hartington?"

"Yes, sir; I have. It struck me as important—even of first-rate importance. And the present state of affairs is so bad that there's bound to be an end to it soon, one way or another. It's better that the change should come from inside the Service than from outside."

"You think it's as bad as that? But no one outside knows anything about it."

"They will, sir. It is so bad that one day someone will wake up to it. The Press may get hold of it."

"We don't want the Press in the Service."

"No, sir. That's why I think this business ought to be stopped from inside."

"There are regulations on flogging. . . . However, what is your third cause? I think that is the right way to tackle the problem—see the causes, then root them out."

"The third cause, so far as I can see, sir, is that the Service is so isolated and so specialized. Put briefly, it's a government without opposition, with the usual result of tyranny. And in the Service we have no contact with any interests but our own—no books or pictures, no women, if you see what I mean, sir."

"No women?"

"Only the physical."

"Ah! you mean we lack the refining influence!" The Captain smiled.

"I shouldn't have put it that way, sir. I mean that if men are left too long with men they are liable to become beasts." An illustration of his point flashed across Hartington's mind. "You know what it is, sir, after dinner in England, when the ladies are gone. It begins in talk almost at once. And, left together long enough, men become cruel."

"That's true." The Captain ran his tongue across his lips. "But you spoke of books and pictures."

"And plays and music, sir, and walks in the country, and games, and riding—but chiefly books and pictures, plays and music. They are the best products of civilization."

"And we live among the worst—guns, torpedoes? Is that the idea? But you can have books and pictures in the Service?"

"You can have a few of your own, sir; but that's not the

same thing as meeting them at every turn, in every house. We are outside the atmosphere of——'' Hartington broke off suddenly. This was a senior naval officer to whom he was speaking. Almost he had forgotten that.

"Go on," the Captain said. "The atmosphere of——?"

"Outside the atmosphere of beauty," Hartington said reluctantly. One does not wisely speak of the atmosphere of beauty to post-captains.

But the Captain did not smile until he said: "You put it strangely, but I think I understand you. We are brutalized, in fact?"

"No, sir, I don't think so. If we were brutalized we should be brutes ashore and brutes consistently on board. We are neither one nor the other. It's this—that one branch of us is starved, stunted, so that it can't grow, and consequently the other branch develops abnormally."

"And I can see no cure for that. We have our job to do. There is very little time for anything else. Of course," the Captain added, his words coming slowly, "when you come to think of it, our job itself is ethically indefensible."

They pondered that overwhelming statement in silence, each momently unconscious of the other's presence. When at last Hartington met the Captain's eyes he saw in them a strange expression, half guilty, half amused.

"I'm afraid that's true. We have probably struck bedrock," the Captain said, with a smile. Then, suddenly serious, he added: "That goes no further, Hartington."

"No, sir."

The Captain laughed—nervously, Hartington thought. "And since we can't abolish the Service, Hartington, or the forces behind that make it necessary, let us return to practical politics. Taking your causes in reverse order: We can but nibble at the third. You recommend that the Gunroom should be made tolerable. That's something. A decent place to live in, so far as its size permits—some of the amenities of life preserved—not utterly a bear-garden. Further, I propose to help, if I can, by having the snotties to dine in here, and talking books, or games, or travel, or the theory of cruiser screens—anything, in short, but everyday shop and everyday women, the Gunroom topics. A clean napkin, a smooth shirt-front, and bright glass and silver have an extraordinarily civilizing effect. Besides, to a snotty's mind, these quarters of mine seem spacious, and room to move is room to think. And your job consists in

making your own personality felt; stop them talking and
thinking filth eternally. But you are up against it, Hartington;
the China Station, the naval officer's Mecca, because on the
surface it seems slack and pleasant, is a test—but more of that
later on. Your second cause—the pressure of work, the sense
of war, and a break-up of all our lives being so close that the
'long view' is unattainable. Eat, drink, and be merry, for
to-morrow we die; be cruel, brutal, at any rate, unheeding,
for to-morrow—God knows what may happen! That's the
attitude. Frankly, I don't know how to change it. Religion,
any kind of religion, any quick sense of worlds outside our
own and of time beyond our time, might change it. But that's
hopeless in a Gunroom. There can be no God where there's no
privacy. Do you realize that there is no place in this ship
where midshipmen can pray? By their chests, in a public
passage, with marines in hammocks blaspheming above their
heads? Or they could pray on their backs in their own hammocks if they remembered. But they are tired and sleepy, and
they forget—so the fact stands. I dare say they could do
without formal prayers. But no one can do without occasional
seclusion. They are for ever rubbing shoulders with their own
sordidness, until at last they come to think they are all sordid,
and care to be nothing else. That's the root of the snotty's
tragedy, Hartington. I'm sure of it. He's never alone—never,
from the moment he comes on board to the moment he gets
ashore. His mind hasn't a chance to expand—to stray out into
the vague purposelessness from which, if you can trace them
back far enough, all right purposes spring.''

"I've given two of them—Lynwood and Fane-Herbert—
leave to use my cabin whenever I'm not there. There isn't
room for more, sir.''

"No, there isn't room for more,'' the Captain said. "I dare
say some of the Wardroom would do likewise if I dropped a
hint, but, though it is some gain, there's no real seclusion in
another man's cabin. That problem's insoluble, Hartington,
while ships are built as they are, and so they must be built if
they are to be efficient fighting units. It brings us back again
to the essential immorality of our calling, and—and to the
forces behind that make our calling inevitable. Doesn't it?''

He broke off, smiling.

"There's the solution of leave, sir,'' Hartington said boldly.

"I know,'' the Captain answered. "I've thought of that.
And I agree: the snotties must have all the leave we can

manage to give them. But there are two difficulties. First, officers often stop snotties' leave—it's the recognized Service punishment, and the alternative is flogging. Second—— You've never been on the China Station before, Hartington?"

"No, sir."

"I have; and I'm not sure that short leave is much better than no leave at all. I can give them four or five days now and then, but you know what happens—Hong-Kong, Shanghai, they are Hell. Japan's better; but even there unless by chance they go into the country, there's Yokohama and Number Nine, or Tokio and the Yoshiwara. The East's a bad atmosphere through which to see life for the first time. Let loose from the ship's confinement into a strange land with an unknown language—not even a comprehensible theatre—what is there but bars and women? What's needed is long leave among their own people, their own women—sisters, mothers. In the Home Fleet where distance makes that possible the drive of work makes it impossible. What do they get—an average of fourteen days a year, or a bit more if they are lucky. And out here, England, Home, and Beauty are thousands of miles away."

The Captain stood up. "But, as for your first cause," he said, "as for the Service tradition and the chasing of midshipmen to produce efficiency, I can do something about that in my own ship. Fortunately all our snotties are of the same seniority, so that there can be no seniors trampling on juniors 'to get a bit of their own back.' And so far as you yourself are concerned—well, I know your somewhat unusual views. But other Subs may join us later on, or even the Wardroom may demand that the snotties be shaken. And I want you to understand that, no matter what may come—even if you get orders from the Commander himself, you are to stand out against anything that follows the principle of 'the young gentlemen must be broken.' The fact that these things were done in Nelson's day doesn't weigh with me. I will have none of it in my ship. Is that understood?"

"Quite, sir."

"I shall hold you personally responsible."

"Yes, sir."

"And, apart from any order of mine considered as an order, I want your promise. You know as well as I do that the order is one I can't enforce from day to day. The Service etiquette keeps the Captain well aft. I can't see what goes on."

"I'm as strongly against the system as you are, sir."

"That settles the matter, then, for one ship among hundreds. Good-night."

"Good-night, sir."

Hartington walked towards the door. Because a question in his mind remained unanswered he hesitated visibly.

"What is it?" the Captain asked. "Another 'cause' to baffle us?"

"There was a question, sir."

"Yes?"

"You spoke—twice—of the forces behind the Service. I was wondering, sir——"

The Captain shook his head. "No, Hartington; we haven't time to try to unravel that mesh. Besides, it savours of politics, which are not for naval officers. I have said enough already this evening—perhaps too much unless you are discreet. Good-night, again."

"Good-night, sir."

Chapter XIII
Looking Beyond

I

Those streets at Singapore where the harlots of East and West sit at their doors and in their verandahs, stretching out their whitened arms towards the passers-by, were investigated and discussed by the Gunroom. They are investigated and discussed by most Europeans who pass through Singapore, and they remain and will remain. Cunwell thought them funny; Dyce was curious, and desired information; Sentley, who had entered them inadvertently, left them in haste, fearful and embarrassed. John and Hugh, who drove through them together in rickshaws, were glad when they were clear of them.

"My God!" John said, "isn't it amazing how beastliness spreads?"

"The women?" Hugh asked.

"No; at the moment I was thinking of Krame. But the women, too, if you like."

"Oh, be damned to Krame! We are free of him."

"Yes, we are, but others are not."

"I'd forgotten them."

"One does forget."

Hugh looked at him. "Cheer up, John," he said, "the sight of the women has made you miserable. It's no good being miserable about them. There's nothing to be done."

"I'm not miserable about them only. I'm angry because they are helpless, and we are helpless. I'm angry for all helpless things. They would probably tell you that they would never have come to this if they had had plenty of money. Sweated labour would tell you that what it wants is higher wages. And—though my reason tells me it's all a lie—I myself think that if only I had more money I could do the

135

work I want to do and be happy. We all look to money for help—that's why we are helpless."

"Then it's our own fault."

"Oh, it starts higher than that. It's older than we are. The Golden Calf is the established creed. Put it wider than just money; call it gain—any material gain: temporal power, private land, national territory, influence; and those nights we had in the *King Arthur*, and what other snotties are going through now, and the streets with their harlots—they are just fragments of the result. . . . I'm looking forward to seeing your sister again. She is the only person I have met who, in her heart of hearts, seems not to care for wealth."

"But she has always had everything she wants," Hugh said.

II

Later in April they made Hong-Kong, where they joined the squadron. Being in time for the Japanese summer cruise, they sailed a fortnight later for Yokohama, whither the squadron had preceded them. Throughout the voyage the *Pathshire* was active in preparation for the time when she would be called upon to compete with other ships in Fleet Evolutions; and General Quarters, Fire and Collision Stations, and other exercises were continually practised.

The whole of May was spent out of China. In Tokio a party from the fleet was officially received and entertained. Each British officer was assigned to a Japanese officer of corresponding rank who remained close to him always, providing him with food, drink, and information. The arrangements were perfect, and mathematically precise. The motor-cars were filled but not crowded. Much was shown, but not too much. The programme, of which every officer was given a copy typed in English, was accurately followed. Not a moment was lost. Dinner was taken between the acts at the Imperial Theatre.

Though, after the official reception, John went often to Tokio, and found that the Japanese citizen was peaceful enough, he could never shake off his first impression of a nation essentially military, encouraged by its recent victories over Russia, ready for further wars should they come. Far inland such an impression might have been contradicted; but in Tokio, the centre of official life, it was continually reinforced. It was remarkable and terrible that the Japanese military mind was not even choked, as were the minds of Western nations, by official pomposity. It seemed faultless. Salaries were small, offices unpretentious. The nation was as an athlete stripped.

"Just as well these fellows are our allies" said Aggett in the Wardroom.

Nick Ordith had much leave in Japan; indeed, from the day of the ship's arrival to the day of her departure his messmates saw little of him, save when he came on board for a few hours to deposit one bag of papers and to carry off another. Sometimes Aggett accompanied him; but Aggett, not being supernumerary, and having ship's duties, could not take all the leave he desired. Nick called at many important offices, and in all of them was amicably received. It was to be understood, of course, that he represented no one; but, nevertheless, the Japanese were aware of the existence of Ibble's and of Ordith's. In those days, Mr. Fane-Herbert being as yet far away, perhaps Nick allowed Ordith's to eclipse Ibble's, telling himself that, the understanding between the two firms being so cordial and complete, he could do so with an easy conscience. Further, he had prospects, sprung from his own inventive mind, which were but indirectly connected with either firm. He wanted experiments made, but these must be unofficial. He had ideas to sell, but, realizing the prior claims of his own nation's firms, he could not part with them unreservedly. All his negotiations, which involved so many conflicting interests, were complicated and slow, but before the *Pathshire* put to sea he felt that he had made preliminary progress, some of which he would report to Mr. Fane-Herbert.

III

Sailing by way of Nagasaki, the squadron reached Wei-hai-wei on the first morning of June. The Fane-Herberts, who had travelled overland, were already established there, having taken a small house and equipped it with Chinese servants. Mr. Fane-Herbert had urged his wife not to settle down in a place so deserted. In the absence of the squadron, he told her, there would be little company but that of the somewhat distant regiment. But she had made up her mind, and was not to be dissuaded. The squadron would be at Wei-hai during a part of the summer at least, and, if rumour spoke truly, the *Pathshire* was to winter there alone. Both she and Margaret wanted to

be near Hugh, and taking into consideration the probabilities
of the squadron's ever uncertain movements, they seemed
likely to see more of him at Wei-hai than elsewhere. . . . But
he couldn't do his business at Wei-hai, Mr. Fane-Herbert
remonstrated; the boy was quite capable of looking after
himself.

"You are quite free," Mrs. Fane-Herbert had said, "to
move about independently of us. If the *Pathshire* leaves
Wei-hai for long we will come anywhere you like, and return
when the *Pathshire* returns. We shall have enough time in her
absence to see Japan, and Hong-Kong, and Shanghai, or any
other places you feel we ought to see. At present I want to see
my son. Wild horses shall not move me."

She had had enough of travelling. She liked to be settled in
a home, and did not intend to trail about the seas at her
husband's heels.

Nick invited himself to dine, and John and Hugh, who
would not ask for late leave that night, went ashore in the
afternoon.

"Mr. Alter is always talking of you," Margaret told him
when, after tea, he had her alone. "He wants more of your
work, and he has given me this letter for you."

"I have done no more work," he confessed.

"None?"

"None."

"Didn't you get my letter. I addressed it to Colombo."

"Yes, I got that. I took it up to Kandi with me to read. I
made wonderful resolutions that night."

"And haven't kept them?"

"No."

"John, you are hopeless."

He defended himself as best he could. "I can't help it," he
said; "I have tried to write and I have tried to read. I have
read spasmodically. But it seems useless. I started this naval
business too early. My education has been a naval education,
and—what is more important—my life is a naval life. If you
can't be alone you can't think; if you can't think you are a
fool to try to write. Besides, to write you must read and read
and read. You must see life from a thousand angles—not
from one professional standpoint. And you must feel that, for
better or for worse, you are master of yourself—not necessarily of your actions, but of your thinking."

"But you have written in these very circumstances. Why can't you write more?"

"For the same reason that a man who chances upon an occasional phrase can't write an epic. Literature isn't luck; it's the result of substantial effort."

"Others have written who had other things to do than write."

He wondered if, after all, he was overrating difficulties in order to shield a lack of courage. "Yes," he said, "but out of their office, or shop, or factory, their life was their own. They went home—to some kind of home. At any rate, it was theirs. A snotty's life is never his own. He lives in his office the whole twenty-four hours. He never 'goes home.' "

"Then what are you going to do?"

"Nothing."

"So you give up?" she asked.

"Yes. What can I do?"

"And you are not nineteen yet. What's your life going to be?"

"I may get to like it. Perhaps in the senior ranks it will be better."

"It won't."

"I know. Of course it won't."

She was tempted to be angry because he had so early abandoned hope, because he was not putting up a fight; but she saw that he was opposed to forces so much stronger than any he could command that by no courage could he unaided stand against them. Then she remembered a source whence help might come.

"John," she said, "I want you to fight this out."

"Fight?"

"Because I believe it's worth the fighting. You feel hopeless now, partly, I dare say, because your other work prevents your writing, but chiefly—isn't that true?—chiefly because you don't feel sure that you could ever write. . . . You can write, you know."

"What guarantee have you of that?" he asked, in a tone that was unusually hard, because he did not feel hard. Her presence, her voice, her repose above all, affected his uneasy mind profoundly. It was amazing that anyone should care two damns whether he wasted his life or not.

"I think I had better tell you," she said. "I didn't intend to. There's a sort of convention that you mustn't tell people good of themselves, but I shall tell you this now. I have Mr. Alter's guarantee.''

"Because he said he liked my work? It's so easy to say that.''

"No—more than that. He said you were an example of godless waste.''

"Good heavens!'' John exclaimed with a laugh.

"And he said,'' she went on, "that he believed you could, if you would, be a great man. I asked him at once what reasons he had for saying that. He gave me certain points in your work: I shan't repeat them or you will strain after them and exaggerate them. But he thought them decisive. He showed your work to other men whose opinions confirmed his own. . . . What now?''

"It's wonderfully good to hear,'' John said unsteadily. "Margaret, tell me the special points he hit on. I don't see how it is possible to be sure at this stage.''

"I'll tell you one point—too general for you to exaggerate and spoil. He said that you wrote naturally, established a curious intimacy with your audience, and that yet what you said was momentous—the rarest of combinations. And he repeated what you heard him say that night at dinner—that your images were chosen with the eyes tight shut or wide open—the full vision, inward or outward. He gave instances.''

"What instances?''

"Those I can't tell you. If I did you would be bound to imitate them.''

He thought over this in silence. "Margaret,'' he said, "may not this be mere talk? You know how great men love an occasional enthusiasm. Mr. Alter is in no way bound by what he says.''

"He acts on it, at any rate. He went to see your mother about it.''

"She wrote that he had called.''

"He has called often,'' Margaret said. She smiled as she remembered his words, spoken after one of those expeditions to the country. "Mrs. Lynwood is delightful,'' he had said. "She understands everything except her son. She wishes he would settle down to the Navy—a fixed income and an open-air life. She smiles at his poetry, and says, 'Yes, I dare say it is good, Wing, and I'm glad he does it so well; but there's no money in it. And we are dreadfully poor, you know.' ''

Margaret told John nothing of this. If Mrs. Lynwood did not see fit to mention to her son that she had known Wingfield Alter long enough and intimately enough to call him "Wing," she had probably good reasons for concealing the fact.

"I must think over all this," John said. "I want to tell Hartington about it. Hartington is the Sub."

"The Sub?" she said in surprise. "Does the Sub listen kindly to poetry?"

"Yes, thank Heaven. You must meet him soon. . . . And I'll try to write to-night, Margaret."

"No; don't *try.*"

"But I want to write now. I am so suddenly happy. I have been longing and longing to see you. And when you come you bring this wonderful news."

Near at hand the gulls were crying, and sampan men crooning to themselves as they rocked their bodies over their stern oars.

"Come and tell me about England," he said; "the Thames, the bridges, the lights, the trains; and pictures and music, and books and plays, and carpets and rugs; and little narrow country lanes, and hills, and being free, and——"

"But I can't tell you everything at once!"

"Oh, splendid!" he exclaimed. "I guessed you would say that. I have guessed it every night for weeks and weeks. 'But I can't tell you everything at once!' Now it's coming true. You see," he explained, "I have been looking forward to this."

A tremor of joy passed through her because she had made him happy. She began to talk eagerly, so that, for a time at least, he might forget the ship, and might not remember, what she understood now, that "for weeks and weeks" there had been nothing but this meeting to which he might look forward.

From the bridge of the *Pathshire* Nick Ordith was surveying the shore through a telescope.

"Dull spot, Yeoman," he said.

The Yeoman of Signals rubbed his hands. "Precious cold in the winter, sir."

IV

John returned to the ship in a spirit of exultation, intoxicated, not so much by the heady wine of praise as by the discovery that he was not altogether alone in his difficult world. Margaret cared what became of him; apparently Mr. Alter also cared. But it was Margaret's interest and her personality that filled his thoughts to the exclusion of the colder critic. He sought out Hartington, and laid the matter before him, reading aloud Mr. Alter's letter, and repeating the passages in it which seemed to him unusually important.

"DEAR LYNWOOD,

"*I am sending this letter by Margaret lest it follow you from sea to sea. If she does not meet you at once, she can at least discover your whereabouts.*

"*I have shown your work to several friends—all creative artists, not critics only. Their opinions support my own. Probably in your present situation you have no one to whom you can go for counsel, so I have taken upon myself the duties of adviser. You must read. I don't care about the quantity, but your reading must be regular and sound. The modern men are excellent when you have found your own feet, but before you are twenty you are prone to imitation of their extremes—probably the worst of them. So go back to men whom you will not be tempted to imitate. Read the* Actes and Monuments, *Swift, Addison, Walton, Goldsmith. Burton's* Anatomy of Melancholy *has been an inexhaustible quarry for later essayists. If you must have the living, try Mrs. Meynell for her prose. Go to De Quincey for speed and amazement, Poe for short stories, Fielding for action—Fielding, in fact, for most things. In poetry, take Shakespeare—enough, believe me, for your present needs.*

"*As for a method of writing—whatever I tell you, a thousand others will tell you I am wrong. Fast or slow? Rough-hewn or polished? That you must find out for yourself. I believe* le mot juste *is well worth long seeking in chilly, critical moments. But if you feel excited about what you are writing it's best to use a slack rein. Never be afraid of the whip—it's very good to write a 'portion' every day, if you have the courage to destroy it when necessary in the evening. The wastepaper-basket is a good, silent friend whom it is folly to despise.*

"*Write to me whenever you care to, and send me the little that the wastepaper-basket does not swallow up. I have been seeing much of your mother lately, talking of old times and of you.*

"*Yours,*
"WINGFIELD ALTER.

"P.S.—If you can find a place to do it in, read your work aloud to yourself—especially verse. I should have told you to read the Bible and Thomas Hardy and Murray's translations of the Greek. Robert Bridges will teach you much of metre. Try Clutton Brock for scholarly prose. Margaret is taking out a supply of my books for you. Talk to her when you can, but don't believe all she tells you about literature—and don't accept what I tell you as anything but a foundation upon which to build up your own tastes. I think you might read Conrad, too, if you will promise to stop when Marlow begins to dominate you completely.—W.A."

Hartington who thought that by this time he had a fairly accurate understanding of the working of John's mind, was at first astonished by the extraordinary elation of which this letter was the only apparent cause. It was natural that John should be pleased by the approval and interest of a man of Alter's standing, but his changed mood, the laughter, the quickened speech, the heightened colour, called for an explanation more personal. John spoke of Margaret as "Fane-Herbert's sister" when he spoke of her at all.

"So Alter advises you to talk to Miss Fane-Herbert when you can?" Hartington said. "What's the exact meaning of that?"

"She knows a good deal of books," said John easily.

"But he doesn't suggest that you should be tutored by her?"

"Oh, no."

"Then it's her talk that's to do you good?"

"Yes."

"Because it is *her* talk—not for the sake of her knowledge?"

"I suppose so."

Hartington smiled. Between them as they sat in the small cabin hung a large red-paper lantern, lighted by an electric lead. Hartington touched it with his foot, and set the light and shadows chasing each other round the Fiesole paintings and Dürer's *Hare*.

"Do you think I might ask you an extremely rude question?" he said. "It's important. I think it's relevant."

"I know what you are going to ask," John answered. "About Fane-Herbert's sister? I suppose you think I am a fool to be in love with her."

"It makes the whole business more complicated. It means

that half the time when you think you are wanting one thing
you are really wanting another. Now any consideration of the
future will be hopelessly entangled with consideration of
her.''

John explained that, in truth, Margaret simplified the issue,
because, as he said, her own ideas were so very like his own.
He elaborated this theory until he could elaborate it no more.
Then he stopped suddenly.

''It's so exciting,'' he said, after a pause. ''Everything is
so exciting.''

The excitement of it took his breath away. He steadied the
red lamp, and watched its light glow through the tips of his
fingers. Obviously he had forgotten that his life did not
consist entirely in Margaret and literature. Of what use was it
to remind him now that he was a midshipman, very young
and altogether unknown, who earned one shilling and ninepence
a day? of what use to speak of Ibble's and Ibble's wealth?
Hartington decided not to trouble him that night, to leave
unshattered so long as they would endure his vain, happy
dreams.

''Do you think,'' John said, ''that Mr. Alter would put in a
word with a publisher about a novel?''

''Probably. Have you written one? Have you a great work
stored away secretly underneath your private till?''

''No,'' said John seriously; ''but I could write one. A
hundred thousand words. Suppose I did a thousand a day—or
even five hundred—a couple of quarto pages. . . . There
might be money in that.''

He turned into his hammock that night to lie long awake,
dreaming of title pages, bindings, and press-cuttings, and
calculating royalties. He was generous to himself in the matter of royalties, for so much money would be needed before—
perhaps a play would be better, after all. . . . Very carefully,
mindful of Hartington's warning, he excluded Margaret from
his consideration of these practical matters. But when at last
he fell asleep and could no longer deceive himself, he dreamed
of Margaret only. He dreamed that she kissed him, not that he
kissed her; of a hundred tendernesses of word and deed that
were outside his experience. They had a house in Westminster. . . . She looked down from behind the grille on to the
floor of the House of Commons.

V

Margaret sat very still on the edge of her bed. The last word she had heard her father speak that evening came back to her like a tawdry tune.

"The most steel-like mind I know."

That was Mr. Ordith's. Steel-like: strong, supple, elastic, highly finished. He had, too, some of the splendour, even the poetry, of machinery: accurate, clean, with no uncertain edges, without misgiving. And he had power.

He was a man to whom one might go confidently in any worldly difficulty. He would know what ought to be done, and would do it at once. He would see quite clearly one side of every question. In a way, she supposed, it was a compliment that one who had so wide a field of choice should have chosen her.

Then she remembered how he had watched her. She saw again, as if they were watching her now, those large dark eyes, with their lower lids slightly raised and puckered. It gave one a sense of being a specimen, of being exposed. She shivered, stood up, walked to the window and closed it. The night was hot, so she opened the window again.

"Anyhow," she said, "*he* doesn't want help from anyone." She blew out the candle and got into bed. There were so many people who wanted help—John among them; so many, that one might as well give up trying to help them. With Ordith it would be an easy passage in a comfortable ship that he would steer.

The bedclothes were tucked into place with a little jerk. She pushed back a wisp of hair from her face as if she were angry with it. Then she shut her eyes—tight. No need to think. No need to worry yet. Sleep.

But she opened her eyes again, and stared at the little white mountain of her pillow.

Chapter XIV
Waste and Wonder

There is something in physical drill before breakfast that dissolves the fabric of dreams. This John had discovered long ago, turning out of a hammock in whose warm comfort all things had been possible, and becoming, in the twinkling of an eye, a bare-footed, sleepy midshipman, in dirty flannels; and this he realized afresh on that June morning when his meeting Margaret, his letter from Mr. Alter, and his lamp-lit talk with Hartington had become affairs of yesterday. He went into the Gunroom, drank cocoa, smoked as much of a cigarette as time allowed him, and went with the others on to the Upper Deck. Here all was hosepipes and holystone—gritty to the foot. Ordith, in new sea-boots, was walking up and down the quarter-deck sniffing the morning air. When the midshipmen began their drill, he watched them for a moment, and then turned away.

"Stoop-fallin'—place!" commanded the Instructor. "Feet placin' forwards and backwards. One—two! One—two! One—two!" The midshipmen, on all fours, moved their legs in and out lazily, reflecting that their anatomy was remarkably unlike that of a frog. In any case—and this, perhaps, was one of the more subtle reasons which inspired the authorities to order physical drill—it was impossible while so engaged to imagine one's self addressing the House of Commons, or falling in love, or writing a book, or, indeed, doing anything but sprawl on the deck to the accompaniment of the Instructor's unceasing "One—two! One—two!" At Osborne and Dartmouth, of course, where physical drill had been properly done, it had not been unattractive; moreover, they were healthier in those days. But now drink, tobacco, and lack of exercise had made drill an uncomfortable process. It was useless, too, for they "sloped" through it, and none cared so long as the young gentlemen obeyed regulations by being on the quarter-deck in flannels for a stated number of minutes every morning. The fact that they "sloped" was the young gentlemen's fault; but not theirs alone.

None cared. The senior officers had other things to do than dry-nurse the young gentlemen. If they eluded the regulations concerning wine bills, whose fault was it? Whose fault if they were so bored and had so lost interest in themselves that in their spare hours they nipped, and smoked "chains," and talked women? At Osborne and Dartmouth they had been educated. At the age of seventeen and a half they had come to sea, and their education had ceased. The senior officers had other things to do than worry about the young gentlemen's education. From time to time the Gunnery-Lieutenant would dictate obscure notes about guns that the midshipmen had never seen; or the Torpedo-Lieutenant would mumble over again lectures on Balance Chamber Mechanism and War Heads, of just such a kind as had been given in the training cruiser. There was no system, no syllabus, no timetable, no programme. Sometimes, to the active irritation of all concerned, there was a lecture; more often there was not. There were the yearly sights to be worked out; but these were accomplished on the communal system, and were usually worked backwards, for reasons that will be clear to seamen. Life was a haphazard business, in which the only regular intellectual process was deterioration. One day John discovered that he had forgotten how to integrate, and that all his mathematics was slipping from him. Mechanics, too, was a thing of the past; even the elementary formulæ were forgotten now. Electricity had gone; German had gone utterly; French was going; Chemistry was no more than a vague recollection of apparatus and of the red tie worn by the master who had taught him.

"I've forgotten everything we ever learnt at Dartmouth," he confessed.

"So have we all," Dyce answered.

Borne in the flagship was one Naval Instructor, who was responsible for all the midshipmen in the squadron. Perhaps he taught the flagship's midshipmen; but his visits to the other ships were so rare that he was unexpectedly popular. Because it was impossible for him to be in two places at once, it happened that, when the flagship was in one port of the Station and the *Pathshire* in another, the *Pathshire*'s midshipmen were delightfully free from his ministrations. Outwardly they rejoiced at this emancipation, complaining only that threepence a day was deducted from the pay of each one of them in order that, in accordance with regulation, the Naval Instructor might be fittingly rewarded for being at Hong-Kong while his paying pupils were at Nagasaki. This seemed unjust.

"Our pay from a grateful Admiralty is twenty-one pence a day," Dyce remarked, "on which, apart from what our people provide, we live like officers and gentlemen. And out of the twenty-one pence three go every day to the upkeep of this N.I., who comes near us about one morning in three months. Now, why the hell should I pay one-seventh of my total income for an education I never receive?"

"Lord Almighty!" Cunwell exclaimed; "you don't want the damned N.I., do you?"

"No. But threepence nearly buys a glass of port."

"Well, let's put in a moan," Fane-Herbert said.

"Moan!" Dyce laughed. "We shan't get much change."

However, after further discussion, their complaint seemed so justifiable that they laid it before the powers. The powers considered it, and decided that midshipmen in ships other than the flagship should pay the Naval Instructor only when they were in company with the Flag. This change was certainly an improvement; but still, when the squadron was at sea, John paid threepence a day for the education he did not receive from a man who sailed in a ship one-fifth of a mile away.

The apparent charm of the China Station was that there was nothing to do; its disadvantage, discovered by experience, was that the whole day was spent doing nothing. Occasionally there occurred "spasms"—periods of remarkable gunnery activity, when the midshipmen spent hour after hour on watch or at their guns, waiting for the watch to end or for the deliverance of the next meal. One of these "spasms" took place soon after the *Pathshire*'s arrival at Wei-hai-wei. The ship cruised all the week in the neighbourhood of Waterwitch and Four Funnel Bays, and returned to Wei-hai-wei on Friday nights. But even this activity was powerless to check the growth of the conviction which was finding a place in John's mind that all his preparation at Dartmouth was to be wasted, and that, so far as the Service was concerned, his intellectual development had come to an end. And from this conviction proceeded a feeling that his youth and all the energies of youth were purposeless and useless. Day after day went by and he was never called upon to use his brains. There was routine to be followed—so many hours on duty, so many hours standing about, so many hours of waiting. And in the intervals there was the Gunroom, where one slept, or threw dice for sixpences, or listened to lurid tales.

As time went on the aspect of the Gunroom became more strange and more terrible. Usually John was not aware that anything was wrong. Life seemed slack and easy, and he did not complain. But there were moments when he realized suddenly that young men not yet twenty do not naturally sleep through the daylight hours. Dice for sixpences became poor sport; poker began; the stakes rose; a card-book was started in which were recorded debts a midshipman's income could not discharge. The defaulters satisfied their creditors by keeping their watches and running their boats for them.

Conversation became incredibly filthy. Even the elements of wit disappeared from its indecency. The intelligence of the midshipmen was applied to the invention of new blasphemies, the foulness of which was the measure of the audience's applause. There came moments when even that Gunroom was stricken to silence; and, for a day or two, certain expressions had to be paid for by a democratically imposed fine.

"I'm sick of it all," Hugh said. "there's no earthly point in it."

"This isn't a Mess of women," Cunwell protested, though that was not the expression he used.

"I dare say it isn't. But the fact is that our pretty language wouldn't pass muster in a room full of men. We are miles outside any possible limit."

Driss opened sleepy eyes. "There's nothing else to talk about," he observed, "so we talk like this. We are all sick of it—the same as you, Fane-Herbert. But we shan't stop. We can't stop. It's a habit now." And he rang the bell for cigarettes.

Hartington was powerless; the causes of change in the Gunroom were such as his influence could not affect. A hot climate, monotony of labour, and the absence of any kind of intellectual exercise or stimulus brought the midshipmen to such a pass that first they described their own minds as being "like cesspools"—stagnant and foul—and then ceased to care whether their minds were like cesspools or not. From this it was a short step to carelessness about those things for which in other circumstances, they would have been greatly concerned—their hair, their hands, the linen they wore, and the sheets in their hammocks. Their health suffered, and they did not care. In body and mind they became flabby and slack; and still they did not care. Rapidly they were losing their self-respect.

When they were ashore the deterioration seemed to have gone not so far, and yet far enough. There were in those parts no women with whom they could go, but at the Club were armchairs, and a bar where cocktails had nothing to do with their wine bills. When John went to see the Fane-Herberts the change in him was remarkable. He would wash, shave, and dress himself more carefully. For a couple of hours, perhaps, his speech would be clean. But consciousness of the ship's life never left him, and he felt in Margaret's presence always at a disadvantage, as if he had entered a drawing-room in dirty boots. Self-respect is not to be laid aside and instantly reassumed, and John was for ever sensible of a kind of inferiority to which he could not believe others were blind. As a result he became abnormally sensitive, interpreting a momentary silence as purposeful neglect of himself, and imagining deliberate coldness whenever Margaret was less responsive than he desired.

When Ordith, too, was there, John found it impossible to meet him on even ground. Ordith was a Wardroom officer, and aware of the conditions of life in the *Pathshire*'s Gunroom. No doubt he looked upon the midshipmen with contempt, and smiled to think that one of them presumed to be his rival. Little by little John fell into the background. Margaret, wondering at his lack of enterprise, and not understanding its true cause, was led to imagine that he had ceased to care. His conversation with her became colourless, his manner nervous and embarrassed. As the weeks passed they fell further and further apart.

To this estrangement between himself and Margaret John ascribed a false cause. He regarded it as a consequence of his own insignificant position as a midshipman without money. He was not cynical and foolish enough to imagine that Margaret deliberately excluded him from her consideration because he was poor. Rather, it seemed, the practical hopelessness of any love for him prevented its growth as naturally as darkness stifles a flower. How should she learn to love him when every circumstance of her own life and of his association with her was evidence that such love must be vain? The sight of Mr. Fane-Herbert was enough to shatter any dreams. Never was a man a more loyal citizen of the "world as it is." To look at his gold watchchain was to remember your poverty; to hear him speak of success, of the men who "got there," of the "youths who were likely to do something in the world," was to become vividly aware that you had neither succeeded, nor got there, nor were likely to do anything in the world. When Mr. Fane-Herbert's business gave him a short respite, which he spent at Wei-hai-wei, Margaret seemed more than ever unapproachable and Ordith's position more than ever assured.

Confronted for the first time by the problem of a woman's mind, and having no woman to whom he could go for counsel, John was guilty of an error in judgment almost as often as he and Margaret met. To him, in his present mood, every sign seemed a sign of ill-omen. If she went out of the room when he was there he thought she wished to avoid him. If she was not at home when he called he imagined that she had foreseen his coming. To his ears she seemed never to speak of Ordith save with approval.

In the meantime, Ordith made regular, methodical, and carefully recorded progress. Margaret could not understand John. At a time when she had been most eager to help him he had become suddenly uncommunicative, and lately, without any kind of explanation, he had ceased to come to the house more often than mere politeness demanded. Her father regarded him "as one of those snotties," no more and no less. And Ordith never missed an opportunity.

He would come continually to the house. He would talk to Margaret throughout the long summer afternoons, talk about himself, his future, his ambitions—just such talk as, modestly spoken, flatters any woman into interest. He would ask her advice, making her feel that her decision was indeed of importance to him. He had an air of letting her share his secrets, and a power, that amounted almost to genius, of making his secrets not only important but amusing.

At the dance which the Admiral gave in his flagship he took entire charge of her. She could not help noticing that in the flagship the personality of Ordith had made itself felt. And he was in excellent form that night, laughing, dancing

with extraordinary swing and rhythm, awakening in her an
excitement that brightened her eyes and brought a hot flush to
her cheeks. Through many of the long hours in which she
danced John was in charge of the *Pathshire*'s picket-boat,
lying alongside the flagship, waiting until, the guests being
ready to leave, the boats should be called to the gangway. He
had undertaken this duty, which was not properly his own, in
order that he might avoid a direct decision as to whether he
should attend the dance or deliberately absent himself from it.
He had lacked courage either to compete with Ordith, or,
without some excuse of "duty," to leave the field clear for
him.

"Not going to the dance?" Hartington had said.

"No."

"Why on earth not? You are a dancing man, aren't you?"

"I am running the picket-boat," John had answered.

But Hartington had seen deeper than this poor excuse.

"Couldn't you have got someone to run it for you—if you
want to go to the dance?"

"I am taking it for someone else."

"Oh! Not your own job?"

"No."

"You are an uncourageous fellow."

For a moment John had remained silent. Then he had burst
out: "Oh, it's no good. You don't know Ordith. You don't
know old Fane-Herbert. The odds are too big."

Hartington had shrugged his shoulders.

"That's for you to decide."

So John waited in the darkness at the flagship's side.
Above him the quarter-deck was gay with red and white
bunting, and brilliant with electric lights. John wondered if
coachmen and chauffeurs felt as he did. The colour and music
were close to him, but he had no part in them. He saw
shadows move to and fro on the decorative flags, and wondered if that shadow were Margaret's, and what she was
saying and doing at that instant. Certainly, he reflected, he
could not be entering into her thoughts; and yet it seemed
strange, almost incredible, that she, of whom he thought so
insistently, should occupy her mind with other things—an
experiment in a new dance-step, perhaps, or the effect of her
dress, or the excellence of supper. This thought, as it were an
arm that thrust him back into the darkness from which he
desired to issue, quickened his sense of remoteness. He saw

all his hopes and desires objectively, as if he looked down from a barred window on to a world he could not enter. There, on the quarter-deck, within a few yards of him, was Margaret; he could not attain to her, he could not make her hear; she was dancing and laughing, eating and drinking, unconscious of his proximity, forgetful of his existence.

He did not see her until the dance ended with an abruptness peculiar to entertainments on board His Majesty's ships. At once the sea, which through the hours had lapped quietly against the steel plates, was thrashed to foam by the propellors of the waiting steamboats. It happened, as John had scarcely doubted it would happen, that Margaret and her mother went ashore in the *Pathshire*'s picket-boat. John, who stood where the light fell on him, watched Ordith escort them down the gangway. He saw that Margaret's eyes were tired, as if she had undergone some strain, but this appearance he attributed to physical weariness. She said nothing to Ordith but a short "Good-night" scarcely audible. Then, as she stepped on to the deck of John's boat, she looked directly at him where he stood beside the engine-room casing. She looked at and beyond him as if he were not there, and disappeared into the cabin.

He drove the boat angrily, using too much helm, and brought up by the landing-stage, not by slowing and then stopping his engines, but by a sudden stoppage and immediate reversal at full speed. All went well, as if the Devil were directing his judgment. The stem swung in accurately, the engines stopped, and the boat came to rest with the foam boiling around her. The passengers clambered out with the extraordinary nervous clumsiness of landfolk in boats.

For a moment John was tempted to draw attention to himself by saying good-night to Mrs. Fane-Herbert and Margaret. Then he changed his mind, and kept his place by the wheel, where the brass funnel hid him. Margaret had seen him alongside the flagship. She must have recognized him, and she had given no sign of recognition. He would not press the matter further.

He had other boat-trips that night, but he remembered nothing of them afterwards except a vague irritation because he could not shout at the shrill, silly women in his cabin to keep silence in the boat. When he returned finally to the *Pathshire* he was conscious of that odd despair and misery that sometimes attacked him with irresistible force if he awoke in his hammock in the dark of the early morning. He seemed to have no reserve of will with which to combat it. The Gunroom was closed, and he went into the Smoking Casemate, where he sat down on an upright wooden chair. The room was dirty with the litter of the day. Cards and newspapers lay on the deck and on the chairs. Cigarette-ends exuded their juice among the dregs at the bottom of wine-glasses. From the half-deck, where the midshipmen's hammocks were slung, came the sound of regular breathing, and once the cry—almost the cry of a child, John fancied—of one who dreamed unhappily. He sat staring at the six-inch gun that gleamed beneath the yellow beam of an imperfect police-light. What, in God's name, was this leading to? From the cruelty and degradation of the *King Arthur* he seemed now to be degraded through his own fault. No need to sink into slackness of mind and body; no need to drink rot-gut liqueurs in the forenoon; no need to gamble for stakes he could not afford, or to let his thought and speech be filled with beastliness. His own fault, he supposed; his own fault, he tried to confess in his eagerness to avoid the finding of excuses for himself. And yet—he glanced through the half-curtained door beyond which the others were sleeping—were not they similarly affected? In other ships were the same Gunroom conditions. There must be a reason for it, outside and beyond them all; a force greater than their wills, bearing them down, stifling and slowly destroying the instincts for cleanness and energy which had once been lively within them.

And suddenly John perceived that his stream of life had become stagnant and foul because it was dammed, having no outlet in hope. His care for Margaret, his desire for poetry, his longing for progressive intellectual work which had been allowed to develop at the training colleges, were checked now. In his present life, and, so far as he could see, in the future life the Service promised him, there could be no spiritual or intellectual expansion. Day after day routine would repeat itself. The end towards which all effort was directed was war. War—and what then?

He could not face the questions that were crying unanswered through the passages of his mind. He began to reckon his gains and losses at cards, and frowned because the card-book, into which he would have liked to look, was inaccessible within the locked Gunroom. And presently he began to ask himself what offence of his had caused Margaret wilfully to disregard him that night.

Perhaps for ten minutes, perhaps for an hour or more, he had sat thus, thinking with desperate rapidity, when he looked up to find Hugh, bare-footed, and clothed in torn pyjamas, standing at the Casemate door.

"I saw you from my hammock," Hugh said. "You look pretty miserable, sitting there."

"I've been running the picket-boat," John answered, as if this were sufficient explanation. "You were at the dance, weren't you?"

"Yes. I had to go because my people were going. A flagship dance is no place for a snotty—too much gold lace and aiglettes."

"I took your people ashore."

"I know. I saw them go down into the *Pathshire*'s boat."

"Did you notice anything?"

"Notice anything?"

"About Margaret?"

"No. What of her?"

"Merely that she looked straight at me, saw me, and wouldn't recognize me." John laughed shortly. "I wonder what crime I've committed."

"I think she was excited to-night. Sometimes when I spoke to her she answered me in that vague way of hers, as if her thoughts were far away. Do you remember how strange she was that Sunday after our dance in town? It was the same thing to-night."

"Ordith?"

"Perhaps. She danced with him. I remember, as they passed me, I heard her laugh—higher pitched than usual." And Hugh added, with a touch of embarrassment: "Almost as if she was afraid."

John paused to consider. He saw her in Ordith's arms, moving to the music, her head thrown back a little, laughing. Then, with directness that surprised himself, he asked suddenly the question he had long desired and never dared to ask:

"Hugh, do you think she is in love with Ordith?"

"He is with her."

"I know. That wasn't my question, though. You know why I ask it."

"She has never said a word to me about it."

"She's not likely to. . . . But what is your opinion, based on what you've seen and heard?"

"My dear old fellow, how should I know? It does no good to make yourself wretched."

"But you think there's cause?"

"Well, there's a kind of glamour about Ordith, you know. And Margaret is very young as yet. I don't suppose her mind is made up in any way."

John rose and shivered. "We had better turn in," he said. "The half-deck sentry thinks we are mad. I saw him look round the edge of the curtain just now."

Chapter XV
Trafalgar and the Red Lamp

Though assuredly not with fear, nor with any sense of impending dissolution, the officers and men of the *Pathshire*—and, perhaps, of the whole Navy—regarded war with Germany, in more than one respect, as they regarded death, and assumed that the same certitude existed in their shipmates' minds; so that the end of peace was no more questioned than the end of life, but only the manner of that end and the hour of its coming. Moreover, as from men's ordinary speech speculation concerning the after-life is excluded, so these seamen did not speak, and seldom thought, of the time that would come when the war was over. The tale that German officers toasted "The Day" produced in the British Navy sentiments altogether different from those with which it inspired British civilians. In Service messes they smiled the national smile at this effusiveness of foreigners, just as they would have smiled at the gesticulations of Frenchmen or the exceeding politeness of Japanese. To them it seemed pompous and laughable to drink solemnly to War; they would as soon have been ceremonious concerning a Gunlayers' Test. But this German proceeding aroused in them neither fear nor the resentment that springs from fear. They regarded the Germans who were said to drink this toast, not as wicked men rejoicing in the prospect of wickedness, but as professional men who overstepped somewhat the boundaries of "good form" in their too dramatic attitude towards their profession.

So long as they remained in or near their ships—that is, within the atmosphere of which Mr. Alter had spoken, and beyond the influence of their civilian friends—naval officers saw the coming war with such concentration on its professional aspect that observant visitors were amazed and sometimes shocked. War would come; Germany would be the enemy and the aggressor; but the certainty of this aggression seemed no better reason for bitterness than a chess opponent's initial move of his King's Pawn. It was attractive to wonder whether the King's Pawn would be moved or whether some other opening would be selected. It was delightful to suggest the defence that Jellicoe and Prince Louis would adopt. But, just as chess players are careful for the game's intricacies and not for stakes, so naval officers thought of the war in terms of manœuvred battle squadrons and destroyer flotillas rather than of the destinies of nations. And they assumed that German officers, being likewise professional men, were no more interested than they were in those aspects of war that were not strictly professional. They imputed to the Ober-Leutnant as he stood, wine-glass in hand, no motive more sinister than a desire to prove professional superiority; and, being themselves convinced that they could out-manœuvre and out-gun him, they were unperturbed that he should drink to his sentimental heart's content.

On the China Station the naval officer's concern with war was, perhaps, more exclusively technical than elsewhere. In home waters the Germans were as unfamiliar as bogey-men, and the English newspapers were near at hand. A speech or leading article was potent to awake, even in the naval mind, some of those vague misgivings concerning Wilhelmshaven upon which vulgar opinion on foreign affairs was at that time based. But the newspapers that reached China were stale and little read; and—most powerful antidote for political animosity— the German Fleet was a familiar sight, and its officers were frequent guests.

The field of thought concerning war was thus circumscribed. When the time came, the China Squadron would fight its own independent battle in its own waters. The chess-board was set. The opposing force was known and visible. Many a time in Wardroom and Gunroom were the *Scharnhorst, Gneisenau, Leipzig,* and *Nürnberg* compared, knot for knot, gun for gun, armour for armour, torpedo-tube for torpedo-tube, with the *Pathshire* and her comrade ships. No doubt the Germans made similar calculations; no doubt they, too, cast their eyes sometimes towards Japan. But, in a subtle manner, the very closeness of the association of those who were ultimately to be enemies robbed that association of bitterness. The Germans were excellent seamen, and pleasant companions at dinner. They danced well, drank well, laughed well, and could sing a good song. When Fate ended both dance and song the ensuing duel would be a gentlemanly trial of skill, intensely interesting, a settling of knotty arguments, a test, for instance, of what the Engineer-Commander could do with his main engines. The gun-fire silent at last, the survivors would be picked up and given whisky, or, if the weather was cold, sloe gin. The battle, important to civilians for its effects upon trade-routes, Eastern prestige, and a vast complexity of political issues, would be to those who took part in it a thrilling conclusion to a technical work which for many weary years had been hard reading.

It would be a conclusion, an end of a book to which no sequel had been planned. After it, as after death, would be but that blank fly-leaf whose whiteness is more emphatic than the written word FINIS. A man whose whole life has been devoted to one object scarce dares to look beyond its attainment. The business man speaks uneasily of the years that are to follow his retirement; the historian wonders how he will occupy his time when his great work has gone to press; the mother turns from contemplation of the hour in which her child, made man by her pain and endeavour, goes from her into the world. And the naval officer looked infrequently and with reluctance beyond the crowning of his work.

But there were moments when it was difficult so conveniently to restrict the vision of the future. Rumours of war were continual reminders of war's imminence, and, therefore, pointers towards the years of undefined purpose that would succeed it. As each rumour was proved false, it was impossible, in the days of reaction, to avoid some speculation as to the results which would have ensued had the rumour been well-founded; just as it is impossible for a man who has survived an attack of that disease by which he knows his end must come not to look a little wistfully beyond the gates of death. And soon after that night on which John had, for other reasons, asked himself to what end his present life was directed, there came whisperings of war to make the question more insistent. Once again the rumour was seen to lack foundation; a leaf in the great technical volume was turned excitedly; but not yet had that page been reached upon which was written CHAPTER THE LAST. But John knew, as did they all, that they were near the end now—very near the end.

"I hope it comes," he said to Hartington, "before we leave

China. Out here it will be on a smaller scale. We shall be able to see the whole battle at once, and it will be *our* battle. It will be simpler, more clearly cut than that vast affair in the North Sea.''

"Do you look forward to war?"

"What else is there to which we can look forward? It's our training. It's what we are here for."

"It means untold suffering—mourning, poverty, bitterness for years to come."

"That may be," said John, "but it's our job."

"You are a queer fellow—an idealist one moment and a shouting militarist the next."

"No, I'm not a militarist, though I do say I want war. I shouldn't want war if there was anything else on God's earth that I could want with a reasonable hope of obtaining it. I should take no pleasure in war itself apart from the momentary excitement of the thing; and certainly I'm not dreaming of political gains through war, which is the part of the genuine militarist. I want it just as one wants a thunderstorm to break quickly that one knows must break some time. I'm sick of the tension, of wasting precious years in preparing and waiting. If the end of all our work is to be 'mourning, poverty, and bitterness for years to come,' if that's what we are living for, I want an end of it. I don't know what is beyond. I don't care. But, at any rate, it will be a clean sheet—a clean sheet to spoil may be, but a chance to make a fresh start."

"A chance for you to make a fresh start?"

"I mean—I mean the world in general."

"But you?"

"Oh, I'm a naval officer for good and all. It's different for me."

"Our trade's going to be an odd one after the war. It may become more or less superfluous. There may be a great pensioning-off."

"I've thought about that—'after the war.' But I dare say there'll be work for us to do."

"Yes," said Hartington, "but work with what object? Think of it: the work we do from day to day gives precious little satisfaction in itself. I suppose everyone—no matter in what line of business—has one supreme ambition that overshadows all other ambitions. But in most lives, while a man waits for his Great Attainment he is kept going by smaller successes, intermediate achievements that have at least some of the qualities of permanence. The statesman waiting to pass his Great Reform passes smaller measures that are *something*— something that stands. Or the novelist writing his intermediate novels, or the architect designing the houses that are to precede his Great Design, or the shopkeeper, even, opening a new branch here and a new branch there, stepping-stones to the Great Store of his dream, but each a substantial achievement in itself; all these people know that, even if the Great Dream comes to naught, they have constructed something more durable than themselves. But the naval officer accomplishes nothing by the way. I suppose Guns is glad if a battle practice goes well, but it all ends in a round of drinks; no one is the happier for it. No one is a whit the happier for anything we do.''

"The practical economists would tell you that we are indirectly constructive because we protect commerce,'' John said.

"The boy who frightens birds with his clacker is constructive in that sense. So is the hangman with his rope. No, that's too shallow a foundation on which to build comfort. All our eggs are in one basket. War is everything to us. And when the war is over and we can say there will not be another war for fifty years, perhaps a hundred years—certainly not in our time, what then? How are we going to live through routine? What heart shall we put into preparation for a remote possibility?''

"And we shall still be young men.''

"We shall have all our lives before us.''

John rested his head on his hand as if he were tired. "And even now,'' he said, "when at least this wonderful achievement of ours is in the future and not in the past, it seems a poor thing to me. I may be a Sub when it comes, or I may be a Lieutenant—anyhow, a cog in the machine.''

"The Lord knows when it's coming. We may be Admirals by then.''

John thought. He was perceiving a revealing truth. "I don't want to be an Admiral,'' he said.

"But that, in a naval officer, is heresy and disaster,'' Hartington answered, with a hidden smile. "You ought to want to be an Admiral. At the age of twelve you promised, as it were, to love, honour, and obey.''

"I did want to be an Admiral—then.''

"But you must want it now. You must make yourself want it.''

"Because there's nothing else to want?''

"Just that." Hartington was determined that, for his own sake, John must be made to see his position with perfect clearness. "But in time of war," he went on, "an Admiral's position is different from his position now."

"The chances are heavily against his having a command."

"Oh, for that matter, the chances are heavily against success in anything. To reckon on that basis is hopeless. It's no good to count on failure. . . . Imagine you have absolute success, and reckon backwards from that, if you like. Imagine that there is war. You are the Admiral commanding the Home Fleet. You have—you have the destinies of the world in your hands: it would be little less than that. Doesn't there seem something fine——"

"Assuming, for the sake of comparison, an equivalent success elsewhere, I'd rather shape destiny with other tools."

"As Prime Minister?"

John smiled for a moment. Then he said seriously: "Or write a great book. Or—oh, there are dozens of better implements."

"But suppose—and this is the ultimate test—suppose you won a Trafalgar?"

John looked up quickly, realizing whither he had been led. Their eyes met. "I don't think Trafalgar would make me happy," he said.

He picked up the red lamp that was swinging within a few inches of the cabin floor and placed it on his knees. Hartington settled himself deeply in his great wicker chair.

"If that's so," he said, "you ought not to be in the Service. You ought to get out of it, and try to write that great book."

John put the lantern from him hurriedly and rose. "Do you think I don't know that?" he demanded, with a tremor in his voice.

"You didn't know it sixty seconds ago."

"I did. Good-night."

"Good-night."

John paused with one foot outside the cabin door.

"Do you want to be an Admiral yourself?" he challenged.

"That question does not arise," Hartington answered.

Because he could not trust himself to speak again John went out, his eyes aching as before a storm of tears.

Chapter XVI
The Engines

I

About the middle of July the squadron left Wei-hai-wei to visit Chemulpo and Seoul. John was now attached to the Engine-room staff. He kept no more watches on the Upper Deck, attended no lectures, and ran no boats. His connection with the executive branch was limited to the writing up of his log-book, the taking and working out of sights, and to certain gunnery duties of which more shall be said. The executive officers, who objected strongly to the system under which midshipmen were withdrawn periodically from the Upper Deck, and by which they were thus deprived of a full comple-ment of messengers, boat-runners, cocoa-makers, and general assistants, had contrived on this occasion that no more than two, John and Driss, should go below. This arrangement, which John had at first welcomed, was soon found to be less advantageous than he had supposed.

The control of engineering midshipmen had passed into the hands of Aggett. He disliked all midshipmen trained under the New Scheme with the instinctive dislike of a small-minded man for those who, in their education and upbringing, have been more fortunate than he. He objected to these "young gentlemen"—the phrase sounded unusually venom-ous and scornful as he pronounced it—he objected to their very presence in his Engine-room. They were intruders. At heart they were executive officers. Their interest—if, indeed, this Lynwood had interest in anything but his stuffy books— was in Gunnery, Torpedo, and Seamanship. It was more than likely that, in their own Mess, they referred to engineers as "greasers." Damned insolence! he thought. Damned inso-lence! He'd teach them. . . . To them, of course, the Engine-room was attractive only as a shelter from the fury of the

Commander, a place in which they might smoke on duty. Aggett was under no delusion on that point. They thought they could loaf while they were engineers, and get ashore more often in harbour because they would have no boats to run. Not one in twenty of the New Scheme midshipmen was keen of engineering. They looked down upon it, they dared to turn up their noses at *his* profession. Aggett had an uncomfortable feeling that they despised him—that they gave him salutes which were somehow less respectful than those they accorded to officers of his rank on the Upper Deck.

Moreover, Hartington pampered the little pigs. Midshipmen ought to be flogged; flogging, sound and frequent, was the only way to break them. This, in Aggett, was not mere brutality but an article of faith. He saw in the *Pathshire*'s midshipmen, several of whom seemed likely in any case to be strangely hindered by temperament from conforming easily to his ideal, young men handicapped by faulty training. He did not believe that a sound officer could be produced unless in his days of apprenticeship he was broken in.

He remembered how he had asked Hartington, early in the commission, for an introduction to Little Benjamin, this being the name given to the stick kept by most Subs for the flogging of midshipmen. Little Benjamin, our Ruler, it was customarily called by midshipmen themselves, or, with familiar affection, Benjy. Within Aggett's experience Subs had been proud of this implement. They chose it with care, fed it with oil, put whipping on its end to prevent it from splitting, and exhibited to all comers its balance, flexibility, and other attributes. Aggett had seen a tea-party of lady visitors excited to gurgling laughter by one Sub's scientific application of Benjy to a dusty armchair, and by the historical anecdotes with which he had coloured his performance. One lady had collaborated by providing with her own shrill voice the cries of the imaginary victim. And the other ladies, somewhat shocked perhaps by this uproariousness, had smiled, nevertheless, behind the teacups above the handles of which they crooked such genteel white fingers. It had amused them to think that the young men, ranging in age from eighteen to twenty, who came into the Gunroom now and then and went out quickly that they might not interrupt the Sub's party, were treated as the dusty armchair was being treated then. They had seemed to think it right, Aggett reflected, and they were thoroughly respectable women.

Aggett had asked to see Hartington's Benjy, intending only to offer advice as to its treatment and care. Besides, as a point of politeness, one asked to see a Sub's Benjy just as one asked to see a woman's last-born babe. And Hartington had said curtly: "I haven't got one."

"Then what do you beat the young gents with?"

"I don't beat them."

"Never?"

"Never yet."

"Why not?"

Hartington had wanted to say, "Because it makes me feel sick," but, realizing in time how odd Aggett could make such an answer seem in the Wardroom, he substituted, "Because I have seen no need for it."

"Easy enough to *find* a need, ain't it?"

"Perhaps."

"Well, why don't you? It does 'em good. You're not doin' your duty by them."

"Thanks."

"But," Aggett had persisted, unable to restrain the curiosity which the discovery of so eccentric a Sub had aroused in him, "but suppose the officer of the watch or the Commander sends a snotty down to you to have a dozen—what then?"

"It hasn't happened yet."

"But it licks 'em into shape," Aggett had suggested good-humouredly, believing what he said. "Spare the rod and spoil the child, you know."

"I disagree absolutely. . . . Besides, they are not children. They are out in the world. My help is scarcely needed in the hurting of them."

Once again, in a scene that has already been recorded, Aggett had returned to the attack, frankly amazed that any attack should be needed. Couldn't this fellow Hartington see for himself that what midshipmen needed was firm treatment? It seemed so obvious . . . And now the engineering midshipmen had been placed under Aggett's control. Lynwood, Hartington's friend, and Driss—that chin-tilting Irishman—were his to train. He'd train 'em! He'd show 'em! And if they weren't more tractable when he'd done with 'em, well——

So John and Driss were ordered, while at sea, "to keep watch and watch, the Afternoon kept"—that is, they were to be on duty in alternate watches day and night, with this relief, that in the afternoon, from noon to 4 p.m., neither went below. In these circumstances, to suit their own convenience, and to vary the rotation of labour, they regarded the two Dog Watches as a single watch of four hours. By Service custom they were excused early morning physical drill, one being on watch at the time and the other not having come off watch until 4 a.m.

They made out a table of their watches for forty-eight hours thus obtaining a graphic representation of a routine which, while they were at sea, repeated itself every two days.

Date
14th Forenoon Watch . . 8 a.m. to Noon . . Lynwood.
    Afternoon Watch . . Noon to 4 p.m. . . . No Midshipman.
    Dog Watches . . 4 p.m. to 8 p.m. . . . Driss.
    First Watch . . 8 p.m. to Midnight Lynwood.
15th Middle Watch . . Midnight to 4 a.m. Driss.
    Morning Watch . . 4 a.m. to 8 a.m. . . . Lynwood.
    Forenoon Watch 8 a.m. to Noon . . Driss.
    Afternoon Watch Noon to 4 p.m. . . . No Midshipman.
Date
    Dog Watches . . 4 p.m. to 8 p.m. . . . Lynwood.
    First Watch . . 8 p.m. to Midnight Driss.
16th Middle Watch . . Midnight to 4 a.m. Lynwood.
    Morning Watch . . 4 a.m. to 8 a.m. . . . Driss.

"Keeping the First *and* Morning," said Driss, "will be hell."

"After all," John said, to encourage himself, "it means only twenty hours on duty in forty-eight. Average of ten in twenty-four. Not so bad."

Driss smiled. "Now let's make a summary. First, how many hours are we going to get in our hammocks? Don't forget that one has to have a bath to get the filth off after every watch. Follow through your case on the timetable from 8 a.m. on the 14th. After your first watch you come off at midnight, turn in at twelve-thirty, and sleep till you are called at ten-to-four—*three hours and twenty minutes*. On the 15th you finish the Dogs at eight p.m.; dinner at eight-thirty; asleep, with luck, at ten-thirty; sleep till ten minutes before midnight—*one hour and twenty minutes*. On the 16th you finish your Middle at four a.m.; asleep by four-thirty; sleep till hammocks are made up at seven-fifteen—*two hours and forty-five minutes*."

They added together the three periods of sleep, and wrote down as a beginning of their summary:

Time in hammock during 48 hours = 7 hrs. 25 mins.

They stared at that.

Then John said, rather hopelessly, "Oh, well, it's getting on for four hours' sleep a day. I believe some K.C.'s, when the House and the Courts are sitting, do with less than that."

"But when they are on duty they are not in an engine-room or a boiler-room—not in that temperature—not standing all the time."

"No. . . . I dare say we shall get some sleep in between—in the Smoking Casemate or on the Gunroom settee. I can sleep through any noise."

Ten hours of watch-keeping in twenty-four seems not terrible, but two facts throw light upon its meaning. First: the Service, which does not pamper, allotted eight hours in twenty-four to stokers—trained men, inured to the task. Second: "Watch and watch"—twelve hours in twenty-four—was ordered as a severe punishment to midshipmen on the Upper Deck in harbour, not in the Engine-room depths at sea.

Moreover, ten hours of watch-keeping did not mean only ten hours of work. The engineering midshipman not on watch at the time attended Divisions and Quarters. He took charge of the stokers during Dog Watch Evolutions. He wrote up his log-book, a slight task; worked sights from time to time; and each week completed an Engineering sketch.

Aggett was careful that the sketches should not be too easy. He demanded scale-drawings of machines in pen and ink, coloured, and with dimensions. Perfect accuracy was essential. It was necessary to know every detail of construction and working, and to be prepared to support Aggett's searching cross-examination. John's first weekly sketch occupied thirty-two of his spare hours.

They found, too, that in addition to their engineering duties they were required to attend the guns. The four midshipmen remaining on the Upper Deck were not enough, the executive officers declared. So, whenever "General Quarters" was sounded—and at that time it was sounded once and sometimes twice a day—John or Driss, whichever was not in the Engine-room, went to a gun for the long hours of the gun-practices. Time after time the hours which were theirs for rest

or sketching were occupied in this manner; they standing—
and they seemed now always to be standing—not in the
Engine-room but on the sighting platform.

In the Engine-room from breakfast to lunch; at his gun
from lunch to tea; Quarters and Evolution from four to nearly
five; Engineering sketch from five to seven; dinner from
seven to seven forty-five, when he put on dirty clothes; in the
Engine-room from eight to midnight, and again from four to
eight—that was an example of such a day as came to John
three days in six while the ship was at sea. On the alternate
days he was less below and more at his gun. There was little
difference in effect.

The effect was dull, unspeaking misery; eyelids that closed,
and, being forced open, closed again; limbs gnawed by weariness; a weakness of control that brought hysterical tears and
laughter very near. The mind strayed back to childhood and
leapt out in jagged flashes towards licentiousness. Aggett
could do what he liked with them. No insult could provoke
now any desire to protest. They obeyed like whipped curs.
"Yes, sir. . . . No, sir. . . . I'm sorry, sir."

"It's taming 'em," said Aggett.

Nervous exhaustion, so potent to produce obsessions, urged
John to the reading of books in snatches and Driss to intermi-
nable calculations of minutes. Driss analyzed his day with
pitiless accuracy. He would confront John with pieces of
paper on which he had written in his neat round-hand the
number of minutes he spent in sleep, in watch-keeping, in
standing by his gun, in drawing his sketch, in eating his
meals. And John, seeing from these tables that there was no
time for reading, became, for that reason, the more determined to read. He read at meals until Hartington, who, when
he was present, insisted that the Gunroom should observe at
least some of the conventions, told him to put his book away.

"It's the only time I can read," John exclaimed. "You
know it is the only time I have."

"I'm sorry," Hartington answered; "but I'm not responsible for your routine. I can't have reading at Mess."

And John, made unreasonably angry by this excellent rule,
read at odd moments for five or ten minutes at a time,
crouching on his sea-chest when he came off watch at midnight, wasting the precious interval before he went below
again at 4 a.m. He read, too, between breakfast and Divisions,
between tea and Quarters, between Sunday Divisions and

Church. He turned to his book with almost fierce devotion on occasions when no one else would have thought it worth while to open covers that would so soon have to be closed again. And he wrote—wild blank verse. The scansion missed sometimes, but he did not care. He would write no lyrics now; his indignation would not pause for rhymes. Never had his mind been so full of themes demanding expression; never had words come to him like this unsummoned. Tremendous phrases woke him in the night, so that he lay in his hammock, his head a little raised, listening. He heard nothing but the engine's throbbing and the faraway clashing of the revolution-telegraph. And he would lie down again and hide his face, wondering how, even for a moment, he had been amazed and excited by a phrase which, as he considered it, he saw to be without shape or meaning.

It was not safe, he knew, to take any book he was reading into the Engine-room. Its cover would betray him to the Warrant Officer who kept the watch, to the stokers who worked near him, and to Aggett should he enter suddenly. It was impossible to read on watch. . . . But he found that he could write with impunity. He took with him a small, marble-covered notebook of the pattern customarily used by midshipmen for rough engineering sketches—diagrams of the lead of pipes, plans of the boiler-rooms showing the feed system, and the like. To make these sketches during the idle stretches of a watch was regarded, not as an offence, but as a sign of laudable enthusiasm. So long as the usual pattern of notebook was used everyone assumed that only professional matter was entered in it; and John encouraged this belief when he was writing by moving his position from time to time, by stooping with an air of curiosity and interest over auxiliary engines that his eyes scarcely saw, and by gazing upward occasionally in the direction of the pipes that he might have been sketching.

Everyone was not deceived. After the performance had been repeated through many watches a Warrant Officer said suddenly:

"You'll be gettin' the hang o' them pipes before long, Mr. Lynwood?"

"Yes," said John. "Just a few sketches in case Aggett asks questions."

"But always the same pipes?"

"Oh no."

The Warrant Officer seemed to smile. "Makin' a specialty like o' the condenser connections?"

"No. Why?"

"You've been payin' 'em partickler attention these last watches you've had with me."

John wondered how much was known. He went away to feel the crank-head bearings, leaning far over the guard-rail, his hand stretched out so that the warm, revolving brasses swept against his fingers. As his eyes stared down into the crank-pit, where a dark liquid slushed to and fro with the rolling of the ship, he wondered how many men, engaged as he now was, had slipped, lost their hold on the guard-rail, and fallen below the crank to be mashed instantly to death. Would a man so falling have time to cry out? The engines would be stopped, not because the stopping of them was of any use, but because some drastic unusual action is demanded by the sudden entry of death. There would be momentary commotion. Stokers would stare, their shiny, sweating faces lurid beneath the electric light; and, as they recovered from stupefaction, a wave of pity would pass over them as they stood transfixed among the steel. The auxiliary engines would rattle more loudly in the main engines' silence. Water would trickle down the gleaming rods from the piston glands. And presently the engines, with a little hiss and groan, would start again, and the blood be pumped out with the bilge.

Overpowered by this dreadful vision, John screwed up his eyes as if to shut it out. He walked towards the Warrant Officer, intending to ask if ever in his experience this thing had happened.

"Have you ever——" he began; but the roar of engines drowned his words, so that the Warrant Officer did not know he had spoken.

"How's the poitry progressin', Mr. Lynwood?"

"Poetry?"

"That you writes down here."

With a queer wrench John established the connection with their previous conversation, but his mind was now so full of what he had seen in the crank-pit that he cared not how much had been discovered.

"Yes," he said simply. "I do write poetry down here. What are you going to do about it?"

"Do?" The Warrant Officer regarded the defiance in the weary, drawn face raised to his—a face, he reflected, almost comically like those of the half-starved urchins in the back streets of Portsmouth who had looked up at him often enough with just this expression of defiance that was a thin cloak for a spirit near to breaking. "Do? What d'you think I'm goin' to do? Go to Aggett and give him another chance to have at you?" His voice dropped to as confidential a tone as the noise allowed. John felt his breath upon his cheek. "I served my time on the Lower Deck as a youngster, Mr. Lynwood, an' I knows how it is with midshipmen. The Lower Deck sees a lot that the Gold Lace don't care to see. And it ain't against midshipmen. Them that suffer ain't against them that suffer. And—if I may say so, by the way—don't you forget *that* when you get to the Wardroom. It's the men who don't forget that the hands 'll run for. . . . And as for our Mr. Aggett," he went on, "as good an engineer he is as I've ever known— smart as they make 'em—but not a nice man, not a gentle- manly man, to my way o' thinkin'. I wouldn't deliver a midshipman into 'is 'ands, nor any human bein'—not a puppy, even. No, Mr. Lynwood, you needn't have fear o' me. You write your poitry and so long as your job's done an' you enters up the log at the end o' the watch there won't be no complaints from me. But don't let the stokers catch on. An' don't you let Mr. Aggett find you at it."

John gave indistinct thanks.

"Are you feelin' poorly?" the Warrant Officer asked.

"N—no."

"Well you looks precious bad, an' Mr. Driss too. It's a shame this watch an' watch. We in the Warrant Officers' Mess wouldn't stand it—unless the Service had special need. The stokers wouldn't stand it; they'd be fallin' in before the Captain in two ranks. Only the midshipmen stand it. He wouldn't try it on with no one else. Last night we was sayin' at Mess we wondered the midshipmen didn't take it before the Captain."

"We couldn't."

"Couldn't?" said the Warrant Officer, not realizing that John had meant "wouldn't." "Why there's not a man or boy in this ship that hasn't a legal right to take his complaints to the Captain. Couldn't? How d'you mean?"

"It can't be done in our case."

"Well, I agree in part; I don't hold with officers comin' up with complaints. It's bad for discipline. . . . But there is a limit to what any man can stand. This very mornin' when I came down here at 4 a.m., I found Mr. Driss goin' to keep

the watch with me. 'When did you come off your *last* watch?'
I asks. 'I kept the First,' says he. 'I turned in at twenty-five
minutes after midnight. I've been asleep for three hours and
twenty-five minutes'—all spoken cold and thin, like someone
sleep-walkin'. It ain't natural, Mr. Lynwood. I don't like to
see him—or you—white as ghosts, ready to drop, stumblin'
half blind round an' round my Engine-room. It makes me
feel a brute for keepin' you here. But if I sent you up, the
first thing Aggett would say, if he came down, would be,
'Where's the midshipman o' the watch?' ''

He paused dramatically.

"It's too much," he said, "to keep eight hours below
between eight in the evenin' and eight in the mornin'. An'
you at your guns when you *are* off watch. The Captain
wouldn't have it, if he knew."

Looking at John's hollow cheeks, he thought, "There'll be
an end to it soon."

But before the end came disaster. Two days later, John, in
a corner by the evaporators, was writing in that marble-
covered book. The mood in which he wrote held him captive.
He was conscious neither of the engines' beat nor of the
ringing of the telegraph. He saw with intense vision, only the
scene he described.

"Makin' notes?"

Aggett, with low waistcoat and bulging shirtfront, stood
there, his hands thrust in his pockets, his chin pushed forward
over a choker collar. He must have come down as soon as
dinner was finished and the wine passed.

"Gettin' keen on engineerin'? Let's see."

He held out a hand into which, without hesitation, John put
his book. There was a long pause.

"Often write this balderdash on watch?"

"Two books full, sir, and what you see."

"Why?"

"I get an idea and I write it down, sir."

This was Aggett's chance: At last he had caught one of
them committing a really serious offence. Officers were required when on watch to give continuous attention to duty.
Hartington could not get out of this, Aggett reflected. He tore
out a blank sheet from the notebook.

"Pencil," he said, stretching out his hand.

He wrote on, and folded, the paper.

"Take this to Hartington. When he's finished with you, report down here again. I'll wait."

John climbed the steel-runged ladder and, passing through the great heat above the cylinders, scrambled on to the grating which the windows of the Engineers' Office overlooked. In the Chest Flat he found Driss beginning to undress before turning in.

"Do you know where Hartington is?"

"In his cabin, I think. Aggett's below, isn't he?"

"Yes. He has just bowled me out writing verse on watch. Sent me up with this chit for Hartington."

"To be beaten?"

"I suppose so. Good-night."

"Good-night. . . . I say, Lynwood, it's rotten luck. Come to my hammock before you go below again and tell me what happens. Will you?"

"All right. Personally, I don't care very much what happens."

John went to his chest, changed his boiler suit and dirty shoes for a monkey-jacket, a scarf, and pumps. While he was thus engaged Driss reappeared.

"Hartington hasn't beaten any of us yet," he said hopefully.

"No; but he must this time."

"I suppose so. I should put some padding in, if I were you, Lynwood."

John smiled. "It isn't the pain I care for," he said. "Besides, I've made up my mind."

"Made up your mind?"

But John offered no explanation. With a towel thrown over his arm he was already on his way to the bathroom to wash his hands. Presently he was tapping at Hartington's door.

"Hullo! I thought you were keeping the First below?"

"I am. Aggett has sent me up with this message for you."

Hartington unfolded the paper and read:

"I have just found Mr. Lynwood neglecting his watchkeeping duties. He has been writing verse in an engineering notebook, obviously for the purpose of deception. He tells me that he has two more books stowed away somewhere, so this writing on watch is a practice of his. I do not wish to harm him by making an official report. A dozen cuts would meet the case.

"W. AGGETT."

"Why did you give him this chance?" Hartington asked. "It's what he has been waiting for, you know."

"I'm sorry," John said.

"But why did you do it? Why did you take the risk?"

Feeling dizzy, as if he were about to fall, John said: "Do you mind if I sit down?" and, without waiting for an answer, fell heavily into a chair. Leaning across the table, he let his head fall on his arms. Then, fearful lest Hartington should think he was acting in order to win sympathy, he overcame his exhaustion with an effort that sent a tremor through his body, and sat up. "I don't think I can argue it. I'd rather you got it over. We can talk about it some time—some time later."

"May I see the book?"

John fetched it from his chest, where it lay in the pocket of his boiler suit, and, having handed it over, waited listlessly. The emotion of the last quarter of an hour had so added to his fatigue that, as if a high fever were upon him, he desired nothing now but to be alone where he could lie down and sleep. He was not thinking of the flogging; it would be a flogging in dream. He was altogether careless of consequences, of the future that seemed so far away, to-morrow morning—beyond the infinite reaches of that night. There were yet two hours of his watch. Twice the slow hand of the Engine-room clock must creep round the dial. . . .

"What is the sequence of this?" Hartington asked.

"There are different tales, jumbled up. A bit of one and a bit of another. I dare say they could be pieced together. But there are gaps in all of them. I write down any scene—just as I see it."

"Some of it is bad—incoherent."

"Yes."

"And some of it is filthy."

"You needn't read that. One writes anything—anything that's vivid enough to swamp the moment."

"And some of it is—— Lynwood, why didn't you tell me you wrote this? Why haven't you read it to me? I judged you only by the gentler stuff. And now, here are passages flaming with vision: the speed and pause, the song and shock of blank verse. Do you realize——"

"Yes—yes; I realize."

"And you didn't show it to me?"

"It was my own; a kind of sanctuary. Peace there . . . everyone shut out by flames."

John was huddled in his chair, his feet drawn up, his eyes gazing out above his knees. Hartington looked at the lines the writing of which had been interrupted by Aggett's arrival.

"Could you go on from here?" he asked, and read them aloud.

"No; not now. But don't read them. Aggett's waiting."

Hartington stooped over the table and picked up a pen.

"I am afraid it is inevitable that you should make an official report," he wrote.

"Take that to Aggett."

"You are not going to beat me?"

"No."

John delivered this reply, and Aggett immediately left the Engine-room. He jerked back the curtain of Hartington's cabin so that the rings clashed on the rod.

"What's the meaning of this?"

"Surely the meaning is clear."

"You won't beat him?"

"No."

"Why?"

"My reasons are my own."

"You'll be made to give them."

"Oh!"

"By the Commander."

"You intended to take this to the Commander?"

"Certainly I do; and a pretty fool you'll look, young man. This obviously is an offense that can't be passed over. There's nothing for it but beatin'. The Commander will send you his orders. . . . Wouldn't it be easier to give way now than then?"

"I shall not give way then."

"Refuse to obey the Commander's orders?"

"In this case—yes."

"On what grounds?"

"That depends. If it is to be in any way a personal matter I have my explanation. If the Commander makes it a Service point—strictly a question of discipline—his definite orders refused: well then, Aggett, I take it to the Captain."

"A real sea-lawyer, eh?" said Aggett. "It's pig-headed drivel. And, you mark my words—it won't do any good. If you take that stand you may avoid this beatin', but the Commander won't forget it, and the Captain won't forget it."

"As a point of fact," Hartington said, "this is all heroics. The contingency won't arise. This matter will not be taken to the Commander."

Aggett grinned. "Then I send Lynwood to you again?"

"No. That isn't what I meant. I am not giving way. But I think its as well we should understand each other. Sit down, will you?"

"I prefer to stand. And no sort of compromise 'll do for me—see?"

"All right. . . . Now this is not going to the Commander because you won't take it to him."

"That's all you know!"

"You won't take it to him because you know that, if you do, I force it to the Captain. And that brings me to the other point. I don't pretend to minimize Lynwood's offense. He is altogether wrong to do what he has done on watch. And I don't wish to argue with you about the life snotties lead under your orders: that's your affair, not mine. But I do refuse definitely to be your accomplice in producing their misery. They are ill; they are overworked to a degree you dare not make public; it is preying on their minds. If they don't collapse physically and go on the sick list they will go mad."

"It's not for you to interfere in my routine."

"I know. That is why—although I think it's an open question whether a Sub, who is in some measure responsible for the snotties, ought not to interfere in these circumstances—that is why I have kept my mouth shut hitherto. But beating is within my province——"

"I've a damned good mind to beat him myself."

"If you try that I go straight to the Captain."

Aggett shrugged his shoulders. "You're an obstinate mule, aren't you?" Then he allowed his anger to take charge of him. "You're an obstinate mule, aren't you?" he shouted. "Don't you see that what I'm doin' is bein' done for the boy's good?"

"That's for you to judge. I judge about beating. If you take this matter to the Commander, I take everything—*everything*, remember—to the Captain. If the snotties were being treated reasonably I should have beaten Lynwood for this—much as I dislike beating my friends."

"You admit the crime, and you won't punish it. I didn't think you were a fool."

Hartington drew his finger across his chin. "Why don't you mete out a Service punishment yourself?"

"Beatin' is the proper punishment for this kind of trash."

"Trash? The poetry? It's not that, Aggett."

"That be as it may. I don't care if he's writin' bloody Keats. What I care about is that a snotty should be a scribbler at all. The sooner he's broken o' *that*, the better for himself and everyone else."

"You and I seem likely to disagree on every subject," Hartington said. "But you haven't answered my question: why not a Service punishment?"

"What?"

"Well, on the Upper Deck we give more watch-keeping."

"They are keepin' watch and watch already, as near as may be; you know that."

"Yes," said Hartington, "I know that. It is difficult to punish them more than they are being punished already."

"If I chose that they should keep watch and watch," Aggett cried, perceiving that Hartington was amused, "it's none o' your business. This goes to the Commander." And he went out of the cabin, purposely leaving the curtain undrawn.

Hartington rose and drew it quietly. He undressed, curled himself up in his wicker chair, and began to read the marble-covered notebook.

The Commander heard nothing officially of John's behaviour. Ordith's advice was sought.

"My dear Aggett." Ordith said, when the situation had been explained to him, "you will forgive my saying that you have made an ass of yourself."

"I asked you what I should do."

"You seem to be somewhat disarmed. Why not stop his shore leave?"

"Then he'll sit on board and write more drivel. Besides, the punishment is inadequate."

Ordith spread out his hands. "It is all you have left."

So the leave which John might have had when the ship reached harbour was stopped indefinitely. Ordith promised himself that he would make a pretty story of the occasion of the stoppage when next he met Margaret. It would be good to make Lynwood and his poetry appear ridiculous.

Then, partly in generosity, and partly with a desire to irritate Aggett, Ordith said one day to John:

"If you want a quiet place to write in, and Hartington is using his cabin, you can sit in mine, Lynwood, any time I'm not there."

II

The end to Aggett's persecution, which the Warrant Officer had said must soon come, came unexpectedly. The ship was out of sight of land. Divisions and Prayers were over, and, there being no Gunnery that day, the hands had been told off for their forenoon duties. Driss, who had kept the First Watch and the Morning, came up from the Gunroom at about ten o'clock. He stood on the quarter-deck, drinking in the fresh air, and wondering how many minutes he might thus spend away from the Engineering drawing which he had deserted. Because he was very tired and thought himself unobserved he was unseamanlike enough to lean on the quarter-deck rails.

"Mr. Driss!"

He turned to see the Captain standing a few yards away from him. He sprang to attention, and saluted.

"Have you nothing to do this forenoon except lean on the quarter-deck rails?"

But Driss was not afraid of the Captain. "I have nothing to do this forenoon, sir, except an Engineering sketch. I came up for a minute to get some air."

"No lecture?"

"No, sir. Midshipmen engineering don't do School. We do the sketch in our time, sir, working it in as we like."

"So you came up to get some air?" the Captain said, looking steadily into Driss's face. "Don't you feel well?"

But one does not betray anyone to the Captain—not even Aggett.

"Yes, sir," said Driss in such a tone of surprise as he might have used had his cheeks been rosy.

"Quite well?"

"Quite, sir."

"Sure?"

"Yes, sir."

"When did you come off watch?"

"Eight bells, sir."

"You kept the Morning?"

"Yes, sir."

"And your watch previous to that?"

"The First, sir."

"First and Morning? Are you making no mistake?"

"No mistake, sir."

"How many midshipmen are doing Engineering duties?"

"Two, sir."

"And you keep watch and watch?"

"We both stand off the Afternoon, sir."

"But haven't I seen you at a gun in the Afternoon?"

"Yes, sir. The midshipman not on watch attends his gun when there is Gunnery."

"I see. . . . Are you undergoing any kind of—er—punishment at present, or is this the customary routine?"

"We are not under punishment, sir."

"And you feel fit?"

"Yes, sir."

"And happy?"

Driss, genuinely surprised, looked up at him, and after an instant's pause answered, "Yes, sir," in a voice which was somehow not so steady as he could have wished.

"I see. That will do."

The Captain swung round on his heel and went below to his cabin.

"Messenger! . . . Tell the Engineer-Commander to speak to me."

The messenger fled like the wind. He knew the Captain, but failed to recognize this mood. Ordinarily the Captain would have said, "*Ask* the Engineer-Commander. . . ."

The Engineer-Commander, stirred to unwonted activity by the boy's breathlessness, came quickly.

"You sent for me, sir?"

"Engineer-Commander, are you personally responsible for the routine of midshipmen performing Engine-room duties?"

"Mr. Aggett is directly responsible, sir—under me, of course."

"They are keeping watch and watch night and day. Are you aware of that?"

"The Afternoon is regarded as kept, sir."

"So I am told. . . . In addition to their watch-keeping they do an Engineering sketch each week?"

"Almost inconsiderable, sir."

"You forget that they come to me for initials every week. They are elaborate drawings."

"A few hours, sir. . . ."

"Let that pass. . . . They attend Divisions and Quarters. They are in charge of the stokers at Upper Deck Evolutions. And they attend their guns. All this is in their watch off."

"I am not responsible for their Upper Deck duties, sir."

The Captain's eyes flashed. "That was unnecessary, Engineer-Commander. It is your duty to make your orders conform to circumstances. Have you realized that these young officers get less than eight hours sleep in forty-eight?"

"Surely, sir——"

"I worked it out while I waited. There are the figures."

"I didn't think, sir——"

"It is extraordinarily necessary to think when you have young lives in your hands."

"I will instruct Mr. Aggett at once to make some modification, sir."

The Captain took back the paper on which his figures were written. "These officers are ill," he said. "I may as well tell you that I was led to make enquiries entirely by the astonishing appearance of a midshipman I found standing on the quarter-deck. He was whiter than I care to see my midshipmen."

"I will make a change, sir."

"Yes. . . . In future, midshipmen will do duty in three watches, and they will not be below after 10 p.m. or before 5 a.m. That will ensure that they get a night's sleep every other night."

"I will give your instructions, sir."

"And take the control of midshipmen entirely out of Mr. Aggett's hands. Take charge of them yourself."

"Yes, sir."

"That is all then, Engineer-Commander."

The Engineer-Commander hesitated. Then he gathered courage. "If I might make a suggestion, sir: in the circumstances, you having spoken to a midshipman—probably the Gunroom is talking about it—would it be wise to make this change at once? And from the disciplinary point of view, sir, to take the midshipmen so suddenly out of Mr. Aggett's hands might look like—like an aspersion, in the circumstances. A little delay, sir?"

The Captain shook his head.

"In the circumstances, Engineer-Commander—no delay."

Chapter XVII
Decision

I

When John said to Driss that he had made up his mind, he thought that the decision at which he had arrived was unalterable. If it were possible, he would leave the Service. The resentment he felt against Aggett coloured his dreams of an impossible future, in which he was to be free to learn and to write, free to build, free to love, free to fight at no permanent disadvantage for the possession of whom and what he loved— free as no one of his generation could ever be. But even before relief came by the Captain's orders he had begun to reconsider his decision, determined that a step so momentous and irretrievable should not be taken in hot blood. By the rules of the Service he, a midshipman, was unable to resign. Midshipmen must be withdrawn by their parents, and this implied that John could act only through his mother. If the responsibility had been his own he would have accepted it at once; for his own needs, and, he thought, the price he would have to pay for their satisfaction, were indeed clear to him. A price, however, would be demanded not of him only. His mother was glad that he was in the Navy, settled in a profession that would provide him with shelter and clothing, food and drink; and now so far advanced in it that in less than two years she would cease to pay the annual fifty pounds demanded by the Admiralty of the parents of midshipmen, and John, receiving the daily five shillings that was the pay of sublieutenants, would be able to keep himself. His mother had been so generous to him, had given him so much of the little she possessed, that John could not bear to demand more of her. The education received by him at Osborne and Dartmouth had cost the State more than his mother had paid. If he left the Service before the Service had had time to reap in his labour an interest on its outlay, the Admiralty would mostly require of his mother that she should make good at least some part of its loss. She would be forced at last to draw upon that small capital which, for all her need, she had never touched. John knew that the Admiralty, a stern, and yet on occasion a strangely generous department, was sometimes disposed to waive its rights; but he could not imagine his proud mother in the part of the suppliant widow. She would make no appeal for sympathy or exceptional treatment. "They have a right to this money," she would say, "and they shall have it in full." And she would add: "I'm glad to pay it, John, if it makes for your happiness." John could hear her saying that. It gave him pause.

This preliminary cost of freedom it would, however, be possible, though inconvenient, to pay. Beyond it lay a problem not easily soluble—perhaps impossible to solve. By leaving the Service he would cut himself off from the only profession for which his specialized training had fitted him. He would have to be educated again, apprenticed again. At a time when he might have been earning enough money for his own support more money would have to be invested in his career. It was probable that, for all his mother's good-will, the money could not be produced. The meshes of the net were close and strong.

So John fought to reverse his decision and succeeded at least in postponing the letter by which his mother should be made aware of it. Delay was easy, almost pleasant; for he dreaded above all else the answer, which despite his hopes he felt was inevitable, that his financial position made his second apprenticeship, and therefore his withdrawal, impracticable. Such an answer would shatter in a moment the dreams by which he now lived. Until it came hope would endure; by its arrival hope would be definitely banished. He dared not think of his life after that. He must leave the Service soon or not at all, for every year would make a fresh start more difficult. If he was forced to realize that he could not be withdrawn as a midshipman it would be made plain to him—so plain that he would not be able to deceive himself—that he must be a naval officer so long as he lived. His visions of Oxford, of the House, of miraculous literary success, extravagant though he knew them to be, were yet based upon possibility. This possibility once removed, as it would be by his mother's negative, the visions themselves must perish and their consolation pass away.

Not till August was nearly over did the time come when action could no longer be delayed. An incident entirely unconnected with John's desire to leave the Service impelled him to write the letter in which his desire was expressed. The squadron had been carrying out Commander-in-Chief's firing. It had fallen to an elevation party from the *Pathshire* to board the tug which towed the target, and to spot the fall of the flagship's shot. John and Cunwell had gone with Ordith. It was their duty to sit aft in the tug so that they were in line with the target, and to record by means of a stop-watch and the Rake instrument the time and effect of each salvo. Ordith was to observe, calling to John, who would write them down, the errors over or short in yards. Cunwell was to keep his eyes on the flagship and, as the guns flashed, say "Fire," John pressing the knob of the stop-watch and entering the time on his sheet.

Rain fell so fast during the forenoon that it had the effect of fog and made firing impossible. The elevation party went to the *Pathshire* for lunch, and, the rain having by then ceased, returned in the afternoon to the tug. The target was towed by a wire hawser, which was intended to ride from side to side over the great hoop-shaped girders with which the tug was fitted. It had been found, however, that if the wire were given free play, instead of passing evenly over the riding-hoops as the tug altered course and the target shifted from one quarter to the other, it held up momentarily in the centre, swung across at high speed, and was thus subjected continually to sudden stresses that threatened to break it. To prevent this, the wire was secured by port and starboard steadying-lines, and, no longer free to travel over the riding-hoops, was kept rigidly amidships. This arrangement was itself dangerous, and the tug's crew were warned that in no circumstances were they to go aft of the point of attachment of the steadying lines.

When the elevation party reached the tug there was still some time before the firing was due to begin and they spent it with the lieutenant in command—whom Ordith knew as Toby—sitting in deck-chairs and smoking cigarettes. The sun had broken through a stormy sky, so that there was golden lace on the rim of each dark hollow in the sea, and the rigging was fringed with glistening drops that, as the vessel rolled, fell in showers on to the deck.

Presently the "Preparative" was hoisted by the flagship.

"Time to begin," said Ordith, and stretched himself. "Everything ready, Lynwood—paper, pencil, stop-watch? We'd better be moving aft."

"There's plenty of time," said Toby, "time to finish your cigarettes."

Ordith drew slowly at his, and watched the smoke swept aft on the wind. Like a cat he lay contented in the sun.

"I'm not keen on you fellows sitting aft of those steadying lines," Toby said. "If one of them parts, the wire will move like—like the blade of a guillotine."

"I confess the position is not one I should have chosen," Ordith answered. "But where else can we work the Rake? I don't want my valuable head removed."

"I think it might be possible—God! there goes the tow!"

Toby sprang up as a tremor passed through the tug. No sound had been audible. John, who had caught a glimpse of Toby's suddenly white face, moved to follow him. Cunwell, too, was on his feet.

"Unnecessary panic," said Ordith. "It's only one of his damned steadying lines."

The Engine-room telegraph had clanged, and, the engines being stopped, the tug rolled heavily. Through the silence came a voice that contained a suggestion of doubt: "Man overboard!" Then a moment later, loud and clear:

"Man overboard!"

Toby, whom they could not see, shouted: "Away lifeboat's crew—no, not all of you—blast your eyes! . . . Make a signal to Flag for boats and doctor. Keep a look-out from the bridge. . . . Find out who's missing, Hogge."

Ordith, moved at last, went aft, followed by John and Cunwell. Toby, standing near a blood-soaked body that lay on the deck, was questioning a seaman whose nerves had gone.

"You shouted 'Man overboard!' didn't you?"

"Yessir."

"Did you see him go over?"

"Not *see 'im*, sir, as you might say. Thought I saw a splash, sir."

"Splash—in this sea?"

"Well, sir—seemed a splash like."

Toby resisted a desire to stamp his foot and shake his fist.

"Did you hear anything?"

"Wouldn't 'ear no splash in this sea, sir."

"No," said Toby, "quite right; you wouldn't." Then, taking breath, he continued more calmly. "There's nothing more to be done—the boat's away; this man's dead; take your time: I want to find out if there's a man overboard or not. What made you think there was? What made you shout 'Man overboard'?"

"Well, sir, there was two standin' there talkin'. I seed 'em on'y a few minutes gone. An' when the accid'nt 'appened, sir, 'an I looked again, there was on'y one"—he glanced at the body, and finished lamely—"on'y one, as you might say, sir."

"Then one's gone, unless he moved away. Did you see who they were?"

"There was Skidd, sir—that's Skidd, lyin' there."

"I know. The other?"

"Didn't see no face, sir. Didn't notice."

Toby ran a handkerchief over his forehead. Hogge had come up.

"Well? Mustered the hands?"

"Owlett's gone, sir."

"Owlett? Sure he's not away in the boat?"

"No, sir; 'e's not in the boat, sir."

"Right. . . . Was every man warned not to go aft of the steadying lines?"

"Yes, sir. Accordin' to your orders, sir."

"You could swear to that, if need be?"

"Swear't on the Bible, sir. Warned this Owlett meself, sir. Never was one to take 'eed."

"Very good." Toby saw Ordith, and greeted him as if almost surprised by his presence. "Hullo Ordith. . . . Poor fellow! gone down like a stone. They'll never find him. . . . Fool to stand there—damned fool! Oh well!"

"Head off?" said Ordith, pointing to the now covered body.

"Nearly. . . . Good seaman, that. Wife and three children."

Ordith turned for'ard as Toby left him on his way to the bridge. "Five minutes later, might have been me. . . . This valuable head," he added, a little shaken. "And Aggett rummaging my cabin." He patted his pockets. "By Jove! left the keys, too." Then, suddenly perceiving Cunwell, he gripped his arm. "Don't care for Aggett," he said confidentially; "do you?"

He returned to his desk-chair.

"Wonder if we can help Toby at all? . . . No."

He moved his shoulders as if adjusting the set of a coat, opened his cigarette-case and shut it again with a snap.

"Oh well!" He sighed, leaned back, interlaced his fingers behind his valuable head, and, because the sun was strong, tilted his cap over his eyes.

II

That evening two Wardroom Officers came into the Gunroom to play poker. At the end of the table which the game left free, John sat down to write his letter. He had been too near to death that afternoon to waste more time.

He wrote the date and

> "H.M.S. 'Pathshire.'
> "China Station,
> "At Wei-hai-wei.

"Dear Mother,—"

(Then he paused. Usually he wrote "Darling Mother," but after consideration he decided not to change what he had written.)

"I have just had your letter telling me of your work, and your holiday, and your talks with Mr. Alter. It was such a plain, interesting letter full of news that I hate myself for writing any other kind."

(That was a poor sentence—but let it stand.)

"But I don't honestly think it would be fair either to you or to myself to postpone writing about what I have to say this evening. The facts are plainly these, and I suppose I may as well come to the point at once."

(It was time to turn a page, and John saw his mother's face as she turned it.)

"I am writing to ask you if I may take the very serious step of leaving the Service. My reasons for asking this are chiefly these: I am not keen on the Navy. I don't want to succeed in it—that is to say, the prospect of becoming an admiral doesn't attract me. If I became an admiral I shouldn't be very glad or very happy. If I won a Trafalgar I shouldn't be very *proud. And I think the sooner one leaves a profession one doesn't want to rise in, the better.*

"*It is not a case of sudden impulse—I have felt very much the same about it, though I haven't always been quite so explicit with myself, ever since I came to sea, or, at least, ever since I began to realize what this job leads to. If I have stood it so long, why not longer? I have tried to fight it down. But, although I might make myself do a great deal of work, I can't make myself care for it, and, after very long and careful consideration, I have come to the conclusion that the end must inevitably come.*

"*The great problem is that of money. I have always realized how much trouble you have taken, and how much money you have spent, in starting me in a profession, and I know that throwing it over now means a great sacrifice for you. First, there's the cost of getting me out—the Admiralty will want something; then, if I am to enter almost any formal profession, the cost of training and educating me all over again; and lastly, there's the uncertainty—instead of the present certainty—as to how much money I shall ultimately earn, and when I shall begin to earn it. It seems all money.*

"*Of course, what I want to do is write—you have known of that fatal desire ever since I could hold a pen. And I want to be free—but let that pass now, since this is almost a business letter. I should like to go to Oxford, but I'm afraid that's impossible. So I think the best thing is to get out first—that's the essential. And then, with a little help from you as a start, I could take rooms in a far corner of London and start in journalism. The future would take care of itself. I think Mr. Alter would help with advice as regards journalism.*

"*I am very, very sorry for all this. I know the trouble and worry I must be causing you. If I tried to explain in detail what has led up to this I should never end: the causes go back further than I can trace them. It may be quite impossible for reasons of money that I should leave. If so, tell me, and I shall manage to settle down as I am. But I had to ask in case, just for lack of asking, I was letting slip the one chance of another start.*

"*I will send some little news very soon.*

"*J. L.*"

"Jack Pots!" cried a poker player. The chips rattled into a

saucer. "What about some drinks? . . . Drink for you, Lynwood?"

"No, thanks very much."

He put his letter into an envelope, stamped and addressed it, and scribbled "Via Siberia" across its corner. Then, having dropped it into a hollow-voiced letter-box, he left the Gunroom. The decision being now inevitable, he dared discuss it with Hartington.

"Can I come in, Hartington? or—or are you reading?"

"I was. But come in and talk. Move those things from your chair on to the bunk."

After a short silence, John said: "I've written to my mother, asking her to take me out."

Hartington moved suddenly, his eyes shining.

"Oh, splendid!" he cried. "I am glad. I wondered if you'd ever have the guts to do that. Which is it to be—Balliol or Univ.?"

Never had John felt more gratitude than he did for this enthusiasm.

"You think I'm right?" he asked, for the pleasure of hearing Hartington answer: "Yes, of course you are right. Go and order some drinks, and then come back and tell me what you are going to do—all your plans. And we'll drink to Oxford and the Great Work. We'll drink to all our dreams—yours, coming true—and mine, very like yours once."

The drinks were ordered, and John returned.

"Probably my mother won't take me out," he said.

"Yes, she will. She's bound to if you've made her understand—she wouldn't be your mother otherwise."

"It's a question of money."

"Oh! . . ."

"Oxford's impossible, anyhow."

"Then, damn Oxford! . . . Lynwood, you *must* get out. I didn't. Something interfered—never mind what. And now I know. . . . You must escape somehow."

Then slowly John explained much that, even to Hartington, he had never spoken of before—how little money there was, and how little influence. He talked of his mother and of Mr. Alter.

"I believe Alter would help but I don't like to ask him."

"Why not—if you're going into journalism?"

"I know; but, you see," John said, with hesitation, "I

think Alter was in love with my mother at one time. I'm not sure he doesn't love her still. One can't ask favours.''

They talked until near midnight, when John rose to go.

"Even if I do get out soon," he said, "I have a horrible feeling that one doesn't escape very far.'' And, blind to Hartington's questioning eyes, he went on, speaking a part of his thought. "The powers that encompass us are devilish strong: the Service, Fane-Herbert's father, Ordith—all the ring. One doesn't defy them easily. One gets caught again . . . in the net.''

Hartington dragged from his shelf a book that John had never before seen in his hands. He opened it where an envelope marked a place.

"Read that—from the second verse—*'They all lie in wait.'* ''

" *'They all lie in wait for blood; they hunt every man his brother with a net. That they may do evil with both hands earnestly, the prince asketh, and the judge asketh for a reward; and the great man, he uttereth his mischievous desire: so they wrap it up.'* ''

"Go on, it's most important to go on.''

" *'The best of them is as a brier: the most upright is sharper than a thorn hedge: the day of thy watchmen and thy visitation cometh; now shall be their perplexity.'* ''

"That's where you stop,'' said Hartington. "And you are going to get out, Lynwood. Good luck!—and dreams of Oxford.''

When John had left him, Hartington sat down by his writing-table, and, in his capacity as "Lynwood's Sub,'' wrote a long letter to a man he had never seen.

"I'm probably making a fool of myself,'' he thought; "but it's a chance—and the need's pretty desperate.''

Chapter XVIII
In the Cross-Passage

I

There was no Gunnery after the first days of September, and on the fifth the squadron sailed for Yokohama in order that it might send representatives to the Mikado's funeral. The Gunroom was cheered by the prospect, though the enthusiasm of the midshipmen who were then attached to the Engine-room staff was somewhat damped by the thought of so many days continuously at sea. John, however, had by now returned to the Upper Deck, and to him watch-keeping on the fore-bridge had ever been the most attractive of his duties. By night it was even pleasanter than by day; for then the bridge's isolation was accentuated; there was no routine, no hurrying to and fro of the hands; no Commander, no Captain, no Navigator, save in exceptional circumstances. The Gold Lace, together with all that the Gold Lace implied, was securely packed away. The officer of the watch and his midshipman drew closer together, the barriers of Service were dissolved, and personality lived again. Sipping the cocoa that John had made, he and his officer would stoop over charts of strange regions and weave tales of the places whose names they found; or, together on monkey's island, they would exchange reminiscences of Dartmouth and the *Britannia;* or discuss books, women, politics, or spiritualism, according to the officer's taste.

In the *Pathshire* the relations between Wardroom and Gunroom were excellent—a circumstance which, as had been said at that last dinner in the *King Arthur*, went far towards the making of a Happy Ship. There was not one watch-keeping Lieutenant with whom John was reluctant to spend four hours on the bridge. It was necessary, when the watch began, to make a swift estimate of his officer's mood, and to regulate his conduct accordingly. Sometimes the four hours were allowed to pass almost in silence, and, in any case, it was not the midshipman's part to begin anything but a strictly Service conversation. Often it was cocoa that loosened the officer's tongue.

"Well, young fellah-me-lad," Dendy, the ship's rake, would begin. "I'm damned bored, I don't know about you?" This would open the way for tales of Dendy's invariably triumphant loves—tales which John had found he was required, not to comment upon, but to believe. Dendy had his moments of seriousness, too, when he would take hold of John's arm and explain that love could not always be lightly regarded. . . .

Lanfell, a stolid salt-horse, was a less amusing companion. At times when other officers were more carefully dressed, Lanfell had a habit of appearing in a sweater and scarf, an incredibly old monkey-jacket and trousers, and a pair of sea-boots. When at sea he would ask his midshipman how he would moor ship, or rig sheers, or lay out a bower anchor, and the watch was liable to degenerate into a peripatetic seamanship lecture. If he could think of no more questions he would sometimes consent to be diverted into lighter paths; but even then his imagination led him with painful regularity to a football field. He was never tired of explaining that he was neither a mathematician nor a theorist.

"I can't chase X—never could," he would say. "And in a destroyer with a sea running I'd rather have a drop o' rough seamanship than all your ballistics."

"Then you don't believe in specializing, sir?"

"Specializing? Oh, I don't know. I suppose the specialists have the pull. But there's still room for the seaman—more room than most fellows think."

There were times when Lanfell's faith failed him, and he saw himself as a salt-horse eternally waiting for promotion; but such misgivings he drowned quietly. His skin would become pasty and opaque, his eyes heavy, his movement cumbrous. Then, by taking violent exercise and cold baths, he would restore his health and hope. The Service suited him, and, save in those periods when his wine bill mounted prodigiously, he was happy.

The most exciting watch-keeping partner was undoubtedly the First Lieutenant; but his visits to the bridge were voluntary, and unfortunately few. He would appear at odd hours—

usually at night when he had been unable to sleep. At first he would take no notice of anyone, but stand at the end of the bridge, staring down upon the chains. Then, rousing himself jerkily—every movement of his was a jerk—he would do breathing exercises, a performance so strange that the Quartermasters shook their heads and sometimes tapped their foreheads significantly.

When the breathing exercises were finished the First Lieutenant would turn swiftly, his cap over his eyes, and rattle up to monkey's island, where the officer of the watch and his midshipman were standing by the compass.

"Ee!" he began. This was a strange sound, peculiar to himself, which was forced from his throat—apparently in spite of some physical obstruction. "Ee! Finish your watch for you. You go below. Anything to turn over?"

"Can't you sleep, Number One?"

"No. Ee. Yes, I mean. You push off. Mm?"

One night, after such preliminaries, the First Lieutenant being left on watch, he rapped out at John:

"Ever seen a sea-monster? . . . Ought to see a sea-monster. . . . No, boy, don't look amazed. This isn't a Peter-Piper-Picked-a-Peck exercise. Common sense. Ought to see a sea-monster. Good for snotties. Mm?"

After a pause. "Seamen's fairies. Believe in fairies. Believe in fairies, believe in God. Look for sea-monster and you have your eye on the Devil. Catch sea-monster; catch Devil by tail."

Other midshipmen had been known to laugh, as they thought, politely; but John knew the First Lieutenant too well. Left alone he would presently become comprehensible and interesting. Interruption would drive him into silence.

Soon he began a rambling disquisition upon the probable anatomy, functions, and habits of sea-monsters. His talk was full of the technicalities of doctors and zoologists. The longer a word the more rapid his pronunciation of it. . . . From sea-monsters to prehistoric beasts, and thence to were-wolves and vampires was an easy progress. Of the supernatural he spoke with none of the nervous suggestion of one who visits séances. He did not persuade or argue, and his tales, frankly imaginary, seemed to be told to himself rather than to John. They were wonderful tales.

"D'you read Algernon Blackwood? . . . Ee. . . . More fun to spin the yarns yourself. Mm? Now, if ever you get writing, don't lose a sense of Eternity. That's what the modern people lack. Brilliant enough: dozens of women—acid mostly; brilliant like chandeliers, though—not stars. So taken up with their own few years they forget the rest. Scramble for the nuts; forget the tree; forget the forest; forget the hawk overhead. That's why Hardy sits in the inner parlour with the giants and all the others rattle their mugs in the taproom. Know Hardy? Every word a new link in chain from Adam; every kiss taught by Eve. Sense of Eternity. . . . Sense of Eternity makes a watch pass quicker. Read Gibbon, boy, when the Commander curses——"

"Light on the port bow, sir!" sang the lookout in the foretop.

"Aye, aye. . . . Take a bearing, boy." He took off his cap and flung it on to the bridge below. "Ee. . . . Signalman o' the Watch—my cap. Dropped it. Bring it." And when the signalman had come and gone he added to John: "Must keep them awake. Must remind 'em I'm here. They like it. Bad for morale to stare too long at the sea. Breaks the morbid current if you bash things about. That's why Cabinet Ministers ought to have Jesters with balloons. Smack on the head with a balloon restores sense of proportion. Mm? . . . What was the bearing? . . . Take the Corporal of the Watch with you and go the Rounds."

Almost any occasion—especially the solemn and pompous—might be enlivened by the flight of the First Lieutenant's cap. Once he had hurled it, without explanatory comment, into the midst of the ship's company when they were engaged in prayer during quarter-deck Church.

"Sorry, padre," he said afterwards. "Forgot about you. Fellow talking. Had to stop him. No other means of communication."

II

After the Mikado's funeral the *Pathshire* visited Vladivostok and Nagasaki before returning to Wei-hai-wei. The way of life ran smooth, and seemed to John to run the smoother because for him its direction might so soon be changed. His hope, at first so weak, of a favourable answer from his mother, had fed upon itself, until at last it had become almost a conviction. He had ceased to think of his future as that of a naval officer.

This sense of approaching emancipation and the thoughts of independence by which it was accompanied changed his attitude towards Margaret. His hope had so grown that now once more it included her. From a midshipman, from an officer who throughout his life would be dependent upon the pay of his rank, she was separated by impassable barriers of wealth, influence, and competition. But now, in the light of his new hope, the barriers between him and her seemed no longer impassable. He would at least have the chance to construct ladders of fame and money before it was too late. He would be able, too, to bring those ladders near. The Service etiquette and tradition would bind him no more. Ordith, for instance, would cease to be his superior officer. He would not be borne away to sea, nor would his shore leave be stopped at the moment when he most wanted to see Margaret. Mr. Fane-Herbert, whom it was impossible not to regard as some kind of naval chief with additional advantages of wealth and civilian freedom, could not continue to treat him as a junior officer of no accounts. The blind alley would open into a clear field. Opportunity would increase.

Or, at any rate, this is how John's sudden optimism led him to regard his future.

Margaret was one of a small party that came on board to tea with Hartington early in October. It was a Gunroom party, to which Ordith was not invited. Its beginning had been difficult because civilians seem always to require so much space that a warship cannot provide. The chairs, which had been comfortable enough until it was necessary to invite ladies to sit in them, appeared suddenly to be in a shocking state of disrepair. Never had Gunroom china seemed so thick or Gunroom fare, for all the preparations that had been made, so brutally masculine. The corticene, scarred with burnings of cigarette-ends, cried out for rugs to hide it.

The ladies, however, were tactfully blind to these deficiencies. The tea had been a success. At Hartington's suggestion the party broke up so that the guests might "see over the ship," he having conveniently forgotten that they had "seen over" it many times before. He himself took charge of Mrs. Fane-Herbert. Margaret was left to John.

Having examined the Upper Deck twelve-pounders in the view of all the world, he took her into the ammunition and cross-passages, where he knew none other would be. The electric lights flared from polished metal and white enamel;

the atmosphere was heavy; their lightest footsteps clattered and resounded. But John was oblivious to all this.

"I've never seen you in such good spirits," she said. "Tell me why."

"Because I am going to leave the Service."

"Leave it—for good?" She drew in her breath.

"Yes. I've never told you. I haven't had a chance to tell you. My leave was stopped for a time, and I never seemed to be able to get near you. You know why my leave was stopped?"

"Yes. Nick told me."

Nick! So it had gone thus far. "What did he say?" John asked.

"He said that what you did was a serious offence—technically."

"Technically?"

"I mean he seemed to sympathize in the circumstances. He told me about Mr. Aggett and the watches you were keeping. He told me everything."

"And he sympathized?"

"Yes. You needn't say it like that, John. I believe it was he who persuaded Mr. Aggett to stop your leave instead of taking it further."

"Did he tell you that too?"

"No; but I read between the lines."

"Ah!"

"And father said he thought you had been lucky."

"So Nick told *him*?"

"I don't know who told him. Nick may have done. It's been the talk of the fleet."

John winced under that.

"I'm sorry," she said. "We oughtn't to have talked about it. I've made you wretched."

"No. I don't care now—now I'm going to get out."

"When is it to be?"

"I wrote home at the end of August. The mail takes just over a fortnight each way. I might get an answer—to-morrow."

She said after a moment's thoughts: "Oh, I am glad, tremendously glad . . . for you."

The thought of John's leaving China, of his returning home, troubled her. It brought Ordith and the inevitable decision nearer. Somehow John's absence—though lately his presence had meant so little to her—would weaken her own defences. Now that he was breaking free of his net, his company and the likeness of his situation to her own as she conceived it had become suddenly more valuable to her. A safeguard, she told herself. . . . And yet, more than a safeguard. . . . She looked at him nervously. She wanted him not to go. She would be alone when he had gone.

"You know," she said, "this—all this life—doesn't suit me better than you. We're together in that. And you are escaping."

"It's no good without you."

He had spoken on the instant. There was no going back. He said, before she could interrupt him:

"Margaret, you must listen. One can't go on alone. I can't. I don't believe you can. We are both caught the same way. I'm getting free. You must, too. Oh, you must, Margaret!"

"It's impossible."

"Now, yes. But couldn't we come to an understanding now? And later——"

He was stricken by doubt for the meaning of her word "impossible." He tried and failed to read her face.

"Or did you mean——"

"You are not out of the Service yet, John," she said.

He was sure now that she had intended to check him. That reminder of the Service—which she had spoken partly to gain time, partly to drag back her own thoughts to realities—seemed to him a deliberate thrust, well aimed. He was still in the Service, still a snotty—powerless. It became a source of embarrassment that she was beautiful and wore beautiful things. His imagination drew for him a picture of her dressing-table, spread with silver; of her furs; of her soft dresses, orderly and exquisite; of her maid brushing that wonderful hair—and of the vast house in London, with its stone steps for ever in the twilight of a frowning porch, and its stern door, of which the handle was but an ornament not made to turn. In contrast were his barbarous sea-chest and hammock, his own small home tucked away in the country, and his one shilling and ninepence a day.

He had been a fool to think that she—oh, a thousand times a fool!

Feeling that the moment and, above all, her cruel thrust had given him the right to say what for long years—until he was more than a snotty—he might not say again, he flashed out:

"Come what may, Margaret, you're the best I have on earth."

And he turned away, leaving her to follow him out of the ammunition passage. She, not knowing how she had wounded him, not realizing how her one word "impossible" had been misinterpreted, moved her lips to speak. His last phrase—a direct statement rather than an exclamation—thrilled her. He had meant every word of it. It was the finest tribute a woman could hear spoken; and he had given it finely—every syllable swift and clear-cut like sharp-edged flames. And yet——

She did not speak. She stood without moving. Already he was a few paces away—the nozzle of a fire-hose glinted between them: and he did not turn around. There would have been no need for speech had he turned. She would have run to him. They would have made great plans, too brave to be impossible.

But he did not turn, and in a moment she began to follow him.

Chapter XIX
Crisis

I

Mr. Fane-Herbert had recently returned to Wei-hai-wei after what his household was led to believe had been a prosperous absence. He bullied the Chinese boys with cheerful energy; he patted Margaret's hand, and chuckled at the jokes which he gave her to understand he would have made but for her innocent presence; he allowed his moustache to rest a little longer than usual on the forehead his wife raised to him each morning when, after entering the breakfast-room, he exclaimed, rubbing his hands, "Ah, nice hot coffee! Nice crinkly bacon! What more can a man want? . . . Well, well—good-morning, everyone. Morning, my dear"—all these being signs that the world was revolving as he wished it to revolve.

Ordith had immediately been in attendance. One morning soon after the Gunroom tea-party he and Mr. Fane-Herbert were shut up together for three hours.

"That dreadful business!" said Mrs. Fane-Herbert. "Why can't your father take a rest, I wonder?"

"He likes it, mother."

"Yes, dear, I'm afraid he does. It seems odd—looking back. Times change. Things take a grip on one as one gets old."

"Not only when you get old, mother."

"No? . . . Oh, Margaret, darling, are you happy? I do so want you to be happy. If you let anything spoil your life it will be as if mine were spoiled a——" She dared not say, "a second time"; but she went on quaveringly, determined to say now what she had in her heart lest afterwards she had not the courage to say it. "I'm not very strong, you know. I may not be able to do all I should wish for you."

"But, mother, you were strong enough in refusing to follow father from place to place when he came here. You put your foot down then, didn't you? And you won."

"Ah, yes. But that's like choosing furniture, or moving from place to place, or any of the small things. I can win because your father yields. He doesn't really mind. He is very kind about such things. But on *matters of essential principle*"—how often and often had she heard that ugly phrase, spoken as if by a dictatorial Chairman to a subservient Board?—"on matters of essential principle I don't oppose very firmly, not now. It only makes trouble, and does no good in the end. . . . He always makes me feel that perhaps I'm wrong, after all. He's a very clever man, you know, dear—your father; clever, and strong. He knows more than I do of the world."

"Dear mother!"

"So, Margaret," Mrs. Fane-Herbert went on, "you must fight your own battles. And be strong. And whatever I say afterwards—for I'm not often like this . . . now—remember what I think. . . . And that I do love you. . . . And that compromise with truth is no good—ever. Once beaten, always beaten."

She rustled into a chair, her white fingers clasped on her lap.

"Fear is—oh, dreadful! like a foot in the door. You can never shut it out. You never seem to be—to be quite alone again." Then, with an expression of appeal and warning in her eyes, she added: "That's all I can say—I think that is all I can say."

There was more finality in her tone that was warranted by the closing of a conversation. When the door had shut softly on its latch and Margaret stood alone, she realized that her mother had spoken to her as she was not likely to speak again.

With a sensation of sadness creeping over her she went out into the garden—its cool air, its pale sunshine. As she passed the window of the room in which Ordith and her father were discussing business she thought she heard her own name—"Margaret." Why were they speaking of her? Perhaps her imagination had cheated her. Chance anyway!

With a little toss of her head she walked down the gritty path and paused, turning her face into the wind, which blew cool on her forehead and throat. The clouds were like great tigers springing up from behind the hills. The water was flecked. The ships' white ensigns were driven out on the wind so that they seemed stiff, like toy flags painted on tin.

II

When, after many congratulatory farewells and an exchange of confident good wishes for the future, Ordith had parted from Mr. Fane-Herbert, he saw Margaret in the garden. He paused with his hand on the outer door, which he forebore to close lest the sound of its catch should make her aware of his presence. Her right shoulder was turned to him, and she was looking seaward. He threw over the slim form, slightly inclined against the wind, a glance both critical and passionate; for it was a peculiarity of his mind that, unless he were in wine, its faculty of criticism was little affected by desire. Yet, even as he thought calmly of her beauty and the amazing excellence of her body's pose against that pale, tawny sky, the idea of possession—or, rather, an impulse towards such an idea, for there was nothing deliberate, no defined imagining in this—came to him, and passed over him like a cool hand, infinitely light of touch, causing him to shiver imperceptibly and his eyes to narrow as if they were about to close. His throat opened slightly to receive a breath quick drawn through the mouth. He became conscious of the solidity of the brass knob against his palm, and, as his fingers moved a little, of the chill of the metal they had not previously touched. Then he closed the door, and went forward.

"You, Nick! How long have you been standing there?"

"Standing?"

"I—I had an idea that you had been."

"No, this moment I shut the door. What made you think that?"

She moved her shoulders and smiled, dismissing the idea.

"You're not staying to lunch?"

"No, I'm lunching at the Club. I'm coming again in the afternoon."

III

He summoned Aggett by signal to share the meal, and when he arrived gave him cocktails and a carefully censored account of the business negotiations with Mr. Fane-Herbert. For several days, well aware that negotiations were in progress, Aggett had pressed for information, only to be met by a shaking of Ordith's head.

"Not yet, my dear fellow. Honestly, I don't know how we stand. I'm not clear in my own mind how far Fane-Herbert has advanced. All in good time. As soon as I have anything definite to tell you, I shall let you know at once."

Aggett had waited impatiently, but with a show of patience. Upon Ordith's good-will depended his chances of leaving the Service and of obtaining a position on the technical staff of that imaginary firm, Ibble and Ordith. He had, therefore, a personal interest in the foreshadowed amalgamation. He knew, too, that until these arrangements for amalgamation reached their final stage Ordith and Mr. Fane-Herbert, though they were ostensibly allies with regard to the Eastern Contracts, would continue to provide for the competing interests of their respective firms, strengthening each one his own position in preparation for the ultimate settlement.

Aggett feared that this rivalry, conducted under the cloak of friendly co-operation, might cause a rupture. Ordith, confident of his own powers, might snap his fingers at Ibble's; or Mr. Fane-Herbert, relying upon Ibble's weightier establishment, might decide to remain independent of the younger firm. Amalgamation was almost certainly to the interests of both parties; without doubt it was to Aggett's interest. Breakdown now would be disastrous, and Ordith, he knew, was prepared to go far to prevent it. But could he be trusted?

Aggett was not without misgivings. A disagreement in detail, a slight on Ordith's pride, an angry word—Aggett imagined his friend gathering up his papers and walking out of Mr. Fane-Herbert's room, never to return. Moreover, Aggett perceived clearly by what personal, as distinct from commercial, motive Mr. Fane-Herbert was urged towards the amalgamation. He had no son worthy to receive his vast bequest of influence and wealth—for Hugh's powers were obviously inadequate. And the firm of Ibble was to him more than a business. It was his life's work. For its sake he had sacrificed many things that when he was young he would have sworn never to sacrifice. In it he had invested not only money, but an unrealizable capital of labour and affection, and his sentiment insisted that, when he was gone, Ibble's should continue to be identified with one of his own blood. Yet, if none of his own blood possessed the necessary ability, outside help must be accepted. There was but one way to compromise. His daughter must carry on the personal tradition; her husband must provide the administrative capacity. Also, because Mr. Fane-Herbert had learnt not to give without receiving, he was determined that the husband must bring with him more than brains. He must add like to like, possession to possession. And the choice had fallen on Ordith, who was qualified in youth, ability, and endowment.

But Mr. Fane-Herbert's view of the world led him to believe that the amalgamation without the marriage ought to be opposed. If she were not tied to Ordith, Margaret might marry any fool, and cease to exercise the influence on policy which her immense holding would place at her command. She might even sell out, and devote the proceeds to God knew what ridiculous frippery. The Fane-Herbert tradition might come to an end. He might lose his immortality. . . . The projects of marriage and amalgamation were therefore inseparable in Mr. Fane-Herbert's mind. This was the fact upon which Aggett dwelt. Ordith must act, must act immediately. Every moment of delay was dangerous, pregnant with discord. The marriage once effected, the settlement once made—the settlement was the point—there could be no retreat from amalgamation.

As Aggett came ashore he had decided, at the risk of unpleasantness, to draw Ordith's attention to this aspect of the matter; but he was soon to discover that the risk was unnecessary. Lunch was a tedious meal, at which conversation on engrossing topics was debarred by the presence of others, but when it was over, and the patron saints of armament firms had been invoked, in silence but with perfect understanding, over many a glass of wine, the two men returned to their quiet corner and were again at ease.

"It amounts to this," said Ordith presently. "Point one, the Eastern Contracts: he has been doing good work, so have I. There's much yet to be done, but the outlook is excellent."

"Does he know that you have been squaring your own yard-arm when he wasn't looking?"

"He does. I know as much of him. That cancels out."

"Right. I don't like it—I'll tell ye why in a shake. But go on."

"Point Two, the Amalgamation: we have both agreed to support it—I, of course, on my father's behalf—but on one condition. Point Three, Yourself: your billet is fixed. You go on the permanent staff. Start at fifteen hundred—I'll get seventeen-fifty for you when it comes to the point. Rises after that by agreement. As for those plans and gadgets in my cabin, there's nothing said yet. Nothing can safely be said of them till the amalgamation's completed. But you stand in with me there. You'll have to trust me. . . . Satisfied?"

"Yes," said Aggett, "though I fancied two thousand. . . . But what about Point Two and that condition? You skidded over that, sonny."

Ordith laughed—perhaps with embarrassment. "Simply a—er—personal matter," he said, and stopped.

Aggett glanced sidelong without moving his head, and winked. "What's up with ye, Ordith? Think I don't know? Stammering lover, eh? The part don't suit ye. . . . Bo-oy! Couple o' cocktails. . . . Yes, you son of a——, two piece, two peecee! Chop chop!" He held up two fingers at the blinking Chinese waiter. Then to Ordith: "That's to celebrate."

Ordith smiled. It wasn't worth while to get angry with Aggett. "It was rather odd," he said, "I didn't care to be too direct about the—about my personal point. It's devilish difficult to introduce your own marriage into a business discussion without making it sound too businesslike. Oh yes, you may grin. It's damned easy for you to be cynical at long range. . . . But to me, although you may choose to think otherwise, and although I may at times have given you reason to think otherwise, to me this marriage is something more than a business proposition. I nearly left it out for decency's sake; very nearly decided to take my chance without preliminary safeguards."

"But you didn't leave it out, after all," said Aggett drily.

"No, Aggett; as you observe, with such sympathetic understanding of my character, I didn't, after all. You never know; the most callous father may be touched by sentiment and drive a hellish hard bargain at the last moment. Then I should have looked a pretty fool. Besides——"

"Besides, I've always read in the pretty storybooks that all the best brought up young gents approached the parents first. So you're in good company." Aggett drained his glass and shouted for more cocktails. "Drink up, ol' man, and come to the point."

"Well, I was infinitely tactful—screwed up my courage and shied off again half a dozen times. Then, thank Heaven! Fane-Herbert opened the subject himself. I thought he had been keeping something back. 'Ordith,' he said, 'you must pardon my questioning you on a side-issue. I shouldn't venture to do so if I was not reasonably certain of being able correctly to anticipate your answer.' "

"Sounds like a lecture," said Aggett.

"Probably he had thought it out. He was talking at the picture above my head. 'I think we'd better be frank,' he went on. 'I think you ought to know that I regard your marriage with Margaret as an essential adjunct to any scheme of amalgamation.' Then he explained why. He as good as told me—but polite as the Devil himself, mind you—that he wouldn't associate Ibble's with Ordith's unless he had guarantees that I should look after the Fane-Herbert interest. And, where I am concerned, he regards a husband's self-interest as the only reliable guarantee."

"D'ye blame him?"

"No," said Ordith, with faint irritation.

"Then the thing's fixed."

"You think so? There's another person concerned, you know."

"The girl? She's as keen as mustard. Besides, she'll do as she's told."

"The last statement may be true," Ordith said, with his trick of formality. "The first is, unfortunately, a lie."

"I've watched her dance with ye."

"But dancing is not marriage."

Aggett exposed his teeth. "Less difference than ye think," he rapped out.

Having reached a stage of mental development at which virginity seemed an unjustifiable defiance of manhood, he delighted in the marriage of any woman he had known unmarried. He was satisfied by it as numberless people, who had no interest in legislation or in the constitution, were satisfied when the House of Lords had its wings clipped. He never refused an invitation to a wedding unless it was that of a widow.

Margaret was a girl the prospect of whose taming particularly pleased him.

"You mark my words," he said. "She may jib the first time. But you stick to it—it won't last long. If she tries to stand out, she's got no one to talk to, not a soul to plot her little rebellion with. Ye soon get fed with rebellin' alone. The girl don't stand a chance."

"Very pleasantly put to the prospective husband. . . . Incidentally, the father isn't a brute."

"How d'ye mean? Surely he's fixed? You said he was fixed?"

"He might conceivably unfix. He can't exert pressure beyond a certain point. What's more, Aggett, I don't want him to."

"Now that's generous of ye, that is—not 'beyond a certain point.' God! Ordith, old man, that's you all over. But don't ye see that there's no goin' back for Fane-Herbert now? It ain't jus' a pers'nal question. He's got Ibble's behind him."

Ordith nodded. He reflected that he himself might have conducted this affair differently if Ordith's had not been behind him. . . . And yet—well, it was no damned good to sentimentalize now. He called for more drink as a set-off to Aggett's frequent generosity, settled himself in his chair, and, banishing misgiving as only the greatly successful men of this world can banish misgiving, allowed Aggett to talk.

Aggett liked to generalize on this his favourite subject. His aids to the imagination and the care he took that his friend's glass should not long remain empty produced in Ordith a brightening of the eyes and a certain fixity of smile. From the state of mind of which these were the outward signs Aggett drew vicarious pleasure. He explained, with careful avoidance of personalities which Ordith might have resented, his theory of the advantages to be obtained by impetuous attack upon girls of the difficult kind.

"No good hummin' and hawin' from t'other end of the room. They can hum and haw better than any of us. 'Engage the enemy more closely.' That's the signal. I always have a feelin' with the villain in the story-books. I like the breakin' of these proud young things."

Never a word of Margaret herself.

Ordith was scarcely listening now, but, as the speaker intended, his thoughts followed Aggett's, though with change of phrase and manner—followed them through the succeeding talk until at last he rose to go.

"Go an' prosper, sonny," Aggett said; "an' Ibble an' Ordith's and all thy gods go with thee."

Ordith started on his way to the Fane-Herbert's. It was irritating to one on his quest to be reminded of the assistance of these gods. He didn't like to think of Margaret in their net— compelled. "She's got no one to talk to," Aggett had said. "It ain't jus' a pers'nal question. He's got Ibble's behind him. . . . The girl don't stand a chance." Poor little Margaret! Poor little——

But Ordith dragged himself out of that slough.

"Ass!" he said. "No good whining that drivel. Too many cocktails."

He took off his hat, stood still, and gathered self-control. Then, looking at his hat, he thought it a pity that he was not in uniform. Even upon Margaret, used to it as she was, the blue and gold would have produced effect. As he approached the house his mind was clear and calm.

IV

Margaret knew in an instant for what purpose he was come. As he crossed the room and placed himself on the hearthrug she knew that the crisis she had so long expected was upon her at last. Though he spoke of a dozen trivial things of which he had spoken many times before, there was no doubt in her mind that this speech was but preparative to attack. There was a stiffness in his pose like that of an actor who is ill at ease. His feet were apart; his body was inclined slightly towards her; his hands were behind his back. She found that, despite herself, she acted and thought defensively—and in the bottom of her heart was a feeling that even her defense must ultimately prove of no avail.

She heard him telling her calmly that he loved her and wished to marry her. Then she heard him giving reasons, outlining the future, speaking at last as if she had given her consent. His eyes were fixed on her and held her; but, with an effort that was a physical shock, she broke free of his gaze. At least he should not assume consent. She would not be edged by this slow process into compliance. She would say something—anything to break the intolerable evenness of his speech. She let go of the back of the chair by which she had been standing.

"No. . . . Wait, Nick. . . . I——"

He waited not an instant, knowing that he must give her no opportunity to recover herself or to reorganize her defence. He put his arms outside hers, and swept her to him. Mind and body, she seemed enveloped, borne down. The strength, the impetus of him overwhelmed her as flames and smoke, bursting suddenly forth, overwhelm the opener of a door in a burning house. She was too sick and faint to do more than force her head a little backwards, and, catching sight of the black and white notes of the piano, attach to them the strange significance which belongs to things far, far distant from us—the significance that the cool frosty stars possess in the mind of one who perceives them from the window of a room in which fire has trapped him. In the same second Ordith was aware that her body, become limp, reposed almost its whole weight on his arms.

And she heard him urging her with words that seemed to grow more and more musical until at last she was listening pleasurably to them. His nearness, his strength, his tenderness even—for where there was no struggle there seemed now no kind of brutality—were becoming sweet to her—just as the snow becomes warm and comforting to the wanderer who, sunk by the roadside, is about to cross the line of sleep and death beyond which is no waking, no resisting, no troubling any more. It was so good to yield, so easy to say the one word he was demanding with murmured reiteration.

But she did not say it. She knew she must hold out, as the lier in the snow knows he must keep awake. "Keep awake!" The words themselves seemed part of a dream. She tried to put up her hands to thrust him away, but the impulse led to no more than a faint movement of her fingers. Then, as she opened her lips and no sound came his kisses fell on her mouth and throat, and her poor little struggle flickered out. She had said no word, but the thought came to her, as of a thing accomplished, "That's over. . . . Of course . . . I knew. . . . His wife—his wife. Always." Whereupon the consciousness that he was still holding her reasserted itself and filled her with sudden horror and fear.

Then miraculously—for she remembered nothing of the movement that released her—she found herself standing clear of Ordith. He had let her go. In the open doorway, upon which Ordith's eyes were turned, stood Hugh, an amazed, embarrassed Hugh, who was saying, "Heavens! I'm sorry. I didn't know . . ." and hastily shutting the door.

For the first time Ordith was at a loss.

"Well?" he said.

She sank down in a chair.

"Please go away."

At his last movement towards her she sprang up, white and trembling, but calm of voice.

"No. . . . I can't bear it. . . . And please never come back—never."

"But you said——"

"I said nothing."

"No—not said, but——"

"Oh!" she exclaimed quickly; "I may have been wrong outwardly. But don't blame me for having deceived you. You were never deceived."

He smiled at her as at a child momentarily in a foolish mood, and went out of the room. On the stairs he met Hugh.

"I'm awfully sorry, sir. I had no idea."

Ordith laughed. "Nothing," he said, "nothing at all. . . . By the way, there's nothing official—no definite engagement as yet, so don't go and worry her about it. Better act as if you hadn't seen, unless she speaks to you of it. . . . You weren't meant to see."

So Hugh was bound. Ordith went on his way to report to Mr. Fane-Herbert the development of the campaign. Together they considered the position and reassembled their forces after the not unexpected reverse.

"The difficulty," said Ordith, "is that she forbade me to see her again. Having regard to the standard of honour by which we live, that's something of a tail-twister."

"You will, of course, continue to come to my house on my business. The rest follows in time."

Ordith turned the pages of a magazine. "The sad thing is that in five minutes or less she would have consented."

"You're a queer fellow, Ordith. But there, I suppose you are in love with her; I'm sure I hope so. Five minutes or five months, what does it matter? Obviously she doesn't know her own mind. I'll talk to her this evening."

Ordith, his head bent over an illustration, looked up under his eyebrows. The most amazing trait in Fane-Herbert's character was his complacency. There he stood, unruffled, speaking of Margaret as of a baby who had been naughty but who would in time learn to distinguish between right and wrong.

"I'll talk to her this evening."

"Oh well," Ordith thought in excuse for himself, "she's got to live either with you or with me."

V

Margaret said nothing to Hugh of what he had seen, nor

did he question her. She made no attempt to argue with her father, for there was no arguing against what he called his "plain statement of facts, spoken for her own good." By this she was given to understand that, in rejecting Ordith, she had acted with rash impetuosity which, on account of her youth, her father was ready to pardon. Next time—and she smiled at the authoritative tone in which he spoke of this second opportunity—next time, of course, she would revise her decision. As for her having forbidden Ordith to see her again— that was ridiculous, childish.

"In any case," Mr. Fane-Herbert said, "you understand that he is a friend of mine, and the business we are conducting is most important—of the utmost importance. Therefore he must come to my house. You do not intend to shut yourself in your room, I suppose?"

The incident of that afternoon was not afterwards mentioned. Mr. Fane-Herbert would neither himself remember that Margaret had refused Ordith nor would he allow others to take the fact into account. After a decent interval Ordith began to visit the house again. He met Margaret so often, and with such smiling tact, that some kind of reconciliation became inevitable. She met him first in her father's presence. The encounter was unexpected; there was no retreat; and it was impossible to pretend that she was unaware of Ordith's presence. Her choice was between a scene, in which her father's intervention was probable, and a recognition friendly enough to make complete estrangement impossible in future. And she shrank instinctively from such a scene.

The absence of any apparent breach in his sister's relations with Ordith caused Hugh to assume that, though some difficulty might have arisen, the incident he had witnessed was at least a prelude to the engagement of which Ordith had spoken. For long he said nothing of this to John, but at last the rumour which Aggett had put into circulation made an explanation inevitable.

"They say Ordith is engaged to Margaret," John said. "Is that true?"

"She has told me nothing of it," Hugh answered.

"But you know——?"

"I saw ——"

"What? Tell me. There's no harm in telling me now. The whole ship's talking of it."

"So far as I know there's nothing definite. I haven't heard

Margaret or my father or my mother say one word about it. All I have to go on is that I saw him kiss her, and he still comes to the house, and they seem friendly enough. There may be a hitch. Ordith said it was unofficial; and it's not for me to question Margaret. There it stands. You know all I can tell you, John. These good people may be beforehand with their rumour, but I'm afraid they're on the right track.''

"Thanks," said John, after a pause; "now I know, anyhow."

Chapter XX
Wingfield Alter

John's request to leave the Service did not find his mother wholly unprepared. Her realization of the mistake he had made had been earlier than his own, and for many months now she had considered the possibility of obtaining his release should he demand it. The difficulties were, as John knew, wholly financial. She could afford to pay the sum which the Admiralty would require as the price of his liberty, but she could not re-educate him as she felt it was essential he should be re-educated. If he abandoned the Service he would have to earn his living as an unqualified man. Journalism? She had heard enough from Wingfield Alter to teach her the meaning of life in the lower ranks of provincial journalism. And the alternatives for the unqualified were a clerkship in a City office or manual labour.

To Wingfield Alter, from whom she might have sought the advice and assistance she so badly needed, she would not go. On the evening after the arrival of John's letter her resolution on this point nearly gave way. The need was imperative. It was her son's need, not her own. And Wingfield Alter would help abundantly and willingly—she knew that. Yet, it was impossible to approach him. If it had been no more than advice she needed she might not have hesitated; but it was money—money. No fair words, no tact of his or hers could disguise that fact. And before he helped her son he would ask her to marry him. She foresaw that quite clearly. Her request for help would, in effect, be a request for a proposal.

She closed her eyes, pressing the lids tightly together.

When she opened them her mind was made up. Years ago, when it was impossible that they should marry, she and Alter had cared for each other too well and with too much silent restraint for her to spoil it all now. Because she had been married no word of love had passed between them. When the strain became unendurable, he had gone away with his wife, leaving her to dream through a few months, and then to marry John's father. And now, John's father being dead and Alter's wife too, they met again. She knew he loved her still, but he had said nothing. Why she could not imagine. He must *know*; he must have seen. She had no doubt of him—why should he have doubt of her? Why? Heaven knew! She would do no more. She would not go to him.

She could not go to him.

Meanwhile, Alter was waiting for signs and failing to recognize them. He was not, he told himself, the man he had once been, and to his eye she seemed to have changed very little in all the years. Moreover, the fact that there had been real affection between her and her husband made her seem difficult to approach. He was by no means convinced that her old love for himself had survived. It was natural that their present friendship should have taken its place, and any attempt on his part to insist upon love might sever the friendship for which now he chiefly lived.

Then came Hartington's letter. John needed help. It gave Alter his chance, his opening. But he could not be blind to the fact that, if he offered to help the son, the mother, in accepting, would feel that she had placed herself under some obligation; and, whether the offer of marriage were coincident with or subsequent to the offer of assistance, the acceptance of one would at least be a powerful argument for the acceptance of the other. And he wanted her choice to be free. He wanted her to accept him for his own sake, not for that of her son. Yet, apart from all other considerations, he was eager to help John because he felt that John was worth assistance. Alter had reached the point in the lives of successful men at which the highest good and the most intense personal satisfaction seem to spring from the help it is possible to give to others.

Far into the night he sat with Hartington's letter on his knee, considering how best to help, and cursing the impossibility of frankness in this instance. It would have been so easy could he have gone to John's mother and have said: "You can count on me. Have the boy out. I'll see him through Oxford. I'll give him the start which, as I understand him, is all he needs. And all this you will please regard as a side issue. It has nothing whatever to do with our relations with each other. There's no kind of obligation on you." But that was impossible. This, by the evil decree of Fate, was a question of money, and money set up an obligation which, where man and woman were concerned, no good-will or friendship could nullify. Hartington said that John had written home. The letter must have arrived. If he went straight to her now, making no mention of his knowledge, she would inevitably look upon him as the man who was able to solve the problem with which her son had confronted her. Her decision would be influenced one way or the other. And, what was more, she would tell him about John; she would feel bound to tell him. He would have to confess foreknowledge, and unending complications would ensue.

No; there was one thing to be done, one thing only. He went to his table and wrote to Hartington.

"His mother cannot possibly afford to re-educate him. Therefore, she will certainly refuse to apply for his withdrawal from the Service, and she will persist in this refusal unless extreme pressure from him forces her to act at last against her better judgment. You and I, Mr. Hartington, must pull together in this matter. I am interested in Lynwood; I am sure he has real ability; and I am willing and eager to take full responsibility for giving him a fresh start. But, for reasons of my own, I cannot at present approach his mother on the subject. Before I go to her it is necessary that the prospect of her son's leaving the Service should be banished from her mind. She must feel that a decision has been taken in which Lynwood himself has acquiesced, and that the whole matter is over and done with. Then, and not till then, I can go to her.

"Your job is to obtain Lynwood's complete acquiescence. You must say nothing of my intent to help him. You must persuade him to bow to the inevitable with the best grace possible. In other words, when his mother's refusal arrives— and it should reach the ship in the same mail with this letter of mine—he must write again to her, accepting her

decision, and—for the sake of her peace of mind—accepting it willingly. . . .

"It is not necessary for me to give in detail my reasons for requiring this of you. I suspect that you have already guessed them. It is enough for me to say that I wish Mrs. Lynwood to be under no obligation to me. Also, when I go to her, I want her not to be thinking of her son's future. She must feel that that is settled, and that young Lynwood himself is satisfied with the settlement. Then, knowing her to be a free agent, I shall be able to act more easily. . . .

"Write to me at once and tell me what Lynwood does. Give me, too, your considered opinion upon the question of his leaving the Service. It may be a little difficult, when the time comes, to persuade Mrs. Lynwood that her son's acquiescence was not indeed the result of a change of mind. Like most women, she thinks the Navy an ideal profession for men. A letter from you, telling me of the circumstances in which Lynwood was persuaded to accept his mother's decision, and giving a definite assurance—supported, if possible, by his own words spoken privately to you—as to his real inclination, might be needed to persuade her that, for all his apparent consent, he is still at heart eager to break free. . . ."

Having finished his letter, Wingfield Alter returned to those words he had written, "break free." They implied more than he had meant to imply; but, as he considered them, he had no desire to weaken his phrase.

"My God!" he said aloud, "the younger generation is in a hell of a mess!"

He picked up an envelope and laid it face downwards on the mantelpiece. On its back he wrote:

"Children of Capital; Children of Labour. They suffer in the transition. They pay for the bitter triumphs. They are weighed down by the pride. If the young men could but learn that gain is without profit they would know that force is barren. When all the world has that knowledge" . . .

He tore up the envelope.

"But that's the coming of the Kingdom," he thought. Did he himself believe, with absolute belief, that force was barren? It was easier to compromise, to risk nothing, to wait;

safer to go slowly. Everything would right itself in time. That was a comfortable thought—but a lie.

He shifted his feet on the carpet, and, turning, peered beyond the soft blur of his reading-lamp into the dark room. And a phrase came upon him suddenly, like galloping hoofs ringing close in the dark against a frost-bit road. Its strange rhythm startled him as if it had been the clatter of horses riding him down.

". . . Finally to beat down Satan under our feet . . . finally to beat down Satan under our feet . . ."

Chapter XXI
The Currency

I

It happened that his mother's reply, reaching the *Pathshire* in the middle of October, came to John soon after he had learnt of what he believed to be his irretrievable loss of Margaret. With her loss his need for her became more instant. While she had belonged to none other, and his own future had been at least not closed to dreams, he had hesitated to admit, even to himself, that he loved her. The lesson of the complete insignificance of midshipmen, which the Service teaches with such energy and eagerness, had been so deeply impressed upon him that, even in a matter so personal as this, he had been unable to forget it. "For drill purposes," as the Service says, snotties did not love—they had women; and it was indeed ridiculous in one whose pay was twelve-and-threepence a week to contemplate any love that might lead to marriage. Moreover, John had felt that Time was on his side, and Chance as yet not a declared enemy. He had dreamed of a swift end to his snotty days, of expanding fortune, of reinforced hope. He had wished to justify his claim to Margaret before making it.

It had seemed enough that she should stand for the imaginative, the creative, the permanent—a contrast to that professional side of his life which he took to be destructive and ephemeral. But now all these things were changed. By his mother's letter it had been made clear that there would be no expansion of fortune, no reinforcement of hope, no breaking free into a new world. Margaret ceased to represent the possibly attainable.

The outlines of his vision of her were thus sharpened. Now that she and his hopes for the future were at once taken away from him he saw her as he had never seen her before. Her personality stood out more clearly. A new fierceness and impatience entered into his thoughts of her. That the worldly difficulties in the way of his claiming her were as great as ever mattered no longer. That he was still a midshipman mattered not at all. There was no denying now that he loved her—that fact dominated all others, sweeping aside doubts, and arguments, and misgivings.

For a time this singleness of purpose was a source of happiness, a stimulant, the effects of which rapidly passed away. At last John went to Hartington, and showed him the fateful letter.

"Well," Hartington said, "what are you going to do?"

"It's definitely the end," John answered. "It's no good to go on hoping to leave the Service. I'd better settle down to it, I suppose."

"What are you going to say to your mother?"

"Oh, some lie. I don't want her to worry her soul out. Better make her believe I've changed my mind. How does one change one's mind convincingly?"

Together they planned his reply.

"It's all very well for me to say I will settle down," John said, "but there's no incentive in this job. I shall always look outside it. And yet, God knows, I shall take it lying down like the rest of them: grumble and grouse, but never break free, never rebel. Isn't it odd how one submits and submits, until at last the average N.O. begins to believe, 'Oh well, it isn't so bad, after all'?"

"Even the cabhorse gets accustomed to his cab—perhaps gets to like it in the end."

John answered: "I begin to see the wisdom of breaking snotties while they are young. I suppose it's kinder in the long run."

II

As autumn drew on to winter, the cold of Northern China closed down on Wei-hai-wei, and, after a short cruise to Ching-Wang-Tao, the *Pathshire* lay in harbour until Christmastime. John saw little of Margaret, and never saw her alone. To meet her now was an exquisite agony, for her beauty, of which he seemed never before to have been fully aware, had that amazing power to baffle and astonish which is the attribute of ghosts. For him the former Margaret still existed, but under a cloak of unreality. Her friendly smile, her deep, quiet eyes, that reflected laughter as a great lake reflects the lamps swinging on the boats of *fête*, her manner of giving him her hand, of inclining her body a little backwards as she spoke, these things were familiar with the familiarity of a persistent memory—in the light of circumstance they were no more substantial than this.

The cold became intense; there were enormous stoves in every part of the ship; the ice made the scrubbing of decks impossible; officers kept watch in hoods and gauntlets of fur, and the men were shrouded in wool. In such weather there could be little activity. The Gunroom found nothing better to do than smoke, and gamble, and drink, and tell stories of women who were now inaccessible. And with Christmas Day came an opportunity for outbreak. To-morrow they were to sail for Woo-Sung—that is, for Shanghai. Christmas was their last day in harbour, a climax, an end to many months.

In accordance with Service custom the men had decorated their messes, and the Captain, followed by all the officers in order of seniority, inspected them. The mess-tables were covered with good things—cakes, jam, cigarettes, tobacco. At the end of every table stood a man with a plate containing samples of the mess's Christmas fare, and from every plate each officer as he passed by was compelled to take a morsel. They ate what they could, and carried the rest in their caps.

When Captain's rounds and Church and Divisions were completed, the Gunroom was entered by the Wardroom. John drank cocktails with everyone, drank so many that he lost accurate count of them, and emerged with nothing but a vague consciousness of the figure eleven. He refused to believe he had drunk so many, for he was strangely sober. His speech was a little quickened, but his legs were steady and his brain was clear. Oh yes, his brain was clear. And he wasn't making as much noise as those other fellows. They were further gone than he; the Wardroom was further gone than he. . . . And the Wardroom was drifting into the Gunroom; hospitality was being returned: cocktails were circulating again. . . . What about wine bills? Would they run their wine bills over? . . . Wine bills be damned! All these cocktails were going down to the Mess. Hartington had said so. They would be charged on the Mess share. And anyhow, seeing it was Christmas, the Captain——

"Thank God we're going to Shanghai tomorrow!" Dendy exclaimed. "Then to Hong-Kong. Life moves again. Here's to the pretty ladies what takes pity on the lone, lorn N.O.!"

John had another cocktail from the tray presented to him by the Chinese boy. He must go steady with those cocktails. Three since he came to the Gunroom; the third must be made to last.

"What about putting in for leave together at Shanghai?" said Dyce's voice. "What about night leave?"

"Could we get it?"

"I have friends there—genuine friends. We could say we were going to stay with them."

"Commander'd see through that."

"Commander doesn't want to. . . . Commander knows snotties' human beings—animals, like the rest." Dyce put down his glass on the table. "Anyhow, means getting out of the ship for a night. . . ."

"D'you know where to go?"

"Find out from Dendy—he knows the ropes."

"I——"

John drank, that none might read in his face the workings of his mind.

"That fixed?" said Dyce.

"Yes."

A great shout went up at some joke. Heads were thrown back, slack mouths were opened. Someone slapped his thigh to show his appreciation of the current wit.

"That's good . . . hellish good! . . . D'you know the one about the Irish girl who——"

John's glass slipped from his fingers and broke with a clean, tinkling sound. A heel ground the fragments. . . .

The Wardroom officers went their way. The Gunroom sat down to lunch. There was a basket of champagne, brought by the Captain's steward. . . .

Through the long afternoon the Wardroom and the Gunroom slept. Through the dog watches they slept. A few stirred for supper.

III

Night leave was granted at Shanghai. As many midshipmen as could be spared from ship's duties accepted it and went ashore. They went with a light conscience, for this affair of women had long ceased in their eyes to have any connection with right or wrong. They regarded it neither from the social nor from the moral standpoint. They did not consider it more seriously than a civilian considers a visit to a theatre. To them it was a break in routine, an escape from sameness, an obtaining, in the only accessible form, of that change of association which is as necessary to the mind as is change of diet to the body.

"In the only accessible form"—in that phrase was the essence of the truth. When first they went to sea they had no taste for drink, no habit of women. What relief they needed from the inevitable hardness of work and discipline they found as other men find it, in the company of those whose interests differed from their own professional interests. According to their tastes they read, or played games, or danced, or flirted. They talked to their mothers or their sisters, and forgot; they went to a theatre and forgot; they saw colour, silk, pictures, furniture, and forgot; they hunted, or read some poem, or walked on high hills, and they forgot with the saving and strengthening forgetfulness of sleep. So men live; such is the meaning of recreation.

In Gunrooms these things, which have in common that their appeal is imaginative, do not exist; and the inhabitants of Gunrooms—and not of Gunrooms only—because the imagination must needs be fed somehow, seek relief where they may. The *Pathshire's* midshipmen were not naturally drunkards or gamblers, nor were they naturally corrupt. When they had gone home on leave from the *King Arthur* they had not drunk or womanized; when they returned from leave they had found the tone of the whole Gunroom temporarily changed. Leave, a chance to break free, an opportunity to meet women other than harlots, had cleared their minds as the opening of a window clears a foul atmosphere. For a time blasphemy had been unpopular, foul language infrequent. But by the pressure of circumstance they had been driven back into the old ways. Now they thought lightly of drinking in excess and of going with women.

"You R.N. snotties," a merchant service officer had told John, "have the filthiest minds I know."

That night on which leave was given Hartington dined with the Captain.

"Well," he said, "what of your snotties now? I suppose they are off with the women. One can't blame them. There's nothing to be done out here. They can't be given home leave. . . . But the devil of it is, Hartington, that even in home waters they don't get leave worth speaking of. . . . The fact of their having women doesn't worry me. The trouble is that snotties' minds, their whole manner of life, their outlook— it's like a gradual debasing of a currency. . . . They are strange people, the Powers-that-Be. Give them an invention or a strategical idea and they'll work on it untiringly, develop it with amazing ingenuity and care. Give them boys, as fine human material as is to be found in the world, and for four and a half years they educate them magnificently. Then, before they are eighteen, when their minds are in a most impressionable stage, these boys are sent to sea. They are subjected to persecution; they are flogged continually for no specific wrong-doing; they are deprived of all opportunity for solitude or thought; they are put in a crowded mess where they are cut off from intimate association with men older than themselves, from women of their own kind, from art and culture, from trees and hills, from all legitimate amusement. And the Powers know it. They have absolute authority in the Service, but the evil continues. Wine bills are limited on board, and there is a free issue of prophylactics, but the evil continues. I know the difficulties—the inevitable conditions of sea-service, the need there is that snotties should be taught discipline by a short method. But it's an odd thing, Hartington, that men with ability and power, who have the interests of the Service at heart, should be unable to find any means of preventing that waste and wrong.''

Chapter XXII
Margaret in the Net

I

In the early days of the New Year, when the *Pathshire*, after her voyage to Woo-Sung, had proceeded to Hong Kong to refit, Margaret found herself singularly alone at Wei-hai. Her mother and father were with her, but their presence accentuated rather than lessened her sense of isolation. She could never shake off her consciousness of the opposition of their wishes to her own. They did not argue with her or seek to persuade her. They gave her no opportunity to state her case. Instead, by their kindness, by their consideration of all her inessential interests, they made her understand that if she would repent and make reparation they were ready to forgive and forget.

Forgive! . . . There were moments when she rebelled in her heart against the idea that she stood in need of forgiveness. But her rebellion lacked support and objective. If her mother had sought to persuade, she too could have persuaded. But this tacit assumption that she had done wrong and foolishly, this treatment of her as a child with whom it were idle to negotiate, this slow pressure of silence and unwelcome generosity—there was no fighting against these things.

She began to understand the secret of her father's power over men. He did not threaten, he gave no opening for retaliation; but he impressed upon her continually and with infinite patience a sense of the extent of his own resources and of her lack of resource. It was as if she fought one possessed of unlimited reserves. She might hold out a month, she might hold out a year, but the time would come when she would fail and yield, and abandon all she had defended.

Why, then, struggle? . . . Was that the question that all the opponents of her father were at last persuaded to ask themselves? . . . It would be easier to yield. She had only to accept Ordith in order to escape for ever from the intolerable atmosphere of coercion which filled her own home. As Ordith's wife she would be, in many respects, independent. If she could but overcome her increasing fear of him, her instinctive shrinking from his touch, her dread of his presence, she might be happy. . . . And what was the alternative? So long as she was unmarried she could never escape from her home. Her thoughts went out to John, but there was no help in him. He was caught as she was caught. Through different channels the power of Ibble's was exercised over them both.

"Some day," she said suddenly to her mother, "some day the young men will break free."

"As one gets older one learns the meaning of compromise. I have learnt it myself," Mrs. Fane-Herbert answered.

"That may have been true of the last generation."

"It's true for all time."

"But don't you feel, mother, that everything is going to change? There's going to be a catastrophe, a great breaking-up. And at first it will be a tragedy—flat tragedy. We shall pay for all that's gone by—the young men will pay. And out of it will come——"

"Nothing will come of it. Revolution, chaos, a military dictatorship, and then slowly back to a system essentially the same as the old."

"I'm not speaking of a political revolution—only. Not a change of means, but a change of motive."

Mrs. Fane-Herbert smiled at her. "You strike truth, Margaret." Then, swiftly serious, she touched her daughter's hand. "You know what you are asking for—a revolution for Christ?"

"Yes."

"Do you believe that possible?"

"I——" For a moment Margaret could not speak. "It must be made possible. It can't go on like this. We must substitute the motive of Sharing for the motive of Gain. It's the only way out. It's the only way to stop the cruelty everywhere—in slums or in the Congo or in Gunrooms—that horrible kind of cruelty which is half-excused by a plea of the necessities of competition. . . . I suppose it does mean a revolution for Christ. . . . Mother, why do you make it all seem so difficult?"

"Because I didn't want your father's daughter to starve for a dream. There is no leader for such a revolution."

"But if Christ came again?"

"To end the world?"

"No; if He came now—as a man."

The elder woman's eyes filled with fear. Her white fingers trembled on the necklace she wore.

"Did I ever give you that idea—that hope? Is it your own?"

"Yes, it is my own. Why do you ask? Why do you look like that, mother dear? Are you afraid. What have I done wrong? Tell me."

"I had that hope when I was a child. It is like knowledge of sunshine in a darkened room. But you are tied down, Margaret. You can't move. You can't pull back the curtains. It is terrible to be aware of one's own captivity."

" '*As the fishes that are snared in an evil net,*' " Margaret said. "Mother, I don't believe—I believe there *is* a breaking free. I believe——"

"Ah!"

It was like a cry, soft, from a great distance, almost inaudible.

II

For several weeks Margaret would lie awake through the early hours of the night. At first she strove to think connectedly, to lay plans and make resolves; but always she would fall to wondering whether her mother, whose girlhood must have been strangely like her own, had made these very decisions, and, when the test came, had failed to give them effect. And by this wonder her mind was carried towards acceptance of the inevitable. There would come blank periods in her thought when, oppressed by what seemed a clear perception of the futility of effort, she would see her own life as a cockleshell adrift upon the seas of Time. She had no recollection of a Departure, no sure hope of a Landfall. God had closed His eyes, was sleeping; and she was alone, unguarded, unperceived.

Unperceived. This thought clung to her through the night on which her father told her that Ordith was coming on the morrow. It made easy the acceptance of ease. She lived in the moment, noticing with unprecedented pleasure certain details of her room's appearance—the soft roughness of the blankets, the beading on the brass handles of her dressing-table, the pale lights of blue and gold that mingled in the bevel of her mirror. She undressed slowly. Once, with her hands and arms raised above her head and her chin thrown back, she watched the light and shadow move over her bosom and throat as she drew breath. . . . A sudden weakness overcame her; her arms dropped; she was surprised by the strange, wild expression in her reflected eyes. Her face seemed thinner, her eyes more deeply set; upon her lips pallor had fallen. This would be her appearance when she was older; this, a little accentuated, would be her appearance as she lay dead. . . . Something she wore brushed and hissed against the eiderdown. She turned quickly and laid her outspread hand upon the bed, so that light billows of satin rose between her white fingers. She touched her arm with a slow caress. With her nail she caused a long, shrill sound to issue from the silk.

Frightened by the unknown spirit that possessed her, she stood in the middle of the room, swaying from her feet, her lips parted, her eyes wide. The intolerable stillness within, the lifeless folds of the flowered curtains, that would hang in just those folds though she slept, though she died, laid some spell upon her, and she strained her ears for the low murmuring of the sea. A board creaked beneath her. There, close to her, in her own room, were evil presences—or was it that a Presence was withdrawn and the room empty, and she alone?

Unperceived. . . . She crouched beside her bed because as a child she had thus knelt to pray. The scent of linen, the pressure of her finger-tips upon her forehead, the fragrance of her own hair—why did these memories of childhood's bed-times come back to her now with mockery and sadness? Their significance was changed, and their sweetness gone from them.

"O God, make me pray. Take away this insistence of touch and sound and sight. Make me believe the Spirit is powerful still, and can prevail . . . and shall prevail; and that life is not just living in the body and the hour. And give me——"

It was as if she had been speaking to one who, unperceived, had gone from the room. She had not been heard. Throughout the prayer she had been thinking how the pile of the carpet was pressed down by her knees.

For long she remained kneeling, her face hidden, her hair

dark over her hands. She knew what she would do: she would
take Ordith. She might be afraid at first, but soon he would
win her, soothe her. Of course she would take him; that had
been planned, preordained.

She was almost asleep. Her weight pressed the edge of the
bed. . . . Ordith would teach her, hold her. She would give
herself—— "God, why am I so hedged round—forsaking
what is lovely, though I see its loveliness—like all the young,
because I must. Jesus, pull me out of this even now—so
late—even now."

Her lashes moved against her palms. The light came through
the pink edges of her fingers. . . . Was that only hypocrisy?
Was she willing, after all? A tremor of excitement ran over
her, and she pressed her elbows into the bed and shut her eyes
again. . . . Anyhow, in fifty years it wouldn't matter. . . .
And Christ would not come again. It was foolish to—to
starve for a dream.

The room was cold. Her shoulders were bare, and her feet.
This physical consciousness was like the touch of a hand.

III

Throughout the morning Margaret looked forward to her
encounter with Ordith with that mixture of passivity and
restlessness which alternately lulls and excites the sensitive
boy who, something of a hero among his schoolmates, awaits
his flogging. After breakfast Ordith and her father disappeared; after lunch they disappeared again. She and her mother,
possessed by a common thought which neither would express,
faced each other in a silence that was half-nervous, half-
determined.

Early in the afternoon her mother complained of a head-
ache, and went to her room.

"You might have my tea brought up to me, Margaret."

"Poor mother!" Margaret thought. "She's hoping that I
am going to be sensible. Ought I to tell her I am going to be
sensible—just to set her mind at rest?"

But she did not move. She let the silence of the room close
round her. Presently, after many hours it seemed, the door of
her father's room opened and shut, footsteps sounded in the
hall, and Ordith entered.

"Alone?" he said.

It was strange that she felt so calm, so decided, so completely mistress of herself. A twist of annoyance because he asked so unnecessary a question—that was all.

"Are you ready for tea?" she asked.

"Indeed I am."

"So you lay aside the burdens of state. Is father coming?"

"I expect he is."

"I don't," she said, under her breath. Then, aloud: "I'll go and ask him. You might ring."

She looked into her father's room. He was sitting by his desk, a spiral of blue smoke rising from the ash-tray at his side.

"Tea, father?"

"Yes, you might send in a cup to me. No milk, no sugar, and strong, *doushka*. I'm dead tired."

He had used the Russian word which had been his pet name for her in the nursery, which she could not remember his having used since she was a child. She went to him and stood by his chair, wishing she could love him.

"You are not ill, father?"

"No—no."

"I think you ought not to work so much. Surely you have earned a rest?"

"I couldn't retire, darling. You don't understand."

"I'm beginning to understand—how it holds you. Couldn't—wouldn't it be possible, father, for you to throw your mind back to the old days and what seemed worth while then?"

"We are not young twice," he said, trying to laugh.

"No . . . but that's true of the young as well as of the old."

He would not understand her. She withdrew a pace from him and steeled herself.

"You want me to marry Nick," she said, and went on: "You know what it means, and that he doesn't love me. And you know what that means."

"I think he does love you."

"Physically. . . . I'm going to say it, father. I'm going to be straight this once. . . . A girl can tell what a man's thinking about her. And if it's . . . what Nick thinks . . . it's like being stripped—there—in the middle of the room." When her breath came more evenly, she said: "And when you think that the girl was once a little child extraordinarily in touch with Christ, made for sunshine and flowers, and warm affection—almost a part of Him, wondering for the first time about stars and distances, and so—without fear—about death, and love, and time——" She broke off. "That's the chance, the raw material of the spirit. And then fear creeps in, and the craving for power—they creep into the nursery. We start compromising because others compromise; we are cruel in self-defence, evil for the sake of good—and our motives are confused until we don't know what's right or wrong. Our seeing of Christ is out of focus, and we talk—honestly as honesty goes—of a man's being 'too Christian,' of 'adapting Christianity to the needs of the day.' And so at last I don't think badly of you for wanting me to go—in there." She made a gesture towards the room where Ordith was. "I make excuses for you. It seems quite reasonable. And, more amazing, you don't think badly of me for consenting. . . . Yes," she added, meeting his quick glance, "I do consent. You needn't worry."

IV

She turned to Ordith with high confidence. The Chinese boy who laid the table was sent to her father with tea, and she gave orders that a tray should be taken to her mother's room. When the boy had gone, she leaned over the fire with hands outstretched.

"Cold?" Ordith said. "Sit by the fire, then—there, on that long thing. I'll manage tea."

From his chair he could look down upon her. For a time they scarcely spoke. He was content to watch her; she to submit. His empty cup tinkled on the saucer as he set it down.

"Do smoke."

He leaned forward.

"Have you forgiven me?"

"Yes." She would not give him the pleasure of a fight.

"Quite?"

"Quite."

Unprepared for this acquiescence, he was disconcerted. She smiled as, without looking at him, she became aware that he was ill at ease. For the last time, perhaps, he was suppliant now. Soon no mysteries would divide him from her. Soon——

But she liked him for being afraid, for his embarrassment, his momentary helplessness.

"You old fool, Nick!"

"For doubting? Then—Margaret, I'm ghastly afraid of frightening you. But I do love you. I do love you, Margaret. You're different from me—on a different plane—that's what makes it difficult. But I love you, body and soul. Margaret——"

"And soul!"

The implication stung. "You mean——"

"Never mind what I mean. I'm not quite sure myself. I don't care."

He could not wait to think it out. Perhaps she had meant nothing. He said:

"You know what I am asking."

"I don't love you," she said, before he could speak, "nor you me."

She faced him suddenly.

"There's one question I want to ask you, Nick," she said evenly. "Whatever your answer may be it will not affect my answer. So the truth . . . If I consented to be your mistress, would that be enough? Would it?"

"Good God, Margaret! what a question! No, a thousand times, no!"

"Put aside the business aspect of this marriage. Think of the personal only. What is it you want in me?"

"All of you."

"Body and soul?"

"Yes."

She bowed her head. "I wonder if you believe that. I think you do." Then, in a flash, "Oh, Nick, we do lie to ourselves! I was wrong in a way. It's possession you want, isn't it? —abstract possession—ownership—gain!"

"Is that wrong?"

"You're a man," she said simply, and, with caught breath, "Thank God for that!"

He was careful, in the light of his experience, not to approach her, not to touch her. This time she should come to him.

"Come, Margaret," he said; "don't let us be fools."

She looked across at him. So she was to move towards his chair, and sit at his feet—and sit at his feet. He would touch her hair, her hands, her shoulders. That would be yielding. That would be, very quietly, the end. . . .

That would be extraordinarily like an oleograph—"in the firelight."

She thrilled to laughter, and slowly, like recognition of an unfamiliar acquaintance, laughter came. It was as if she had wakened from some ridiculous nightmare; as if a shaft of light had fallen across a dim room, revealing countless absurdities that the dark had concealed. And laughter fled suddenly—stifled her a moment, and was gone.

In the stillness, she remembered—as something long passed—the sharp sound of her merriment. Looking round the room, she saw the piano standing open, and beneath its polished lid the black keys and the white. First it was their sharp contrast that seemed to interest her; then, as her attention dwelt on them, they assumed a certain power of reminiscence, of suggestion, as if they were symbolic of something outside themselves, something in the past peculiarly significant to her. With a mental process similar to that by aid of which dream and reality are separated until they stand recognizably on either side of the line between sleep and waking, with the laborious thought of one struggling against the last influence of a drug, she remembered how those black and white notes had imprinted themselves on her consciousness when, on that other occasion, Ordith had so nearly mastered her. The days intervening between that time and the present ran before her in swift procession. She saw herself as she was then; as she was now—then, fighting, determined, clear in mind; now, with even her will gone. By subtle process she had been changed, for the circumstances were unaltered. Slowly, day by day, by patience, by silence, by implied menace, by the bluff on which her father's power depended, her fortress, unknown to her, had been undermined. Her father had come very near to winning, very near.

He should not win!

If she had not seen herself as a figure in an oleograph and laughed. . . . The ways of salvation!

She laughed again. Ordith, with the first laugh still ringing in his ears, moved as if to come to her. But, on the instant, the tension that had held her failed. With the sob, not of a woman but of a little girl, she drooped and trembled and hid her face in her hands. She was crying like a child who, having come through some great fear, breaks down under confidence restored: tears of relief, of sanity snatched back, held—just held.

"Margaret!"

She dropped her hands, raised her head. Her eyes were

swimming and glistening with tears, her cheeks flushed as if with happy excitement.

"Oh, leave me alone, Nick—please—please! Nick—please. Promise you will leave me alone always. . . . I'm frightened. You could get anything you wanted at last. But you don't want me—not really. It's so much to me; so little to you. Please, Nick, is this the end?"

"If you wish it."

She seized his hands between hers. "Even if he persuades?"

"Yes."

"Your word? He's so strong. . . ."

"My word. . . . Margaret—oh, you child!—I do care for you now more than ever."

Suddenly he kissed her.

"There. . . . Have your own way. I'm not a devil, Margaret dear. But your seeing is different from mine—and your gods, I think. They won't have us together."

"No." She looked up with sudden curiosity. "Nick, you are superstitious like all great men? You—you wouldn't have me now if I asked you? Would you? Would you?"

He smiled at her with understanding, and admitted, "No."

"Something—inside you—says 'No'?"

He nodded.

"Then I'm safe—quite safe."

This amazing childlikeness!

"As your gods keep you," he said.

And she, with the embarrassment of one who returns a formal congratulation, answered: "And yours . . . and yours, Nick. You've been good."

Chapter XXIII
An Instant Free

I

Mr. Fane-Herbert decided to be in London with the spring. Ibble's and Ordith's were to remain independent, an arrangement of which both he and Nick Ordith saw the advantages, and which Aggett alone regretted wholeheartedly. Three weeks in Japan would complete Mr. Fane-Herbert's work in the East, and to Tokio he went, with Margaret and her mother, at the end of February.

Soon afterwards the *Pathshire*, having finished her refitting, sailed for Yokohama, and on the first Friday in March, John and Hugh, who had obtained week-end leave, arrived at Kamakura. That evening, when the hotel dinner was over, they sat together in the verandah of John's bedroom. Below them stretched the lawn, its size exaggerated by the semi-darkness, its nearer edge gloomy under the hotel's shadow, slashed, where the gleam of windows fell upon it, with parallelograms of yellow light.

"They come to-morrow," Hugh said.

"This will be the last that you'll see of them before they leave for home."

Hugh nodded. "Margaret will be glad to go."

"Because Ordith stays?"

"Partly—though I think she has cast off Ordith and the thought of him. . . . But she'll be glad to be rid of the place and its associations. London will give her something else to think about."

"It's almost incredible," John said slowly, "that anyone out here now should be able to reach London within seventeen days. It seems further away than that."

"But I like the East," Hugh protested.

John laughed. "Good God!" he exclaimed, "so do I; but that has nothing to do with it." He knocked out his pipe against the verandah rails. "Anyhow," he said, "it's a long lie-in to-morrow. Throw us a cigarette, Hugh."

He looked out across the lawn, across the broad belt of trees that stood between the garden and the beach. The sea was near—not that sea into which steel ships vomited their bilge, but the quiet sea of kissing sands and straight horizon which had been his first love. To-morrow did not matter; that darkness, those stars unsnared by sextants, that sea undivided into ranges, were suggestive of too many to-morrows, too many yesterdays. From an open window came voices and laughter, and the tinkle of a curtain being drawn.

"Women," Hugh said.

John leaned over the rail.

"That curtain has cut a patch of light out of the lawn. They'll all go out one by one."

"Ours won't—not yet. I'm not going to turn in for hours."

"I know," John said, reading his thought. "I hate wasting leave in sleep. Even if I turn out late, I like to wake early, and imagine the Reveille sounding and the calling of 'Guard an' steerage.' 'Show-a-leg, show-a-leg, lash up and sto-ow!' —and you lying in bed, with the whole day before you— away from the ship."

"This being Friday," Hugh observed, "we have to-night, and Saturday night, and Sunday night—two clear days."

"I wonder what would happen if we didn't go back—if we hid somewhere and never went back—if we started on our own. Why should we go back?" John said, for the sake of saying it.

"If we didn't, we'd be caught. If we weren't caught, we'd starve. . . . The extraordinary thing is," Hugh went on, in a puzzled voice, "that we can't stay as we are. I'm happy as can be sitting here; yet I shall get up presently and put an end to this evening by going to bed. I don't want to move. It's glorious here in the dark. . . . Look at the lawn—like a great pool."

"You want to lay hold on the instant," John said. "You can't any more than you can lay hold on eternity. They are the two infinities that meet somewhere. Probably from some point of view—if only you could reach it—the instantaneous and the eternal appear as one and the same. But the proofs we have of that are pretty vague: there's that extraordinary consciousness—coming for no apparent reason—that a given instant is of tremendous importance, that it is going to be remembered, that somehow it's a source of unknown events to come; then, at the other end of the scale, there's the recollection of certain instants—more than mere memory, a kind of preservation. An instant years-old by the measure of time, remains intact, perfect; and you know that it's never going to perish or fade. Usually the occasion was trivial. . . ."

"I wish," said Hugh out of the silence, "the Commander could hear his young gentlemen talking like this."

John laughed uneasily. "I had managed to forget the ship."

"All the same," Hugh went on "I like vague talk. I like listening to you—even though I don't understand too much of it. Vague talk gives me what I imagine you were driving at, what you spoke of before—a sense of eternity."

A watchman's bell rang faintly in the distant village. When it could be heard no longer, John said:

"A sense of eternity—what a phrase that is!"

Light, quick footsteps sounded on the path; then the heavier tread of a man. The girl stopped suddenly, touched her companion's arm, and, when he looked down, laughed breathlessly—an odd laugh, half-confidential, half-embarrassed.

"Oh, Torwood," she exclaimed, "I do so *love* this East!"

He threw his arm round her, and, with a tremendous air of proprietorship, almost dragged her indoors. Little gasps of excitement were her show of protest. As they passed through the room below the man could be heard speaking quick words to her, in a voice unevenly controlled; speaking with strange disregard for the public room's bleak emptiness and for the stare of electric bulbs, which, when they shine singly over places deserted till the morning, have so intent an air of watchfulness and curiosity.

II

On Saturday evening Margaret and Mrs. Fane-Herbert reached the hotel. After dinner, Mrs. Fane-Herbert said to John:

"I hear you changed your mind about leaving the Navy."

"It was scarcely a question of my changing my mind. It didn't get as far as that. You see——" He looked aside and saw that Margaret was watching him. "At any rate, I am settled down to it now," he said.

Hugh broke in with talk of Kamakura.

"When does your leave end?" Margaret asked.

"Monday."

"You must go back to your ship, then?"

"Yes, by noon."

She turned to John. "And you, too?"

Something in her intonation caught his attention, and he looked swiftly at her.

"Yes," he said. "You must send us news of London as our share in your home-coming. . . . I want to hear of your great-grandmother's welcome."

"Her great-grandmother?" Mrs. Fane-Herbert put in.

"The portrait, mother—the one over the stairs." Then to John: "She'll give me comments with her welcome, a lecture for her runaway."

There was a hint of bitterness in that; but John's remembering that conversation on the first evening she had known him stung her with the sting—half-pleasant, half-painful—of childhood days recalled in dark moments. For now she was easily stung to sorrow or to a kind of fierce joy. She had wanted desperately to talk, to tell someone how free she was—Ordith being gone. Untold, her freedom seemed incomplete. But neither her father nor her mother had spoken. They had learnt the facts, accepted them; she had attempted no explanation; not one word had been said. This silence had a hardening quality. Her experience, the vivid remembrance of which might have flowed easily away, was somehow frozen in her mind, like a sin unconfessed. There was no one to whom she could go. Warmth of heart, comradeship, the simplest affection she starved for. But this being left alone, this frigidness of spirit, this intolerable independence. . . .

John had known, at least, that her heart was full. It was as if she had seen a friendly face in the midst of a vast unnoticing crowd. When she said good-night to him she gave him her hand with new confidence. Then, out of his sight, she was suddenly angry with herself as for a foolishness, a weakness for the first time realized. An instant she stood unmoving outside her bedroom door—her mind tripped somehow, taken unawares.

And in the morning she settled at once to a book, glad of an occupation so isolating.

"You're very deep in that book, Margaret," Hugh said, as he passed her. "Aren't you coming out?"

"I want to finish it before lunch. Do you mind?"

"I see the last of you and mother to-morrow."

"I'll come this afternoon, . . . or shall I come now?"

He looked into her upturned face. Her hand was on the arm of her chair to raise herself.

"No, you odd sister. . . . No; you're not to come—of course not."

She went late to lunch, and was surprised to find Hartington at her mother's table, with John and Hugh. He said that his leave lasted only till that evening.

"Can't you stay and go back with us to-morrow?" Hugh asked.

"No." He shook his head. "But I wanted to see the homeward goers before they went. That's really all I came for."

The meal over, he had no difficulty in seeing Margaret alone, for she felt that it was to see her he had come.

"Well," she said, "secret emissary, what is it?"

"You know there's something?"

"You are full of suppressed news."

"Yes; good news—oh, such good news!"

"Thank God for that!" she breathed.

"You expected bad?"

"I fear it always. There's nothing definite that I expect. But somehow——"

"No," he said quickly. "This is good, anyhow. Lynwood is free—through Wingfield Alter."

She gave no sign of pleasure so eager was she. "How? Really free?"

"Really free," he smiled. "Are you beginning to disbelieve in freedom? . . . The mail came in after Lynwood left the ship. A letter for him from his mother, and a letter for me from Alter. I have them both here. Alter is to marry Mrs. Lynwood. He has taken the first definite step towards getting Lynwood out of the Service."

"When will he be free? Will he come home with us?"

"Not possible. It takes time. But now it is only a question of time—a couple of months, perhaps."

"You haven't given him his mother's letter?"

"No."

"You haven't told him?"

"No; I came to you first. I want you to tell him."

Something stifled her inclination to ask "Why?"

Hartington went on hesitatingly: "It means so much to him, you see. It's such tremendous news, because he has no hope or expectation of it. So . . . Miss Fane-Herbert, I want you to tell him."

Her eyes widened for a moment. They looked out beyond Hartington. Then, with abrupt decision, she said, with a fluttering, pleading gesture towards him: "No; you. You must tell him. It's your right. You brought it about."

"I wrote to Alter—that's all."

"It came about through you. Oh, long before the writing of that letter, you helped him—didn't you?—perhaps not deliberately. You don't realize how much you have done for him. Certainly you don't realize what he feels for you—the strangest mixture of affection, and admiration, and respect—but overwhelming. You are all that's best in men for him! And he'd like you to bring this news. He'll be glad, years on, that it was you who brought it. Friendship between men is so much more substantial, more secure. You must tell him," she concluded. "It's your right."

"Why do you insist so much on right? I waive it if it exists. That's why I came here."

"Oh," she cried, with a smile in acknowledgment of his unveiling of her half-pretence, "I want it to be you!"

He laughed back at her, so that her colour came. . . .

He took John away into the country roads, where the cherry-trees were in blossom and the sun lay flat on the long, low, irregular branches, reminding them of illustrations in Japanese fairybooks. There, as they walked, the news was given, the two letters read.

"You've done all this," John said, and remained speechless.

"I can't help wondering what it is exactly that I have done or helped to do. What's it going to lead to?"

"What do you mean?"

"I mean that this—the breaking free—is a beginning, not an end."

"I know. . . . But there's time enough to think of what's to come. I won't think of it now. . . . Hartington, couldn't you come too?"

"No; we shape different courses now."

"But we three shall see each other often—in London. I've never seen you in London. And at Oxford, you must stay with me there."

Hartington looked wistfully at him. "Oh yes," he said, "we shall see each other often."

They found on their return that the others had finished tea. Only Hugh remained by the empty cups. He sprang up to meet them.

"I am glad, you civilian! Margaret told me."

"She knows?"

"I told her," Hartington said. Then, "Have I stolen your news?"

"There is no one left to tell," John answered, laughing. "I want to tell thousands of people."

Later, he asked: "Where is Margaret?"

"I don't know. She disappeared after tea."

They sat smoking. Everything was pleasant to John now: the click of a cigarette-case being shut, the tapping of the cigarette, the long silences in which none of them had need of speech. The afternoon had begun to fail. The sun slanted yellow across the window-panes and fell in rippling beams of light and shadow upon the pale matting. Outside, the lawn and distant trees had taken on those soft golden tones which, at the approach of summer's dusk, flow across English fields, investing them with kindly magic. Then the church tower seems more than ever still; the churchyard silent, but not terrible. The bird rustles in the hedgerow; you imagine his bright eyes. The cricket stumps yellow against the green; the shadows flicker on the pitch; the bat sounds clearer, sweeter; the ball runs smoothly, and with peculiar ease; the players and the umpires in their white coats grow nebulous and vague.

" 'And a ghostly batsman plays to the bowling of a ghost,' " John said.

"Back in England already?"

"This summer in England!"

He went bareheaded into the cool air, across the lawn, springy under his feet, down the path among the trees where the white sand lay heavy, on to the shore. There was Margaret, near the waves' edge. He approached her, and, because she was so still, touched the billowing muslin she wore.

"You know?"

"Yes. John, how happy you must be! Always you'll remember to-day. It's your hour—one of the three or four. They go by so soon."

"And you? Are you not happy? . . . You are free, too."

He faltered as he spoke of this, of which she had never spoken.

She shivered, as if a cold breeze had struck her.

"Yes. . . . I understand. . . . I, too, am free. I know."

She turned to him eyes full of light.

"Oh, Margaret," he cried, his arms outstretched, "don't look towards the future. To-day's enough, Margaret. What is it you are afraid of?"

She said, trembling under his touch, close to him so that her dress brushed lightly against his coat, "What is it we're both afraid of? We are both afraid."

For answer, in his primitive wisdom, he swept her to him, overwhelming her thought. Lip to lip they clung, she imprisoned, silenced, caught up from fear. His arms about her in fierce pressure were a whole armour against doubt—more than armour, a charm, for the arrows themselves were diverted and flew wide of her, forgotten. Flames ran down her as his mouth burned against her throat, and her lips, opened now, were full of the sharp sea-wind.

She fell from him a little, still held.

"That once," she said, with caught breath, "that instant lives. That stands. Nothing can touch it or steal it. . . . Don't let me go—not yet, my darling—don't let me go!"

He drew her close again, but more gently. And she said:

"It's our victory."

"Nothing reverses it."

"Tell me——"

He told her his love again and again, her arm drawing him down so that the fresh scent of her hair was over him.

"Nothing takes those words back"—his kiss fell on her—"or the touch."

"But here we begin," he protested, wondering at the jealous terror that possessed her. "We shall go on from this for ever. Nothing is taken away. We build and build. In a few years, when I——"

"Oh!" she cried, "in a few years—who knows? We don't break free so easily as this, John. The net sweeps wider than we know. It yields—that's its strength. And presently it draws us in again. So it will go on—till the breaking. . . . You see, even you and I go on strengthening it, making new meshes despite ourselves. If ever we are to stand together in the world, first you have to gain money and power. You have to fight. Then—it's inevitable—we would have to teach our children to fight—equip them for 'the battle of life!' And they would look round to find themselves in *our* net.

"But it's going to end. The world will change its motive when this motive of gain has made it suffer so terribly, so obviously, that it realizes the cause of its suffering. We have to suffer—we or our children. It's near now. The whole system may smash—the good with the bad—perhaps that's the only way; and we may slip back into the Dark Ages again. I don't know. . . ."

"But now——" John said.

"Now? Yes—that's ours. . . . Oh, for God's sake! touch me and hold me as if you would never, never let me go. . . ."

And presently, standing away from him, she was saying with composure: "Let's go back. It's getting dark. Look how the colour is fading from the sea."

They went up the beach to the edge of the tree belt. There she checked him. Turning, they looked down upon their tracks to where, in the instant now gone by, the sand had been roughed and broken by their feet. Soon the water, which from the gathering darkness had drawn its first gleams of phosphorescence, would smooth their footprints away.

Chapter XXIV

One Year Later: The World In The Net

"Our fathers understood not thy wonders. . . ."—PSALM CVI.

"Our fathers have trespassed . . . our fathers have fallen by the sword, and our sons and our daughters and our wives are in captivity for this."—2 CHRON. XXIX.

"We have sinned with our fathers. . . ."—PSALM CVI.

Under the hot sun of an early August day in 1914 John walked from Parliament Square towards Whitehall. More than a fortnight earlier he had gone to the Admiralty and offered his services for the war. His name had been added to a long list of applicants for whom employment could not immediately be found. The same morning he had offered himself as an infantryman to a corps which was awaiting permission to form new battalions, and his name had been taken again. Now an official telegram had brought him to London.

In the forecourt of the Admiralty he met Tintern, who had entered at the corner nearer to Trafalgar Square.

"You, Lynwood—I thought you were at Oxford."

"Not yet. I've done the exams. I was waiting for the term to begin in October."

"What are you doing now? Volunteering?"

"Yes."

"I nearly chucked the Service myself a few months back. Glad I didn't now. War breaks the monotony of routine. It's what we, who stayed in the Service, have been preparing for. And even you, who made up your mind to break clear away—you have been roped in again. It comes to the same thing in the end. . . . They've emptied the college at Dartmouth, you know—all the cadets going to sea.''

Together they went up the steps into the great building, through the many passages of which, after enquiries made of a messenger, they began uncertainly to thread their way.